Why didn't he trigger the ~~alarm~~

Anyone who could penetrate the safeguards of her haven was a deadly enemy.

I have to kill him. Now. Somehow.

She pulled her close-up knife from its sheath. If she died now, she'd suffer uncounted years of torture because she'd failed to redeem her soul. Even worse, she would have failed in her attempt to destroy the seven demons.

A tear slid down her cheek. *Jake, I thought you were the one.*

DARK TIME

Praise for Dakota Banks's first MORTAL PATH novel

"A passionate, fascinating story packed with action and history."
DAVID MORRELL, author of *The Brotherhood of the Rose*

"A novel to be savored for both its edge of suspense and the pure joy of its storytelling."
JAMES ROLLINS, author of *Altar of Eden*

"Seductive, sophisticated, and imaginative."
STEVE BERRY, author of *The Charlemagne Pursuit*

By Dakota Banks

Mortal Path

Book 1
DARK TIME
Book 2
SACRIFICE

SACRIFICE

MORTAL PATH

BOOK TWO

DAKOTA BANKS

An Imprint of HarperCollinsPublishers

EOS
An Imprint of HarperCollins*Publishers*
10 East 53rd Street
New York, New York 10022-5299

Copyright © 2010 by Dakota Banks
Cover art by Don Sipley
ISBN 978-0-06-168732-7
www.eosbooks.com

First Eos paperback printing: September 2010

10 9 8 7 6 5 4 3 2 1

To a special person who believed in me:
Diana Gill

ACKNOWLEDGMENTS

I'm pleased to bring you *Sacrifice*, the second adventure of Maliha Crayne and her friends. I hope you'll find Maliha's story rich in emotion, suspense, action, drama, quests, friendship, and love. It's the kind of story I love to read, full of conflict and moral dilemmas, and I've done my best to convey all of these elements to you.

I'd like to thank the readers of the first book in the Mortal Path series, *Dark Time*, who responded so enthusiastically and encouraged me to continue the exciting quests Maliha faces.

My agent, Jill Marsal of the Marsal Lyon Literary Agency, provided valuable feedback that kept me on track. I'd like to thank her for working with me. Diana Gill, Executive Editor at HarperCollins, took what I put down on paper and helped me shape it into the book I had in my mind. For this and in particular for your patience and understanding: Thank you, Diana.

I'm grateful to my husband, Dennis, for those long breakfasts and all those notes on napkins that got me through the tough spots.

*When the beginnings of self-destruction
enter the heart it seems no bigger than
a grain of sand.*

JOHN CHEEVER, *The Journals*

*In this desert there are a great many
evil spirits and also hot winds; those
who encounter them perish to a man.
There are neither birds above nor
beasts below. Gazing on all sides as
far as the eye can reach in order to
mark the track, no guidance is to be
obtained save from the rotting bones of
dead men, which point the way.*

CHINESE MONK FA XIAN,
DESCRIBING THE TAKLIMAKAN
DESERT, 5TH CENTURY

SACRIFICE

Prologue

The diversion would be the wet and bloody kind, though not something that really sang to him. Too impersonal.

Dr. Mogue Kane was impatient. He'd had enough of the brown unchanging view, the soft sound of the wind playing in the sand, ripples of heat on the horizon, and the rank smell of the mercenary crouched next to him. In the encroaching sands of the Sahara desert in the Darfur region of Sudan, where the temperature was somewhere north of 110 degrees, any diversion would be welcome. When it was over, he could get out of the sun, the sweat bath he was taking, and the invasion of his personal space by a sniper who went by the name of Long Shot. What little cover there was in this godforsaken shithole had to be shared.

The man probably doesn't realize the double meaning of his nickname.

The doctor wasn't used to these dismal conditions. Experimenting in an air-conditioned laboratory was more his style. But the money was good and this appointment—as he called his contract work to imbue it with an academic aura—offered opportunities to watch people die for the purest of reasons: medical research.

Mogue was formerly a member of the Internal Security Unit of the Irish Republican Army, ferreting out British spies through chemical interrogation. Once he'd obtained a confession, the spy, who may or may not have been engaged in espionage, was executed. Then the IRA had gone political and disavowed violence. Mogue, an anachronism from the violent days, was cut loose. As an extraordinarily gifted researcher and not the type to twiddle his thumbs, it didn't take him long to settle into another organization where his many talents were appreciated.

Long Shot tensed and alerted Mogue with a slight nod of his head. A convoy of Land Rovers, two dozen of them at least, made its way toward the dry riverbed at the bottom of the hill. The riverbed, a remnant of prehistoric times when the area was favored with an inland sea, provided a relatively easy, if meandering, route for travel where there were no roads.

He saw the mercenaries on the hill across from him adjust their positions to focus their sights on the convoy. The two-man crew of an M240 machine gun on a bipod readied for action. Mogue's hand strayed to the Browning HP 9mm holstered at his belt. It was the same type of pistol used by Saddam Hussein, and that was a source of secret glee whenever Mogue handled the gun.

The twenty or so Land Rovers in the middle of the line bounced along transporting a World Health Organization team and their densely packed supplies. One vehicle at the head and one at the rear carried hired security guards. Where the nearest hospital was hundreds of miles away, the WHO team was a lifeline, one that Mogue was about to sever.

Mogue licked his lips, tasting salt from the sweat that had dried there. He itched to launch the attack, casting himself as Lawrence of Arabia shouting "No prisoners!" Without a word from him, rifles were fired, and then the machine gun came to life, spewing eight hundred rounds a minute into the valley of death.

The windows of the guards' vehicles exploded inward, hit from both sides by simultaneous fire. The guards, hit by multiple bullets, jerked helplessly in their seats. The vehicles sank to the ground as their tires deflated, like awkward camels lowering themselves to the sand. The mist of blood in the air settled. In a scant ten seconds, the hired guards were dead and the medical team was left without protection.

In between the two disabled vehicles, the remaining Land Rovers halted. Deeply tinted windows revealed nothing. Mogue imagined the fear of the people pinned down inside the Rovers. His senses were feeding him information in vivid detail intense enough to make him feel in the middle of the action. He'd experienced the sudden acuteness before and wished he could remain in that state all the time. This was living! He hummed to himself. *Memories are made of this. . . .*

The wind brought the scent of blood up from the river-bed.

The shattering of glass broke the silence. Someone had smashed the pane of one of the vehicles from the inside. The barrel of a rifle emerged and a couple of shots were fired. A volley of bullets from the hilltop answered. The rifle slid from the loosened grasp of a dead man in the vehicle and landed in the dirt.

Mogue nudged the man next to him. "Do something. It's hot out here."

Giving no sign he'd heard Mogue, Long Shot squeezed off a round from his rifle and the driver's window of the dead man's vehicle split into shards. It was a catalyst for panic. Doors were flung open and the staff emerged, running for shelter that was nonexistent in the valley. Some fired handguns upward at the hilltops. A bullet pinged a rock near Mogue. He huddled closer to Long Shot, earning a grunt of disapproval. A shooting gallery opened up as mercenaries picked off individuals.

Then all was quiet again as the last passenger emerged from a Rover. It was a woman dressed in a flowing white desert robe, baggy trousers covering her legs. She was stiffly erect, shoulders back, her head carried high. She took a few steps, her dignity forming a fragile shield around her. No one fired and she kept walking, gaining some confidence.

"Shoot her," Mogue said. His voice was husky, but not from the dry desert air. He was aroused. This was better than killing faceless people inside Rovers.

The man hesitated. Mogue pulled out the Browning, took aim at her torso, and fired at her from the back. The bullet smacked into her hip, twisting her sideways as blood spread across her white robe. She fell heavily, screaming in pain but far from dead. Mogue wasn't a good shot. One of the snipers put a bullet in her brain and she lay still.

Mogue made a clinical observation. *Blood has no time to pool in the desert. The sand is thirsty.*

An hour later, the Land Rovers had been pushed or driven into several tight clusters and covered with desert camo nets. The corpses rested inside, bloody cherries wrapped in metal instead of chocolate. A new medical team, Mogue's, was on its way.

Chapter One

Maliha Crayne drove through the Massachusetts countryside on a crisp October afternoon, patiently keeping pace with the outsiders who clogged the roads on fall color tours. Her black McLaren F1 was made for speed on deserted stretches of highway, not this tourist shuffle, but she didn't have far to go until she could turn off onto her private road.

In the Northeast, people who hadn't been born there or at least put in a couple of generations or a few decades on the land were still treated as outsiders, because families there had deep roots. Maliha was no outsider. She'd been born there in 1672.

She had three hundred acres, a mixture of orchard and forest. A farmer, the third generation of his family, ran the apple orchard for her. He kept all the profit and paid no rent for the house where he and his wife raised two children. It was a generous arrangement and returned in kind by scrupulous care of her land.

When she reached the turnoff she had to get out and unlock the gate. Winding through the apple trees, she rolled down the windows and breathed in the air free of car exhaust. On a whim, she stopped and picked some of the heritage apples she'd brought over from England in the mid 1700s. Biting into a Margil apple's yellowish flesh released an aroma that brought back memories. Juice dribbled down her chin.

She sat in her car for a time watching the clouds move with a high, swift wind barely felt on the ground. She

cleared her mind of what was ahead and thought of the
recent past instead. The last time she'd seen her boyfriend
Jake Stackman, a Drug Enforcement Administration agent,
she'd stabbed him.

*Did I act too soon? Should I have given him a chance to
explain?*

On a hill far from the farmer's house, she parked the
car and walked a short path to an area with tall maple trees
and open areas of grass. Among them were two small slate
gravestones, worn and thin, but standing tall. Recently fallen
leaves covered the graves. The sight of the leaves cascad-
ing down from the trees brought a small smile to her lips.
Maliha had brought flowers, but they seemed unnecessary
with nature already providing such fine decoration.

When she got within ten feet or so of the graves, it was
like passing through a tangible emotional barrier, a bubble
that surrounded them and kept the memories fresh and raw.
Her hand flew to her chest, where her heart pounded, each
beat heightening her fear.

Dragged from my bed in the middle of the night . . .

Another two steps closer.

The accusations, the trial, my husband turning away . . .

Her feet shuffled in the leaves. Although she'd come here
before, many times, it was still hard.

*Tears streaming down my cheeks and onto my stillborn
daughter, lying on the dirt floor of the jail cell.*

"Constanta! My baby, my little one." Maliha's head
hung, her eyes staring at the ground, unable to read the
writing on the tombstones just yet. Her tears mingled with
the yellow leaves. She walked the last few feet in a rush and
sat down.

The memories of the stake and the flames came next, and
she endured them, crying out at the smell of her own flesh
burning. Maliha stretched out her hands to her husband's
tombstone and placed them over his carved name. The slate
was cold to the touch, cold enough to keep the flames at bay.

"Here lies Nathan Layhem," she said without looking at
the words. She'd memorized them. "Who was released from

a troubled life on October fifteenth 1708, in the thirty-eighth year of his age. Misfortune shadowed this man's past, he met the King of Terrors at last."

She was the misfortune in Nathan's past. As his wife, she'd been accused of witchcraft. His life in the village after that couldn't have been easy.

Her hands moved over to the next tombstone and when she touched it, pain stabbed through her lower abdomen. Here beneath the ground was the child she'd carried in her womb, her daughter.

The only time in her long life that she'd carried life within her.

"In memory of Constanta, daughter of Nathan Layhem"— she traced the carving with her fingers—"who was Still Born August third 1692. In hope that her rest is peaceful and her spirit be not vengeful."

Her name was not mentioned on the tombstone. It hurt, but she knew it was the only way Nathan could get the baby buried at all. Otherwise the unwanted, bewitched body would have gone to the trash pit with the afterbirth. The townspeople had no doubts that Maliha was a witch. They'd seen her step naked and powerful from the flames that should have blackened her body and ended her life.

Maliha stretched out on the leaves that covered her daughter's grave, getting as close to Constanta as she could. Though several feet of earth, hundreds of years, and the specter of death separated them, she felt her arms wrap around her baby. Comforted by the feeling, she remained there for hours.

The night was cold and clear when she rose. The full moon lighted her way back to her car. Moving from country road to country highway to interstate, Maliha headed home, for Chicago, over eight hundred miles away. She intended to be in her lakefront condo before lunchtime. The McLaren was in its element, flying through the night like a black arrow. She rode with the windows down, drowning out her memories with the white noise of wind rushing past the car.

Pain streaked across the side of her neck, and then sliced across her left temple. She put a hand to her neck and it came away bloody. Maliha braked hard for an upcoming turn and struggled for control of the car as pain blackened her vision on the edges. She felt the impact as the car scraped along the road-side barrier and then punched through it. When the tires left the road, there was a heart-stopping moment when the McLaren seemed to hang in midair before gravity took charge.

Chapter Two

The car's cockpit safety net, a body-sized spider web, sprang toward Maliha. Expanding foam rushed into the compartment, rapidly chilling her and blocking her view. She was barrel-rolling down the hill, blind and pinned tightly to the seat. The McLaren's frame shuddered as it came to an abrupt stop.

The net loosened and Maliha slumped in her seat, barely conscious. In a few minutes, she began to move around. The foam had already started liquefying. She was very dizzy and resisted the urge to throw herself from the car as fast as she could. Instead, while the foam drained, she checked her body. The neck and scalp wounds she'd felt before the crash were bleeding, but her skull was intact and so were her major neck veins and arteries. The shots had been fired at an angle and neither bullet had entered her body. Her left arm had been twisted oddly when held in place by the net, and was temporarily numb. Other than that, she was sore everywhere, like someone had done a thorough job on her with a baseball bat. She flexed her arms and legs and found that she could move.

No broken bones, but I'm one big ball of pain. Not that I'm complaining. I could have been facing much worse pain for dying before my quest is over.

"Thanks," she whispered, tapping the car's misshapen dashboard.

Someone hired an assassin to take me out. Ironic, considering.

Maliha was a former assassin herself, a superbly trained and effective one. Having the tables turned didn't appeal to her, and she started to feel angry about that and about interrupting her trek from the tombstones with something as crass as a contract on her life.

Either an assassin who's a really bad shot was assigned to me, or the shooter misjudged my speed.

She'd been going about 120 miles per hour, a romp in the park for the McLaren. At that speed, she'd be a very tough target. If she'd been the shooter, she would have waited for a better opportunity.

When her dizziness began to ease, she left through an open window and moved away into the brush, leaving no trace of her passage. She felt like a giant walking bruise, but at least the feeling had come back in her left arm. From thirty feet away, she examined the wreck by moonlight. Her car had come to rest against a tree, its roll cage badly dented but still intact. Every extra safety measure she'd installed in her car had come into play. The McLaren had given its all. She blew it a kiss.

If I were the sniper, I'd verify my kill, so I'd be on my way down here right now.

Some of her weapons were in the car and irretrievable. She had only those she regularly concealed on her body, a small knife strapped to each calf, a few throwing stars and darts in a leather pouch inside her waistband, and her whip sword, flexible bands of sharpened metal that curled inside a sheath at her waist. It was more than enough. In the mood she was in, it would be rewarding to throttle the shooter with her hands.

Twigs snapped uphill from her.

Too confident of a kill. Unprofessional.

Maliha ignored the complaints streaming in from all parts of her body and silently climbed a tree. While waiting for the shooter to arrive, she snapped off a handful of twigs. She plotted his route easily after listening—he was heading straight for the wreck. When she saw his shape in the moonlight, she let go of the twigs, making a noise like a footstep right below her. He altered his path, moving to investigate the sound.

She dropped on him, slashed the arm that held the rifle, and put a knife to his throat. The motions came from deep in her memory, carried out without thought. She was trained for this and she'd shed blood. Any threat to her life should be met in kind. He yelped in surprise, as if he were in the grip of a ghost, and he wasn't far wrong. As an Ageless assassin in the service of a Sumerian demon, she had gone by the name of the Black Ghost.

She kicked the rifle out of reach. Wrapping one of her legs around his, she effortlessly took him down. With one leg clamped over his lower body and his slashed arm twisted tightly behind him, she secured him. With the point of her knife delicately resting on his carotid artery, she could feel his pulse hammering. Before she killed him, she wanted information.

"Who hired you?" It was the Black Ghost's voice. There was no answer. She drew a drop of blood from his throat. "Don't make me ask again."

"Nobody hired me. I'm here on my own. You killed my great-grandfather." He'd managed to put some defiance in it, and given his position, that earned him some points with her. She loosened his bleeding arm to relieve a little of the pain.

"Explain."

"You mean you don't know? Your family kills so many people they lose track?"

My family? "Humor me."

"Loon Lake, 1910. Ring any bells?"

The mention of Loon Lake brought back vivid memories. She'd taken a life that day working for Rabishu, the demon who'd controlled her then, but saved another life. It had been the start of the awakening of her conscience, questioning whether her Ageless life was worth it if bought with so much death. "What does something that happened a century ago have to do with me?"

"With you, nothing. But one of your ancestors stabbed J. H. Sawyer to death the night my grandfather was born.

His wife, Lucy, saw the whole thing. She swore to get vengeance."

He means me. He just doesn't know I was around then. "What's your name?"

"John Sawyer."

"How did you find me?" The Black Ghost had slipped away. This wasn't the time for a killing machine. She needed reasoning and judgment.

"Lucy wanted to find the killer. She kept records of all the guests at the Loon Lake Resort. Only one turned out to be using a false name. That name turned up somewhere else, on the deed to a plot of land in Massachusetts, and it kept turning up there. Property transfers. Inheritance. Sales."

Shit. So much for sentimentality.

"You have no idea what went on back then."

"And you do?"

"We have our family stories, too. Did Lucy ever tell what really happened that night? She was in labor and the baby had the cord wrapped around his neck. The killer stayed and saved the baby, your grandfather. If not for the killer, you wouldn't be here. A life for a life. The score was settled long ago."

"I never heard that. You're sure?"

"What reason do I have to lie? Don't live out someone else's obsession. Drop this and get on with your life. Come near me again, I'll have to kill you." She stood up, shoving him away from her as she did. He nodded, but was that enough?

Will I have to keep looking over my shoulder for this guy?

There was still time to kill him. He could carry on his vendetta and get better at it, even pass it on to his children. Every twenty or thirty years a new Sawyer family member could be looking for her, and she wasn't about to give up owning or visiting her Massachusetts land. She focused on a point beyond him on the hillside and let her eyes relax. His aura, the luminous radiation surrounding his body, came into view. It was mostly yellow and orange swirled together, which she interpreted as intelligence and the desire for a successful life. Overlaying these basic pieces of John's personality were his feelings of the moment, long tendrils of black and red that flicked like small whips—anger and hatred at what she represented—feelings imposed by Lucy, long in her grave. As she watched, she could see these tendrils begin to fade. It was a promising sign.

But there's too much at stake here. John could have put an end to everything for me over this. I haven't earned back my soul yet and my quest to eliminate all the Sumerian demons left on Earth is far from complete. All because of Lucy. I should have let her baby die back then!

John was walking up the hillside toward the road. Maliha fingered her knife, undecided, and then drew back her arm and launched it toward John's receding back.

No!

The instant the blade left her hand, she changed her mind. She raced the knife up the hill, using a burst of speed far beyond human capabilities. Before the knife could strike John's back, she deflected it with the back of her hand. The knife missed him and struck a tree nearby. The skin on Maliha's left hand was torn open where the blade had skittered along it.

He deserves a chance to come to terms with the new version of his family history. I think he's a good man who grew up in Lucy's very long shadow. I'll take the risk.

When John finished his climb, he turned around and called back to her. "Sorry about your car."

It wasn't until later, when Maliha was walking along the edge of the highway, that she realized he had apologized for wrecking her rare and expensive car but not for shooting at her head.

Men.

Chapter Three

Three days later

Maliha Crayne didn't have a clear view of the terrain rolling by beneath her, so she put her foot on the copter's skid and leaned out the door. The hot downdraft from the whirling blades overhead buffeted her.

"Hey!"

She felt Hound's sizable hand grab the back of her waistband.

"What the fuck. Don't scare me like that. You don't have a safety line or anything."

"I have good balance. Do you want me to find her or not?"

She looked back over her shoulder at him. Every inch of his body language screamed *Hell yes!*

She leaned farther out, trusting him. There was some muttered profanity behind her, but no more complaints.

Then Hound moved close behind her in what in other circumstances would have been a lover's ardent clasp, especially with his hand taking liberties on her ass. He clipped an anchored lanyard to the D-ring on the back of her full body harness and let go of her.

"Lean all you want. Fall out, I don't give a shit."

She knew that wasn't true. She and Hound had known each for a long time. He was upset and angry at the world in general because his partner, Glass, was down there somewhere in the dark, kidnapped by a mostly Arab militia in Darfur. He and Glass had been together for years but recently things had heated up between the two of them and Hound had finally forced the M word out of his mouth.

Glass delivered medical supplies for the World Health Organization. Her last known location was in the Darfur region of Sudan, near a town named Duraysah. The village she'd been assigned to had been discovered burned to the ground. Glass's engagement ring was pressed into the dust on the path out of the village. It wasn't accidental. The ring lay within a hastily drawn letter "G," establishing hope that Glass had left the village alive.

The theory was that Glass had been taken by the Janjaweed, the militia members responsible for attacking and burning the village. They routinely raped their female victims, mutilated men, women, and children with machetes, and then killed them or left them to fend for themselves, bleeding from severe wounds. The Janjaweed members didn't have the latest military equipment. Bullets and rifles cost, but one terrorist weapon every militiaman possessed was a prick. Raped women underwent terrible social stigma, most of them becoming outcasts, disowned even by their husbands. Rape as a terrorist tactic demoralized both sexes and tore gaping holes in the Darfur social fabric.

Nice guys. I hope to meet them very soon.

Maliha's hand strayed down to the throwing knives strapped to her thighs and then to a belt slung low on her hips that had a knife for close-up work and a holstered Glock machine pistol along with several spare extended thirty-three-round magazines. She brushed the thin, flat handle of the whip sword that curled around her waist. In use, its two flexible blades snapped through the air like whips, with a buzz-saw effect on the target. Her skin was protected from the blades in a sheath made of intricately carved yak leather, three times as strong as ordinary leather, lined inside with metal.

She'd been trained with edged weapons three hundred years ago, and the first-learned lessons stuck with her the most.

She brought the eyepiece of her handheld night vision monocular to her right eye. The full moon and the washed-out field of stars provided enough light for the device to gather and amplify.

The copter came over a rise, and there it was—the sign Maliha was looking for. Cooking fires. Half a dozen at least. The Janjaweed operated hand-in-hand with the Sudanese government. There was isolated resistance to the militia, but in this region they had little reason to be cautious. They made camp, cooked dinner, got drunk, and turned to their captives for the night's entertainment.

"Back off. We're too close." Maliha gestured at Hound, emphasizing the urgency. The campsite was about half a mile away. The monocular had picked up the bright fires.

Hound relayed the message. The copter made a wide swing away from the camp. She and Hound would be going in on foot.

"I hope they didn't hear us," Hound said.

"We were close enough to hear. The Sudanese government uses Russian MI–24s to support some Janjaweed raids, so the sound of an isolated helicopter might not alarm them. They'd just think their buddies are flying over."

"Did you find Glass down there?"

"Not a chance. Too far away."

In the moonlit interior of the copter, she could see Hound's face well enough to tell that his eyes were closed. She didn't know what was going on behind those eyelids, but she didn't think it was benevolent thoughts about the Janjaweed.

Odds are Glass is already dead.

If she was alive, they might rescue her in time to prevent gang rape, but if Hound didn't already know about that, this wasn't the time to tell him.

She reached over and took Hound's hand. He squeezed hers back, and she took it as a call to action.

"Better watch out, motherfuckers," Hound said, his words catching in his throat. "We're coming."

By the time they reached the drop site, Maliha was

streaking her upper face with black and brown camo paint. Although he was black, Hound still needed the paint on puckered pink scar tissue on one side of his face. Maliha tucked her black hair, worn in a long braid down her back, under the collar of her shirt and then pulled on a dark mesh hood that left her eyes exposed.

Maliha went first, locking a carabiner on the attachment point on the front of her harness and adding the descender and static rope. The spotter, a friend of Hound's, told her to use three tugs, and she stepped out into the night.

She enjoyed roping off a copter or parachuting at night, but the seriousness of this mission wiped away all thoughts of fun. The layer of heat she encountered on her way down promised discomfort to come, between the tactical clothing she was wearing and the equipment that went with it. She'd never seen Hound show an outward reaction to any sort of weather condition.

On the ground, she unfastened her line and tugged three times on it. As her rope was disappearing skyward, pulled up by the spotter, Hound landed beside her.

"I hate this shit. Reminds me of in-country."

There was only one "in-country" for Hound: Vietnam. He'd been a medic, and had come home broken in body and soul. He was a private investigator now and didn't do fieldwork like this often. At least, she thought he didn't. He did some government work she didn't know anything about.

Maliha drew her thumb and index fingers across her lips, signaling silence. Hound nodded. He had the GPS unit, so he took the lead. The GPS device wore a mesh hood, too, to shield the light from its screen.

The two of them walked only a few minutes before the heat of the surroundings caught up to Maliha. Even though it was dark, in October the heat was oppressive near the equator. Her sweatband was soaked and a waterfall cascaded down her spine. She couldn't stop her body from sweating—wouldn't, even if she could, because she would overheat—but she shoved aside the sensation of walking on coals.

In ancient times, when Sudan was known as Nubia, the lioness goddess Sekhmet inflicted her fiery breath on the land in the summer. In order to keep her from making their world uninhabitable, Nubians appeased her with elaborate rituals so the Nile floods would occur in the fall. Sometimes the appeasement was unsuccessful, and in those years of drought the bloody goddess took her toll in lives. Maliha was ready to make a sacrifice to Sekhmet now: a band of Janjaweed.

Around them, bushes, islands of grass, and scraggly trees were mixed with stretches of bare rocky or sandy soil.

Not much cover. Not the best for us, but not good for them hiding out either.

She could see Hound's body stiffening with tension the closer they got to the campsite. She closed the distance between them and tapped him on the shoulder. He turned to face her. She indicated she wanted the GPS and that she would take the lead. His eyes, normally very expressive, swallowed the moonlight and didn't acknowledge her right away. Then he blinked and handed over the device.

I should have left him in the copter. Tied him down if I had to.

"You don't have to worry about me. Just help me get to her."

She said nothing about his whispered comment. It was as though he had read her mind.

Checking the GPS, she found that they were only a hundred yards out. She suspected that security was a bit lax after the raid.

The small grove of trees they were in, none of them more than eight feet high, seemed like a good place to stop and plan. She'd tried to discuss that with Hound in the helicopter, but his idea was to get in, grab Glass, and get out. Focused, but short on details. They had to know numbers, weapons, layout of the camp, sentry positions, and whether Glass was with this group or not.

She turned around and signaled Hound that he was to stay put and she was going forward to reconnoiter. He shook his head, and kept shaking it as she repeated the command. She planted her hands firmly on his shoulders and pulled his face down to hers so that her lips were close to his ear.

"If you don't do this, I'll cut you so you can't go any-where, and then you'll be out of the action. We're not charging in there without intel, Hound. If Glass is there, she could die."

He twisted out of her grasp, leaned against a tree and answered her in a voice that was more of a rumble than a whisper.

"Fuck. You come back for me, you hear? Fuck."

She nodded.

All in black, Maliha moved like a cat's shadow across the land, heading for a high point she'd spotted a while back. Near the top of the rise, she stretched out on the rocky ground and inched forward until she could see into the valley on the other side.

The campsite spread out below her. She rapidly assessed the opposition's strength: about fifty men, mostly in one part of the camp, some sitting around the scattered fires. Thirty hobbled horses were in a makeshift corral just out-side the camp. There were plenty of automatic weapons in view, probably AK–56s sold to the Sudanese government by China. Sudan had begun exporting oil to China and import-ing outdated Chinese automatic weapons. China was happy to unload them, especially for oil to fuel its emergence onto the world stage.

Maliha had been in one place long enough. She retreated from the top of the hill, marked it in her mind as her six-o'clock position, and walked in a broad arc toward three o'clock.

She heard the guard before she saw him. He was urinat-ing. Drawing her knife, she approached, adjusting her path so she'd come up behind him. If Glass's life weren't on the line, had this man not been a member of the Janjaweed, Maliha might have knocked the guy out and gone on with the mission, hoping a scorpion would sting him on his ex-posed dick for picking the wrong side in the battle. She slit

his throat and he fell to his knees in midstream. She lowered
him quietly to the ground.

Maliha searched for the other sentry, but the man she'd
killed was working alone tonight. Still on the high ground,
she got on her belly and peered over again for a look into
the camp, letting her eyes relax into a soft focus this time.
The campfires blurred into reddish-orange clouds. She
stared at the closest person, an old man sitting cross-legged
in front of a fire. Then she moved her gaze through him
so that her focus was on a point beyond. His aura, the luminous energy that surrounded him and radiated outward
from his body for a distance of about two feet, became
visible to her.

The old man's aura was a medium brown with strong
veins of red and black. Black meant evil and hatred. The
bright red, in combination with black, indicated deep-seated
anger. Brown, the dominant color, told Maliha that he was
a selfish man who lied to further his goals, the kind who
would stab his mother in the back if doing so bettered his
life.

Maliha let her vision float around the camp, seeking
out other auras. It was the surest way to find Glass. In the
crowded northwest corner of the camp, the auras were
tightly mingled and individual identities were lost in the
throbbing dome of muddied red: machismo, and lots of it. It
had to be where the women were kept.

Moving to the three-o'clock location, she found two
sentries chatting together and smoking, the red glow of their
cigarettes obligingly marking their locations as targets.

As she crept closer, she could hear them talking. Maliha
was fluent in Arabic and stayed her progress long enough to
listen for scraps of helpful information. She shook her head
in disgust. It was nothing but crude boasting about what
they would do after their duty shift ended and they joined
the celebration.

Two slender throwing knives spun through the night and
landed with precision, impaling two hearts drenched with
evil. The men fell simultaneously. Maliha followed in the

wake of her knives. She retrieved her knives and wiped them clean on the dead men's clothing.

Onward to twelve o'clock?

It's what she would do if she were alone, but with Hound waiting for news, she'd already been gone too long. She headed back. To her relief, he was right where she'd left him, agitated and digging a hole in the ground by shuffling his boots—a way to take action without going anywhere. She made some noise so he would hear her approach.

He stopped shuffling. A red dot from the laser sight of the Israeli-built Tavor TAR–21 assault rifle he carried marked Maliha's heart as a target.

"Hound." The circle fled from her chest.

"Damn, woman, don't sneak up on me like that. I could've plugged you."

"I doubt it. I could have gotten to you first."

"Bullshit. Is she there?"

"I . . ."

"Time to move out. We can't just stand here while . . ." His voice trailed off.

She quickly told him about the camp, the sentries, and where Glass was. They each checked their weapons and then headed out silently.

When they passed the corpses of the guards Maliha had killed, Hound grunted in satisfaction.

At the twelve-o'clock position, they were so close they could hear the Janjaweed in action: fists and sticks striking skin. Hound, kneeling next to her, was primed for action.

"What're they saying?" he whispered. There were no guards and no one could hear them over the raucous noises.

Hound didn't speak Arabic. "Better not to know."

"Fuck."

"Pretty much their plans, when they get done softening up the women by beating them."

Now that she could see the situation close up, Maliha felt the only way to proceed was to attack, distract, and try to get Glass out during the mayhem—basically, Hound's original plan. Hound agreed, even considering the risk that Glass might not survive a surprise attack. After all, the Janjaweed could blast away with their rifles, but she and Hound couldn't return fire indiscriminately for fear of killing Glass and the other women.

She reminded Hound of his promise when he'd badgered her to come on this rescue—that it was her show and his role was to watch her back. She'd do the attacking and Hound would go after Glass. Then she moved away from him so the same burst of gunfire wouldn't wipe them both out.

Just as she arrived at her new position, she saw Hound running into the clearing, shouting as if the hounds of hell were after him—or he *was* the Hound of hell.

No way is that watching my back.

For a moment she was frozen with fear for Hound's life. She watched him mow down several militiamen at the nearest campfire. The noise of the gunfire was like using a hornet's nest for a piñata—suddenly men were running everywhere, taking up weapons that had been set aside for the evening.

Maliha sprinted into the camp, sending her throwing knives at two men who were about to take aim at Hound. Not waiting to see the result, she drew the Glock with her left hand and used her right hand to pull the whip sword from its sheath around her waist. Keeping an eye on Hound, she picked off three more of the scrambling men and then another two who were heading for the horses to escape. Bullets puffed the dirt at her feet and whizzed by her, one leaving a streak of pain.

She kept on the move, closing out the screams and the moans of the dying, killing in a bubble of total concentration, a berserker's trance without the uncontrollable rage. When she got close enough for personal combat, she put the whip sword into action. As she swung the double-edged blades around, they bit into flesh at the throat or knocked a weapon away, along with the arm that held it. The whip sword whirled around her faster than the human eye could track, with only her skill in wielding it keeping one of the blades from slicing her own throat. Blood sank into the thirsty soil beneath her feet.

Glancing at Hound, she saw that he had reached the area where Glass should be. She also noticed the red spreading rapidly on his clothes. He'd taken at least one bullet on the left side and was probably lucky he hadn't been cut in half by automatic fire. Maliha needed to be where he was, and fast.

Using the supernatural speed that was a remnant of her Ageless time, she sped toward him, a blur weaving through the camp to his side. The effort weakened her—not a good thing in a firefight like this. But there were times when the trade-off was necessary.

She arrived near him in time to blast one of the Janjaweed coming up behind Hound with, of all things, a spear. She noticed that the tip of the spear was bloody even though it hadn't touched Hound. It must have been used on the women. Angry, Maliha pumped another couple rounds into the dead man at her feet.

"You okay?"

"Yeah. Glass is . . ." He swayed a bit on his feet. ". . . over there."

Maliha spotted Glass not far away, sitting propped up against a tree. She was cradling an AK–56 in the crook of her arm and popping off short bursts at men who had been tormenting her only a few minutes ago. She looked dazed, and she wasn't hitting many of her targets, but she was keeping them at a distance with her sporadic fire.

"That's my woman."

Glass's condition hadn't registered on Hound yet because he was so glad to see her alive. Maliha took in everything.

Bad. Really bad.

In the light of the cooking fires, she could see that Glass had numerous bruises that were going to look a lot worse in a few hours, including on her face. Blood trailed in thin streams from multiple cuts on her body. Glass's head rocked forward in either dizziness or drowsiness, making Maliha suspect a head injury. Glass was holding and firing the gun with one hand because the other hand was lying limp on the ground. Spread out in front of her were two twisted and mangled legs showing splintered bone. The Janjaweed sometimes broke the legs of any woman who dared to fight back or tried to escape.

Looks like Glass put up one hell of a fight.

Hound went rigid beside her. He was finally seeing with his eyes in addition to his heart. Maliha grabbed an AK–56 from the loose grasp of a corpse and pulled Hound down into the shelter of a rock that wasn't quite big enough to conceal both of them. He winced at the movement. Maliha squeezed as small as possible and tugged his bulk behind the rock just as bullets hit where his foot had been.

"Take Glass to the evac point." She pressed the GPS into his hand. He'd need it to find the coordinates of the pickup site.

Hound shook his head.

Not again.

"Don't give me that shit! You nearly got us all killed. You get her to evac and do it fucking now!"

"I meant, what about you?"

Oh. "I've got your back."

"There's at least twenty-five . . ."

"I can count. Besides, I'm not wounded."

"You dodge faster."

"Get going. Starting cover fire in three . . ."

He pulled her into a rough embrace. "I'll always love you."

A surge of emotion blurred Maliha's vision. She could tell that he thought he was saying good-bye forever. She'd loved his bravery and selflessness since the day she'd saved his life in Vietnam, then later loved him with deep passion and with loyal friendship. She traced his lips with her finger, saying all she needed to say without words. He pressed her hand to his lips and kissed it.

"Go save your woman. Cover fire in three, two, one."

She moved to the side and laid down thirty seconds of fire, three hundred bullets on missions to steal lives. Hound scrambled toward Glass and made it safely. He was limping on the left side, though.

I hope he can get himself *to evac.*

Three Janjaweed had come out of hiding and were heading after him as he escaped from the camp, and he wasn't making swift progress. Maliha ran to intercept them. One went down after a flying kick to the head and the other two with twisted necks.

A fourth man shot Maliha before she had a chance to deal with him. Automatic fire stitched a zipper down the outer curve of her right thigh and a sliver of flesh separated. Maliha dispatched the man with a kick that shattered his trachea and sent him to the ground choking for his final breaths.

Quickly she felt for the extent of her injury. A chunk the size of a well-used bar of soap was gone, leaving a shallow crater. Expecting another assault any second, Maliha tore a section from the shooter's clothing and tied it around her thigh tight enough to apply pressure to the wound but not tourniquet tight.

About twenty of them left.

Thinking about the way these men had beaten the women they'd captured, and the plans they must have had for rape before being interrupted and attacked, she vowed that the only way any of them would get past her and pursue Hound and Glass is if she were dead. She was no stranger to torture and knew what awaited them if they were captured.

A single tree nearby offered a good view of the path Hound had taken. She would have climbed it for an aerial view, but like other vegetation here it was stunted by the harsh climate. Still, it was as good an observation point as she could find.

She waited behind the tree, watching the camp for signs of pursuit. Five minutes later, much sooner than she expected, a line of men on horseback came into view. Hound didn't stand a chance of outdistancing horses.

Jump out and kill everything in sight with automatic fire? Too risky at twenty to one. Some could slip by.

She was keenly aware that if she were alone, she'd take that risk, and more.

This business of watching over others will be the death of me.

She needed an edge, the advantage of . . . a horse. Instantly the plan fell into place. Ambush the last rider. Pick off the others from the rear. She moved silently and waited for the horses to pass.

Go.

Maliha ran toward the horse, stopped just short of a collision, and sprang upward, her right leg arcing over the horse's rump. A fresh burst of pain came from the wound on her right thigh, nearly crippling her with its intensity. She pushed away the pain and slit the rider's throat before he could yell a warning to the others. Maliha lowered the body slowly toward the ground. The horse reacted to a dead weight sliding down its side by snorting, tossing its head, and skittering sideways. As soon as Maliha was able to drop the dead man, she leaned low over the horse's neck, calming it. Then she urged the horse forward to catch up with the others.

She took the next rider by surprise. She thought of tying his horse to her own but figured that would cut into her maneuverability. She pointed the riderless horse back to the camp and lightly slapped it.

Unfortunately, the two riders at the end of the line had pulled up side by side to talk. The picking-off stage was over. Maliha was about to dig her heels in and bring her horse to a run, but was upstaged by the horse she'd sent back toward camp. It had turned around and now came flying past her at a full gallop, then past the pair of militiamen, and on up the line.

The jig's up.

Reacting quickly, Maliha slid down her horse's left side, away from the men, and clung on with her left foot in the stirrup. The startled animal took off running, appearing as a second riderless horse to the Janjaweed. It would buy her a few seconds to switch plans.

Suddenly a fierce pain struck the center of her body, so overwhelmingly powerful no amount of meditating or training could shut it out. Her arms and legs went limp and her head dipped perilously low to the rocky ground.

No! Not now!

The horse, further alarmed by the shifting weight of its rider, veered to the left, swinging Maliha into some bushes and knocking her loose from her already tenuous position. She rolled awkwardly, her arms crossed over her painful midsection. A bullet slammed into her right leg, sending her sprawling backward on the ground. Ripping at her clothing, she yanked the cloth away from the source of the pain on the front of her body.

She knew she'd lost her chance to stop the Janjaweed. Knowing what was happening didn't make it any easier to accept. Carved into Maliha's skin from between her breasts to just below her navel was a scale put there by Rabishu's fiery claw when she'd given up her immortality. In the pan on one side were miniature figures representing the people she'd killed as a demon's assassin. The other pan held people she'd saved after becoming mortal. The deal for breaking her contract with Rabishu was that she had to reposition the scale—saving as many lives as she'd taken— before she died, or suffer terrible consequences at his hand for eternity. She didn't get rewarded one-for-one. Anu, the chief Sumerian god, had his finger on the scale and determined the extent of her reward.

Her scale had come to life. The lines traced on her skin glowed red, lit by the fires of the Underworld. Animated figures were on the move across her belly from lives taken to lives saved. Every Janjaweed she'd killed would have been responsible for multiple deaths in the future. The figures left burning footprints, like drops of acid on the skin, as they moved. As she writhed on the ground, she was a helpless target.

Maliha was dimly aware of other centers of pain— sudden sharp impacts, including a staggering one on her head. She managed to raise her arm to cover her face, and a rock struck her wrist, bringing blood. They were stoning her! It had happened before, on the terrible day centuries ago when she was declared a witch. Even her husband had cast a stone. The Janjaweed must have decided they wanted nothing to do with the demon of a woman who had flames dancing across her belly.

The last figures had climbed into the pan on the saved side, and the scale was rebalancing itself—another round of agony as the pans swung through an arc on her skin.

The stoning abruptly stopped.

They've gone after Hound. No . . .

She heard a sound that was familiar but puzzling. A sword powerfully swung, impacting flesh. She heard it again and again, and now picked up shouts abruptly cut off and the lesser sounds of the dying.

Just then the second part of the demon's bargain hit: the ticking clock. Whenever she saved a life, she aged an unpredictable amount of time, making it harder to save more lives. Age meant vulnerability, slowness in moving and in healing. Eventually, there would come a time when she couldn't take on a band of Janjaweed.

Maliha felt the tug of moving forward in time. Sounds faded and all she could see was a gray tunnel stretching out in front of her. She advanced in the tunnel as though there were a tether around her waist, reeled in by some unimaginable force at the end of the tunnel. Then the tunnel dissipated, leaving only the desert around her. Anu controlled her erratic aging, too, and she hadn't traveled far—barely aged at all—this time.

When she became aware of the real world again, a man's body fell heavily to the ground just inches away from her. A second or two later, his head landed.

The swordsman!

She reached for the only weapon she could use in this position, her knife. A hobnailed sandal pinned her arm before she got anywhere near the sheath.

Her heart beat against her ribs and her mouth was dry. Every muscle in her body tensed in anticipation of the sword's descent. Decapitation was a sure way to end her life—there was no way she could heal from that.

The end to her dreams was at hand. She'd lost her bargain

with the demon, just as he'd said she would. Looking up to greet her death with eyes wide open, Maliha gasped at what she saw.

Standing over her was a Roman centurion. His silver armor gleamed in the moonlight and blood dripped from the long sword held at his side.

Must've hit my head . . .

She felt powerful arms gently lifting her body, mindful of the hurts she'd suffered.

Must have really *hit my head.*

Chapter Four

Maliha tossed back the thin blanket, pulled up the hospital gown she was wearing, and checked her injuries. There were bruises and shallow cuts from the rocks thrown at her, and the top of her head was tender where she'd been hit by a stone. Most of the bruises were fading and the rest would be invisible within hours. Pressing on the neatly bandaged bullet wound on her calf, there was no sharp pain. It would heal in two or three days.

She couldn't say the same for the thigh wound. She peeked under the dressing and found a red crater in her flesh.

No bikinis anytime soon.

She usually avoided hospitals and doctors because she didn't want any witnesses to the speed or manner of her healing. Maliha sat up and swung her legs over the side of the bed, grimacing at the pain emanating from her thigh.

At least they didn't give me any painkillers. Can't afford to be both injured and sluggish.

She tried putting weight on her right leg and found that the pain was bearable by her standards. She was mobile. She went in search of clothing but was prepared to make her exit in the undignified gown if she had to. There was a noise at the door to the hall. Maliha slipped into the bathroom and pulled the door closed so that she could just see out.

"Miss Winters?" It was a nurse checking on her.

Maliha used the identity Marsha Winters as her public

identity, the one who actually worked and provided a livelihood that justified a wealthy lifestyle. Marsha was a novelist who wrote popular pulp-fiction books featuring Dick Stallion, intrepid adventurer and crime solver who galloped through his cases with his libido leading the way. Her income as a novelist, while substantial, was a just a cover story for the massive wealth accumulated over centuries of collecting and investing, everything from pirate booty to precious gems to stock purchases. She'd had three hundred years to amass a fortune, and her methods in the days when she'd been a demon's slave weren't always pure. In fact, they'd rarely been pure.

"I'm Winters, right here." Maliha stepped out of the bathroom and sat down on the bed.

"How are you feeling? You should probably not be out of bed until the doctor approves."

"I had to pee. How are my friends?"

"You are in the finest new hospital in Khartoum," the nurse said, straightening her back and lifting her chin with pride. "Fedail Hospital. You and your friends are receiving top-quality care. Your woman friend is in the ICU. The man is with her most of the time."

Khartoum. I came out on the evac copter then. I don't remember that. I must have been out cold.

"I need to change your dressings. Would you lie down please?"

Maliha remained seated. "Who do I need to see to pay my bill?"

"I hear from others that you have already paid, plus made a donation to the hospital's good works. Do I need to call an aide to ensure your cooperation?"

Amaro must have sent money. Lots of it.

Amaro Reese was the second of Maliha's loyal trio of friends, the people who knew Maliha's story and had joined her struggle. It didn't hurt that she'd saved all their lives, too. Amaro and his sister Rosie were Brazilian orphans brutalized by gang members until Maliha intervened. She brought the two to America, where Amaro discovered his knack for all things computerized and Rosie discovered her knack for having babies. She was married and had recently given birth to her third child.

Maliha locked eyes with the nurse, who was a middle-aged woman with a no-nonsense demeanor. "I have to leave now," Maliha said. "Is there a robe or clothing in the room? Otherwise I will leave in this immodest way."

The nurse moved to a phone by the door. Switching from English to Arabic, assuming that her American patient wouldn't understand, she requested a security guard in the room.

Maliha sighed. It would be easier to go along than make a fuss, and there were patients in nearby rooms she should consider. Some of them might be disturbed if she got tough with the guard. "Okay, you don't need a guard. See, I'm lying down now."

"Thank you." The nurse changed the dressings and commented that Maliha was healing well.

"Due to your top-quality care. Now, the clothing?"

"Right here." She handed over a zippered bag from a drawer nearby. "This is not a good idea until the doctor releases you."

Maliha deftly wrapped the length of red and yellow cotton inside the bag around her body like a sari, but left her head and face exposed for now. It wasn't the first time she'd worn desert garb.

"Where are the things I came in with?"

"The man took them."

Getting in to see Glass in the ICU took some persuading, but finally she fell into a chair next to Hound at her bedside.

"It's good to see you," she said. Some of the tension went out of his body when he heard her voice. The niche next to Glass was empty, and Hound had taken over the space. He'd pushed the empty bed out into the middle of the workspace, forcing someone to move it away.

At least I hope the bed was empty. He might just do that with someone in the bed, though.

"How are you?" she asked.

"Me? I'm okay. Some damn nurse keeps pestering me about my dressing, though. You look good in that outfit."

"Really? I never thought yellow and red were my colors."

He smiled, and it warmed her heart. Hound was doing okay.

She noticed that he was slanted in his chair, his shoulders more uneven than usual, favoring his left side. He was wearing several layers of gowns, alternating opening in the back and opening in the front, and a robe over that. Changing his dressing would have been a major excavation job just to get down to skin level.

His eyes reassured her she needn't worry about him. She turned her attention to Glass. She looked far better than the last time Maliha had seen her. Pristine white blankets concealed everything but her neck and face. No twisted legs visible, no limp hand, no ripped clothing. She was awake, although groggy with painkillers.

"Glass, can you hear me?" Maliha said.

Glass's head turned toward her, but without any sign of recognition. She murmured something Maliha couldn't make out.

"What's she saying?"

"I think it's 'canteen.' That's about all she says, plus something else that sounds like 'dead.' We figure she's either delirious or thinks she's still in the desert or something. I don't think she's physically thirsty. With all those la-la drugs and fluids they're pumping into her, there's no telling what's she's saying."

Hound put his face to Glass's ear. "It's okay, everything's going to be all right."

He straightened up and motioned for Maliha to step out of the room with him. She did, and they talked in the hall.

"I don't want her to hear us, in case she's awake enough. There's a chance she'll lose her left hand," Hound said. "Her legs are in temporary traction splints. She'll probably need several surgeries on her legs but since there wasn't any major bleeding, other things have to come first. The problem is the head injury. A CT scan detected a small amount of bleeding in her brain. Right now it's not a big problem, but pressure could build up."

"A subdural hematoma."

Hound nodded. "The doctor says he doesn't think there's major brain damage underneath it."

"That's a relief."

"I don't know about continuing to treat her here. They did all right patching her up from the field, but for the complicated stuff, I don't know. Could be okay, could be not. I want her to have the best chance. I'd like to take her to that clinic you arranged for me the time my hand got crushed. I have confidence in them."

Maliha nodded. "Clinique des Montagnes. Is Glass safe to transport?"

"As far as I can tell from the docs here, yeah, although I'm worried about the altitude and the brain swelling. But it's got to be done soon." His eyes dropped to the floor. "Uh, there's a problem. A guy like me can't afford—"

"Enough. You don't have to ask." She stood up. "I'm going out to find a phone. I'll be back soon."

The clinic, hidden away in the Swiss Alps, catered to the rich from all countries. Outside those circles, the place didn't exist. Marsha Winters called and informed them that she was checking in a family member and his wife as soon as she could get them there. She gave a brief description of the situation.

"Do they both need to be treated by Dr. Corvernis?"

There was one doctor on staff who treated her and was sworn to secrecy about it, guaranteed not to reveal anything due to the perfect snare she'd trapped him in: she gave him money for his clinic and kept silent about a scandal in the doctor's past that she was aware of from a previous life of hers. Dr. Corvernis provided medical support for Maliha without questioning her healing prowess. A few times she'd recovered from broken bones at the clinic, treating her stay like a luxury resort with a little health care thrown in.

"No. The woman I'm bringing is a kidnap victim with multiple traumas. She's been treated physically here in

Khartoum, but I suggest you start from the beginning. There is some question about her transport. I need to have one of your doctors contact the hospital here and give the okay. The man is her . . . husband, and he has a gunshot wound. Bring in any specialists you need. I'll have this hospital send her CT scan. You'll send the jet, right?"

The clinic had a private jet that picked up and delivered patients.

"Pick up location?"

"Fedail Hospital in Khartoum. We'll need a copter to the airport. Transportation is to be secure and discreet. I want a full emergency medical team on board."

"No problem. I'll have our transportation director make the arrangements himself."

Back in the ICU, an hour went by while she and Hound talked quietly.

She told him everything she'd done in Darfur, through taking a horse and pursuing the Janjaweed, and the attack with the militiamen clustered around her.

"I got hit on the head," she said. "I don't remember anything after that."

"Then let me take it from there. When I saw you next, the evac copter was twenty feet off the ground and all of a sudden you appeared at the end of the clearing with a lit flashlight tied to your belt. We touched back down for you."

The centurion bent down, the crosswise brush on his helmet elegant and untouched by the gore of battle. Stars sparkled in the sky behind him. He sheathed the sword and leaned toward her.

"I must have gotten away but with a concussion from being stoned. When I got to the clearing, I collapsed."

Hound nodded slowly. "Plausible, especially since you're not going to tell me the real story. After the evac, I sent a team back to finish off anyone who was left and search the place in general. They were all already dead. So you killed them all after they had you on the ground throwing stones at you? With a concussion? You're good, woman, but maybe not that good."

Maliha was ready to sputter and deny that she wasn't telling him the real story, but Hound waved the subject away.

"Keep your secrets. I've sure as hell got mine."

Relieved, she nodded. "We have twelve or thirteen more hours to wait for the jet to get here. I think we should both try to get some sleep."

"You go ahead. I'll wait here and just sleep in my chair. Hope my snoring doesn't disturb anybody."

"You don't snore."

"How do you know? You've never stayed around long enough to find out."

Not true. I've watched you sleep for hours. I just wasn't there when you woke up.

She and Hound had been lovers, since long before Maliha knew about his relationship with Glass. As Hound and Glass headed toward marriage, Maliha had eased out of the picture. She'd had enough of love triangles in her lengthy life and was always the one to duck and leave.

Back in her room, Maliha slept ten dreamless hours and popped awake suddenly, with the feeling that she'd just put her head on the pillow a few seconds ago. In the ICU she found Hound asleep in his chair and sat next to him. When she got news that the jet had arrived, she shook him gently.

A buzz of activity began to prepare Glass for transport. When things got busy, Hound handed her a couple of duffel bags and asked her to bring them while he located some clothes.

"I'm gonna strip one of these doctors if they don't have a decent pair of pants around here. I'm not wearing one of those wraparound things you have on."

Maliha moved out of the way and examined the contents of the bags. Inside, Glass's clothing had been tossed in, down to the boots she'd worn, her medic's vest, and her blood-spattered shirt and trousers.

In a separate bag next to Glass's, Maliha found her throwing knives, whip sword, and pistol. Hound's search team must have brought them out. She rested her hands lightly on them, feeling the familiar textures under her fingertips, glad that Hound had arranged this for her.

Digging around in Glass's bag, she came across her survival gear. Among the items was a canteen. Maliha remembered Glass talking about a canteen. She picked it up and shook it. There was a sloshing sound from inside, but it sounded like something thick, like Jell-O that hadn't quite set yet.

Maybe she's not delirious. Maybe there's something important about this canteen.

Maliha was curious and started to open the canteen. She twisted the cap until it was almost off, then thought better of it. Glass might have added something to the water, or done something else to it, that was important.

Something that could condemn the Janjaweed even further and draw attention to Darfur. It's worth a try.

Maliha asked a nurse for a bag that would seal, a medical isolation bag. With the canteen safely preserved, she prepared the rest of Glass's possessions for shipment back to the U.S.

She called Amaro. After telling him the latest news, she asked where her private jet was.

"You mean you don't know?"

"It's never where I want it to be, when I want it. Just check, would you?"

She heard the tapping of keys.

"It's in Cairo, where you left it six weeks ago. Do you even know where I am, or did you misplace me, too?"

"Of course I know where you are. You're in Seoul at some conference."

There was silence, meaning she'd gotten it correct. "As for the jet, I would have made it back there sometime. Tell the pilot, Jackson I think, to come here and pick up some things I want flown back to Chicago. The package—it's a duffel bag—will be left with the clinic receptionist. Remind him he has to get permission to land here. Tell the pilot I want that duffel bag delivered to the University of Chicago medical school, professors Tyson and Claire Rainier. I'll get in touch with them so they know to expect the bag."

"What's so important about this duffel bag that it gets a private jet across the Atlantic?"

"It's just some beat-up clothes with Janjaweed cooties on them, plus some kind of strange desert glop. I'd rather preserve them now than wish I had done so later. Maybe they'll be evidence."

Amaro snorted. "Like you're going to bring the Janjaweed to international justice? Get real, Maliha. Besides, the men who beat up Glass are dead."

"There are more where those came from."

Amaro sighed. "Okay, I'll take care of it. How's everyone doing?"

"You know about Glass. Hound has a bullet wound, and I'm missing a pound of flesh."

"What?"

She told him about her injury.

"Well, no bikini for you for a while."

"My thoughts exactly. Listen, I haven't had a chance to make plans for the other women who were abducted along with Glass. I want excellent care for them, physical and mental, and I want resettlement somewhere that isn't in a refugee camp. See if they have relatives elsewhere. If not, figure something out."

"I will. I'll follow up and keep following up. I should probably fly in there. We can't undo the trauma they've been through but we can make a fresh start for them."

"Don't forget they are widows now. Even if their husbands are alive, they won't have them back. The younger girls are orphans. Same thing, with their parents."

"I understand what you're saying. I'll do the best I can."

Next she phoned Ty. There was no answer, so she left a message. "Ty, it's Marsha. I'm sending you and Claire something to analyze for me. Some kind of goo in a canteen." As an afterthought, she said, "Be careful with it. See you soon."

She hurried out the door and made it to the roof just as the helicopter arrived. It was an uneventful trip to the airport.

With Glass settled aboard the jet and the clinic's medical team fussing over her, they took off into the night sky. Hound promptly fell asleep. Maliha withdrew to the rear of the cabin, determined to alleviate her thigh pain, which had grown worse with increased movement and her lack of attention to it. She estimated it would be about four days before the edges of the wound closed, leaving a pocket underneath to heal at a slower pace.

Closing her eyes, she began to meditate as Master Liu, her Ageless martial arts instructor, had taught her a long time ago. First she slowed and deepened her breathing, then relaxed muscle groups in her body. After reciting mantras about healing and the perception of pain, she reached the deepest level of her meditation. Mentally, she turned on one of the concentration points she used, an infinity symbol that pulsed with a golden glow that matched her lowered heartbeat.

Pain receded from her mind. Focusing all her attention on the infinity symbol, she let it expand into the dark corners of her thoughts. With her senses tuned in to the throbbing glow, she opened her mind to whatever experience came her way. This time, she had an unusual vision of walking on the surface of her brain. Under her feet was a rainbow, with each successive color of the spectrum lighting up and clicking into place as she traversed it. When she had all the colors in place, they melded into white and the radiance extended outside her skull, further and further into the world, then beyond the conscious plane. She had created the experience of a fully realized being, if only for a while. It was good imagery that left her refreshed and with less pain.

For several days at the clinic, Maliha did nothing but heal, write, support Hound, and be frustrated because the Rainiers were away at a conference and hadn't done any analysis on the canteen sample.

Glass was gradually weaned off the barbiturates that had kept her in a coma while her brain swelling decreased. One evening when Maliha entered her room, Glass was not only sitting up, but chatting as though she wanted to make up all the time she been in the coma in one evening.

If Maliha didn't look too hard, she wouldn't notice that the arm tucked under the cheery blanket covered with daisies had no hand and the legs under that blanket were extra large due to casts. Hound was beaming, his lopsided grin showing more teeth than a beauty contest winner.

Hound's just so happy to be with her. I wish Jake were here, grinning at me like that. I miss him.

Maliha kissed Glass on the cheek and patted her right hand, which was whole. She noticed that Hound rested his hand on the blanket on Glass's left arm above the amputation. Because of his service as an Army medic in Vietnam— more of a calling to him than a job—Hound acknowledged traumatic injuries with candor.

"From the copter," Glass said, "it looked like the village had been melted. The bodies on the ground, I mean. Then I spotted a survivor and decided to set down. I should have just shot her from the air. Turns out her guts were falling out. She was dissolving right in front of me." Glass turned toward Hound. "She was just about our daughter's age."

"Hannah's safe," Hound said. "She sends her love. She's staying with your sister Ginny."

"I know, you big idiot." Glass smiled at him, or what passed for a smile with several teeth missing. "Anyway, I figured it might have been some new kind of napalm that dissolved flesh instead of just burning it. I poked some of what was left of the girl into my canteen. You still have that, right?"

"Sent it off to a lab," Maliha said.

Glass nodded slightly. "Good. That's when I saw the guys in suits. They were burning the bodies with flame-throwers, and they were between the copter and me. I hid in something I think was a big oven. I heard them blow up the copter. I figured I was going to get baked in that oven. What a fucking dumb place to hide."

Maliha could see that she was really into her story, reliving it. Glass was breathing deeply and her face was flushed.

"When it was dark, I came out and started walking. I ran into some Janjaweed who'd rounded up a few people who had escaped. I don't think they had anything to do with the attack. They were on their way somewhere else. They killed the men. I was lumped in with the women. I think you know the rest."

Glass's voice wavered to a stop and her head dropped back on her pillow.

"She needs some rest," Hound said. "Let's move next door."

Next door was officially the room that Hound was supposed to be recuperating in, but he'd changed it around to resemble an office more than a hospital room.

"If it's true, this is far worse than a simple Janjaweed attack on a village, as bad as that is. It's clear that it was a field test of a biological or chemical weapon," Maliha said.

"Damn cold-blooded," Hound said. "They put that killer stuff on those villagers or in them or something, and watched them die. Probably took pictures, made a nice scientific record. We gotta find those motherfuckers and blow their heads off. Are we all infected? Wait—what do you mean 'if it's true'?"

"Let's not jump to conclusions," Maliha said. "One thing you have to consider is that Glass is fresh out of a traumatic experience and a coma. She could be disoriented about some things. Even if she isn't, we don't have any physical proof of her story—yet."

"We have that contaminant in the canteen."

What a cold way of referring to the deaths of hundreds, contaminant.

"The unexamined contaminant, at least so far. Let's think it through. Was there any radio or other contact with the villagers before Glass got there?"

"Yeah, that was the procedure," Hound said. "She'd check in the day before to make sure the village was expecting her. She didn't want to be shot at or anything, and the medical team had to be there to receive the supplies. She wasn't supposed to leave them just with the villagers. Too much chance the supplies would sprout feet and walk away."

"So assuming she made the call, there was no problem the day before she flew in, and a medical team was there," Maliha said. "I think when she contacted the village, somebody there would have mentioned that they were in the middle of a horrible medical emergency. That means that all the deaths happened after she called, from one day to the next. Very fast acting."

"We picked up Glass almost a week ago, and nobody has gotten sick since. We should be all right," Hound said.

"I'll arrange some tests from a specialist to make sure. The European Centre for Disease Prevention and Control in Stockholm would be a good source," Maliha said. "I sent Glass's possessions to Chicago. Including the sample from the dying girl. If anything's capable of spreading this 'Darfur Death,' that sample is the prime suspect."

"What'd you have to do that for? Fly that shit all over the world? Might as well have dropped it out of the plane over New York." Hound wasn't happy, whether it was at the thought of the tests Maliha had mentioned or genuine concern about spreading disease, or both.

"At least I packed it in an isolation bag."

"Well, that certainly saves the day. A zippy bag to the rescue."

She was ready with a smart retort, but looked at his aura instead. Hound's aura was always complex and difficult to sort out, but the clear, vibrant tendrils of fear were unmistakable. He was worried about Glass and the new issue of some kind of toxin. She bit her lip and discarded the retort.

"My wife is our canary in the mine then. She's got a couple of days' jump on us, so we'd have about two days of warning."

He said my wife. *First time I've heard it.*

"Generally that would be true. Whatever happened, it could progress differently in different people, like faster in people with weak immune systems." *Or not at all in me.*

"Do we have to tell the docs?"

"Definitely. But only the one we can trust."

Hound raised his voice. "How do you know who to trust? It was probably some doctor who invented that killer stuff in the first place."

A nurse stuck her head in the door. "I heard noise from

out in the hall. It's late and we do have other patients here
who need their rest. Any problem in here?"

"No, nothing's wrong. We'll keep the noise down. Would
you have Dr. Corvernis join us, please?"

"He's not on duty. Visiting hours are over."

Maliha decided to ignore the crack about visiting hours.
"Call him then, Nurse Stocker." The woman had an ID
badge that omitted her first name. She must like being ad-
dressed by her title. "Tell him Marsha Winters needs to see
him right away."

"He is the head of the clinic. I don't want to disturb him
unnecessarily. I'll just call the attending on duty."

Maliha let her eyes focus on a spot past the nurse. Her
aura came into view. Nurse Stocker's aura was partly green,
a healer's green, but there were strong elements of light
brown for insecurity, dull yellow for selfishness, muddy red
for anger.

She's carrying around a lot of baggage. Problems at home?

"Call him. Trust me, he'll come."

The nurse left without a word.

Maliha shrugged. "She must be new around here. The
staff is supposed to know that Dr. Corvernis and I have a
special arrangement."

The nurse returned and said Dr. Corvernis was on his
way in and would be joining them in about ten minutes.
Her words were professional but the tone was resentful. Not
only had her judgment been questioned, she'd no doubt been
reprimanded in harsh terms for it.

"Fine. Would you ask someone to bring us something
to drink, Nurse Stocker? I think we're going to have a long
discussion when the doctor arrives. Water's fine."

"Certainly." Her tone was chilly.

"That's one pissed-off woman," Hound said after the
nurse left the room. "Maybe we should have the water
checked for poison."

Maliha walked over and closed the door. They were
broadcasting their business too carelessly.

"Simmer down. The only one we speak to here is the

good doctor. That remark about killer stuff a while ago might have been loud enough for other patients to hear. The nurse certainly did."

Conversation came to a halt while Nurse Stocker brought in a tray of glasses and a pitcher of ice water.

Dr. Corvernis rushed in, a little red in the face. "You needed me?" He glanced around the room. Normally he spoke to Maliha in private. "Are you ill?"

"I hope not. That's what we need to determine. Hold on a second."

Maliha went over to the closed door, treading softly. She opened the door suddenly. Nurse Stocker was outside. She'd been standing with her ear close to the door.

"Can I help you?" Maliha asked.

"Just . . . just checking back to see if you needed any more water."

"Who's out there?" Dr. Corvernis said.

Maliha stepped away from the door, revealing Nurse Stocker.

"What are you doing? Never mind. You're dismissed for the night, Mrs. Stocker. Go home. I'll talk to you in the morning."

She pinched her lips together, turned on her heel and left.

"I don't know what got into that woman," the doctor said. "The staff knows patient confidentiality is guaranteed. We treat celebrities here. Royalty. Heads of state. I'll bet she's trying to sell something to the tabloids. 'World-famous author has hemorrhoids' or something."

"Does she?" Hound said. He was smiling, the first smile Maliha had seen on his face for a while.

"No." Maliha and the doctor answered in unison.

An hour later, after hashing out procedures, a specialist was on her way from Stockholm. She had agreed to a news blackout, even to her own organization, under very stringent conditions. If there was a problem of any kind, or if she even suspected any problem as soon as she arrived, she was free to call in her organization at any time and get to work.

Even with a plan of action in place, Maliha didn't feel

reassured enough to fall asleep that night. Her mind raced with plans. What she really wanted was to put all of it behind her and go home. She didn't like the turn things had taken from a horrid but at least understood Janjaweed raid to something that might be a new terrorist tool for use on a large scale.

Five tense days later the canary was still alive and the specialist went home. Glass was getting the best of care and Hound was at her side, so there was no reason for Maliha to linger in Switzerland. She was ready to fly back to Chicago. Since her jet had ferried Glass's possessions to the other side of the Atlantic, she booked first class on a commercial flight.

All of first class. She liked privacy.

A couple of Asian businessmen had to be displaced, but were persuaded to move into business class with credits to their accounts after being told that a member of the diplomatic corps required the entire first-class section for security. Maliha allowed them a quick glimpse of her as she boarded, but drew the line at posing for photos.

I'm on my way home!

Her heart was light for the first time in days. Analyzing the canteen sample had fallen to a lower priority because Glass, who'd been closest to the material, breathed it, walked through it, had been cleared of disease. Maliha settled into the new style of first-class surround seats, fully reclining with dividers for privacy and even a seat for a visitor.

At home she could catch up with life in "RandyWorld," as she'd dubbed the trials of her twenty-something friend's dating life, and do some writing on her latest Dick Stallion novel, *Too Big To Be True*.

There was also something she'd been putting off. She was long overdue for a talk with her boyfriend Jake Stackman, a Drug Enforcement Administration agent. She needed to ask some tough questions and kept putting it off, partly because their schedules had pulled them apart.

Admit it. The main reason is I don't want to know the answers.

She summoned the male attendant.

"Mr. Peeters, was it?" Maliha said in her sweetest voice, the one that melted men into compliant puddles. "I'm in the mood for champagne and chocolate."

"Right away, miss. You can call me Jens, if that's not too familiar." The handsome attendant returned with a glass of champagne and two delicate truffles on a lace doily, all on a silver tray.

The champagne and Neuchatel truffles were excellent.

"Bring me a bottle of champagne, Jens," she leaned closer to whisper although they had the first-class cabin to themselves, "plus a glass for you and the box of truffles these came from." Although Maliha rarely drank, there didn't seem to be any threats around miles up in the air and she felt like relaxing.

Jens was glad to be of service. "You know, miss, what goes nicely with champagne and chocolate?"

"No, tell me."

"I'd rather show you."

He started with a slow, sensuous foot massage. It was a long, pleasant flight.

Chapter Five

Mogue considered what the woman had said. So far, he hadn't gotten rough with her, so he still had her confidence. The twenty thousand euros on the table between them kept her talking.

Martine Stocker was the type of person who stood out to Mogue's eyes as though she had a neon sign floating over her head. He could easily pick out such women: needy, poor in a spiritual or material way, weak-willed, with a streak of meanness usually concealed. But not from him.

Mogue maintained a network of informants in hospitals and clinics around the world that catered to the rich and powerful. Such people were most vulnerable when they were forced to face the prospect of death, because the Grim Reaper is the one thing they can't bribe, cheat, or cajole. Mogue's informant at the Clinique des Montagnes was the pilot of the courtesy jet, Edmund Kappel. He was the first to know what prince or sheik or Hollywood star or music diva would be checking in for discreet services.

Edmund reported that he'd picked up three wounded Americans, one of them severely injured, from a private Khartoum hospital. Mogue put that information together with the report from his cleanup crew about a helicopter at the test site that shouldn't have been there. The fools had blown the copter up, but Mogue put two and two together and came up with five: there was at least one American witness to his work.

Enter Martine Stocker, a nurse with a perfect vantage point for information gathering and a serious weakness for jewelry she couldn't afford. Not that she had anywhere fancy to wear the jewels. Either she wanted the gems for their intrinsic beauty or she hoped to have a place to wear them in the future. Mogue didn't care about her reasons. He never did.

"The woman who was injured the most was Alexandra Trent, but everybody called her Glass. I guess that Trent name could be fake because the whole thing was so odd. Another woman, Marsha Winters, has been to the clinic before, and she has some kind of secret arrangement with Dr. Corvernis. It got even stranger. They made some remark about killer drugs or something, and they flew in some woman from Sweden who started doing tests and ordering everybody around. What a bitch she was."

Mogue took in everything with no visible reaction. He could see that his silence made her nervous, which is exactly what he wanted. Nervous people want to fill a silence with more words. Mogue got some of his most useful information without asking questions.

"So is that enough? I can get my money now?" Her eyes dipped again to the stack of money on the table. Lying next to it was the partial recording she'd been able to make before being discovered. The recording device, as he'd instructed, had been hidden behind her ear. He'd frowned when she'd described how she'd been caught—with her head leaning toward the door!

Stupid woman. So obvious. All they had to do was a quick search and the device would have been found, and that would have led to questions. Questioning Stocker was like squeezing a cupcake.

She'd agreed to meet him in the kitchen of a restaurant closed for the night, and never questioned the location. She was inexperienced at selling information or she would have thought the location, surrounded by knives, cleavers, frying vats, and food grinders, was an unusual place for their underhanded business.

"Yes, you've been very helpful. Go ahead and take the money."

When she reached across the table, Mogue reached too. He'd been holding a lovely titanium boning knife, borrowed from the restaurant's ample supply, in his lap. He jammed the knife through her hand and into the wooden table.

Her eyes widened in pain and surprise. She yanked her hand back, but the solid little knife held and tore her flesh. She didn't scream, but she made an anguished moan. Tears began to run down her cheeks.

Mogue watched objectively, trying to decide if the tears were from pain or from the realization that she wasn't going to leave alive. An experiment was in order. From his pocket he took a delicate pair of pliers. Clamping the jaws on one of her fingernails, he twisted his wrist quickly and pulled out the nail.

That got a scream out of her. The tears were probably from pain, then, not the anticipation of death.

Lack of imagination. Even now she is unable to see what lies ahead.

Chapter Six

When she got into O'Hare International, Maliha called the lab where Ty and Claire Rainier worked. No one answered. She called each of their cell-phone numbers and left messages.

Calling a few contacts at the university, she learned that both of them had been away attending conferences, and had intended to take a few days of vacation after that. Recalling her phone message to the Rainiers from the clinic, Maliha hadn't indicated any real urgency about examining the canteen specimen, so they'd probably continued with their plans.

The Rainiers were a brilliant and eccentric couple. She prized their out-of-the-box thinking and the independence with which they worked. That very independence made them a little prickly to deal with. If she seemed to be pestering them, they'd do the exact opposite of hurrying.

Maliha arrived home late on an unusually warm November afternoon. She loved having Chicago as her home base. For a woman who'd traveled so much in her life, and lived in all the cosmopolitan cities of the world, it was nice to claim a place as her personal backyard. At least, during this cycle.

As people aged around her and Maliha didn't keep up, she had to reinvent herself every twenty or thirty years, and that usually meant pulling up stakes. She would have to dispose of her temporary identity—Marsha Winters—and emerge somewhere else in the world with a new name and a new background. She kept access to her fabulous wealth by a variety of techniques. It was a lonely existence, but now Maliha had friends who would carry over from one cycle to the next. A complication, but a rewarding one.

The doorman she'd known for years, Arnie Henshaw, was on duty. He tipped his black shiny-brimmed cap to her.

"Take your bag to the thirty-ninth floor, Ms. Winters?"

"Yes, please, Mr. Henshaw."

The instructions were for the benefit of the assistant, summoned with a crisp snap of Arnie's fingers. Maliha's relationship with Arnie was well established. He was on the fringe of her secret life but didn't know the details. He was well aware that there could be all kinds of weapons, legal and illegal, in her bags. Arnie had known her for fifteen years, but she hadn't aged much at all in that time. Whatever he thought about that, he kept to himself. He knew she led a shadowy double life, but not the details of it, and that suited both of them just fine.

Arnie also knew the truth about her life at the Harbor Point Towers—that there were two places she called home. One was her public apartment on the thirty-ninth floor, sometimes shared with Hound, Amaro and Xia Yanmeng, the third of her trio of close friends. Maliha rescued Yanmeng and his wife, Eliu, from certain death in a prison during the Chinese Cultural Revolution. With three men occasionally staying and working at her place, she'd needed more room. She'd bought the apartment next door, an expansive three-bedroom space, when the owner moved to Barcelona for the climate. Remodeled and immense, her public home now had a private suite for her, plus three guest bedrooms and a communal space. She liked all the room, but it wasn't where her heart lived. That was reserved for her secret haven, where she surrounded herself with treasures she'd collected during her long life. The haven was the center of her life as a former assassin and the base of her quest for redemption.

It was also the place that Jake Stackman had broken in to the last time she saw him. Not to steal anything, but just because he figured out how to get past her advanced security measures and wanted to surprise her. He surprised her, all right. The secret haven was designed to be impenetrable by humans. Maliha assumed anyone who got in had to be Ageless, the servant of her own or another demon, sent to kill her since she'd told Rabishu where he could shove her contract.

A rogue, that's what they called me now. Not quite Ageless, not quite human either.

The secret haven was just nine floors above her public home. She headed there now. She'd bought two condos on the forty-eighth floor and torn out their guts to make one large, semicircular space with a coveted view of Lake Michigan. It was a view for which others would pay extravagantly, but for Maliha security came before scenery. The window was coated with a blast-resistant film and covered at all times with special cellular shades that were metal on one side and decorative cloth on the other.

She entered numbers into a keypad at the door and placed her eye up to the retinal scanner. The door, steel-plated and bomb-hardened, slid aside. Bright lights in the foyer came on, intended to blind anyone who wasn't expecting them. Light bounced off the metal floor and ceiling of the foyer, multiplying the effect and turning the brightness level to near lightning-bolt intensity.

Maliha threw herself across the light chamber and pressed a nearly invisible switch that disabled a nasty "welcome mat"—waves of darts shot from the ceiling, leaving an intruder both blinded and pin-cushioned. In a final safeguard, if the disabling switch wasn't pressed, the lobby sealed into a steel box and air was pumped out of it. An Ageless person could survive the darts, but even the Ageless had to breathe.

Her safe haven was surrounded by a metal tube exactly like the foyer, meaning that anywhere the safe room touched another wall, there was a buffer zone that could be filled with darts and evacuated of air.

The bright light faded and Maliha entered a short hallway that ended in a sharp left turn. Once in the main area, there was a cocoonlike feeling due to walls and deep carpets the color of eggshells and black cellular shades on the windows.

"Lights, soft."

Twinkling low-voltage lights suspended from the ceiling came on, along with a band of light built into the walls that was adjustable in intensity. Although the space was large, it was defined by the different uses—bathing, food preparation, sleeping, weapons cache, exercise area, and private museum.

Maliha put her shoes in a bin near the door and dropped her clothes into another bin. Usually she went naked in her haven, or wore a light robe. This time she picked out a robe and set to work cleaning the few weapons that had survived the car crash and the stint in Sudan. Master Liu had impressed on her that her weapons came before leisure, and it had been bothering her that she hadn't had an opportunity to clean them before this.

A sharp thwack across the back with a fighting stick brought her aware. Master Liu had returned. His face was as fierce as she'd seen it, but he didn't shout. His quiet voice was lash enough.

"Your comfort is never to be placed above your duty to this school or the respect you pay to your weapons. Look about you."

The floor was blood-smeared in places and so were some of the swords, knives, sticks, and other weapons used during the marathon session. Her uniform was marked with red from wounds beneath it. Maliha pulled up to her feet and began to work. At the first light of dawn, she fell asleep in her cot in the cabin behind the school. An earned sleep, with the school's floor and weapons spotless and her body freshly bathed.

When her weapons were spotlessly clean, she restored them to their places in wall and shelf displays, where they shared space with an assortment of edged weapons and modern ones, gleaming swords and dull black Special Ops pistols, side by side.

Her wounds inflicted in Darfur were feeling much better,

especially the bullet wound in her calf. The thigh wound, with the chunk of flesh removed, was still giving her trouble, but she could ignore it if she set her mind to it.

Maliha showered and called Randy Baxter, her connection to the normal twenty-something world, the one where it was possible to have fun that didn't involve body-slamming someone unless it was foreplay.

"Are you alone tonight?" Maliha said. Randy knew her as Marsha Winters.

"Depends on why you're asking." It was a webcam communication, and Maliha could see that Randy was in the middle of dressing to go out. She fastened a score of buttons up the front of a white cotton dress, and then bent over to shake out her curly reddish-blonde hair.

Maliha peered at the screen. "Is that eyelet lace?"

"Yeah. Shows a lot of me underneath. Like it?"

"It's terrific. Are you going out with Power Balls?" Randy had private nicknames for her guys.

Randy nodded. "You're actually available for a girls' night out?"

"Mm-hmm. And I want to get your take on Jake."

"Already gave you that. Marry the guy."

"You don't know everything about him."

"Yum, juicy. Girls' night out and rampant gossiping. You're not going to freak out and threaten to cut the hands off some guy because he groped you, are you? I mean, that was a little embarrassing."

"Way too mellow for that." *I'll go straight for his dick instead.*

"I can detect the scent of wine on your breath from here. You must have gotten a head start. Let me call PB and tell him I'm sick."

"Call me back when the deed is done. I'll pick you up."

Randy's brow crinkled on the screen. "You shouldn't be driving, Ms. Mellow. Let me get us a taxi."

Maliha hadn't been drinking, and chose her occasions carefully when she did. It didn't make sense when spending eternity as Rabishu's plaything—the penalty if she didn't balance her scale—could rest on a single physical or mental response to a sudden threat.

"I'll come in the limo." *Which reminds me that I need a new car.*

"You are my beloved sugar mommy. Thirty minutes?"

"If I can decide on a dress fast enough."

A quick call summoned one of her limo drivers, positions filled by a married couple who lived in the same building in a one-bedroom condo, courtesy of Maliha. They were highly paid to make sure one of them was available whenever Maliha was in Chicago, trained in defensive driving tactics, and imperturbable. Tonight it was the wife, Ryba, a taciturn Eastern European woman. Ryba knew her way around the personal and vehicular defenses the limo carried and wouldn't hesitate to use them. Having her as a driver seemed overkill for a night out on the town. If Ryba ever faced the baby-stroller-in-the-road challenge, she'd probably step on the gas if the safety of her passenger was at risk. At least Maliha felt secure with Ryba, if not socially correct.

Before getting dressed to go out, Maliha placed a quick call to Amaro.

"Don't you ever sleep?" she said when he picked up promptly.

"Not often. What's up?"

"I have something fun for you to do while you're working on the depressing stuff. I need a new car. You know my car was totaled in Massachusetts."

"No! Tell me about it."

She gave him an abbreviated version. "I was banged up a lot but nothing serious. The car had a great custom crash system. Anyway, I'm thinking of another McLaren or a Pagani Zonda F. Why don't you dig around and see what you can come up with? Don't buy anything, though. I have to make sure my customizer can work with it first."

"You're kidding, right? Can I go on test rides?"

"This is for your spare time. You need to wrap things up with the abducted Darfur women. But yeah, you can do some test rides. Just say you're the purchasing agent for an

anonymous buyer and provide a credit letter from one of my
Swiss accounts you have access to. They'll guarantee that
there is more than enough on deposit to pay in cash."

"Cool. Wait a minute—there are more Swiss accounts I
don't know about?"

"Bye, Amaro."

Maliha was sure she'd have a car soon, and have spared
herself the tedious search. She pulled her thoughts back to
her evening out. Randy was escapism, a way to set aside the
deeper purpose of Maliha's life, and was worth the little pre-
tenses needed to keep up the illusion of normal life. Maliha
picked a long, slinky blue dress with spaghetti straps that
was cut nearly to the waist in the back, low enough to earn
a disapproving look from Ryba.

Maliha loved it when men admired the tattoo on her
back, a hawk that spread its wings over her shoulders. It
was a remarkable gift from Master Liu. The tattoo drew
attention away from the Chinese character branded on her
shoulder, and that was fine with her. That brand was more
private. It was her symbol of acceptance as Master Liu's
granddaughter and a member of his school—the completion
of her training. While it was an honorary title, it was one
they both took seriously. Her scale, her hawk tattoo, and the
shou—long life—character on her shoulder were the tripod
on which her life rested.

*Why didn't I run straight to Jake's arms tonight? That's
where I'd like to be. But we have to clear the air. Why am I
being such a coward about it?*

"So what's wrong with Jake? Does he want kinky sex or
something?"

Maliha and Randy were crammed into a corner of the
Only the Lonely Club, their table no bigger than a hand-
kerchief. The place was packed in spite of its name, which
conjured images of people sitting in silence, one person
per table, the tables far apart and poorly lit. This interior
of this club was brighter than daylight. The majority of
the space was used for a dance floor containing so many

mostly vertical people that they were in three hundred and
sixty degree contact. Having rebuffed numerous requests
to dance, the two women were talking with their heads
tucked close together. Some lipreading was involved, even
at that range.

Maliha smiled. Whatever Randy meant by kinky, she
would bet that Randy's concept was mild compared to situations Maliha had extricated herself from over the centuries.
Jake doesn't even register on the kinkiness detector.

"No, nothing like that."

"'Cause if that was it, you let me know and I'll have a
talk with him and call him·off. After all, I did introduce you
two."

Randy had set up the blind date that sparked the romance
between Jake and Maliha, so she thought she had some
degree of responsibility if anything went wrong. But the
thought of Randy having to protect her from an unwanted
sexual approach nearly made Maliha laugh aloud. She bit
her lip instead.

"No, really. You don't need to talk to him."

"He's gay then."

"Nope. Hey, this isn't an interrogation. It has to do with
his background. When I start seeing a guy, I ask a friend
who does background investigations to check him out. I
have to worry about stuff like that because of my books. You
know, guys wanting to be Dick Stallion in the flesh. I asked
him about Jake, and it turns out Jake has a gap of about five
years during which he didn't exist."

Randy's eyes narrowed. "Did your friend investigate me?"
Of course.

"Of course not. You're a girl."

"Okay then. Forget I asked."

"When I say Jake didn't exist, I mean he had no public
records at all. No driver's license. No IRS filings. No phone
records. No dental records. Poof. Gone."

"That's what's bothering you? That just makes him mysterious."

That's not the only thing that makes him mysterious.

There's the Incident, too. Damn, when I start thinking in capital letters I know things are bad.

"I mean, look at you. You write books. You do research for your books. You write more books. You live a dull life. You need to walk on the wild side. Jake is good for you. The dark, mysterious stranger who sweeps you away to . . ."

"To what, exactly?"

"Something exciting. A different kind of life. Marsha, it's what we all dream about."

"What if he did something bad during those years? He's a government agent."

"You mean like secret missions where he assassinates the bad guys?" Randy's eyes sparkled. "I'm jealous. I should have kept him for myself. Wonder what his nickname would be. Want to part with the anatomical details?"

"You're talking about the movies, Randy. Secret missions and all that. I mean, what if he's a run-of-the-mill murderer?"

"You mean he was in prison for five years and the murders stopped? Or he started a fresh life after doing away with the wife and kids? Now you're the one talking about the movies, Marsha. How likely is that? Do you think our government would let that kind of person be in the DEA?"

In the blink of an eye, if it served their needs.

"I guess not."

Jake's aura revealed a deep, probably murderous evil, overlaid with sincerity about doing his job and concern about protecting people. Maliha had glimpsed that same kind of aura—in the mirror the first and only time she'd tried to assess herself.

Randy tapped Maliha's hand. She'd asked a question. "I said, do you love him?"

"Probably." *Yes.*

"I'll take that as yes. Then you have to love his flaws, too. You can't wait for the fairy tale."

It struck Maliha as something profound, coming from Randy who seemed so casual about her relationships.

Buried in her statement was a genuine longing, something she'd never heard from Randy the Player.

Love his flaws. How about my husband, Nathan? I loved him when he married me and started a child in me. Should I also love that he stoned me and watched me set afire as a witch? I think she's talking about flaws with a little f, not a big F. Which ones does Jake have?

"Hey, let's dance." Randy signaled that the serious stuff was settled as far as she was concerned.

Randy stood up, held out her hand to the first man who approached, and moved away to the dance floor. Maliha did the same, but she sat down after a while. The wound on her thigh was covered over so that it felt normal to her dance partners if they touched her, but it wasn't fully healed underneath. The wound felt pulled in all directions from the dancing, reminding her that only a short time ago she'd been on horseback in the African desert.

Randy found someone to hook up with, so Maliha rode home alone in the limo. All her nervous energy was gone and she was finally ready to sleep.

Alone.

Her haven welcomed her with its understated elegance and environment finely tuned to her solitary moments. With her bare feet enjoying the thick carpet, she wandered among the treasures. On the wall was a panel from the original Amber Room given as a gift to tsar Peter the Great in the early eighteenth century. The Amber Room was made entirely of tons of carved amber, accented with gold and mirrors. Looted and moved by the Nazis at the end of World War II, the room disappeared and its whereabouts have been a mystery since 1945. Most people think it was destroyed when the castle it was in was burned.

Maliha, then operating as Rabishu's slave, was very active during the war, and one thing she did for herself was salvage a panel of the original room. It had sentimental meaning for her. For others it was a priceless treasure, but to her it was something she had stood in front of and admired at a ball given by a friend of hers, Elizabeth,

Empress of Russia, only a few years before Elizabeth's death.

Maliha moved from the carpeted area to the simple wooden plank flooring. It reminded her of the training platform of her martial arts school in the mountains of China, where Master Liu had taken her in as a resentful, awkward beginner. Master Liu was more than five thousand years old, an original Sumerian and priest of Anu. He knew he was the last one left, and he was forced to keep his immortal bargain with Rabishu for a reason far different from anyone else's. He wanted to be alive to welcome Anu back to Earth when that time came, and to be the priest who would help the rest of the world understand the gods of its creation.

Maliha had no argument she could offer against Master Liu's constancy. It ruled his life, and she had no proof one way or another about any return of the gods. She couldn't imagine the experiences of his lifetime. All she knew was that she had felt Anu's hand on her life, specifically on the balance of her scales and the amount of her aging. Even more concrete than that, she had seen and talked to one of Anu's offspring; visited Midworld, where their two worlds intersected; and been thrust briefly into Rabishu's hell, where he tortured those who had fallen under his sway.

She used some of her weapons for a brief, intense workout on the wooden planks, cleaned them so that no drop of sweat remained, and took a shower with the hot water set at such force it felt like it was needling her all over.

In a thin white gown that stuck to her damp skin, Maliha went to her sleeping area. It was a Japanese tatami mat, woven of straw, on a wooden floor. Unrolling a thin futon on top of the mat, she lay down and looked at the sparkling low-voltage lights suspended from her ceiling like stars. After a while, she said, "Lights out."

In the dark, in her safe place, she was free to evaluate her experiences, feeling the doubts, the longings that often didn't get a chance to surface—especially in the middle of a firefight. That included weaknesses of her body that she usually had to conceal.

Never show an enemy a weakness, Master Liu would say, or he will know where to add to it.

She checked over all the parts of her body, working on the hurt places, the wounds, concentrating on helping them speed up their healing. Then she let her mind wander.

All those questions Randy asked about Jake, and then the one thing I was most worried about she just brushed off. He's mysterious, and that excuses a lot. Flaws, phooey.

In her haven, in the dark, Maliha could let the words take shape that represented deep fears.

I bear the guilt of doing great evil. Some days it nearly rips me up inside. All those people, dead by my hand. Why didn't I come to my senses earlier? A century earlier would have meant so many lives saved. Instead I stayed young, had a great time traveling all over, bedding princes and sheiks, and the payment was a growing pile of corpses. Never enough blood to satisfy Rabishu, though. I'm so ashamed. Would any good man want me as a wife, knowing what I've done in the past? Bedmate, yes. But soul mate? Would Jake, if he truly knew me?

She closed her eyes and let tears slide down her cheeks.

Chapter Seven

Maliha awoke before dawn. She'd been restless all night, and knew what she had to do. She got up, turned on some lights, and before she could think of reasons not to, she called Jake. He answered on the fourth ring.

"It's me. I hope I didn't wake you."

"No, no, I was up doing some paperwork."

She could hear the sleepiness in his voice. She pictured Jake sitting on the edge of his bed in boxers, shaking his head, trying hard to sound like he'd been awake.

"Are you alone? I mean, would it be okay if I came over?"

"Yeah, that would be great. Come on over and I'll fix us some breakfast. Or you want me to come pick you up?"

"No, I'll be there."

Maliha decided it was time to stretch her aching muscles. She dressed in black, braided her hair, concealed her knives, and added a sweatshirt for warmth. In spite of the unusually warm weather, cold winds from Lake Michigan could change things quickly. When she left, the sky was the deep lavender that preceded sunrise. Pulling the hood of her sweatshirt up, she sped through streets that were deserted except for early grocery deliveries of fresh produce, milk, and bread. Her thoughts were of her complaining muscles at first and then of the rhythm of her footsteps. When she reached the McKinley Park neighborhood, her feet took her into the park instead of directly to Jake's house.

I could go home. Consider this a morning run. Call Jake and tell him I felt ill or something.

The thought was tempting. She draped herself on a bench near the lagoon. The run had been only a dozen miles or so, not enough to tire her or even break a sweat. He was expecting her for breakfast. She wanted to go in. Her love for Jake had been growing when the wedge between them suddenly surfaced. . . .

Two Months Earlier

She rode the elevator in the Harbor Point Towers building to the forty-eighth floor. At the door to her private and very secure haven, the biometric sensor welcomed her by name after identifying her by retinal scan.

She navigated the trap in the foyer meant to stop unwanted visitors. The spotlights snapped off and the door closed behind her.

"Lights, low."

Instead of moving into the room, she paused. Something was wrong. There was dampness in the air, and the barely detectable scent of the orchid shampoo she used. Yet she hadn't been here in more than two weeks. It was as if someone had been using the haven in her absence.

Her eyes grew wide as she realized the situation. She'd walked into a trap.

Maliha flattened against the wall of the hallway. She was in a bad position, trapped in a dead end area, in limbo between the exterior hallway and a weapons cache right up ahead, around the bend in the hallway.

Whoever was inside knew she was coming. She'd given that away with the flash of the spotlights and then her voice. She could back up, hit the switch to open the door, and then dive out into the hall. Better to leave now, if she could, and return better prepared. She could visit the armory in one of her scattered safe houses and come back prepared, even though she'd still be at a disadvantage.

"You can come out now."

It was Jake Stackman's familiar voice. She'd been dating him for several months.

Her shoulders sagged with relief. Her legs felt limp as the adrenaline rush that had prepared her for action started to fade. Then she remembered the switch on the wall of the foyer that stopped the darts. As fast as her elation had arrived, it now fled.

Jake was inside her safe haven.

Why didn't he trigger the darts? Why is he still alive?

Anyone who could penetrate the safeguards of her haven was a deadly enemy, whether extraordinarily clever human or Ageless. She pressed herself into a defensive position against the wall as her emotions balled into a cold lump in her heart.

I have to kill him. Now. Somehow.

The weapons she had with her weren't promising—only two throwing knives and a short knife for close work.

"Something wrong over there? It's about time you got here, by the way. I've been here for hours."

He was in motion and his voice sounded much closer. He was coming to see why there was a delay—coming to trap her in her dead-end foyer. Getting caught here was giving up. She had to flee or take the fight to him.

She pulled her close knife from its sheath inside the waistband of her jeans and held it at the ready. She pictured the layout. Around the corner was her weapons cache with swords, guns, explosives, things that might give her a fighting chance. The problem was that from the sound of his voice, Jake was closer to it than she was, and an advantage of even a few inches for an Ageless man could be too much to overcome.

The stakes were as high as they could be—if she died now, her quest to balance the lives she'd taken as the Black Ghost with lives saved since she became mortal would fail. She would suffer uncounted years of torture at the hands of Rabishu—she'd lose the chance to redeem her soul. Even worse, she would have failed in her attempt to destroy the seven demons.

A tear slid down her cheek. *Jake, I thought you were the one.*

She pushed away the regret. If she survived, she'd have time for that. Maliha bent her legs, tensed her muscles, and then sprang around the corner. He was there, right up near her—she'd let him get too close. Her judgment was screwed up, and the hesitation was going to cost her.

She stabbed his thigh as she went by, then she hit the wall of the weapons cache and spun around with a sword in her hand. She felt a little less naked.

Jake was down. Against the odds, she'd surprised him and landed a blow. She shoved off from the wall to press her advantage. Half a second later, she was on him, her sword balanced at his throat. The edge of her weapon drew blood. All she had to do was lean her weight on the sword, sending the edge deeply into his flesh.

She'd delayed so long that by now he should have thrown her off. Instead, he went still beneath her.

A ruse?

She saw his lips move, forming the shape of her name with no sound.

Act, damn it—do it!

Her hands weren't obeying her mind, they were taking orders from her heart. The blade broke the skin in a short line that welled with blood but went no further.

What if I'm wrong?

She rolled off him, kept going, and came to her knees a short distance away. Then she rose to her feet and dashed back toward the door.

"I love you," came from the man down on her floor. She hesitated, and then kept going. She had to get away from the shock, the fear that she'd killed the human Jake or failed to kill the Ageless Jake when she had the chance.

Out in the hall, she kept going. She ran down the fire stairs and toward the front door. Arnie, eyes wide at the sight of her with bloody clothes and a sword, tried to wave her down before she made it out the door, but she weaved past him and ran outside.

On the large portico outside, she halted her unthinking rush, realized that heads were turning to look at her, and quickly made it back into the stairwell. Climbing back to the forty-eighth floor, she dreaded what she would find.

"I love you," Jake said. I'm going to find his body, bled out from the leg wound. Or his wound healed instantly and he's waiting to kill me with my own weapons.

She entered her haven with caution. There was neither a welcoming voice nor a cry of pain. Edging around the corner, her sword at the ready, she smelled blood.

And that's all there was, a stain on her carpet. Jake was gone.

The next day she called Jake's number at work and was told he'd taken a few sick days.

"Old leg wound acting up, he says. Would you like to leave a message?"

Maliha was relieved Jake was alive but that didn't go far enough to answer her questions. As the days went by, it became easier to hide behind a curtain of not knowing what had happened than to face the truth: she'd raised her hand against the man she thought was her true love, and had come within milliseconds of chopping off his head.

Where's the trust in this relationship?

She'd kept track of him, had known that between then and now he'd spent most of his time overseas, in Afghanistan working with tribal leaders on deals to replace the poppy crop. She'd been in Africa, with Glass. Lines of communication were shaky, but if they'd both desired it, they could have found a way to talk before now. Before she found herself on a bench a couple of blocks from his house, thinking of calling the whole thing off.

The sunrise brought with it a heavy fog that normally would have been ice laden at this time of year. Instead, it began to soak through her clothing, leaving her chilled. She took it as a sign that she'd dallied too much in the park. She left the bench and headed for the park exit.

Left turn, home. Right, Jake's house.

She turned right and hurried the last two blocks. Jake opened the door before she knocked.

How does he do that? Cameras?

Mundane questions were swept from her head as he pulled her inside and gathered her in his arms. His kiss left her dizzy with love.

Too fast! Get rational.

She pulled back and studied him. At arm's length, his physical presence was as powerful as if he were a giant magnet and she were a pile of iron filings. He was fit, broad shouldered, with a solid abdomen and lean waist. His naturally curly black hair made her want to run her hands through it, but instead she put her finger over the scar on his chin. He claimed he'd smacked it on a car door, but she knew a scar from a blade when she saw one.

But that scar could have been made before he became Ageless. I still have one from my time as a colonial wife.

"Drop your pants," she said.

Jake blinked and stepped back a bit. "I, uh, thought we'd have a talk and maybe some breakfast, but if you want . . ."

"What I want is to see your left thigh where I stabbed you."

"Oh. I think we should talk first."

She edged backward a little and put one hand on the doorknob, the other in position to draw the short knife sheathed inside her waistband. There was only one reason he would be reluctant to show the wounded area.

I shouldn't have come. Too much risk.

"Okay, don't leave."

"Do I have your word you won't attack?"

As though that would do much good if he's evil, but at least it's something.

"Yes, damn it. Get it over with." He unfastened his belt and did as she requested.

Maliha took her hand from the doorknob and ran it up his thigh from his knee to up under his boxers, moving back and forth, feeling for a scar. She heard a slight gasp from Jake, but continued her search visually by dropping to one knee and taking a close-up look at his thigh. Maliha stood, and he pulled his pants back up over the bulge in his boxers.

"Still want to talk? Or are you going to dash out of here?" Jake said, as he fastened his belt.

She'd determined that he had no scar from her stab wound.

"You're Ageless. What else is there to talk about? I'll leave now, and the next time we meet I'll try my best to kill you."

"We don't have to be enemies. I'd still like to have that talk. You know nothing about me."

"I know enough. I know that you're a demon's assassin and the demons know I'm a rogue. I can't imagine any of the demons have warm feelings in their hearts for me."

"They don't, assuming they have hearts. But my demon, Idiptu, no longer cares about what happens in the Great Above. I don't have any orders to kill you. I don't have any orders at all. Come in and sit down. I gave my word I wouldn't attack you."

He extended his hand to Maliha. After a brief hesitation, she took it and let him lead her to an upholstered chair in the living room. He had a fire set in the fireplace, and now lighted it with a long match. She noted that they both started fires the same way, not with crumpled newspaper, fatwood, or commercial fire starters, but with a pile of wood shavings, curled and aromatic, under an expertly placed stack of kindling. He blew a few times until the shavings were blazing, then sat a few feet away in another chair, avoiding the couch where they'd made passionate love in the past. They both watched as flames spread to the kindling. Jake added a few logs and settled back in his chair.

"Not only can I build fires, I can survive on wild berries."

"A merit badge for you."

A smile passed over his face but dissolved into earnestness. "I want so much for this to work out. I love you. If you don't or can't love me, then I respect that and we go our separate ways. I'll get a transfer to another city to make it easier. Ask me anything, Marsha."

The fire was taking the morning chill out of the room. Maliha pulled off her damp sweatshirt to let the warmth reach her skin. "First, stop calling me Marsha. That's my temporary name for the public, and we're beyond that. I go by Maliha Crayne. Explain the rules of your contract with Idiptu."

"My contract is just like the one you had. Obey without question and in return receive immortality and certain other gifts to help with the demon's assignments."

"What are your gifts?"

Jake's eyebrows rose. "You mean the gifts come in flavors?"

"Just answer."

"Extremely rapid healing and movement. Very sensitive hearing. I can hear your blood moving in your body. The hearing operates over a distance, too, but I have to focus on it. Yours?"

Interesting about the hearing. I'm supposed to be asking the questions here. But we can't have a trusting relationship if he's the only one doing the trusting.

"Same healing and speed of movement, diminished now that I broke the contract. I can see auras. I'm not sure if that came with the contract or if it was something I was born with and gradually learned how to use. It didn't lessen after I went rogue."

Jake nodded. "I got my training—"

"With Master Liu?"

He doesn't have the shou *character branded on his shoulder.*

"Yes, and I know what you're going to ask. I don't have the brand on my shoulder that you do because Liu and I, let's say we didn't get along. He didn't ask me to join his school. He knew I wouldn't swear loyalty to him."

"Because?"

"That's something I'll have to withhold, Maliha. Ask Liu. Maybe he'll tell you, but I doubt it."

I'm curious, but curiosity's not enough of a reason for me to know something between him and Master Liu. I've got my secrets, too. She nodded for him to continue.

"After training, I went to work as an assassin for the first couple of hundred years. Then the assignments thinned out, and finally my demon told me that I could live my life as I chose and he wouldn't be calling on me anymore. He'd lost interest in humans and now spends all of his time thinking about older days, when the rest of the Sumerian gods were here on Earth. I think he might be pining after some lover who left the Earth when he got left behind."

"The demons can appear in any form. I don't know if they have gender the way we think of it."

"Okay, *it* might be pining after a lover. Are you an expert on their mating habits?"

Maliha remembered a time when Rabishu appeared in the form of a black panther that had a void in its center, causing fog to swirl away into it like a black hole.

His teeth parted and out came the tongue, red and obscene. It played lazily over her chest, licking up the blood, and then drifted onto her breasts. She felt his agile tail stroking her legs in a sensuous way. Then the tip of the tail, now hard and hot, squirmed between her legs.

She stiffened beneath him and clenched her thighs shut, wondering if he was planning to rape her and what she could do to stop him. So far she hadn't been able to stop him from doing anything he wanted, including driving his claws completely through her flesh, a violation of a different sort. . . .

"Hey, I'm sorry. Let's get off that topic."

Maliha's face must have given away the bad memory. "Good idea. How did you become Ageless?"

The change of topic was good for her, but now it was Jake's turn to reflect on events he'd rather forget. His mouth pinched into a straight line and his eyes grew troubled as he put his thoughts together.

"Do you know the name Taddeo Gaddi?"

"An Italian painter, I think. Before my time."

"Fourteenth century. He did a lot of work in Florence. I was apprenticed to him at the age of twelve. That was in 1332. He had several apprentices, but I was the best of them. I was his favorite, and he made that very clear. Lots of praise. I traveled with him—he even let me do brushwork on his frescoes after he injured his eyes studying eclipses."

"I can see where this is going. The other apprentices were jealous."

Jake nodded. "Then came the perfect opportunity to get rid of me. It was in 1348."

"The black death."

"The city had a high death rate. The others locked me in a small room and told the master that I had taken ill and it wasn't safe for him to see me. At least I guess they did, because I cried out for him and he never came. After a few days, they all came into the room while I was sleeping and stabbed me. I screamed that I would take vengeance, but I died, or nearly died. The demon pulled me to Midworld and I was so angry I took his offer."

"Let me guess. Your first assignment was to kill the other apprentices."

"Broke their necks. I put them out for the pickup of the dead. They went to a mass grave. I told Master Taddeo I was frightened of the plague and was leaving the country. It was hard, especially when he called me a coward, because I loved that man. But I had to get away from there. I learned later that he made it through the plague, and that helped some."

For a while, the crackling fire was the only sound in the room.

"Your turn," Jake said.

Maliha sighed. "Depressingly like yours, based on betrayal. I was a wife and healer in Colonial Massachusetts. In 1692, the witch hysteria swept through my area. A young woman named Alice, who'd been spurned by my husband, accused me of witchcraft. She hoped he would marry her after I was out of the way. I was dragged out of my home in the middle of the night and thrown in jail, where I . . . I gave birth to a stillborn daughter. The trial was a farce. Alice accused me of causing afflictions to her and of plotting to kill my husband with my 'witch's potions,' which were nothing but healing herbs. I wasn't allowed to speak in my defense for fear I would utter curses, and my husband wasn't either, since he was presumed to be bewitched by me. The usual penalty for witchcraft was hanging, but since I was found guilty of both witchcraft and plotting murder, the judge decided I needed something more than a quick snap of the neck. I was burned at the stake."

"I'm sorry that you had to go through that."

"To this day I like my fires confined and controlled." She gestured at the fireplace. "I took Rabishu's deal and my first assignment was to kill Alice. After that, I left town. I had nothing there. My baby daughter was dead, I'd killed my accuser, and my husband had turned against me and tried to stone me."

The emotions came swirling back, and Maliha quickly swiped at the tears that were forming. She lowered her eyes. It was the lowest point of her life she was talking about and it was never easy. Jake started to rise to come over to her, but she raised a hand to signal him to stay put. It was her story. She would deal with it.

"I killed innocents for over two hundred years. I didn't think about it much, just did my work and enjoyed the other part of my life. I took men on my terms and became fabulously wealthy by buying land and collecting gold and rare items. I traded in world markets—London, Paris, Amsterdam—when Wall Street was just a street next to a wall built by the Dutch to defend against attacks by the British. I presume you've done the same, over a longer period of time." Jake nodded. "Then I had some assignments that made me question what I was doing. I started to see the targets as real people whose families grieved for them. I finally got to an assignment I couldn't carry out."

"I never reached a questioning stage," Jake said. "If Idiptu had stayed active and had been giving me assignments for over the full six hundred and fifty years . . ." He shook his head. "I think I would have killed myself."

Been there, tried that.

"I have new goals now. If you don't work for your demon, what do you do with all your time?"

"Study. Travel. Take jobs like the one with the DEA from time to time."

"You don't use your Ageless abilities then."

Jake considered. "Mostly the immortality part. I have my own moral code I've developed, and when that code's being stepped on, I'll do something about it. Can't say it always lines up with the legal codes of the time and place, but it's meaningful to me."

That moral code must be what I'm seeing when I read his aura—that strong desire to help people, but not pure goodness. More like a gray area where the outcome is good but some of the steps along the way aren't. That describes me, too. Sometimes I have to kill people to save others. That's as gray as it gets.

"I think we're alike in that. Jake, I have to ask. What about your missing five years?"

Before answering, Jake put more logs on the fire.

"Easy there, you're going to make it too hot in here," she said.

"I have an ulterior motive. You'll get too hot and take off all your clothes."

In answer, Maliha stretched and pulled her top up over her head. She was wearing a camisole underneath. Jake followed every move closely but didn't budge from his chair.

"I can't tell you about the five years. I'd be breaking too many sworn confidences. I hope you can accept that."

"Then tell me you weren't doing something evil," Maliha said.

"I can say it concerned my moral code."

Can I live with that or not? It comes down to the whole issue of trust. Do I think he's been telling me the truth about everything else? How slippery is this moral code? With my past, I can't exactly demand purity in someone else.

"I can live with that, I guess. Now you have to tell me how you got past my security measures into my private place."

"I love it when you talk dirty. I followed you after you first contacted me about the drug-smuggling scheme. I found out that sometimes you went to one condo and some-times to another. Who has two places in the same build-ing? Someone who's living in one and doing something drug related in the other one, I figured. Since one condo had a simple key and I'd been inside it already with you, I concentrated on the other place. I was in the emergency stairway watching you when you went to that door. You did a retinal scan, and when the door opened, there was a blind-ing flash of light."

"How often did you follow me?" Maliha was chagrined that she hadn't noticed him tailing her. She had a tendency to relax when she passed the doorman and went into the lobby of her building.

That will have to change.

"Only a few times. I lucked out that you went to your hideaway so soon after I started."

"How did you get into the building? It's supposed to be a secure building. All the residents think so, anyway."

"The loading dock in the back. I showed the man there my government ID and he let me go right in. Retinal scan-ners I was familiar with from my work. A microprocessor compares the live retinal scan to a stored eye signature, and a match opens the door. Since your retina was a bit hard to come by, I used a different angle. I know a guy named Stone, a tech genius for hire who doesn't ask questions about how the gadgets he designs are used. Stone's gadget reset the scanner to learning mode so I could add my own eye signature to the scanner's storage. I'm a legitimately enrolled person, just like you, so I can get past the scanner whenever I want."

"Does the scanner still accept you as legit?"

"As far as I know, it does. I came by when I knew you weren't home. I'd seen the bright flash, so I brought a welder's helmet with me to get a better look at what was going on. When the door opened, I saw a switch on the wall across from me. I figured it was a trap and I had to press that switch within a certain amount of time. I opened the door again, made the dash to the switch, and got in. Once I was in there, I wasn't exactly sure how to get out, so I made myself at home. You know the rest."

Maliha thought it over. It seemed doable, even reasonable, the way he explained it. *I'll have to get Amaro to install a high-speed camera in there, one that has a chance of catching the motion of an Ageless.*

Jake rose and came to her chair. He extended both hands to her, and she took them and stood facing him. His hands started to roam.

"Wait a minute! What happened to that breakfast invitation?" Maliha said. "I'm famished."

Jake fixed something for her in his kitchen. She watched him at the counter, slicing fresh mushrooms, sautéing them, then cracking eggs into the skillet and stirring.

This is the man I love and he can cook, too.

He divided the eggs onto two plates and she chided him for salting his. They left the dishes in the sink and went to his bedroom.

Jake was the only single man Maliha knew who believed in the restorative powers of clean sheets and a blanket that smelled like it had been dried outdoors with a pleasant breeze and exuberant sunshine.

The clean linens didn't block his intriguing male scent that stirred her desire. She ran her hand lightly over his chest and abdomen and felt his muscles tighten in the wake of her fingertips. Leaning in close, molding her body to his side, she gently licked the side of his neck. The effect was electric. The hairs rose on the muscular arm that held her.

"Love you," she said. It felt so good to be free of the restrictions she'd placed on herself for so long. Jake was someone who could understand. She didn't have to conceal the kind of person she was from him. She had that freedom with Hound, Yanmeng, and Amaro, but they were family in a much different way.

"I love you, Maliha."

It was a thrill to hear him say it. She could see his face and his eyes totally focused on her, totally desiring her. His hand moved over her body, languishing on the curves of her breasts and hips. Her nipples hardened under his tongue as he gently licked and sucked them. His hand cupped her mound and then his fingers explored the warmth and wetness inside. She slid her leg over his hip, getting so close to him that she could feel the warmth radiating from his groin.

She lay against him and he kissed her deeply as her hand moved to encircle and stroke his erection. Pushing him back against the sheets, she straddled him and took him slowly, deeply inside her, then raised and lowered herself on his shaft. Jake's breathing came faster and faster and then he grasped her hips with both hands and wouldn't let her rise. Unable to move upward, she rotated her hips instead, bringing moans of pleasure from Jake.

He rolled on top of her. He teased her by pulling out and rubbing the head of his shaft against the pulsing nubbin that guarded her entrance. She shuddered with pleasure and anticipation until she couldn't stand it another second, and then pressed her hips up against his. Jake began thrusting hard. Maliha felt her excitement rising, rising, and then an explosion of release as Jake throbbed within her. Waves of pleasure radiated from her groin, traveling up her spine and blocking out every other sensation. She panted wildly, her chest heaving against his.

Jake then supported himself on his elbows, keeping his full weight off her, and when her panting had slowed, he gave her a lingering kiss and moved off to her side.

Maliha had never made love to an Ageless man before, and she hadn't known what to expect. When Jake fixed her breakfast the next morning, she'd learned what it felt like to have his fierce power focused on her. She also had a nickname à la Randy for him: Repeater.

Chapter Eight

The next day passed quickly as Maliha turned over in her mind the events with Jake and added words to her book *Too Big To Be True*.

Amaro called her with three suggestions for her new car: another black McLaren, a silver Zonda F, and a black Zonda F with red interior. The black with red interior caught her attention.

"Where's that last car located?"

"In Naples."

"Florida or Italy?"

"Italy."

"Set up an appointment to test-drive it. I know it's used, but I expect a like-new condition. If you like it, call my customizer." She gave him the name and number. "Ask if the car's suitable for Marsha's package. He'll know what you mean. If it is, buy it."

"Me?"

"Who else? Ignore the asking price. Decide on a price and make one bid. If it isn't accepted, walk away."

"Uh . . . okay."

"Don't worry. The sales consultant will know there are other cars on the market now. If no better offer comes through in a couple of days, he'll call you back. He won't want to lose you. To make it interesting, you keep the money between the asking price and the purchase price for going through all this trouble."

"I don't need any incentive. This is a blast." He hung up.

She called the Rainiers' numbers once more and tried not to grow impatient. Often they turned off their phones while working. Finally, she was ready to visit the professors' lab.

At various times in the past, her fighting outfit had been made of loose cotton, silk, or leather, but it had always been black.

Black to hide the blood, as Master Liu said.

Tonight she slipped on the black cotton trousers of the ninja and tied strings around her calves, nipping in the wide material. The top wrapped around her and secured with ties, and she filled the hidden pockets with throwing stars. Tabi socks and boots, with their traditional split toes for better gripping, followed. The bottoms of her trousers tucked neatly inside her boots, and at the top of each boot she fastened a sheath with a short knife for close-up fighting.

Maliha braided her black hair into one heavy braid down her back, and then tucked it inside the back of her top. She wasn't ready to use the mask and hood, so she put them up her sleeves, held them in place by forearm ties.

With her throwing knives strapped to her thighs, she moved through the lobby of the building and tossed a wink at the wide-eyed door attendant.

"Costume party," she said.

"Uh . . ." he said, and she was out the door into a night with a sliver of moon in the sky.

It was exhilarating to be out on the streets dressed to kill.

Even now I understand the temptation to be Ageless. The power, the fearlessness, the decadence—answering to no mortal, suffering no consequences . . . To be able to turn that on and off like a switch would be interesting, to say the least. Black Ghost on demand.

She shook herself before those thoughts could take hold.

Moving rapidly, her cold breath trailing behind her, she headed south to the University of Chicago. Flitting through the parks that lined the lakeshore, she came to Jackson Park, in the Hyde Park neighborhood. From there it was a straight shot west along the Midway, a large grassy area that was the site of the 1893 World's Columbian Exhibition, an event Maliha remembered well. She'd ridden the first Ferris wheel there and ridden the same one again at the 1904 St. Louis World's Fair.

The route of the lakeshore to the Midway wasn't the most direct way to go, but she felt like running and she liked to stay to the green areas whenever she could. When she passed the crenellated towers of Harper Library, she left the Midway. It was only one long block past the hospital to the Pritzker School of Medicine.

The Rainiers' lab was located in an older stone building with gothic arches. Maliha knew of a window with a broken lock above a side doorway that projected out from the building like a LEGO block stuck onto it. The window had been that way since Maliha moved to Chicago, although it had been fixed twice in the interim—and Maliha had promptly broken it again to preserve her access. Because of the Rainiers, the building was a useful place to her, and it was, after all, in her backyard.

Now for the tricky part.

She climbed the outside of the building, using the ridges and curves of the gothic features as handholds. She didn't have far to go, about ten feet to a flat section of roof atop the projecting doorway. The window was topped by arched glass; she was interested in the bottom panes. She lay down on the rough, gravelly surface and placed her rubber-soled boots on the glass. Pushing up with her legs, she expected to raise the heavy window enough for her to slip underneath it, but it didn't move.

The window's lock had been fixed again.

Impatient to get inside, Maliha didn't want to try anything else, like breaking in through the door. There was an electronic lock on the door, and it wouldn't yield without time and tools. Glass, though, yielded to many things, among them a swift kick from one of her boots. She swept the glass out of the way as best she could, put on her mask and hood, and dropped ten feet to the floor inside the building, landing with the relaxed knees of a trained parachute trooper.

Maliha made her way carefully through the halls, dimmed except for security lights every twenty feet or so. Professors Ty and Claire didn't rate prime facilities, which for Maliha's purpose was fine. Larger, better-equipped labs were crowded with grad students who worked all hours of the night. Most of the time, the Rainiers worked alone.

As she approached the door, she heard noises coming from the lab. The sound of glass breaking was followed by a muffled scream. She ran the last fifteen feet and went flying feetfirst toward the door. She crashed through, tearing the door off its hinges. She landed with a roll, ending behind a solid lab bench.

Taking a quick look, she was horrified at the scene.

Bright lights flooded the lab. She blinked and tried to adjust her eyes rapidly. There were two men dressed in black, but they were blocky and moved with no grace. They were not trained martial artists. She dismissed them, but not the guns they held. Even the hired muscle could get lucky.

Claire was tied in a chair in the center of the lab, her head slumped forward so her chin rested on her chest. Ty was on the ground, clutching his belly and groaning. There was broken equipment all around. A tall, thin man stood next to Claire. His hair hung in greasy lanks and he wore a long, heavy robe. One of the pockets of the robe had a bulge that she figured was the canteen. He turned his face toward Maliha and for the briefest moment their eyes met. His were deep blue but flat and emotionless.

The tall man reacted faster than either of the thugs. He was across the room in no time and slammed Maliha in the belly with his fist. She'd had only enough time to tighten her muscles in anticipation, not to move out of the way. The powerful blow knocked the wind out of her. He didn't press his advantage. By the time the spasm faded, he had disappeared back into the lab. Just as she ducked into the shelter of the lab bench, she saw him pick up a piece of broken glass from the floor.

Maliha knew his intent as though their minds were one.

She rolled out from behind the bench and planted a star in the wrist of the nearest gunman. He screamed and dropped the gun. As she passed by him, she finished him with a blow to the throat, then turned her attention back to the real danger in the room. She launched a throwing knife at the tall man. He was in motion as she threw, and instead of skewering his heart, the knife landed in his arm. It didn't stop him from carrying through the action he'd started. He yanked Claire's head back and slit her throat with the piece of glass.

No!

Claire's frightened, wildly beating heart pumped sprays of blood across the room. Then the flow slowed to cover Claire's chest in blood. Maliha knew her friend was gone.

The other gunman got off a few shots in Maliha's direction. She spun and threw her second knife at him and he fell, the knife buried in his chest. Out of the corner of her eye, she saw the thin man toss the bloody piece of glass on the floor and yank the knife out of his arm. His wrist moved back and she knew what he was about to do. He flipped the knife, spinning it toward Ty, who was still in anguish on the floor. One of her throwing stars deflected it, and the knife hit the floor and slid away harmlessly.

He started running toward the back end of the lab. Maliha didn't know if there was a door there. She hoped he'd be trapped in a storage area. She started after him and then froze.

She'd spotted a bomb stuck underneath the edge of a lab counter. A timer was counting down. Sixteen seconds, fifteen. She automatically started the count in her head. She turned and saw Ty move slightly. He was still alive. Abandoning her pursuit of the tall man, she went to Ty, quickly picked him up in a fireman's carry, and raced out into the hall.

Eleven.

She felt Ty's blood soaking the cloth covering her shoulder, but there was no time to worry about whether she was doing any more damage to him. If she didn't get out of

there, they'd both be in as many pieces as the broken glass
on the floor.

Eight.

Out in the hallway, she accelerated to her full speed,
beyond human capabilities. Every bit of her energy focused
on the exit door, the one she'd bypassed because of the electronic lock system. She had no choice this time but to attack
it with everything she had.

Six. Five.

She threw herself at the door. For the first breathless
moment she thought the door was going to hold, but then
it broke loose and fell, obstructing her path. Tightening her
grip on Ty, she leaped over it and kept going at full speed.

The brilliant orange sphere of the explosion lighted her
way and cast shadows in front of her. Flames from the blast
snapped at her heels, and then the force of it flattened her
into the grass. She shielded Ty as much as she could when
she fell.

Running her fingers over Ty's chest and abdomen, she
found a hole into which her fist could nearly disappear. It was
worse than she'd thought. It was amazing that he was still
alive. Help would be coming soon, in response to the blast.

If he's lived through it so far, maybe he can make it.

It was false comfort and deep down she knew that.
Hunched over on the grass, she held him. His eyes fluttered
open.

"Claire . . ." he said.

"She made it. She's just a few feet away."

A lie to the dying is only comfort.

His voice was weak and he was beginning to shiver.
"Marsha?"

"I'm here. I'm right here. Hang on, Ty, help is coming."

"Not bio . . ." He coughed hard, bringing up blood.

"Hang on, Ty, stay with me."

"Nan . . ." Another cough racked his body. "Tell Claire I
love . . ." He shuddered and went limp in her arms.

*If I hadn't taken the long way here they might still be
alive. If I'd left before dark they would definitely be alive.*

So many years, so many decisions, small and large, had brought her to this place with Ty's blood soaking her shirt.

Maliha could hear sirens coming, and she had something left to do, the last thing she could do for Ty.

She pushed his body to the side and stretched out in the exact spot where he'd died. Suddenly sounds faded and the light from the blaze dimmed even though her eyes were open. She let her muscles relax until it seemed like she'd been poured onto the grass.

A violent death left a psychic imprint on the spot where it occurred, a ghostly recording of extreme emotion. Maliha knew that it was a remnant of the victim's spirit that had been left behind instead of passing to its next destination. Most people would walk through the spot of the psychic scar and feel nothing. A few would feel a vague sense of unease, a very few a disturbing sensation that quickened their heartbeats and made them look around anxiously as though some danger existed.

Maliha could fully experience the imprint. She could move into the lower level of the psychic plane, the state above the physical, just as she did briefly when she saw auras. Her friend Yanmeng had the same capability to shift, but his interpretation of the experience allowed him to do remote viewing.

Ty left a fragment of his spirit behind and now it was drawn to Maliha. She slipped into the imprint, prepared to experience what Ty did in his last minutes of life. It was the only way to make his spirit whole, but to do so she had to experience his death. She had died over and over through the years, using her unique skill.

She reached out for Ty's ragged shred of spirit and let it coalesce around her.

As Ty, she felt a knife penetrate her belly and reached to clutch it with her arms, but something was holding them. Something or someone. She couldn't struggle free. The knife twisted in her belly and then tore upward toward her ribs. She nearly blacked out from the pain, then she felt her head being lifted. A hand under her chin was forcing her head up.

With vision fading around the edges, she looked into the face of her killer. A man, thin face . . . she squeezed her eyes shut to deny him the satisfaction of seeing the light leave her eyes. The hand let go of her chin and her head fell forward, seeing nothing now. Whoever held her up by her arms let go, and she crumpled to the floor.

There was pain, so much pain, there were thoughts of Claire and the certainty of her death, and the smallest relief that she did not see Claire die. Then a wave of pain wiped out all thought, followed by an impression of being off the ground and moving fast.

She felt words coming out of her mouth, desperately wanting to say something, to explain, but there was no time and no breath to do it. Numbness. Her body was shutting down, her heart stopping, her brain dying after that. Finally the pain was gone.

Maliha waited after Ty's death. The fragment of his spirit grew stronger and brighter. Just before the spirit moved on, she felt something extraordinary. Another fragment had been drawn to her, or rather to Ty. It was Claire. The fragments gradually wrapped around each other, leaving her behind. The violent death imprint had been released, and wherever Ty and Claire went, they were together.

Maliha walked away as emergency crews began their work. Hot tears of grief overflowed her eyes.

I should have said no to Rabishu and died in the flames. What joy have I brought into the world since then? What can I point to with pride as my legacy on Earth? A trail of blood.

Maliha had a sudden stabbing pain in her shoulder, the one that Rabishu had gripped with his claws long ago, leaving a scar that even her Ageless body had been unable to heal. She felt that Rabishu was gloating at her setback, at her personal grief, and he was letting her know that he expected to win and claim her soul forever.

She was still coping with Rabishu's gleeful reminder when she was struck with what felt like a flash of lightning across her midsection. Panting, her arms wrapped around her abdomen, she stumbled as far as she could and took shelter between the building and some low bushes. The rhythmic sound of sirens pounded into her ears. She hoped she would be able to move on before the police searched the area.

Mystified at what felt like the action of her scale when she hadn't saved any lives, she pulled up her top. There in the darkness two fiery figures made their way across her skin. Her eyes grew wide as she followed their path. They were going the wrong way!

Anu blames me for the deaths of Ty and Claire. He's punishing me, taking away lives I've already saved.

The pull through time gripped her hard. She hoped she'd aged no more than a year. *It could have been ten or twenty— or a hundred. Who knows what payment an angry Sumerian god would exact?*

When she could move, she slipped away from the growing knot of police cars and fire trucks. The thought of how she'd brought her unsuspecting friends into mortal danger by her careless actions—delivering the sample to them, spending her first nights at home going dancing with Randy and having an orgy with Jake, delaying checking up on the Rainiers until it was too late. Act after act of hers killed Ty and Claire as surely as if she'd sliced them apart herself.

The only thing I can do now is swear I'll bring their killer down or die trying.

Chapter Nine

Maliha made it home that night to find that Yanmeng had taken up residence in one of her guest rooms. Amaro was still in Africa, working with the group of women and girls who'd been abducted by the Janjaweed along with Glass. Hound was at Glass's side, a circumstance that was probably beginning to wear on both of them. Hound, even with the best of intentions, was a man of action, and sitting around that long in the confines of a clinic was going to wear on him. Maliha figured Glass would be kicking him out soon.

Yanmeng came in after she'd flopped on the couch, struggling with her grief for the Rainiers. He sat next to her and wrapped his arms around her. She settled in, leaning against his side, her head against his chest. Without a word, they remained together for an hour. Maliha felt some of her sorrow drain away as though Yanmeng had sponged it up.

She pulled away and searched his eyes, looking for some sign that he'd assumed any of her burden. There was none. His face looked as composed as usual.

Yanmeng tilted her head up toward his and turned it from side to side. "Is any of this blood yours? If so, I'd like to check your wounds."

The sound of his voice unlocked her story. She told him everything, including how Claire and Ty died and how she experienced the aftereffect of their deaths as their spirits gathered to her.

"You're a brave woman," Yanmeng said. "I believe I could do what you describe, but I have yet to find the courage to experience someone else's death and let them use me to move on."

Maliha made no comment. The experience of losing her friends was too fresh for his words to have any impact. She showered, slept for hours, and woke to the smell of her favorite coffee, a rare variety called Kopi Luwak.

"Got some news for you," Yanmeng said when she joined him at the table. "Something the three of us cooked up. Hound's going to try to learn more about the tall, thin man."

"Glass kicked Hound out."

Yanmeng shrugged. "To hear his side of it, she needs peaceful rest and his presence is too distracting. So yes, she kicked him out."

"This tall man is very dangerous. I'm assuming he survived because he set the bomb and ran toward the back of the lab. He must have had an exit planned. Hound needs to research from a distance."

"Noted. Amaro will work on finding out if the Rainiers made any discoveries that they emailed or otherwise distributed before they died. I'm going to get into the burned-out lab to see if anything physical is left that could help us."

"I'm conspicuously absent from the task list," Maliha said.

Yanmeng nodded. "That's because you're taking a break. It's what people do when friends die. They need some time to adapt. You're off duty."

Hey, who's in charge here? "I'm supposed to . . ."

He waved off her comment. "We're having a mutiny. Didn't you say you wanted to make a desert trip this year?"

"Yes, but . . ."

"It's settled then."

An hour after dawn, the punishing heat of the desert was already a burden on Maliha's shoulders. She dropped her kit in the sand and sat on it, stretching her legs out in front of her. Drinking from the collapsible hydration pack strapped under her loose clothing, she savored the feel of the water in her dry mouth and throat.

She was in the Taklimakan Desert, in northwestern China, a desolate place with a name that meant *Go in and don't come out.* Six hundred miles long, two hundred and fifty wide, uninhabited except by a few wild camels and asses, it was a desert that shouldn't be challenged on a whim.

More than thirty years ago she'd retrieved the Tablet of the Overlord from a cave deep in this desert. The tablet was a book-sized slab of stone, an artifact of tremendous power that when combined with a diamond lens would enable Maliha to read the words on the tablet. The writing on the tablet altered its form so quickly it was a blur of motion that couldn't be slowed down by anything other than supernatural means. Comprehension was impossible without using the lens.

In the decades since, she'd come to believe there was more to be revealed in the cave. There was an inscription on the back of the tablet, but it was carved so delicately that she'd needed a powerful microscope to decipher the ancient Sumerian cuneiform. The minuscule carving was so far beyond the capabilities of the time that a human couldn't have written it. Maliha took it as a message through millennia from the Sumerian god Anu, the one who'd made the tablet. The inscription read GO TO SAND.

This desert is the nastiest bunch of sand I've ever seen. Has to be the place.

The last time Maliha was here, she'd come on a camel with local guides, Uygurs who lived in small villages on the fringes of the desert. Once close to the site of the cave she'd left the Uygurs in camp and gone the final distance on foot.

This time she just drove in.

The Chinese government built the Tarim Desert Highway to bisect the desert from north to south and provide a route for trucks. Maliha rented a Chinese car instead of a camel and drove to the way station closest to the cave.

The car, a battered Chery Tiggo, had an overheated radiator when she pulled into the station. She overpaid the attendant to check out the problem and—although she never uttered the words, as to do so would have been to impugn his honor—make sure her car was still there when she returned from the desert trek.

She stood up and shouldered her pack. She'd traveled through the night and expected to reach the cave by evening. There was no shade for shelter in the middle of the day. The surface of the sand could reach 120 degrees or more. Standing still, she could feel the heat penetrating the soles of her boots. It was best to keep on the move, keep drinking water, and plan to recuperate in the coolness of the cave.

Setting out at a comfortable, sustainable three-minutes-per-mile pace, Maliha measured time by the slow, steady beating of her heart and the passage of the sun across the sky. Covered from head to toe as desert dwellers dressed, Maliha had only a small slit to see through that protected her eyes from blowing sand and from the glare of the sun. There was little sound except the soft swish of her boots displacing loose sand, and sometimes the crunch of the mineral crust on stabilized portions of the sand dunes. Every now and then, she felt a faint touch on her shoulder, the sign that her friend Yanmeng was checking up on her by remote viewing.

He'd had the right idea. This trip was good for her, letting her sweat her grief out under the sun and ponder her guilt under the stars.

Pausing on top of one of the dunes as the sun was dipping toward the horizon, she spotted the rock outcropping that concealed the cave. She'd made good time. There were inviting evening shadows in the valleys between sand dunes. Making her way down into one, she decided to pause in the shade for a short break before tackling the last leg of the trip: crossing to the mountainous outcropping, climbing it, and locating the cave entrance.

In the valley, she opened her pack and shook out a reflective blanket. Putting the blanket shiny side down on the sand, to trap as much heat as possible below her, she sat down. Maliha knew the "Cool Rule": the surface of the sand kills—spend your time above it or below it. She couldn't stay long, but she watched the swift descent of darkness. Stars came out overhead, and a quarter moon provided enough light for her to continue her journey. She packed the blanket away and left the valley.

At the top of the next rise, she felt the wind blowing unusually hard. She turned around to check it out and found what no traveler wanted to see: a sandstorm blotting out the stars. The face of the great *haboob* was a tremendous wall of sand several miles high, coming straight at her.

As she sped across the sand, wet, heavy drops of mud began to splatter her shoulders. Most of the time the rain evaporated before reaching ground level, but this time, the rain was severe and coated with dust and small rocks that the wind had kicked up. When she reached the rocky mountain, she decided to climb in spite of the pelting she was taking from the rain. Eyes closed, feeling her way up the mountainside, she relied on memory to take her to the narrow opening that smelled of fresh air and clean water. She crawled in on all fours and collapsed inside the entry.

Maliha turned on a flashlight from her belly bag. A few feet into the cave, the temperature was easily forty degrees cooler than outside. Small living creatures scattered with the touch of the beam of her flashlight, all of them adapted to the cooler, darker conditions of the cave. They wouldn't survive in the hostile world ten feet away.

The opening was small enough that when she was ready to move on, she had to crawl on hands and knees. This left her vulnerable from the front and back, and she scrambled down the narrow throat feeling as if icy hands were wrapped around her spine.

She had a disturbing sense that someone had passed this way not long before her, based on a slight scent in the air that didn't match the pure scent of clear water from the underground stream ahead.

The tunnel widened so that she could get to her feet. Feeling both a little stronger and better about her prospect for defense, she used the flashlight to examine her surroundings in both directions. There was no one present. She expected her anxiety about being the only one in the cave to fade, but it didn't.

She paused at the underground stream. Stripping away her mud-covered outer clothing, she rinsed it in fresh water and stretched the robe over rocks to dry. In a clean camisole and loose cotton pants, she moved toward the room where she'd found the tablet. The ceiling was at least ten feet high, its surface smooth as though polished by eons of flowing water or a burst of heat that carved the chamber. Once past the constricted entrance at the surface, there were no formations, no moisture on the walls, no dripping from the ceiling, and no bats.

As far as she knew, the tablet room was the end of the line. If there was an enemy in front of her, he had to be in there. She was spoiling for a fight, and hoped Evil might be in the tablet room to face her, without any innocents between them.

The room held a pool that glowed with light. A few inches of water covered a base of sand, and the glow came from the sand. The glow wasn't bright, just enough to delineate the shape of the pool. On the left side of the entrance to the pool room, she flattened against the rock wall and peeked around the corner quickly.

No one. Damn.

She took a longer look, then stepped into the room. It was clear of life, human or otherwise, except for her. Sighing, she settled in a corner of the room where she could see the door and consciously let her tension drain away through her fingertips, which tingled with the effort. Maliha closed her eyes so that only slits remained beneath her dark lashes and slipped into a warrior's catlike sleep, from which she could awaken instantly.

Later, she stood at one end of the pool, looking at the depression in the wall fifty feet across the water that had held the Tablet of the Overlord. The torches on the wall still seemed to be in good condition after her last visit, so she lit them. Their clear, golden light spread throughout the chamber and chased the shadows from the corners. She looked closely at the torch nearest her.

I wonder how many times these torches have been used over the years? Does somebody freshen up the place and leave new supplies?

The pool, wisps of steam rising intermittently from its smooth surface, filled the width of the chamber. There was no way across to the wall without going through the pool. In spite of its placid surface, the water was superheated. The layer of sand underneath the water sucked down anything resting on it for more than two seconds. The sand wasn't a natural, passive thing. She knew from experience that the feel of it against her fingers was like grasping tentacles, a very un-sandlike quality.

Sitting cross-legged at the edge of the pool, Maliha leaned over and plopped in a throwing spike from her belly bag, thinking that maybe the sand didn't behave the same way all the time. Two seconds later, the sand pulled the spike down so forcefully that it churned the water, sending bubbles up that fizzed and steamed when they reached the surface.

Okay. Consistency is a big thing here.

She took a piece of paper from the pocket of her loose trousers, a paper that had been folded and refolded so many times it was tearing at the creases. On it was a drawing of the inscription on the back of the tablet, the words that had sent her to this place. She studied them again: *Go to sand.*

I went to sand. I crossed the desert. Now what?

A thought hit her like an unnatural blast of frigid air in the desert. Gooseflesh rose on her arms and her frightened mind pushed away the terrible possibilities unfolding in her imagination.

No, oh no, surely not . . .

She saw what she had to do. If she wanted to follow the cryptic clue, to find out what awaited her in Anu's cave, she didn't have to go *to* the sand but *into* the sand.

This sand, in front of her.

Maliha had to step into the boiling water and let the sucking sand in the pool claim her. Her mind rebelled against it. All of her logic told her that it was a trap. She would die in the sand from mortal injury, or be trapped there until her body aged and died. Yet Anu was telling her to do exactly that, if those were Anu's words on the tablet.

It would have to be a leap of faith.

Chapter Ten

Maliha stood naked at the edge of the pool. Clothes would just restrict her movement. As for weapons, she had a feeling that whatever was under the sand, her weapons weren't going to be of any use against it. She'd have to manage using her wits and her body. That is, unless the only thing under the sand was more sand, continuing far enough down that she'd never make it back to the surface. In that case, she was doomed.

Nothing I've ever dropped in that pool has come back to the surface bearing good news.

She pushed such thoughts from her mind. In taking a leap of faith, doubt had no place.

When Maliha was Ageless, she had been able to heal almost instantly from injuries that would be fatal to humans. Now her healing ability was beyond the human level, but still diminished from her Ageless days. She had no idea if she could survive immersion in boiling water followed by suffocation as the sand closed over her head, but the god Anu had directed her here, and that was enough.

She'd been trying to enter a deep meditative state using a mantra from her martial arts training, but couldn't quite achieve it. She'd succeeded in relaxing a little, but didn't have the depth of control she needed to block input from her senses. That state was something she thought of as floating inside her skin, oblivious to the outer world.

This was something she didn't want Yanmeng watching,

if he was. She held out her left hand parallel to the floor, made a fist, and then extended her thumb and index finger. It was an "L" in sign language, except that she made the sign horizontally, so he could see it from above, rather than the usual vertical position of the hand. She waited a few minutes, not knowing how long it took him to withdraw, or if he was even watching at this time.

She lifted her right foot and held it poised over the water. One foot in. Two.

It was hard to keep from leaping out of the pool when her muscles were screaming *Move! Move!*

One second. Two.

A powerful drag began, as though her feet were weighed down with the Titanic's anchor. Boiling water rose rapidly on her legs. The water sizzled and spat against her skin, the watery equivalent of being burned alive. She must have been screaming, although she couldn't hear it.

Separate from the pain, there was a frightening sensation that the abrasive sand below the water was removing her skin, scraping it off one cellular layer at a time.

How much skin will I lose?

She clamped her lips and eyelids closed in the instant before her head went under the water.

Stunned by the boiling water covering her face, Maliha was unable to do anything but spread her arms out and hope to slow her passage through the sand.

Seconds passed, and the fiery nature of the pain eased the further she sank from the surface of the pool. She reached a layer where the sand felt cool, her skin tingly. Flakes of burned skin were being gently scrubbed away. Her skin was being abraded—ground against the sand, polished like a rock in a gemstone tumbler.

Through her closed eyelids, or what was left of them, she could see a white glow coming up fast beneath her. This was the source of light at the surface at the pool, so much brighter now that she was close to it. Maliha was still holding her breath. Before she had to worry about whether to try breathing in the sand, she fell into the luminous layer and

then into the open. Her reflexes took over and she managed
a rolling landing that broke the fall. She ended up on her
feet, ready for anything. As she examined her surroundings,
she was startled to see a couple of human skeletons near
her feet.

Others got this far but didn't survive the sand.

It made sense to her. The dead at her feet hadn't shared
her healing ability, which must have kept her from losing
too many layers of skin. When these people dropped out of
the cloud above, there was nothing holding them together. It
was a gruesome image and she didn't linger on it.

Checking her nude body for burn injuries, she saw what
looked and felt like fresh skin—pale and soft. She twisted
her head to look at the back of her shoulder and was relieved
to find her hawk tattoo was intact. The colors of the hawk
with spread wings were more vivid than ever.

The glowing white cloud was about ten feet over her head
and it stretched for as far as she could see in every direction.
With its clarity of view, fresh air, clean feel, and the seem-
ingly one-piece marble floor beneath her bare feet, the space
she was in was the opposite of the one where she used to
meet her demon master Rabishu. Since she lived in the Great
Above, where humanity dwelled, and Rabishu was restricted
in most cases to the Underworld, the demon had interacted
with her in a foul-smelling, fog-ridden landscape named
Midworld—an ugly protrusion of the Underworld that they
could both enter. That's why Rabishu needed human slaves
in the first place: to do his bidding in the Great Above.

*If that miserable place was a demon's creation, then this
place must belong to Anu or one of the other Sumerian gods.
It's a . . . temple.*

As soon as the word took shape in her mind, her surroundings changed to match. Columns took shape, easing
up from the marble floor. Statues formed the same way,
sheltered in beautiful niches, with flowers tossed at their
feet. Fountains sprouted into being and began tossing water
in intricate dances. In moments, the space had transformed
itself into her idea of what a temple should look like. Its

form was malleable and shifted to whatever made the visitor comfortable. She wondered what it looked like when Anu last visited here.

Master Liu is a priest of Anu. Perhaps this space looks different to him if he has been here with Anu. Of course! He must be the one who takes care of the cave by putting in fresh torches.

Master Liu had told her that he remained a demon's slave in order to keep his immortality. It was his one goal, as Anu's last priest, to be alive to welcome his god back to Earth when the time came. It was awe-inspiring to realize that this place could be four hundred thousand years old if it dated from the last time Anu was on Earth, yet looked as though it was created yesterday.

Her anxiety faded. Master Liu was somehow connected to this place. She had been his student and was now his proclaimed granddaughter. She didn't think he would set any deadly traps for her.

She explored some of the nearer columns and found them carved exquisitely with scenes of daily life. One segment included columns for each of the primary gods of Sumeria, known as the Seven Who Decreed Fate. She pictured groups of children sitting around the columns, learning from Master Liu.

Anu, the Sky god, and his wife, Ninmah, the Earth goddess, each had their columns. Their son Enlil, the Air god, was next in power and influence, but his column detailed his troubled life.

Enlil had an intended bride, but he chose not to wait for their wedding day and raped her before marriage. Sex was continually tripping up both gods and goddesses, and many of their convoluted stories, relationships, jealousies, accomplishments, and failures came back to who was sleeping with whom.

Enlil was banished to the Underworld for jumping the gun. His bride, Ninlil, followed him into exile, probably because she was already pregnant. Their first child, conceived of the rape, was Nanna, the Moon god.

Their next son was Nergal, who remained permanently in the Underworld as a trade-off so that his father, Enlil, could leave. Maliha knew way too much about Nergal, Lord of the Underworld, ruler over Rabishu and the other demons, and his queen, Ereshkigal. The demons, offspring of Anu and his wife, were deliberately created as lesser beings to be given away as servants to the gods.

The Moon god fathered two more of the top gods, Utu, god of Justice, and Inanna, goddess of Love and War.

That accounted for six out of the Seven Who Decreed Fate.

The last one was Enki, god of the Primeval Sea and Fertility, well known for his rampant lifestyle. He was the twin brother to the Queen of the Underworld. Enki created humans from clay. He did this by mixing the clay with the "life essence" of the primeval sea—his semen or his DNA, depending on the interpretation of essence. There was some trial-and-error involved, because there were several flawed versions of humans before Enki got it right with the help of some constructive criticism from Anu's wife. Enki's emblem was serpents intertwined on a staff, the basis for the caduceus, the medical symbol still in use today.

The gods created humans to be slaves and take over all the work of running Earth. It was not until many thousands of years later that the gods freed humans.

After studying the columns, Maliha sat on the floor to wait, then stretched out to look at the cloud above her. The white swirls were hypnotic and relaxing. The floor beneath her seemed to soften and conform to her body, which she knew was not typical of marble. That didn't seem to matter.

Feeling safe and secure, she felt the marble deepen its embrace and cradle her in a womblike space, with the soothing sound of her heartbeat reflected back to her. She fell into a natural and comforting sleep.

One second Maliha was asleep, the next she was fully alert. It seemed like no time had passed since she had watched the patterns in the cloud overhead. She was lying

on marble that was now behaving like a floor, not a bed.
She felt refreshed and fully charged mentally, physically,
and emotionally.

She heard water splashing gaily, close by, and got up to
investigate. A large fountain had a central column topped
with a ball that had several spigots. As the ball slowly
turned, streams of water spiraled down, filling a bowl
shaped like a shell. Just looking at it made her realize how
thirsty she was.

*I need water, a fountain appears. This is all crazy. I'm
expecting the Mad Hatter to drop by for tea soon.*

She cupped her hands in the water and drank. The water
was colder than she expected, and refreshing. There was
something at the bottom of the bowl, something barely
visible because it was clear and hidden in clear water. She
reached for it, and the instant she touched it, she gave a
whoop of joy.

A diamond shard!

It was one of the seven shards of the diamond lens needed
to read the Tablet of the Overlord. When she collected them
all, Maliha would be able to decipher the moving script on
the tablet and gain power over the seven demons—power
to banish or destroy them. She had one shard and the tablet
already hidden in her haven.

She looked up at the cloud and wondered how she was
going to get back into the cave with her prize. She'd been
so lulled by the time she'd spent in the temple that leaving
hadn't seemed important until now.

Eyeing the fountain, she figured that if she stood on top
of it, she'd be less than three feet below the cloud layer. She
could jump three feet. After clambering to the top of the
fountain—not easy with wet, bare feet—she stood on the
ball. On impulse, she lifted her arm. She could just reach
the cloud, and she waggled her fingers in it experimentally.

Maliha prepared for the leap.

*Most likely I'll just end up on my ass on the marble floor,
and it's going to hurt.*

Her fingers wouldn't budge. She couldn't pull them back

out of the cloud. Instead, the cloud began to twirl and lower toward her, looking like a miniature tornado. Swirls of the cottony stuff curled around her body and lifted her into the cloud.

This time the sand parted for her—or for the shard— forming a smooth tunnel just wide enough for her shoulders and hips to pass through. The tunnel didn't extend up through the water, but when she passed through the boiling water, she found it only pleasantly warm. She stepped out of the pool with the shard in her hand.

Maliha felt renewed, very alive, living in the moment. Her body had no reminders of the burns received on the way into the pool. It wouldn't surprise her if she'd lost years on her appearance, too. She felt as though she'd slept for a week. It was a triumphant moment. She'd suspected the first time she came here thirty years ago that this cave wasn't finished with her, and she was right. Naked and dripping, she twirled around.

Number two is secure! Five left and Rabishu will be groveling before me. Take that, you damned demon!

She stabbed the air with the shard.

Something ripped through her right shoulder, threw her back against the rock wall with the force of its blow, and buried itself in the rock. She was fastened to the wall. Pain surged outward from her shoulder. Through the haze of her suffering, she realized she no longer held the shard. It was a few feet away from her, on the floor of the cave.

There was someone in the cave with her, and he stooped to pick up the shard. She followed the motion upward and saw a man clothed in silver: chest plate, helmet, chain mail, a sword sheathed on his belt, legs that looked as though they'd been dipped in liquid silver. Her eyes fixed on the weapon he held, a crossbow. She'd been shot at close range with a bolt from his crossbow.

"My name is Lucius Antonius Cinna. I have served the demon Sidana for one thousand nine hundred and twenty-six years. He has charged me to make sure you do not collect all seven shards of the Great Lens."

He's Ageless—the Roman centurion who saved me once before.

"I found the shard you're holding," Maliha said between painful intakes of breath. "Give it back."

"No. You will heal and search again, and again I will be there."

"You're telling me you're going to turn up whenever I find a shard and take it from me?"

"That is the order my demon lord has given me."

Maliha shook her good fist at him, sending shockwaves of pain through the right side of her body. "I risk my life for these shards!"

"I know."

His answer infuriated Maliha even more. She started to lunge for him but the dizzying pain stopped her.

He fired another bolt from the crossbow. This one dug into the rock next to Maliha's head. Three inches closer and it would have gone through her eye. "I have heard you are persistent. If you continue in this hunt, at least do not make me wait so long next time."

"What are you talking about?"

"You entered the pool a week ago."

He gave her a long, slow appraisal from head to toe, lingering on her naked breasts, the curve of her hips, and her lean and fit legs. Many men had done so before, but this time Maliha felt as though his eyes were scraping her tender skin.

"I'd look better without all this blood," she said.

He nodded and then he was gone, along with her prize. The only thing left to her was the reality of the bolt penetrating her body.

The longer I wait, the worse this is going to be.

She could only use one hand. She pushed back as hard as she could against the rock wall, gripped the wooden bolt where it protruded, exerted all of her strength, and snapped it off as close as she could to her skin. Pain shot down her arm and back, her vision went black around the edges, and the worst wasn't over. She took a deep breath and began wiggling her body forward, first one shoulder and then the other. When she was free of the bolt, she crumpled to the floor.

For a while she felt terrible sensations of pain and loss. It wasn't for the physical pain—it would pass. It was for the lost opportunity of collecting all the shards and wiping out the demons forever.

She stayed there, naked, wounded, her plans broken, for a long time. Thirst brought her out of it. She left the pool room, went to the underground stream, and drank the cool water until she was sated. Then she splashed the water, first on her shoulder wound and then on the rest of her. Her injury was just beginning to heal. Her resolve, too.

Lucius old boy, don't count me out just yet. I defied my demon. It's going to take more than a threat from you to make me back off.

Chapter Eleven

The shoulder wound from the crossbow bolt ached. Normally she'd try to block the pain but all during the long trip back from the desert to Chicago, she'd dwelled on it instead, and the circumstances of losing the shard.

I should have been more alert. I suspected on my way into the cave that someone was there. When I came out of that pool, I was like a kid with a candy bar—not paying attention to anything. I let my guard down. I'm beginning to wonder if I can do anything right.

The cab from the airport dropped her in front of the Harbor Point Towers building. After getting her luggage sent upstairs, she went back out. She thought a brisk walk might clear her mind. The wind prominent so near the lake made her cold. The warm spell had broken and late November was back to its usual antics in Chicago.

Walking near the shore of Lake Michigan, swinging her arms in spite of the bitter complaints from her right shoulder, she listened to the slapping of waves. It was a natural and familiar sound and she adjusted her walking pace to form a rhythm with it. Then, as her body stretched and warmed, she moved into an easy run she could maintain for hours without thinking about.

Every time I go after a shard I'm going to have to fight Lucius for it. Impossible. Why even try? I should drop the whole lens and tablet idea and focus on trying to save my

soul. Let the rest of Earth muddle along as it has for mil-
lennia. Who says humankind is ready to be freed of all the
chaos, wars, and destruction the demons cause? I could
succeed in wiping out the demons and find humans turning
on each other anyway. And what about my personal quest
if I wipe the demons out? I automatically get my soul back?
I'm not so sure about that. Anu's running the show with my
scale, determining my aging and the rewards I get toward
balancing. Anu's certainly made that clear lately! Rabishu
made a point of saying he had nothing to do with the balanc-
ing process. Even if I succeed with the tablet and the lens,
I might still have to prove my worth to Anu. He might be a
hard sell after I wipe out his seven demon offspring.

It was getting late. Maliha headed back to her building,
thinking of a shower, a cup of tea, and her inviting sleeping
mat.

She paused for a moment and skipped a rock out over
the lake, just barely following its path in the moonlight as
it caught the tops of the waves and disappeared into the
distance. It had taken her years to perfect that toss to catch
the waves just right.

I have to, though. I have to give humanity a chance to
see what we can make of ourselves. I don't think anyone
but a demon's slave or a rogue has the ability to retrieve
the shards. I can't see any demon's slave searching unless
forced to. If Jake found any shards and kept them or gave
them to me, I'm sure his demon would take notice, because
no demon wants anyone to have all seven shards. Jake
would be horribly punished.

Her whole body shivered at the thought of the kind of pain
a demon could dish out. She'd been to Rabishu's hell briefly,
when he was demonstrating to her what would happen if she
didn't balance her scale and redeem her soul. Maliha tried
to squelch the image her brain was dredging up, but it was
too powerful: being squeezed inside a rapidly shrinking cage
made of sharp wire that divided her skin into squares and
then began to saw through. And when it was finished, she'd
become whole again to experience that or a different torture,

continually. The thought of Jake going through something like that blasted all other thoughts from her mind. She came to an abrupt stop, bent over, put her hands on her knees and panted for breath. She wasn't tired, she was horrified.

Not Jake. I can't let him be involved with the shards. I love him, and he loves me, I'm sure of it. I'd sacrifice myself before seeing Jake punished.

When she caught her breath, she moved on. *As for Lucius helping . . . he's a hopeless case. He's out for himself.*

Then she passed a bend in the path, and on the other side stood the centurion.

This time he was dressed in ordinary clothing and not brandishing a weapon, although it was likely he had one or more weapons concealed. She stopped a few feet away from him. Not wanting to appear unarmed, she reached for one of the small knives from its sheath on her calf. If she had to fight him now, she was not in the best condition to do so. Her shoulder was weak from the crossbow wound. He knew that, and as an experienced warrior would come at her from that side.

"Lucius."

"I go by the name L. A. Cinna. For a Roman the first name is for intimate use only."

"I'll stick with Lucius. I'd say anyone who shoots me, steals from me, and saves my life is past the stranger stage. Are you here to give me back my shard?"

Without his helmet and armor he looked less imposing. He was still tall, muscular, extremely fit, and radiated enough pure animal sex appeal that she wondered the wildlife in the park didn't jump him. Without his helmet, she could see that his hair was light-colored, probably blond, and long enough to cover his ears. She had to remind herself that this was no guy looking for a date in all the wrong places, but an Ageless assassin as skilled and enhanced as she had once been.

"No. I take shards, I don't give them back," he said. "This time I'm the one with the questions. I want to know what put you on the mortal path."

"That's easy. I told my demon to fuck off."

His brow crinkled, absorbing this. "You told Rabishu to . . . go away and have sex? How effective was that according to your contract?"

"Look, you may be great with a sword but you're a little dense in other ways. I'm really tired and I'd just like to go home."

Two friends murdered because I sent a sample to their lab that I didn't know anything about and it pulled them into something nasty. It's my fault. Lucius has the luxury of not worrying about things like that. I remember what that's like: no attachments, no pain, no guilt. I don't think I cried once a century, and that was probably when I stubbed my toe or something. I envy his detachment.

Her view of Lucius blurred for a second. When he reappeared, he had both of her knives, and he threw them into the lake.

That's how he did it in the desert cave! He used his Ageless speed. Damn, he could have been right there in the pool room with me when I went into the sand. Letting me take the risk!

"I am hardly dense. Just puzzled," Lucius said.

Maliha wasn't in the mood to trade quips with anyone, even a two-thousand-year-old hottie. "Damn! Don't do that speed thing again. You're starting to piss me off."

The brow crinkled again. "You're going to . . ."

"Forget it. You don't spend much time around people, do you?"

"I perform the tasks I'm assigned. Otherwise, I live as I choose, and I choose to spend most of my time away from people. When I go among them it is usually to kill. Tell me how and why you left the service of Rabishu."

"You'll figure it out, if there is any compassion in you." Maliha shook her head and continued on her way home. Lucius moved out of her way, but the next thing she knew, she was crumpling to the path, her vision fading.

When Maliha woke, she was half-reclining on a chaise longue in a sunroom overlooking a grand view of forested hillsides. The sun glinted on water in the distance, with a hazy area that might be land to one side.

Lucius was sitting on the edge of the next chaise, looking over at her. When he saw that she was awake, he spoke. "Please enjoy my hospitality."

She sat up abruptly and faced him. She was wearing a soft, flowing green gown. It didn't escape her that somewhere between her street clothes and this gown, there must have been a nude stage. That irked her. It reminded her of the first time his eyes had raked across her nude body, in the desert cave.

"You kidnapped me and stripped me," she said, with disbelief and anger fighting for control of her voice. "Whatever you did, you were cowardly enough to do it to an unconscious woman." She pursed her lips. "Where am I?"

"I didn't do anything to you but make you clean and comfortable. I noticed that you did not heal from the crossbow bolt nearly as fast as I thought you would. I have no experience with rogues. I'm sorry to have caused you lasting pain. I'll act with more restraint now that I know you are so fragile."

Fragile! I'll give you fragile! Just wait until this medicine wears off.

"As for where you are, you are on my island home in the Mediterranean Sea. I said I wanted answers, and short of torture, this seemed to be the best way to get your attention."

Maliha looked around. She could see olive trees nearby, with their evergreen leaves and gnarled trunks.

Toto, I've a feeling we're not in Kansas anymore. Or Chicago either.

She shook her head, and regretted it. Dizziness made the world swirl around her.

"The dizziness will wear off. It's from the drug. I'm a skilled physician. You needn't worry about any permanent effects."

"You can take your torture and your permanent effects and this gown"—she grabbed a handful of the fabric—"and shove them up your ass. I'm leaving here now." She stood up and the dizziness was far worse. Sitting back down, she said, "I'm leaving here in a few minutes. In the meantime, you can go get my shard."

"The fragment of the Great Lens isn't on the island."

Maliha was distracted for a moment by Yanmeng's feathery touch on her shoulder. He was checking on her. With her hand at her side, she made an L with her thumb and forefinger and held them out parallel to the floor. It was the sign they'd agreed on for Yanmeng to withdraw. He did so immediately. She appreciated his attentiveness, but there was nothing he could do when she interacted with an Ageless opponent.

Is Lucius an opponent? He's been ordered to collect shards and I can understand that. But what is going on here, with no shard at stake?

"What reason do I have to believe you?" she said.

"Because what we are doing now isn't part of my assignment. I'm not doing the demon's work."

"Then you've got it all wrong. This isn't the Stone Age. You don't knock a woman on the head with your caveman's club, drag her home, and expect cooperation."

"I've taken women without their consent. But I've matured since then."

"That does it. I'm out of here."

She stood up and began to walk away. The dizziness wasn't so bad this time. Instantly he was in front of her, his hand grasping her wrist tightly enough to signal that he wasn't going to let her just walk off the island. Even though it was a restraining move, his touch stirred something in her. There was no denying that she was physically attracted to him. Relaxed in his own home, with the breeze stirring the curtains on long windows, patches of sunlight on tile floors, and the scent of the Mediterranean in the air, he wore loose shorts and nothing else. She could see the mark of his demon on his chest, faintly pulsing with power.

"I wish you'd stop doing that," she said. "I never did anything that annoying when I was Ageless. Are you going to let me leave?"

"I'd rather you didn't."

His grip on her wrist loosened and his hand slid up her arm all the way to her bare shoulder, leaving an invisible trail of sexual sparks.

"We're not finished," he said. "In fact we haven't even started. You haven't answered my questions about your rogue status. Plus, I . . ." He paused and gave her a slow, appreciative look down to her legs and back up again, ending by gazing directly into her eyes. He had expressive brown eyes, and at the moment they were expressing lust.

Maliha's legs felt a little weak and warmth radiated from low in her abdomen.

He could turn on a rock.

His hand on her shoulder strayed and swept slowly across her body just above where her breasts filled the soft gown. And back again.

He was very close to her now, close enough to bend and kiss her shoulder. Then his arm moved around her waist and he pulled her against him.

Whoa, girl, don't forget this is a demon's servant and a stone-cold killer. I think it's time to toss a little cold water. Remember that business about taking women without their consent.

She raised her knee to strike his groin, but he caught her leg and gave it a painful jerk. She ended up on her back on the marble floor. He offered her a hand up. She took it, planted both of her feet into his hard, flat belly, and flipped him over her head. But he twisted like a cat in midair, landed on his feet, and ended with a move that left her arm and shoulder half a second away from breaking. She rotated on the floor to face him, taking the pressure off her limb.

"So you like to play," she said. "I've done this cat-and-mouse thing with another demon's slave and he came out the worse for it. Don't think I can't do the same to you."

His face, so warm and welcoming just seconds ago, now frightened her. She thought of all the destructiveness contained in his body, no matter how attractive the packaging.

"You are mistaken if you think a cat and a mouse are in this room. A tiger and a mouse are here, and I see no stripes on you." The words were delivered coldly. Both his good will and his lust had been switched off.

He pulled her up from the floor, gathered her gown in his fist and kept lifting, holding her a foot up in the air with one hand. Lucius brought her to within an inch of his face and paused there. From the expression on his face, she expected to be flung backward with murderous force.

He hesitated, and that was enough of an opening for her. She reached out and grabbed his head with both hands. This time she caught him off guard. She twisted as hard as she could and felt his neck snap.

His body went limp. As soon as her feet touched the ground, Maliha sprinted away with a burst of speed faster than a human. Then she came skidding to a stop.

Hold on. I could kill him now, while he's unconscious.

She retraced her steps. She had no weapons, and Lucius, lying on the floor in shorts, was carrying nothing but his male equipment. She checked.

Rather than search the house for a weapons cache that would almost certainly be secured, she thought of another way. Sitting on the floor behind his head, she planted her feet on his shoulders and took her head in her grasp. She'd never tried it before but was almost certain she could detach his head by straightening her powerful legs with all the force she had. If her grip on his head didn't falter as she sprang backward, it would be all over for Lucius.

"One, two, three!"

After calling out three, she was still seated in the same position. Gradually her head sank so that her chin nearly rested on her chest.

Master Liu said, "Face death with your eyes open and your heart knowing you have done all that you could. That is an honorable death!" Popping Lucius's head off his shoulders when he's unconscious isn't honorable.

Maliha stood up and gave Lucius a powerful kick in the head.

"That's for kidnapping me."

Another kick. "And that's for taking my clothes off."

She ran out of the house, down toward the shore, shedding the gown as she went. She expected to have to swim to the Grecian mainland, and the voluminous ankle-length gown would impede her. Then she spotted a helicopter, poised on a landing pad not far from the house, and changed course.

Maliha arrived at Athens International Airport as naked as Aphrodite.

Clothed in a one-piece jumpsuit of the type used by airport employees, Maliha was held in an interview room in the airport security section. Considered an intruder in Grecian airspace with no identification and no flight plan, she was suspected of numerous things, ranging from being a terrorist to staging some kind of celebrity stunt due to her exposed body.

Facial identification software showed her to be one Marsha Winters, American writer of erotica. She was mildly insulted. Her Dick Stallion books had plots.

She was allowed to call the American embassy. After much name-dropping, she reached the ambassador herself, who knew her well. Maliha used to visit her father when Anna was a toddler, but the grown Anna didn't remember that.

"Hello, Anna. Marsha here. How have you been?"

"Marsha, what a pleasure to talk to you. Are you vacationing here? Researching?"

"A little bit of both. Listen, I lost my passport. Could you get me out of a sticky situation here? I'm at the airport."

"I'll send over papers for you."

"I could use a cell phone, too. All my luggage seems to have . . . washed out to sea."

"Poor dear. I'll send a phone, a credit card, and some clothes by courier. Will you come over? I'll send a car."

"Of course. I'd like to catch up on little Alexa. Would you talk to airport security?"

She handed the phone to the impatient, glowering security chief who'd been questioning her. His expression gradually changed from intimidating to reluctantly accommodating. The U.S. ambassador went through channels with the Greek government, as she was supposed to, but it didn't take long. Several hours later a car heading for the embassy swept Maliha away.

Chapter Twelve

Dr. Mogue Kane strode across the granite-floored lobby of the Keltner Building in Washington, D.C., with the frustrated air of a man suffering an interruption of his valuable work. Located a couple of blocks from the International Spy Museum, the structure was a hulking presence with little of the gracefulness of the surrounding historical buildings. The Tellman Global Economic Foundation, TGEF, was Mogue's destination. It occupied the first two floors—that is, its public areas did. The foundation also occupied other portions of the building.

He stabbed the button to summon the elevator. His business took him to the top floor, a level that did not date from the late 1800s as the rest of the building did. Alone in the elevator, he inserted his ID card in a slot that opened an access door revealing a button for the top floor, a secure area that had been added to the original roof of the building. He pressed the button and waited impatiently as the elevator car ascended.

He was here to report to the foundation's council. Not the public board that ran the legitimate work of the foundation and arranged building tours to busloads of schoolchildren, but the private group few knew existed.

The Tellman Foundation touted the benefits of having established economies reach out a helping hand to those that were emerging or still awaiting the spark of development. There were a large number of projects going in such countries, but somehow most of the projects never got up to speed due to underfunding. Donors were shown the slick annual report with color photos of newly thriving villages with deep-water wells and start-up businesses run by African women selling woven baskets or cloth, taken at a few token projects.

That was the Tellman Global Economic Foundation's public face, but its private mission was an ironic twist on its name. The secret council meant to change the current global economic foundation, the glue that held nations together economically.

When he got off the elevator, Mogue faced three guards. Two of them stood apart carrying automatic weapons. The third operated an extended booth, more of a tunnel, into which Mogue stepped. He had a full-body scan, no privacy, but the guard was professional about it and Mogue was confident about his equipment even though most women didn't share his enthusiasm.

Must be they don't like my idea of foreplay.

The scan not only made sure Mogue carried no weapons; it also located and stored the identification information on the computer chip under the skin of his right forearm.

Mogue's ID record came up on the guard's computer. Mogue wasn't quite sure how the guard made a decision to let him pass through, but he figured it was facial recognition or the information on the skin chip, or both. Either the guard or the computer could lock the tunnel if there were discrepancies.

The tunnel hissed open on the far side and let him into a hallway. The third door on the left was the council's meeting room. Mogue never met the members in person. They conducted meetings via videoconferencing. The table, a polished wooden oval set on marble legs, had six chairs, each furnished with a computer station that folded away when not in use. For his meeting, each station displayed a monitor with a live image of the person who would normally be sitting in that chair. All except the fifth monitor at the head of the table, and that showed nothing but a blue screen. The leader of the council never showed his or her face. The other board members distorted their images and voices electronically to varying degrees.

Rather than sit in the one empty chair intended for him, Mogue remained standing so that he could pace around as he talked. Disconcertingly, the monitors tracked his movements, so that the others, three men and one woman plus the secretive leader, remained facing him as he moved. He didn't know if there were actually people viewing those monitors yet. The meeting didn't start until the leader greeted everyone.

Tiring of the game of making the monitors track him, Mogue finally sat down. The meeting was ten minutes late. Should he read anything into that or just assume the normal vagaries of business?

Mogue smoothed the front of his perfectly tailored suit. His hair was clean and slicked back and his shoes polished. He almost reached up to stroke his beard before he caught it and suppressed the movement. He hadn't had a beard for sixty or seventy years, but still sometimes had the sensation that it was there.

I sat for hours listening to the meaningless ramblings of those who came to me for healing. I can sit through a council meeting.

He used a technique he considered being two places at once. He kept himself on alert in the boardroom in case there was something traitorous being planned behind those blue screens. The rest of his mind he freed to spin through his memories and pick out ones to relive. This time it was sexual conquests: the women of the Russian Royal Court who came to him and offered their bodily treasures. Who among their husbands could complain when the women sought religious solace from Father Grigori, a renowned holy man? Even though it was no secret that Grigori Rasputin believed that it was necessary to sin first in order to be able to repent and achieve salvation?

He still did, only he no longer worried about the repentance part. The Ageless had no need for such human concerns.

The monitors came to life. Mogue gave his report, answered two questions, and headed for the door.

"Hold." It was the computerized speech of the sole female council member.

With a sigh, Mogue turned around.

"I wish to propose a final test."

They have the nerve to question my results?

"The data would be redundant."

"Nevertheless."

"Your rationale?"

"Fatality rates beyond the targeted area."

"There are no fatalities beyond the targeted area."

"You have assured us of that, but from examining your reports, I don't see where data is included. Can you point me to the page and section?"

Mogue remained silent.

"Council members, your vote?"

All four voted yes. The monitors turned toward the head of the table. It didn't seem likely that the leader would overrule all of them acting together, but it had been known to happen.

"I concur," the leader said. His voice sounded as if it came from deep underwater. "Another test will be performed."

Mogue's mouth formed a tight line of disapproval, but then he nodded. It had occurred to him that if they felt they had all the data they needed, then they didn't need him anymore, especially if he was going to be difficult. He'd violated one of his own tenets: never make yourself expendable.

He'd done that before, in Russia, when he meddled too much in politics. Poisoned, shot, and thrown into a freezing river, Rasputin had met his death in 1916. When he rose from the icy depths and took his first gulp of air as a demon's slave, his task was to make sure that he was convincingly dead. He located a man who looked like him, exchanged clothing with him, shot him in the forehead, and threw him into the same hole in the ice. Rasputin was among those who watched as the Mad Monk's "body" was retrieved from the Neva River.

His mouth relaxed into what he hoped was a convincing smile for their benefit. He wouldn't make that kind of mistake again, especially with this group. Why complicate his work? They were unstable personalities and it wasn't a good idea to appear too controlling.

"What did you have in mind?"

The inhabitants greeted Mogue and company with enthusiasm. They lived in an oasis, a stopping point for travelers, but those travelers generally weren't doctors. In their remote location, getting health care was a once-in-a-decade event, if that.

The convoy stopped at the perimeter and men brought across the border from Algeria began putting up tents for the medical staff, followed by a row of larger tents filled with cots for the injured. In the evening the Algerians were quietly rounded up, marched a mile away, and shot. Paying them with bullets conserved money better spent on ensuring the loyalty of mercenaries. Men like Long Shot bristled with weapons and the will to use them, but the laborers had nothing but their strong backs, and sometimes not even that.

Mogue had been planning to wait until morning to begin medical assessment, but lines had already formed at the entrance to the hospital tent. Mogue began seeing patients by lantern light. A few doctors remained in the tent with him, and the rest fanned out into the settlement.

Mogue retired to his private quarters after a few hours, leaving the rest of the medical staff to work in shifts through the night. He asked his aide—Mogue tried to maintain the illusion of academic research, even in environments that tolerated no pretense—to summon Long Shot.

The mercenary came grudgingly.

"What is it now? Better be fucking good. I was winning at poker."

Mogue smiled, even though he didn't like the implication that playing poker with Long Shot's buddies was more important than a summons from the boss.

The money I'm paying this son-of-a-bitch should buy some respect as well as his trigger finger.

"You'll be compensated. I have a task for you."

"So what's so important?"

Mogue swiveled to reach the briefcase lying on his bed. Long Shot eyed the case with suspicion and took a couple of steps back, ready to bolt if the case held some nasty surprise.

Mogue opened the briefcase. Three gleaming metal cylinders nestled in foam packing. Each about the size of a thermos, their contents were far more dangerous than coffee.

Long Shot extracted one of the containers from the briefcase and held it up to the light of the lantern, as if he could see the contents that way. "What's in these things?"

"I don't pay you to ask questions."

"I just mean, do we need gloves or masks? Is this shit nerve gas or something?"

"Stop waving that around." Mogue took the cylinder, replaced it in the briefcase, and closed the case. "No, it isn't nerve gas. There are three wells here. Pour one bottle down into each of them. Be sure your men are using the bottled water we brought with us."

The mercenary took the case—gingerly, Mogue thought—and left without a word.

A few days later, the oasis dwellers all followed the same path to death. Abdomens caved inward, eyes turned to pulp. Noisome fluids leaked from the ears, mouth, and all other orifices. Medical technicians walked among the dying. They observed, filmed, and sampled, but offered no help to those who pleaded for it. People randomly chosen for autopsy included some who weren't quite dead when they went under Mogue's scalpel. The camera rolled as Mogue worked. Aware that he would not be the only viewer of the recording, Mogue kept the grin off his face and rarely let his scalpel stray in a non-businesslike manner.

The team packed up to leave. The cleanup crew would burn the settlement, making it look like an accidental fire had taken off and spread by desert winds through the vegetation of the oasis. It would raise questions, but there would be nothing left to prove it was other than a natural disaster.

Mogue's team split in two, half following the caravan traffic east and the other half heading west. The council wanted to know whether deaths extended on either side of the oasis in unintended subjects, and if there were transmission vectors other than human hosts. That was the data they felt they needed before moving forward. Mogue could have told them the answers—no and no—and was reluctant to waste time on it at first, but now he was pleased with the opportunity to direct this larger-scale and elegant test.

Chapter Thirteen

ound and Amaro had arrived in Maliha's absence, so it was a full house in her Chicago apartment. Slices of pizza from Brick's were the center of attention and for a few minutes, food was the priority. Once they were sitting back, satiated, it was time for words.

"Where have you been?" Amaro's voice was both concerned and annoyed.

Maliha glanced at Yanmeng. He was the one who'd declared the mutiny, but he shrugged. She'd been gone longer than the three of them expected. Travel time to the desert, a week in the pool, an unknown amount of time drugged on Lucius's island, a trip home from Greece.

I made a little side trip to a Mediterranean island, wrestled with an Ageless assassin, and almost pulled off his head.

"You know I took a little time off after the Rainiers died," Maliha said. "They were good friends."

In the world of computer hackers, Amaro was supreme. He could make the finest distinctions and pick up the most subtle intentions. Outside that world, he was sometimes a guppy in a pool of sharks, and occasionally he forgot to take into account others' feelings.

"What did you learn from the Rainiers before they got blown up?" Amaro said. Yanmeng winced and Hound elbowed Amaro. "What? Oh, sorry. I could have said that better."

What did I learn? So many things. Their devotion to each other and to science, Claire's laughing eyes. That the joy in Ty's face slipped only once in the time I knew him, and that was when his father passed away.

Wordless images of their lives and deaths played through Maliha's mind. She sighed. She was going to have to walk through all of it in detail, and she didn't feel like living it again. But if Glass could relive her ordeal for them, that was the least Maliha could do.

"When I got there, I could see that the lab had been searched. Papers and glass were everywhere. Ty was on the floor injured and Claire was still alive, tied to a chair. It looked as though she'd been questioned hard."

The broken glass bit into Claire's neck and everything slowed down. The sharp edge reached her jugular vein and blood gushed, blood the peculiar maroon color of oxygen depletion. It arced across to the wall and splashed the hands of the man holding the glass. Maliha looked up from his guilty hands to his face. His eyes were fixed on her, not on his victim. He was sending a message to Maliha that Claire died not because of something she did, but because of something Maliha did. Maliha supplied the sample in the canteen and now both Ty and Claire knew too much to live.

"She died right after that," Maliha said.

"Who was in the room?"

"There were a couple of flunkies plus the evil-looking guy in a long robe. If I'd seen him elsewhere, I would have said he was homeless. In these circumstances, he was clearly the boss."

"Can you do a little better than 'evil-looking' as a description?" Yanmeng said.

"Tall, thin, white, unwashed appearance with greasy shoulder-length hair."

"Are you sure you haven't seen a picture of Charles Manson lately and projected it on this guy?" Amaro said.

"No. This man is older than Manson and his face even thinner, like skin stretched over his skull. His hair has gray mixed in it. He moved with an unusual grace, almost like a dancer."

"Ageless?"

Maliha thought of Master Liu. The first time she'd seen him, he appeared as a naked old man washing his clothes at a forest stream. Seconds later she saw him as a muscular young man. Although she didn't possess that ability, Master Liu was at least one Ageless man who could alter his perceived appearance to one earlier in his own lifetime. If the killer was Ageless and could do something similar, it looked like he'd chosen to show himself to Maliha as a ragged old man near the time of his death—exactly as Master Liu had initially done.

"He didn't do anything one way or the other that signaled he was Ageless, like moving impossibly fast for a human. I think he's just what he looked like on the surface, an evil old man who thinks nothing of killing. He had the canteen."

"Shit," Amaro said. "We still don't know if that stuff's dangerous then. I couldn't find any communications the Rainiers made about it. Would have been nice if they'd emailed all their findings to Maliha. If they had any findings."

"I did manage to get into the lab," Yanmeng said. "I went as an arson investigator."

"Cool," Amaro said.

"Nothing left. No notes, no computer files, no samples on slides. But if I could sneak in, so could Mr. Evil's henchmen, so I don't know if the place was cleaned out before I got there."

"Speaking of Mr. Evil," Hound said, "he's not only evil but invisible. I couldn't turn up anything on somebody operating like him from my sources. Yet we know he's involved in these murders and I'm guessing the Rainiers weren't his first targets. I have more to go on with a physical description. Maliha, can you tell us anything else you learned while you were in the lab with him?"

"Bullets were flying. I was kind of busy. Never got a chance to look for anything, once I noticed the bomb. And of course that substance is dangerous. Why else would Ty and Claire have been killed to keep them from talking about it?"

"Maybe the killer was there for something unrelated," Amaro said. "Some other research of theirs."

She frowned at him. "No. It was because of the sample. Otherwise he wouldn't have taken the canteen. Are you guys testing me or just slow?"

"So we assume Mr. Evil got out alive, before the bomb, with the canteen," Yanmeng said.

There was no disapproval in his voice, but Maliha added his words to the guilt she felt about her friends' deaths.

"I had to get Ty out of the building. He was still alive and I couldn't leave him that way. I couldn't chase the killer and look after Ty at the same time. Outside, Ty said some things I haven't had much time to think about."

Yanmeng picked up the guilt in her voice. "You don't have to justify what you did. It was a split-second decision. We trust that you did the right thing," Yanmeng said. Amaro and Hound nodded.

Maliha rested her hand on her belly where she'd lost two figures from the good side of her scales. "Ty said, 'Not bio,' 'nan' something."

And, "Tell Claire I love her." I never had a chance to do that, but Claire knew. She came to him.

" 'Not bio' probably means not biological. So the sample wasn't biologically active. They did make some determination," Yanmeng said.

"He didn't mention 'chem' or chemical, so are we in the clear on that?" Amaro said.

Maliha shrugged. "He didn't have a whole lot of time to talk."

"Who's Nan, then? A lab assistant?" Yanmeng said. "Do you know anyone named Nan in their lives?"

"It doesn't have to be a person. Nan with a little n. A very little n. Maybe nanites," Amaro said.

Maliha seized on it. "Killer nanites. Not biological. It fits."

"A good theory. Something in the victims' bloodstream or cells. Tiny hitchhikers that would go unnoticed in a local Sudanese morgue even if there was something left of the bodies to autopsy. They don't have the specialized microscopes to see them. That equipment is found in research labs. Well-funded labs. An ordinary blood test or an X-ray wouldn't show up nanites. It makes sense," Amaro said. "Glass wasn't affected because she wasn't there when the nanites were distributed. We were never in any danger at the Swiss clinic. They're probably programmed to shut off when their host dies."

"Nobody expected an American woman to suddenly pop in and complicate things," Yanmeng said. "Otherwise no sample would have gotten out, and everybody would have believed the Janjaweed raid story."

"Wait," Amaro said. "The Rainiers weren't experts in nanotech. Would they even know what they had in that sample?"

"Evidently, they found out. The university must have those special microscopes somewhere on campus." Amaro nodded.

Yanmeng said, "Would fire kill the hitchhikers? Maybe they're still in Darfur, in the soil or something."

Maliha was startled with the simplicity of it. No one would think to take soil samples. Everyone thought the Janjaweed had slaughtered and incinerated the villagers and that was the end of it. "We need to send some experts in nanotechnology out there. Amaro?"

"I'm on it already." He was walking over to his computer. "Why not start at the top? I'll find out who the most respected researcher is."

"We don't need to respect him," Maliha said. "Just find out who's good and I'll hop on a plane and drag the guy out to the site. Wait, he doesn't have to go." She rolled her eyes. "What a dummy. I can go there myself and take soil samples. It's hostile territory there."

"Whoa," Amaro said. Yanmeng and Maliha stared at him.

"Whoa, as in don't get soil samples?"

He was staring at his computer. "There's been another incident. They're saying it was a fire wildly out of control. An oasis settlement burned in northeastern Niger. All the inhabitants killed and incinerated in the fire. Sound familiar?"

"How many times does it take for people to get suspicious? Wouldn't there be some investigation?" Maliha said.

"It's Africa. Two different countries. That doesn't make a pattern, not yet, and anyway, it doesn't affect us, so ignore it. That's unfortunately the attitude toward a lot of things that go on in high-poverty areas," Amaro said.

There was bitterness in his voice. Maliha knew he was thinking of his early life in a *favela* in Rio de Janeiro. In those slums life was cheap and the police usually avoided becoming involved. Amaro and his sister Rosie would have died there as teenagers if Maliha hadn't rescued them from gang violence.

"I wouldn't say that as a rule," Yanmeng said. "There are plenty of people who care, like us."

"Hound, how about we go to Niger and take a look? Get some soil samples and generally raise a stink for the press? Amaro, my jet's still at Midway?"

"Unless you took it on a romantic getaway with Jake."

"Not yet. Would you please set up a flight to . . . I guess to Algiers. We'll have to figure out how to get to the settlement in Niger from there."

"You actually said *please*."

"I'm growing polite in my old age." No one had mentioned her appearance, but Maliha had gotten a glimpse in the mirror. Anu's aging for the Rainiers' deaths had not been kind to her. The tiny wrinkles at the corners of her eyes had deepened. Perhaps she was more sensitive to every silver hair or wrinkle than those around her, but she had reason to be. Her powers diminished with age, and there could come a time when the kinds of exploits she now took for granted would be beyond her physically. If she didn't balance her scale by then, Rabishu would win when she succumbed to old age.

*   *   *

Maliha and Hound had just taken off for Algiers when she got a call from Amaro.

"I've got your nanotech expert lined up. Top researcher Dr. Fynn Saltz." He spelled it for her. "Lives in Miami, but here's the thing: He hasn't been seen in the last two months. He could be hidden away somewhere working on the hitch-hiker program."

"Or just decided he needed a little R and R away from the wife and kids," Maliha said. "Either way, he sounds like someone I need to find. We'll head for Miami and I'll get off there. Hound can continue on his own."

With a revised flight plan filed, the jet headed south.

Maliha started with legwork and lying at the University of Miami. She'd learned from Hound never to broach the authorities of an institution, because that's where red tape was purchased in bulk quantities. Instead, she mingled with the students, asked questions, was sent to a couple of dead ends, and then struck dirt with Dr. Saltz's grad assistant, Larry Maybry.

The first thing Larry wanted to talk about was something that both annoyed and worried him. His boss had a research project going on at a different location, or at least Larry thought he did. He hadn't been in contact with him recently.

"I guess I shouldn't feel slighted. Fynn was supposed to get married last week. He never showed up. I wonder what his fiancée thinks about that?" Larry asked.

"Maybe he got cold feet," Maliha said.

Larry shook his head. "Nah. Whatever else I think of the guy, I know he was devoted to his fiancée."

Once he got away from grousing about the boss, Larry loved to talk about his work. She let Larry explain nanotechnology to her to keep from breaking the flow of conversation.

"Nanotech requires you to think on a very small scale," he said. "Smaller than bacteria, smaller than viruses. We're talking about things on the atomic or molecular level, one millionth of a millimeter. That's a nanometer. I'm seeing those beautiful green eyes of yours with light with a wavelength of about five hundred nanometers."

"I've never had anyone flirt with me by describing my eyes as a wavelength." She didn't mind being a flirt. It was the gentlest of her ways of getting information.

"You've never met me before," Larry said. There was no arrogance in his tone, just a statement of fact. "For nanotech, the sizes can be much smaller than the wavelength of visible light. It's like taking a tiny, tiny tweezers and placing atoms or molecules exactly where you want them to create materials. Suppose I wanted to make a strawberry. If I know the chemical components of it, I could assemble a strawberry from water, dirt, and air, and a little bit of energy. Not the way Mother Nature does it with cell division and growth powered by photosynthesis, but it would taste the same."

"Dr. Saltz is working on making manufactured food?"

"That was just an example. But manufacturing—that's the idea. You've seen those big robotic arms that assemble cars, right? They can only handle big pieces, like a steering wheel or something. Shrink the arm down to a hundred nanometers, and now you've got a nanite that can handle atoms or molecules. If you have one nanite build you something that sizable, like a paper clip, it's going to take a long time because it's assembling atom by atom. So have a huge number of them working together—you'll get something that's actually visible to the eye much faster, especially if you can provide some kind of scaffold for them to place atoms in. The little guys could repair themselves or build more of themselves, or cooperate to build a nanite that doesn't look like them. Theoretically, they could even mutate—make a bad copy."

She touched his arm gently. "Go on." She checked his aura. It was mostly a muddy orange, with spikes of dull brown. He was eager for success but lacking in confidence. He'd be the type who would run over others to achieve success. A few streaks of red showed that he was responding to Maliha's sexuality.

He's hooked. But I didn't need to see his aura to tell that.

She was perched on a lab stool next to him, and she casually crossed her legs.

"What are you and the professor working on?"

"I'd rather not say. It's proprietary. But I almost think Saltz has lost interest in it. He's onto something bigger."

"Bigger?"

"I told you earlier he has a project going that he won't let me even look at. I won't get any credit when he publishes, and that ticks me off. He's supposed to be my advisor, and it looks like he advised me right out of the picture. I haven't seen him for a while, so I guess he's working off-site someplace."

"Do you know him well?"

Larry frowned, but it came off as a sneer. "He doesn't let anybody get close except that woman of his. He brought up his son Doyle to follow in his footsteps, but the guy's a bum."

Maliha thanked him and made her way out of the lab, bursting Larry's lust bubble. She was pleased with all the information she'd collected.

Maybe I should apply for a Private Investigator's license and go into business with Hound.

She asked around for information on Saltz's son Doyle and put together a picture of him. He was a college dropout who worked part-time jobs when he could find them. His mother died early in his life, leaving him in the reflected glare of his brilliant father, who had great plans for his son. Those great plans had boiled down to sending his son money every month in the hopes that he'd come to his senses. Dr. Saltz lived in Coral Gables, an upscale community near the university. Doyle lived in the polar opposite, Liberty City, probably just to be spiteful.

Maliha walked through Liberty City after dark. The area had a reputation as crime ridden, but she wasn't worried. Although not dressed in her killing outfit, she had the advantage of knives, throwing stars, and her superb martial arts skills. Maliha garnered numerous whistles and a couple of crude offers, easily deflected. Doyle's apartment was on the second floor of a building at the end of the hall. It was one of the nicest buildings on the block, but had urine stains in the corners and the scratching noises of rodents coming from dark places. As she walked down the hall, she noticed the carpet was worn, the lights dim, and the arguments behind closed doors loud. She'd called ahead, so Doyle was expecting her. His apartment was cramped but clean, except for the layer of marijuana smoke at roughly head height. After the introductions, Maliha sat down on a spongy couch, lowering her head below the smoke layer. He offered her a joint and when she didn't take it, reluctantly put his stash aside.

He was in his thirties, not a people person, but surprisingly willing to talk about his father.

"Yeah, he's been gone since sometime in September. He used to call me every week, make sure I'm still alive, I guess. That stopped weeks ago. I went over to his place and he wasn't there. Wasn't dead either, which I kinda had a feeling was the case. Feels weird to think I'm doing the same kind of shit for him—trying to look out for him and see that he's okay."

"What about the police?"

"They looked into it for about thirty seconds. That was how long it took them to find out that he'd filed for a sabbatical leave of absence from the university. After that they weren't interested. Said he was entitled to his privacy and I should shut the fuck up."

A sabbatical that his assistant didn't know about? Larry was nosy, especially about Dr. Saltz. He would have known.

Maliha spotted a couple of framed pictures showing young Doyle and his father on a deep-sea fishing boat. She estimated the boat at forty feet, and didn't see any crew in the pictures. Dr. Saltz must be experienced to captain his own boat.

A man who hated his father wouldn't have any photos on display, so the relationship between Doyle and his father was more complex than outright rejection.

Doyle isn't making some kind of statement to his father with his lifestyle, it's just the way he is.

"Did you follow your father's research enough to know what he was working on?"

Doyle shook his head. "Not much. I know he was some kind of wizard with nanites. The last thing he was working on was some way to coat the little critters with something so they wouldn't get rejected in the body. Yeah, that was it. He said he could help people with it, like it could fix things in the body. Diseases like diabetes, I think. Maybe something else."

That must be the secret project Larry complained about. If nanites could assemble complex things, they could manufacture insulin in the body. Something to "fix" diabetes would be worth hundreds of millions. Larry was motivated by more than academic pride. He wanted in on the money.

"Did he act strangely before he disappeared? Maybe seem under a lot of stress?"

"He was always under stress. This experiment didn't work, that one was a disappointment. He was very devoted to his work. The weeks before he disappeared he was acting strangely, even for him."

"How?"

Doyle looked off to the side. His features may have been handsome at one time, but now sagged, giving him a worn look beyond his years.

"Nervous. Maybe depressed. It could be hard to tell with him. Would you believe he didn't show up for his own wedding? Now that's gotta be suspicious. I hired an investigator, did I mention that? He came up with nada and charged me a couple hundred bucks to do it. I don't have that kind of money, especially since Dad disappeared. He used to slip me a few bucks every now and then. You said on the phone you were looking for him. You gonna try to charge me, too? I mean, I want to find the guy because I don't think he's on a sabbatical. Would've told me. I don't have anything left to pay. The rent's due."

"I'm not going to charge you anything. He was depressed even though he was getting married? That doesn't make sense. He didn't call her and tell her he was breaking up with her?"

"Nah. All of a sudden she just said the wedding's off. No explanation."

"What's the woman's name? I'd like to talk to her."

"Jamie Blake. She lives in New York. He met her there at some scientific conference. I got her phone number here somewhere." He stood up, crossed the room, and rummaged in a box that served as a desk. "Yeah, here it is. She's a real nice woman. Got a beautiful kid. They were good for each other." He handed her a piece of paper.

The phone rang in another room. "I need to get that. Possible job." He started toward the kitchen, then turned around. "You find out anything, you let me know, okay? I mean, think if it was your father. You can't give up."

"You can't give up," Maliha echoed. "Believe me, I'm going to look very hard for Dr. Fynn Saltz."

He just might be the key to the hitchhikers and exactly what they do. And how to stop them.

Chapter Fourteen

Flynn Saltz's fiancée worked at Columbia University, in the Morningside Heights neighborhood of Manhattan. She had a second floor apartment on West 122nd Street, within walking distance of her job as a biology professor.

Maliha wore a long-sleeved blouse, tucked into trousers, and a light jacket over that. It was chilly, but she didn't want to wear a long coat that would restrict her motion. While walking there, Maliha had a sudden feeling of apprehension about something ahead. She took inventory of her weapons: three knives hidden about her body and the whip sword curled at her waist, its thin, flat handle serving as a belt buckle.

Perhaps this feeling of danger isn't a problem for me, maybe Hound instead. Wonder what's going on with him?

The building had no doorman, so Maliha walked right in and found the name Jamie Blake neatly lettered above the mailbox slot for 2-B. She took the stairs. The building was clean but spare, with art deco details that made it exactly the kind of place Maliha would choose for herself if she were in Dr. Blake's circumstances.

Maliha had phoned ahead, so when she knocked on the door, Dr. Blake opened immediately. She might have been waiting just behind the door. She had blonde hair cut very short, pale skin that must have required sunblock by the gallon, nervous gray eyes, and substantial curves. Maliha thought she was about forty years old, but she'd taken care of herself and could pass for ten years younger. She was dressed well, with a dark silky blouse and an ivory skirt that flattered her legs, probably put on hurriedly for Maliha's benefit because the nice outfit fizzled out at her knees. She wore faded blue socks and sneakers that were past their prime.

A young girl about nine or ten was in the kitchen having a snack, and her mother asked her to go to her bedroom.

"Can I please take my glass of milk?"

"Just this once, go ahead."

Maliha wondered if her own daughter, Constanta, who'd died at birth in a colonial jail cell, would have looked something like this beautiful child. The girl had blonde hair like her mother, but long and wavy, and a waiflike face with large blue eyes.

My girl had darker hair, darker eyes, but so much else would be the same. The intelligent eyes, the angles of her cheeks and chin, the gentle way she speaks. Sweet femininity but strong legs and arms. By the time Constanta was this age, I would have had three other children, maybe more.

She pictured her young family sitting around the table, eating dinner with her husband, Nathan.

A simple life as a healer, a wife, and a mother. Grandchildren, should I live that long! What joy. And when the time came, a place in the cemetery next to Nathan, a natural end to a satisfying life.

The girl smiled at Maliha with a face that already showed the natural beauty of the woman to come. As the girl passed by, Maliha rested a hand on the girl's shoulder for a moment, a moment that would have to do for all the moments in a life that had been ripped away from her.

For a lifetime of the love of a mother for her daughter.

Dr. Blake saw the small gesture and smiled at it. Perhaps she noted the longing in Maliha's look and touch, but Maliha wasn't sure.

When the girl left, Maliha and the professor settled at the kitchen table. The only sign of emotional distress that

the woman showed on the outside was wringing her hands.
The instant she sat down, her hands were lying on the table
pulling and stroking each other. She had an engagement ring
with a large diamond, and twisted it around and around on
her finger.

"Professor Blake—"

"Oh, please call me Jamie. Everybody does, even my
students."

"Jamie then. I'm Marsha. What's your daughter's name?"

"Betty Sue. Her father was from Texas," Jamie said, as
though the name needed an explanation.

"She's lovely. You must be very proud of her."

Jamie smiled and nodded. "She's going to be a musician.
I just know it. She's got a special skill."

"You could be right. Mothers are able to pick that up
sometimes."

*My mother knew my skill very early, back when I was
Susannah.*

1676

A cold night in a long, hungry winter. Susannah
awakened, her stomach cramping, but even at that young
age she knew the family must make the food last all winter.
Wandering from the children's room, Susannah went looking for water to fill her stomach. She filled her cup from the
jar near the door and drank, spilling some.

She went to the hearth, where there was still some color
left among the embers. She stirred them, watching the sparks
and a few halfhearted flames. She crouched to take advantage
of the little burst of warmth. Watching the embers shimmer
in different shades of red, orange, and yellow, sometimes all
three at once, her eyelids began to slide closed. Captivated
by the colors and half asleep, Susannah reached out for one
of the embers. She'd been told not to get too close to the
hearth. At almost four years old there were things she was
expected to do for herself. Her mother couldn't watch her all
the time. She had two other babies to watch.

The ember was so pretty. . . . She picked it up and blew on it to make it glow brighter.

For only a moment, for less than a breath, Susannah held the glowing, jewel-like ember with her fingertips. Then her eyes widened and she dropped it. She stared at the reddened ends of her fingers. Why were her fingers burning hot but there were no flames?

Then the pain struck, the worst in her life. It made her get up and move. She didn't know why, but she knew she needed to get to where her mother had the dried plants she had brought in at harvest. She found the basket and uncovered it. As her fingers throbbed and tears rolled down her cheeks, blurring her vision, she picked up one bunch after another, pressing the dried leaves to release the smell. Finally one was right. On a wooden surface, she mashed the leaves quickly with the heel of her good hand and scooped them into a cup of cool water. She plunged her burning fingertips into the cup and held them there. Gradually the pain eased.

Her mother woke her the next morning. Susannah had fallen asleep with her hand in the cup. Looking at the vague traces of unfilled blisters on Susannah's hand, her mother smelled the cup of water and smiled.

"Benjamin, come see. Our little Susannah is a healer."

"I know this isn't a good time for me to ask questions," Maliha said to Jamie, "with Fynn disappearing like that. But I'd appreciate any answers you can give. Do you think he just couldn't face the idea of a wedding?"

Emotion showed on Jamie's face for the first time, a sense of loss that passed over her face like a spring storm that left no rainbow. "Not a chance. He's very happy about the wedding. We're very much in love."

Maliha noted that she spoke of Fynn in the present tense. She hadn't given up on him.

"Was he in some kind of trouble? His son said that he was nervous or depressed."

"You talked to Doyle?"

"Yes. I told you that, when we talked on the phone."

"Oh. I remember now, you did. Fynn's emotions went on a roller coaster ride depending on how his scientific studies were doing. He was devoted to his work. If he had a success in his experiments, we went out to celebrate. If he was having trouble, the only person who could get him out of a bad mood was Betty Sue." Her eyes darted away, looking at the closed door to Betty Sue's bedroom.

Devoted to his work. Exactly what Doyle said. Is there some rehearsal going on here? Fynn could have disappeared for a reason unrelated to the hitchhikers. What if he was a little too close to Betty Sue? His fiancée or his son could have killed him to stop the abuse. Accounts for the fact that no one persisted with the police beyond that initial missing persons report, too.

Maliha looked through Jamie, as though seeing the wall behind her, and let the woman's aura come into view. The aura was a mix of strong, bright colors. As quiet as Jamie appeared on the surface, she was a flaring symphony of feelings underneath.

Red. She's fearful, anxious, and trying not to show it. Yellow. Her basic success and happiness with teaching. Vibrant pink threads—her love for Fynn and Betty Sue. A little bit of orange for confidence there, but it's way overpowered. She's in trouble. But is it because she knows something about Fynn's disappearance? Time for a lie detector test.

As she continued to view Jamie's aura, Maliha said, "Jamie, I have to ask a difficult question. Did Fynn ever abuse Betty Sue? Physically, sexually?"

Jamie's eyes flew open and her mouth opened slightly in surprise. But Maliha was more interested in what was going on in her aura. Strong flashes of scarlet snapped into being, with flames licking wide tongues in Maliha's direction in the space between them as they sat across from each other at the kitchen table. Jamie was rightfully, powerfully, indignant.

"What are you talking about?" The indignation was

strong in Jamie's voice, too. "Fynn would never do anything like that! He loves Betty Sue. What are you doing, coming here and making accusations like that!"

"Calm down, Jamie. I'm not making accusations, just asking questions to rule things out. You can understand that."

She crossed her arms and leaned back in her chair. "Well, you can rule that out and I don't like you asking. I think that's about all I want to tell you. I don't really know who you are or what you are to Fynn. I think you should leave now." She stood up to end the conversation.

Maliha remained seated. She decided to take a direct approach, since she was about to be thrown out of the apartment and had nothing to lose.

"What are you afraid of? Has someone threatened you or Fynn? Or your daughter?"

When she got to the word *daughter*, Jamie flinched so slightly most people wouldn't have noticed. But Maliha wasn't most people.

"Your daughter then. Tell me about it. I can help you. I've helped other people in situations like yours. It's what I do for a living."

Jamie sat down, her face paler than ever. Indecision fluttered in her eyes.

Maliha reached across the table and rested her hand on Jamie's. "Tell me. It's the best thing you can do for your daughter. For all of you. Doyle trusted me. He sent me here to see you." Maliha could tell that she was losing the battle. Jamie was shutting down, too scared to open up. Maliha dug around in her pocket and came up with a dog-eared card from Hound's private investigation business. It had saved her skin on more than one occasion.

"All right," Maliha said. "I wasn't supposed to tell you. The university hired a private investigations firm, but they didn't want it known. It's not good for their reputation that one of their top researchers disappears. Names like Fynn's bring in alumni donations."

Jamie took the card Maliha held out. "Hound Dog

Investigative Services," she read. "Private. Secure. Don't bother us with easy shit. Extra charge if wounded."

Maliha winced when Jamie got to the easy shit part. She would have preferred that Hound's card said something more professional but she had nothing to say about it.

To Maliha's discomfort, Jamie picked up a phone and dialed the only phone number on the card. Nobody had done that before, at least not in her presence. Someone answered. She hoped it wasn't Hound.

Jamie listened, then said, "Is Marsha . . ." She gestured at Maliha to supply the last name.

"Winters."

"Is Marsha Winters an employee of yours?" Jamie listened for a minute, then said thank you and hung up.

Maliha waited for the verdict.

"It seems you're their lead investigator, assigned to the hardest cases. You have a great record of success. Totally confident, etcetera."

Maliha made a move to take back the business card but Jamie didn't surrender it. She picked up the phone again, dialed information, and asked for the phone number of Hound Dog Investigative Services. She was given a number that matched the one on the card.

"Okay, I guess you're the real thing," Jamie said. "Just because Doyle sent you here isn't reason enough to trust you. Doyle's like a puppy, he likes everybody."

Maliha was impressed with Hound's backup on the business card.

I'm going to have Amaro get me an assortment of business cards with legit offices and scripts in case anybody calls. Score one for Hound, zero for Maliha on this one.

Jamie dropped her eyes. It was easier for her to talk that way. "I don't know if I'm doing the right thing by telling you, but I'm so scared I just have to take a chance. They . . . two of them came. They said Fynn was working for them now and if I wanted to see him again, I should keep quiet about it. Cancel the wedding, tell everybody I changed my mind. If I made any mistakes or went to the police, Betty

Sue was toast. That's exactly what they said, *toast*. That they would . . . I can't say it. I can't even think about it."

"You did the right thing telling me."

"Can you help us? What has Fynn gotten into? Gotten all of us into?" Tears welled up in her eyes. "Is my daughter in danger?"

I don't think those two guys came here bluffing. Can I really protect these people? Before the Rainiers, I would have said yes.

Guilt over her friends' deaths surfaced, but she pushed it back. Her attitude had to be confident no matter what she felt inside.

"You've got to trust me. You've got to tell me everything you know. When did Fynn disappear?"

"I know the exact date. September fifth. The reason I remember is that he said he had one last meeting to attend that week, and then we were taking the rest of the week off together. Like a family vacation, the three of us. Fynn hardly ever takes time off."

"It's been over two months. He hasn't had any contact with you in all that time?"

"No. I haven't gone to the police, either, because those . . . people told me not to. He's a good person. What's going to happen to us?"

"Nothing, if I can help it. Do you have a photo of Fynn I can have?"

Jamie retrieved a photo from a desk and handed it to Maliha. Glancing at it, Maliha saw a picnic with Jamie and her daughter seated at a table, while Fynn roasted hot dogs. Gray hair, glasses, about fifty-five years old, a small belly hanging over his belt. Maliha memorized his face.

"You think he's alive?" The question carried every emotion Jamie was feeling. Love, fear, hope. Hopelessness.

Maliha thought for a moment. *Two months, two recent tests of the hitchhikers. If they're testing—whoever they are—he doesn't have much time left. He's served his usefulness.*

"Yes, I do think he's alive." *But probably not for long.*

"If there's anything you can do . . . I have a little money put aside. Fynn has some, too."

"I don't work for money." Maliha rested her hand across her belly, where the scale that ruled her destiny lay.

Jamie gave her the names of a few colleagues, including a local one at Columbia University. Maliha decided to start there. She phoned Dr. Booker Cobb and he said he'd meet her at his university office, in spite of the evening hour.

Dr. Cobb's office was highly organized. Files in neat stacks, color-coded folders, no memorabilia of his teaching career or the rest of his life, for that matter. On a shelf near the window was a trio of bonsai plants. They were the only things in the room Maliha could relate to, including the occupant. She had a two-hundred-year-old bonsai cherry tree that produced perfect blossoms. It was at least an opening for the conversation.

"I see you are a practitioner of bonsai, Dr. Cobb."

"Oh, those?" He nodded at the plants. "I'm babysitting them for a friend of my wife's who's gone to Paris for three months. Damn nuisance. Have to be watered with an eye-dropper, that kind of thing."

So much for that opening.

Dr. Cobb was worried about Fynn. All she had to do was get him started with a simple inquiry, and then his words tumbled out and provided Maliha with a key piece of information. On the day he disappeared, Fynn had a meeting—that jibed with what Jamie had said—at the Tellman Global Economic Foundation in Washington, D.C. Cobb had joked with Fynn about the foundation luring him away from the university. Fynn had said he was happy at Columbia, but smelled grant money and wanted to talk to the foundation representatives.

"I haven't seen him since. I was invited to the wedding, you know. It's not like Fynn to take off like that. Sabbatical, my, er, behind. I happen to know that it usually takes months to get a sabbatical approved and everybody in the department knows about it ahead of time. I don't believe he planned this months ago and didn't tell any of us. Didn't tell Jamie to postpone the wedding, for gosh sakes."

"Did you go to the police?"

"Jamie begged me not to. I think now I should have."

"Do me a favor and hold off."

"Jamie said you were helping her. She called after talking to you. For her sake, I'll cooperate with anything you want me to do."

Leaving Dr. Cobb to his neat office and the unwelcome demands of his bonsai plants, Maliha called Jamie. She might know more about Fynn's work at the Tellman Foundation.

When she couldn't reach Jamie by phone, Maliha got a queasy feeling in her stomach. She'd been gone less than an hour from Jamie's apartment. Suddenly the apprehensive feeling she'd had earlier crystallized into a fist that struck her in the gut.

No. Surely not.

She took off running, telling herself that she was getting paranoid and that Jamie and her daughter, Betty Sue, had just gone out to eat, or Jamie was in the shower and didn't hear the phone. Maliha's anxiety drove her speed. There were few people out on the sidewalk, and to them she would have appeared as a blur and a rush of wind that left them wondering what had just happened.

Stopping in the entry hall of Jamie's building, Maliha leaned against the wall and gave herself only a second or two of time to think. She didn't bother pressing the button next to the mailbox. She charged up the stairs and pounded on the door.

"Jamie! Open up, it's Marsha!"

When there was no answer, she drove her foot through the door. Both the door and its frame splintered. She dove into the room, hoping that she'd soon be paying Jamie for the broken door. There were no thugs, no evil to fight.

Jamie was at the kitchen table, face down on a newspaper soaked with blood. Her coffee cup sat nearby, undisturbed. As Maliha approached, she could see bullet wounds in the back of Jamie's head. The woman had been executed.

Holding her breath, knife in hand, Maliha moved cautiously toward the hallway to Betty Sue's bedroom. Partway there, caution couldn't hold her back any longer. She rushed to the bedroom and threw open the door.

Relief swept over her. Betty Sue was at her desk with her back to Maliha, watching a movie on her computer, earphones on her head. If she had the volume turned up loud enough, she wouldn't have heard the shots, especially if a silencer had been used. If Maliha could just get her outside without seeing her mother—that was going to be quite a trick. Maliha's eyes scanned the room and halted at an open closet door. An intruder could be in there, alerted by the sound of Maliha's crashing entry through the front door. She slid along the wall to the closet and determined no one was there.

She went up behind the girl and lifted the earphones off her head. "Betty Sue," Maliha said. "I need you to go sit on your bed. Something's happened."

Then Maliha saw the blood splattered on the computer screen. Betty Sue's throat had been cut, saturating the front of her pajamas and leaving the girl to choke on her own blood as she died.

Maliha felt weak, as though her own blood had drained from her body.

Mother and child are dead.

It struck at the heart of Maliha's personal conflicts: the death of her own infant in a dark jail cell; the assignment to kill a baby, which caused her to give up immortality; and her secret desire to regain her life as a normal woman and have a family.

All of it lay in front of her in bloody ruins.

I brought this death here, just like to the Rainiers. Someone must have been watching Jamie's apartment or the place was bugged. Or maybe it had nothing to do with me. Someone is targeting Fynn's family. Why? He's done with Fynn, or close to being done with him, so he doesn't need

*Fynn's family to dangle like a carrot in front of him to keep
him working.*

Maliha put her hands on the dead girl's shoulders.

Constanta.

In her mind she wailed her daughter's name over and
over, her sorrow totally overwhelming her. Then she was into
the imprint of Betty Sue's death. With music from the movie
blaring in her ears, she felt her hair being pulled from behind,
the sudden panic, the hot sting of the blade. Her hand flew
protectively and futilely to her throat, and in the reflection of
the computer monitor, she saw the tall man smiling.

Soon Maliha sensed the girl's spirit around her and
opened her eyes. She was enveloped in a sparkling mist
that felt cool and soft where it touched her skin. Lifting
her head, Maliha remained there as the mist slowly faded.
Pulling herself away from the girl's body, she went into the
kitchen, gently lowered Jamie's body to the floor, and took
her place in the chair.

Nothing happened, and Maliha was about to leave when
suddenly she slipped into Jamie's death experience. The
shots to the head were painful but quick, and Maliha saw
nothing except the newspaper coming closer as her head
sank to the table. She remained in place, waiting for the
spirit fragment left behind to coalesce around her, but there
was nothing except a vague dark fog that stung her skin.
Jamie was gone, or nearly gone, and what she'd left behind
was a cloud of recrimination very unlike her daughter's soft
forgiveness. Maliha tried to pull away, but the fog held her
there for long, uncomfortable moments before vanishing.

Maliha left the apartment and stumbled out into the
night, weak and nauseated.

If someone's trailing me then . . . Dr. Cobb!

Not willing to think it through, Maliha took off at a dead
run to the office she'd visited on the Columbia University
campus.

Outside the office, she stopped and listened. There was
light coming from under the door but she couldn't hear any
sound of struggle. The thought of another death tonight

overwhelmed any planning she might otherwise do. She just stormed the door, knocked it aside with a kick, and ran into the room, a throwing knife in each hand.

Booker Cobb was face up on the floor, his hands and feet bound, his face frozen in terror as a sword descended toward his neck. One of Maliha's knives spun through the air and struck with precision, deflecting the sword blade as it fell enough so that it missed Cobb's neck. The sword bit into the wooden floor to the side of Cobb's head, severing only a few strands of his hair. The second knife, already in the air before the first reached the sword, whirred to its mark, the attacker's throat.

With the momentum of her crash through the door, Maliha's body moved forward and slammed into the assailant, propelling both of them back against the wall of the room. With more presence of mind than she would have given him credit for, Cobb rolled and kicked a chair toward his attacker that tangled the man's legs. Cobb kept rolling, ending up behind a heavy desk and out of the action.

Maliha finally got a good look at the attacker. Tall, thin, stringy hair flying, black robe—she recognized him. With Cobb out of the way, he bore down on her, still fighting with her knife protruding from his neck. He grabbed her and threw her against the wall so hard that she punched through the wall in places. As she slid down to the floor, he yanked the knife from his neck and flung it at her. She managed to shift her head just enough that the knife, aimed straight between her eyes, embedded deeply in the wall.

Mr. Evil wasn't bleeding from the neck. The spot where her knife had been closed up as neatly as if it had been zipped shut.

Ageless. I'm about to die then.

The full weight of the apprehension she'd been feeling now nearly crushed her. She'd sensed her approaching death, through all the despair over the deaths of innocents around her.

He approached her but stopped far out of reach. She drew herself up to face him. She had one thing left to try, but if he attacked from across the room, she was doomed.

"I would tell my demon who sent me back to him, if I knew your name."

He grinned and edged closer, but not close enough. "Mogue is one of my many names. Tell him Mogue sent you."

Maliha felt a rush of air. Unseen in its passage, a crossbow bolt sprouted in the center of Mogue's chest. He roared in anger and clutched at it.

Mogue was distracted and Maliha knew she'd been given a chance. Maliha stepped forward and launched her last desperate effort to kill Mogue. She pulled the whip sword from its sheath and with all the concentration and skill she could draw upon, she sent the blades snaking almost invisibly toward Mogue's neck, one blade on each side, intending to wrap them around his neck and sever his head.

For half a second she thought it would work. But Mogue's hands flew toward his neck and arrived there first. His hands took the brunt of the whip sword strike. The blades tore through the flesh, muscle, and bone of his hands and by the time they struck his neck there was not enough force left to do more than rip a notch on either side.

Maliha had no time to wait around and see what happened next, or to strike again with the whip. She pulled the blades back in a wide swing toward her and let them hit the floor, chipping paths in the wood as they slowed down. She scooped up the blades and spun them back into position around her waist. A glance at Mogue showed his butchered hands holding his head in place as the wounds along his neck began to heal. Some of his fingers were on the floor at his feet. He had plenty to deal with, even for an Ageless one.

Time was up. She pulled Cobb from behind the desk. He'd fainted, probably a good thing. He didn't need to see what had just happened. With Cobb over her shoulder she fled the room, the building, and the campus.

Later, when Maliha's scale rewarded her for saving Cobb's life, she felt it was undeserved. Lucius had saved them both.

Is he really my enemy? Or my greatest friend?

Chapter Fifteen

A man whose ticket identified him as L. Anthony Cinna sat in the train car, half a dozen rows behind Maliha in an aisle seat. With a suit and tie, a briefcase, and a BlackBerry, he looked like any other businessman on his way to the capital, on the Acela Express to Union Station in Washington, D.C. Maliha passed him once, on her way to the café car. He saw her coming and raised a newspaper to his face, feigning intense attention to it. He needn't have worried. She seemed preoccupied and wasn't looking in his direction. On the way back, she was seeing him from the rear and he was just one head of hair among the others.

Lucius had been following Maliha since soon after she left his island. His recovery from the broken neck had been swift. For the Ageless, repairing bone and tendons was, he told himself with a small laugh, a snap. Maliha knew it and knew that a broken neck wouldn't slow him down for long. He was also aware that his life had been in her hands while he was incapacitated, and even after the way he'd treated her, she hadn't pressed her advantage and killed him as he lay on the floor. The bruises she'd given him showed spirit, and anyway, he deserved it. Thinking back over what he'd said, he realized that she could have thought he was planning to take her against her will.

He wanted to talk to her again, but the opportunity hadn't arisen yet. She hadn't done anything lately that he could identify as searching for a shard, so the imperative from his demon, Sidana, wasn't driving him to stay with her.

He had an imperative of his own: a growing attraction to the rogue that was spreading beyond sexual. He admired what she'd done to change her life, and from that and many things—the sound of her voice, the way her hair swept across her cheek when she bent her head, her intelligence, her strength—Lucius was feeling something he hadn't experienced in nearly two thousand years of servitude. He thought he could love again, and that Maliha was the one who could help him experience this very human emotion.

And she's not even fully human.

When she got off the train in Union Station, it was easy to move from place to place in the crowd, never letting her see him.

Just as she walked outside, Lucius felt the tug of his demon summoning him to Midworld. He felt a flash of resentment, of wanting to tell Sidana to leave him alone, but he wouldn't do that. It was always a gut-wrenching transition for him, and when the fog of Midworld coated his skin with unwelcome dampness, Lucius bent at the waist and vomited. When he lifted his head, the demon was already close. The last several times Lucius had been here, the demon had taken the same shape, so he wondered if it was his real shape or at least one that was easy to assume.

The great serpent sliced through the fog, reaching him quickly. He stiffened as the snake began to wind about him, encasing his body in heavy links. They were not the dry, cool scales of a snake in the Great Above, where Lucius lived. This snake was coated with some puslike substance that oozed from between its scales. Lucius felt the slime on his skin, because he was always naked in Midworld, to add to his feeling of total domination by the demon. Sidana curled around his legs, his genitals, his waist, then his chest, climbing the body of his servant. Finally, and most horrible of all, the demon threw a heavy coil around Lucius's neck.

The stench was that of rotting bodies, and it seemed to

him that it exuded from below the snake's scales as if the demon were rotten underneath.

Lucius felt nausea rising again, but there was nothing he could do. He was held upright by the demon, and as his stomach muscles cramped, Sidana tightened its hold around his belly. The snake raised its face to his, its tongue flickering over Lucius's cheeks, eyes, and lips.

It was hard to believe that a short while ago he was in the Great Above, Ageless and supreme among humans. Here he was nothing but a humble slave, immobilized, waiting for the words of his master to intrude on his mind.

Intrude they did. He felt Sidana begin an unsavory journey through his recent thoughts and memories. Then the demon spoke to him, not aloud, but as though the demon wrote the words on his brain.

The rogue has made no more progress.

"Forcing her will not help." When his mouth opened to speak, the snake's tongue darted in and out, tasting him, measuring the truth of his words. "She must search on her own. I am diligent. No shard that she finds will escape my notice."

You took her to your home. Do you desire this woman?

"No."

The coil around his neck tightened, pressing against his carotid arteries and his esophagus.

"Yes. But it will not interfere with my assignment."

Make certain that it does not. I am growing impatient. It has been three months and you have captured only one shard.

"I am not in control of that. She does other things and I merely follow."

Approach her and demand that she devote all of her time to the search. She has a skill for this that you lack.

"It is not common for one demon to meddle with another demon's servants the way you do. There could be a backlash from Rabishu."

Your words are insolent. It is for me to deal with my brethren, not my lowly slave. You are less than the dirt on which I crawl.

Abruptly Sidana squeezed Lucius's legs, making it impossible for him to remain standing. He pitched forward onto the ground, with the snake still wrapped around him.

For your insolence you now have only six months to obtain the Great Lens. At that time you will kill her, whether the Lens is complete or not.

"Six months! Impossible. Ten or twenty years . . ."

Lucius's words were squeezed off in mid-sentence. This time the demon tightened everywhere, compressing his body painfully. He felt the pressure crack his ribs, felt intense pain as his genitals were mashed, and started gasping in vain for air.

I will not be denied.

Lucius choked out his part of the ritual. "I serve only you." He kept his mind clear of anything that conflicted with that.

Locked in his mind, away from the demon's prying, were his secret thoughts. Not long after he began serving the demon, he realized that he had to have a place for private thoughts and ambitions because he was being punished often for them. It had taken him a century to perfect it, the lockbox in his mind with a single key—his.

Killing men in battle was something he understood, as was assassination for advancement, but some of the killings he performed for Sidana were not honorable. He had started to doubt, started to think that the people who died to keep his immortal heart beating had rights of their own, rights to their lives and their happiness. These thoughts were secured in the lockbox.

He wanted to learn how Maliha turned rogue, and why, and to explore a lasting relationship with her. Now he had a time limit in which to do it.

Could I love her the way I loved my wife when we married? I may never find out, thanks to Sidana's order.

When Sidana returned him to the Great Above, Lucius added more thoughts to his lockbox: bitterness. Killing Maliha was a test of loyalty—nothing more—to Sidana.

To Lucius, it was far more. He could never be objective

about Maliha as a target. Of all the women he had been with, only she could understand his true nature and his dilemma, because she had lived through it.

It was a good thing his demon had asked him only if he desired Maliha. Lust was something that often figured in the demon's plans and he understood it well. If Sidana had asked if Lucius *loved* her . . . To reveal his love would show his betrayal of his demon. At the least, things would have become much more complicated. At the most, it would have meant death and eternal torment for each of them in their own hell, and Lucius's greatest torment would be that she suffered because of him.

Chapter Sixteen

On board the high-speed train to Washington, D.C., Maliha thought about what plan she'd use for the Tellman Global Economic Foundation. She tossed out various plans and finally settled on one. It was a stretch, but the least stretchy of the actions she'd come up with.

She called Amaro and asked him to check on Hound by satellite phone. Ten minutes later, she got a return call from Amaro.

"Well, Hound's damn hot, as in sweaty. Peeved that you aren't there being sweaty with him, and that you got to go to places where there's air-conditioning and no blowing sand penetrating every crevice of the body. Once we got past all that, he's okay."

"Has he reached the oasis yet?"

"Nope. GPS says he's about sixty miles out."

She could hear him furiously typing while talking to her. Amaro was a computer security consultant in his day job. Earlier in his life, he'd been a hacker, one of the best in the world. Now "domesticated," as his sister Rosie called him, he worked to protect systems from attack by people just like him. Corporations from all over the world hired him to test their secure systems. He was usually able to hack in past their defenses and show the weaknesses in their systems. Amazingly, even though he'd gone over to the "dark" side, Amaro was able to maintain his connections in the hacker underworld. It was merely a coincidence that most of his clients had recently suffered attacks from one of Amaro's loose cadre of friends.

She hung up, but still couldn't get rid of her feeling that something was about to go wrong. Maliha called Yanmeng and asked him to track Hound.

"I'm at the airport, on my way to Chicago," Yanmeng said. "I'll look after Hound. You're worried?"

"I can't tell you anything specific."

After they hung up, she pictured Yanmeng relaxing in his chair in the airport's gate area, closing his eyes, and looking like he was just an old man taking a quick nap before his flight departed. Instead, he was searching for and then finding Hound, thousands of miles away in the Nigerian desert. The way Maliha understood it, he could only find those with whom he had a strong relationship, and when he did it was like looking down on them from a few feet above. With effort, he was able to extend his presence and touch a shoulder or cheek lightly, just enough to let a person know he was there. He was working on being able to do more than that, such as reach down and grab a bullet or turn aside a knife. It was a long process.

When Yanmeng was remote viewing, he shifted from the plane of the physical to the astral one, separated from the physical by a short distance that wasn't traversable by bones and muscle, only the mind. It is what Maliha did when she read auras or the imprints at death scenes. It was part of the journey Yanmeng was undergoing that would carry him closer and closer, as he passed through higher and higher planes that were grouped into spheres of existence, to being a pure spirit—a god.

He was already in his seventies, and there was nothing that extended his life beyond the norm except, as he would say, good health, clean living, and the love of a good woman. His wife Eliu would dispute the clean living part, no doubt.

Yanmeng didn't talk about it, because it was something that couldn't be put adequately into words, but she suspected that he had made progress and had reached the second sphere, or close to it.

He and Maliha were intimate friends, tied together by a deep platonic love and by their actions and goals.

While his aging followed a predictable path, Maliha's didn't. Anu could be rooting for her to succeed, or not, because her ultimate goal was not only personal redemption but the deaths of Anu's seven offspring, the *Utukki*—Rabishu and his kin. Where did Anu's loyalties lie? With his offspring or with humans?

How long will my concerns be Yanmeng's? How long do I try to bind him to me, if bind *is the right word?*

The time he was with her, before he was claimed by death or by ascension to the third sphere, was hers to treasure.

Not many people could say they knew a god-in-training.

Chapter Seventeen

Maliha sat on a bench half a block away from the Keltner Building in Washington, D.C. December sunshine felt warm on her shoulders as she watched a lunchtime crowd scurrying back to their offices and cubicles.

When Maliha closed her eyes to think, she had to push the memories of Ty's and Claire's deaths from her mind. She'd paid for them with the reverse movement of her scale, but that wasn't everything—there was the guilt. Now Jamie and her daughter had been killed, although Maliha suspected that they would have been targets regardless of her contact with them.

Mogue had a nasty habit of eliminating everyone she turned to for help, and the injuries he'd been given, though dire, weren't going to keep him out of circulation for long. After all, she'd snapped Lucius's neck, something fatal to humans, but he'd recovered from it promptly, as she knew he would. There weren't many ways to kill an Ageless one. Leaving the body in one piece would never work.

I have to set these feelings aside. If I'm paralyzed with regret, I can't act, and even more people will die. I never had this problem when I was Ageless! Things were so much easier without having to worry about collateral deaths.

She had a one-o'clock appointment with Dr. Amalia Ritter, vice president of development at TGEF. Dr. Ritter was responsible for raising money for the foundation, and that involved schmoozing with donors and potential donors, such as Marsha Hughes, a wealthy young heiress with plenty of time on her a hands and a philanthropical bent.

Marsha Hughes, in spite of her wealth, wasn't a social gadabout and rarely left her Italian villa. That made it easy for Maliha to maintain that alternate identity, since the Hughes woman was, conveniently, rarely seen. All Maliha needed were different ID papers, a different style of dress, and some makeup to distinguish herself from her author persona, who sometimes had her photo in the media.

On the last day he'd spoken to Jamie Blake, Fynn Saltz had had an appointment with Dr. Ritter. He'd signed in at the Keltner Building in the early afternoon but there was no record of him signing out. Fynn wasn't a wealthy man and wouldn't be donating so much to the TGEF that it warranted the personal attention of a vice president. She thought he'd been going there not to give money, but to get money in the form of a grant.

Why see Dr. Ritter then?

Marsha Hughes did have the resources and reputation to make a multi-million–dollar donation to the foundation, and Dr. Ritter was going to give her the hard sell this afternoon.

Fynn could have been having an affair with her. Hot sex on the boardroom table? It certainly wouldn't be the first time a man cheated on his fiancée.

Maliha's cell phone rang.

"It's Amaro. Glass is doing great, Hound is on his way back from Niger and says that the oasis site was a trap and that Yanmeng alerted him to it. He was in a firefight but is okay. Good thing we didn't send some unarmed scientists in there. Hound did get a soil sample that he sent on ahead but there were no hitchhikers in it. Finally, Doyle Saltz is dead. He was murdered the same day you talked to him."

Maliha was silent for a moment. *The body count is rising and I'm not even on the scene. Mabry!*

"Check out Dr. Saltz's lab assistant, Larry Mabry. You

might want to warn him to get out of the country immediately and not tell anyone where he's going."

"Will do." Amaro hung up to search out the lab assistant.

Sitting in public, she let no reaction show on her face. Inside, anger and despair warred for control of her feelings. It was a while before she could order her thoughts.

Of course. Doyle was a member of Fynn's family and so the first victim. Or he could have been first because he knew so much about his father's research that Mogue planned to kill him anyway. That would account for the fact that Anu hasn't penalized me—these people were already doomed by Fynn's association with Mogue. Regardless of the reason, it's my trail that's bloody.

She remembered the look of anger on Lucius's face when she'd accused him of game playing. He'd wanted something from her, and she'd misinterpreted. The crossbow bolt he'd fired at Mogue gave her a chance at life while no doubt walking a delicate line with his demon's orders. He'd already saved her from the Janjaweed—how much wiggle room did his orders have left?

I see it now. Lucius has doubts. All those questions he asked on the island—he's thinking of rejecting his contract. And I treated him like shit because of being kidnapped. It has to be Mogue then, flitting from place to place, following me, getting ahead, slaughtering. I must not have slowed him down at all.

Vulnerability was an odd feeling for Maliha. She thought back to her Ageless time, when she walked among humans with such overwhelming abilities that she held their lives in her hands. Yet she'd never developed contempt for humans as inferior beings. She'd never killed indiscriminately, or enjoyed it when she killed on assignment.

Probably because I started out with a normal life, in a loving relationship. What happens if a demon snares someone who is already evil, a true sociopath? That's what I think Mogue is. Give that person a hundred years or thousands of years of unfettered killing with no consequences and it's a nightmare beyond imagining, the perfect tool for a demon who serves the Lord of the Underworld, the god of chaos and destruction.

There was no one near her bench, at least no one she could see.

"Lucius, if you're listening, I'm ready to talk to you. If you're here, Mogue, I'm going to send your soul to your demon's hell, where it belongs."

Brave words, just like the ones I spoke to Rabishu when I became mortal again.

First step: Dazzle Dr. Ritter.

Maliha glided over the lobby's granite floors, a deadly ninja without the trappings. Today she had no hidden weapons to cause the security force concern. No plastic daggers, no clever pieces of a gun to be quickly assembled. Dressed in the unostentatious manner of old money, she could have been a visiting diplomat or trade negotiator. Alert now to signs of being tracked by one of the Ageless, she used her surest method of detecting one. An Ageless person may appear to the eyes only as a blur or not even that due to incredibly fast motion, but movement left streaming aura trails. By opening herself to viewing auras continually, she was able to detect streaks of color across her field of vision where there was no apparent physical presence.

It was a draining experience. In a crowded building, she was assaulted by pulsing colors, drifting tendrils trailing after people, the interaction of auras between people in proximity, and dissonance between what people were saying and what their auras were revealing. Her own aura was in constant motion, making it slightly difficult to know where the boundaries of her physical self were. She could extend her hand to greet someone, for example, and find out that while her aura touched the other person's, her hand didn't quite make it.

She'd done constant viewing only rarely, and there was a reason for that besides the fatigue it produced. She sometimes saw the subdued, ash-gray auras of people who were dying or very ill, whether they knew it or not. As familiar with death as Maliha was, she was never comfortable with it.

Dr. Ritter's office was spare and unfriendly, a surprising point for someone who routinely greeted wealthy donors and made them feel good about themselves as they parted with large sums of money. Maliha couldn't help thinking that the doctor did her real work elsewhere, and that brought back the image of sex in the boardroom.

"Please call me Amalia. Everyone does. May I call you Marsha?"

Amalia was an attractive brunette in her early forties, businesslike in a dark skirted suit, but with a touch of wildness in a leopard-print scarf. The contrast was appealing. Amalia's voice had a professional tone with a hint of Southern charm in it. Marsha found herself relaxing in the woman's presence even though she had every reason not to. Amalia's aura belied the pleasant exterior. Waves of greenish-brown avarice, jealousy, and hunger for power were layered below carefully cultivated yellowish-blue swirls of caring. It wasn't often that Maliha saw such a fine example of what she called a crafted aura—one carefully managed by its owner to conceal the basic personality.

"Certainly. To let you know where I stand, I have a personal foundation with a mandate to distribute a minimum of five percent of yearly earnings to a charity of my choice. Usually I select a charity to benefit for a period of five to eight years. It's a lot of effort to vet these charities, especially since I do it all personally. So once I do it, I stick with that charity for a number of years."

"Of course. Always the best way—see things for yourself. We've already supplied financial statements, Marsha, but your foundation makes, uh, little information available to the public. Would you give me an idea of the level of support you're considering?"

I guess she wants to know how much ass kissing she has to do.

"For a period of five years, that would be about three hundred million dollars total. Give or take."

Maliha didn't miss the flare of the woman's nostrils or the brief glint in her eyes. Apparently, she'd just been put on the A-list. This was a good time to press her case.

"I've read your material, Amalia, but what I'd really like is to see your work in operation. I want a thorough tour."

"Of course. I have a cart waiting outside. This is a big place, and I thought we'd take a ride as an overview."

Good way to keep me from exploring. Won't work, though.

A small golf cart gaily striped in purple and white, the colors of TGEF's logo, came complete with driver. Maliha sat in the backseat with Amalia, and noticed that it was narrow enough that their hips touched.

Intentional? Most of her passengers are men, I'll bet.

The tour proceeded in a controlled fashion that lasted only halfway down the first hall. Maliha spotted a door that said "Authorized Personnel Only" and stepped lightly out of the cart while it was moving. Amalia, taken by surprise, stumbled out after her as the cart came to a halt.

"What's in here?"

"Oh, just the accounting department. Nothing very interesting about a room full of accountants." Amalia tried a wide smile that probably charmed the pants off the male executives she usually ferried around on tour.

"My father started out as an accountant. Nothing dull about them. Let's take a look."

Amalia swiped a card in the security lock on the door and took her inside. Amalia had told the truth about what was behind Door Number One. Maliha made a point of talking to a few of the staff.

The third time Maliha left the cart and asked to be taken inside a locked door, Amalia refused as nicely and persistently as she could. Maliha hinted at withdrawal of her donation, and although Amalia looked frustrated, she didn't give in.

Something interesting behind Door Number Three.

Leaning casually against the door as she chatted, Maliha could feel slight vibrations, as if the door concealed operating machinery.

"It's just a maintenance area," Amalia said. "Nothing to see. Can we move on now?"

Maliha graciously consented. She barely paid attention to the rest of the tour, because she already had her target.

She returned that night, dressed in black and bristling with weapons. It was a rather undignified entry, since she arrived in a delivery truck, stuffed in a crate of cleaning supplies. Once inside the building, she rode the freight elevator to the floor she'd been on earlier that day.

The easy part was over.

The halls were covered by surveillance cameras that were no match for her supernatural speed. To rest and plan her next move, she used convenient camera-free way stations—women's restrooms. She'd encounter more sophisticated security behind the door Amalia had refused to open.

The outer door yielded to the stolen security card of a mid-level manager she'd stopped to talk to during the tour. Maliha's pickpocketing skills had been polished over three centuries and the poor man had no idea that his card had been lifted.

Once inside, she spray painted the camera lens that covered the area. She hoped it would be sufficient to keep the sole guard at the front desk away for the short amount of time she needed.

Where are the big guns for security? I should be running into more resistance.

She faced an inner door that looked just like all the others. Swiping her card, to her amazement, opened the door. Prepared for anything inside, she found only an elevator.

She was beginning to think that Amalia was onto her after all, and she was walking into a trap. A trap had been set in Niger, and Hound had a tough time with it. This might be a pattern, the way TGEF worked.

Warily she stepped into the elevator. She was sure the elevator's motion had caused the minor vibration she'd felt earlier that day. She found the hidden panel door right away, but her card didn't open it.

Now we're getting somewhere. Actual resistance.

Removing a small tube from the bag she wore around her waist, she used the tube like a pencil to draw a line around the hidden compartment. A few seconds later, acid bit into the metal and the panel fell off into her hands. Avoiding the still-smoking edges, she lowered the panel to the floor and inspected the compartment. Inside was a single button for a floor labeled T. She checked carefully for the telltale aura streaks of an Ageless presence. No one was in the elevator with her. Pressing the button, she waited tensely as the car went upward.

T for top floor, I guess.

She took a couple of throwing stars from her bag into her left hand, leaving one hand free to cope with whatever was coming.

The door slid soundlessly open and she faced three very alert guards, who must have known something was wrong as soon as the elevator began to move at an unexpected time.

Maliha wasn't on the guest list.

She ducked instantly and a couple of bullets flew by where her chest used to be. The two throwing stars spun almost invisibly through the air and caught one guard in the hand that was reaching for an alarm button and in his neck. He pitched backward in his chair and then slid out of it onto the floor, clutching at his neck.

Maliha couldn't afford to be backed into the elevator, a dead end if ever there was one, so she threw herself in the direction of the dying man. There was blood on the floor and she slid a little, but managed to get behind the guard's heavy desk while the other two were firing. Lying on her side, she launched a knife under the desk that shattered the ankle of the closer guard. He fell backward onto the floor as her second knife, perfectly timed to his fall, thudded into the side of his head.

The third man stopped firing and as she quickly checked his location, she found that he was heading toward a glass tunnel through which visitors had to pass before entering the inner sanctum beyond. Grabbing up a dead man's automatic rifle, she fired repeatedly at the glass. The guard made it inside, the tunnel door snapped shut, and he began to reach for his radio to call for help. She tossed the useless rifle aside since the glass was barely chipped. Running to the control console for the tunnel, she began wildly punching buttons, hoping to hit one that would open the door for her to follow.

Instead of the door opening, there was a flash inside the tunnel and then it filled with a yellow-tinged cloud, obscuring the interior. A few seconds later, the guard's face smashed against the glass and his hands scrabbled against it, trying to claw his way out. His features were distorted as he choked and gasped, and then he vanished back into the yellow cloud. Then exhaust fans cleared the gas and she saw him lying dead on the floor of the tunnel. The tunnel door *whished* open in front of her.

Come into my parlor, said the spider to the fly.

Maliha wasn't sure if she wanted to go in or not. The tunnel might be set to gas anyone who went into it now that the first use had been triggered.

There's going to be an army of guards here any minute, whether his radio call went out or not. The sprayed camera alone should bring reinforcements.

She glanced around, seeing three surveillance cameras in the space. She might have only seconds. Taking a deep breath she ran in as fast as she could, sidestepped the guard's body, and slapped her hand against what she hoped was a manual release on the far wall.

It wasn't.

Trying a forceful approach, she ran headlong into the door at the far end of the tunnel. Stunned, she fell to the floor, her fall cushioned by the body of the guard. After a moment of disorientation, she saw that the radio the guard had been reaching for wasn't a radio at all—it was a control pad. She snatched it from his dead hand. There was a lighted miniature of the tunnel, so she pressed the spot representing the door she was facing, hoping that she hadn't just set off another gas release. Behind her the entrance door closed, and then the door ahead moved smoothly open. Apparently, both doors couldn't be open at the same time.

Running into the hallway beyond the tunnel, she found a series of doors. Most of them had glass windows so she could see what was inside. Knowing that time was not her friend, Maliha moved quickly down the hall, glancing into each room as she passed.

In one of the rooms was a laboratory and she was shocked to see someone in it—Fynn Saltz. He was at a computer, concentrating on what he was entering. The doorknob didn't yield, so she smashed her fist through the glass and opened the door from the inside. At the sound of the breaking glass, Saltz snatched a jump drive from its slot and stood up.

"Dr. Saltz! I'm here to help you." She approached him but he turned and ran.

"Go away!" he said. "I don't need any help."

She caught up to him, dove at his feet like a runner stealing a base, and slid into a couple of chairs before coming to a halt with him on the ground. Maliha was getting battered on this break-in, and so far she had nothing to show for it but three dead guards.

She got to her feet and pulled Saltz up with her, holding him against the wall with an arm across his neck. "Don't run, okay? I'm not going to hurt you. We have to get out of here right now."

"I can't go. They'll kill my family." He began struggling to get away.

She slapped him in the face. "Listen to me. Your son is dead. Jamie and Betty Sue are dead. They've already killed your family. You don't have anything left to lose."

"You're lying. They don't know what I've got on them. I have to . . ."

Maliha knocked him unconscious. Checking his pockets, she retrieved the jump drive he'd been so eager to run away with, and turned to leave. She had no idea how she was going to get out but didn't think it would be back through that deadly tunnel. She took a few steps away and stopped. She couldn't leave Saltz. She had enough of his family's blood on her hands.

She heard shouts out in the hall. Alone, she might be able to mow the guards down and escape.

With him, not a chance.

Maliha picked up Saltz and moved deeper into the lab, through several interconnected rooms. When the shouts faded a little, she had a few seconds' time to act.

Maliha propped him up in a corner. From her bag she took a coil of C–4 that she'd rolled out before coming to the Keltner Building. Quickly placing it in a circle on the floor, she inserted a detonator and played out the cord. She dragged Saltz back out of the room, found what shelter she could for the two of them behind a counter, and detonated the C–4. The floor shook with the force of the explosion.

With smoke hanging in the air, she went back into the room, lowered Saltz down through the hole in the floor, and jumped down after him. She had just left the top floor and was now in the main portion of the Keltner Building, the ordinary portion with elevators and stairs. The freight elevator took her down to the first level and she went out a loading door.

She was a block away from the building when she saw it—a streak of black that nearly melted into the night. It was heading toward her so fast she knew the Ageless person must be way out in front of it.

Mogue. Or Lucius?

She dropped Saltz against a brick wall and moved in front of him, sensing that he was the target. The Ageless one zipped by her, followed by the black streak, and it wasn't until after both passages that she felt the pain. It was Mogue, all right, and he'd been trying to get to Saltz with a knife. Instead, she'd taken it in the chest.

Chapter Eighteen

When her awareness returned, Maliha was in a dead-end alley. Large buildings lined the alley, with their loading docks jutting out. It seemed like she'd blacked out for a short time, because she couldn't remember getting both of them into a place of relative safety.

Saltz was awake and staring at her as though she'd grown another pair of eyes. He'd been out cold during the time she'd displayed any supernatural abilities, so it didn't make sense that he'd be so wary of her. After all, she had gotten him out of his imprisonment alive.

The knife!

Her hands flew to where she'd last felt Mogue's knife, but it was gone. In its place, there was a tight cloth wrapped around her chest. It felt damp with blood, but at least she wasn't bleeding uncontrollably. She pressed her hand against the bandage and felt the reassuring beat of her heart. Without the healing ability she retained from her Ageless days, she could be lying in the street dead. With the blade gone, the pain was lessened, but she winced as she shifted her position. There were broken ribs involved. With this added to all the insults her body had experienced since she went to rescue Glass in Africa, she was feeling a major strain in healing.

I could use a month without so much as a paper cut.

"Did you do this?" she asked Saltz, with her hand pressed against the bandage.

What a stupid question. He must have. Mogue certainly didn't.

"No. It was that guy at the end of the alley. He won't let me out."

She got to her feet. Her broken ribs made her pay with pain for every movement. She breathed shallowly, but she had to check out their situation. She needed to know if Mogue was blocking them in. If he was, what did he want? She moved down the alleyway, trying to limber up, getting stabbing pains from her ribs for her efforts. She held one arm tightly against her chest, and that seemed to help. Her weapons bag was gone, leaving her with one small knife and her cunning.

The figure at the end of the alley was outlined in moonlight.

Not Mogue, unless he's turned into a bodybuilder overnight.

The man heard her nearly silent footsteps and turned.

"Are you well?" Lucius said.

"Better than I was before you came along. Thank you."

He saved my life again. Mogue could have circled back and killed Saltz and me, but he would have had to get past Lucius to do it.

"Thank you for saving my life. Again." She said it humbly and meant it. "And about on the island. I'm sorry I . . ."

"Broke my neck? It was a warrior's action. I bear no grudge."

"What is it you want from me, Lucius?"

"I've had doubts."

Here it comes. "About what?"

"Killing people. Killing in battle is one thing. Killing men for the advancement of strategy is acceptable. The slaughter of innocents is . . . is not honorable."

"And it took you how many years to figure this out?" Immediately she wished she hadn't let sarcasm slip into her voice.

Am I so different? It took me hundreds of years, so many lives.

He turned away from her. "I've served Sidana without question. It was an oath I took. A blood oath should not be broken."

"You mean the contract you signed in blood?"

He nodded. "I bear the mark of my demon." He touched his chest in the same area where Rabishu had pierced her with a claw and taken her blood for the contract. "Don't you?"

"Not anymore." She put her hand over the spot between her breasts. At long last it had nearly healed, but for centuries had pulsed with the power of Agelessness. The specter of death had left her body through that spot, making her immortal, and later, after she defied Rabishu, it had reentered there.

Lucius was going through the same kind of questioning she'd experienced. Suddenly things crystallized for her. He was looking for a guide, someone who understood, someone who had already summoned the courage to reject a demon's contract.

Someone to push his decision over the edge.

She reached out and touched his arm. "Join me. Renounce your contract and join me in my fight against the demons. If you know of the Great Lens, then you know what it can do."

"You aim to kill the seven offspring of Anu."

"I aim to shed the burden of the lives I've taken and kill the demons, both. I think only rogues can attempt this and I'm the only one now. If you join me, we could make a new world, Lucius. A world without the chaos the *Utukki* have inflicted on the human race. Let's find out what humans can be without that great stone around our ankles holding us back. You know the story of our existence, don't you?"

"That we are created from clay mixed with the life essence of the Sumerian gods. Another thing I have doubts about."

"Assume it's true, because just maybe it is. Follow what happens after that. From the essence, as you say. Translate that to terms now. We have their DNA. They travel among the stars. With no war and evil to keep us down, that's our potential, too."

Moonlight glinted in his eyes. "There is something you forget. For you, there is at least some chance you will reclaim your soul. I have been immortal over six times as long as you have, and have killed throughout that time for my demon. If I renounce my contract, I would never be able to balance a scale that lopsided before dying from aging or another reason. I know what my fate will be like. My demon has shown it to me."

"As did mine. I have to say it scared me off for a time."

"For you that fate in the demon's hell is a possibility. For me, a certainty. By far the easier path is to remain as I am."

"I didn't say the mortal path was the easier one. It is the right one, though, and in your heart you are coming to know that. Together we can find the shards, assemble the Great Lens, and kill the demons. I have the Tablet of the Overlord, Lucius. We can blow those motherfuckers off our world. *Our* world."

"I have much to think about." He stepped forward, took her in his arms, and kissed her. He cradled her gently, aware of her injuries. This time she yielded to his embrace and put all of the passion she felt for her choices, for the mortal path, into the kiss. The kiss signaled her attraction to him, too. She felt him responding and it thrilled her deeply. When the kiss ended, he buried his face in the warmth of her neck and spoke in a whisper.

"Someday Sidana may order me to kill you."

"I know. Do what your heart tells you."

They clung together a little longer, united for a moment against evil. Then in the space of a breath, he was gone.

Chapter Nineteen

Against his wishes, Saltz ended up traveling with Maliha back to Chicago. He was silent the entire way and she let him mourn his family. She was hurting, too, physically. Each breath brought pain from her broken ribs and the knife wound itself ached deeply. She was lucky she didn't have a collapsed lung, too. With the force that Mogue could exert, he could easily have sent not only the blade through her body but his fist behind it.

Maybe he has to do things in a certain order. Finishing Saltz was next on his list and when that didn't work out, he pulled up on his attack.

Maliha spent the flight time quietly doing what she could to speed her healing and answering Fynn Saltz's questions. Maliha wished she'd known him in better times.

Fynn wanted to go to his fiancée's funeral, but Maliha refused. That's exactly what Mogue would expect Fynn to do, and Fynn must have crucial information for them. She wanted to question him, but he was exhausted and depressed.

She had some plans for the day, made before the recent events, before so many had died in Africa and before a comet's tail of personal tragedy developed, following her everywhere.

Yanmeng had a birthday coming and she brought everyone together for cake and a private party. Letting Fynn get the rest he needed, she tried to get into the mood for a celebration with friends.

Hound was back from Niger and rattled off his story of collecting a soil sample at the oasis under fire. Nothing useful had come of it. The soil sample revealed no hitchhikers, or anything else suspicious, like a chemical residue. After that, talk of their ongoing work was banished from the room.

Toward evening, both Yanmeng and the cake arrived. It was a masterpiece, slathered with a whipped-cream icing and artfully decorated and filled with strawberries. And, Maliha knew, the taste matched the appearance. She'd ordered devil's food cake, Yanmeng's favorite.

Shortly after the cake delivery, Yanmeng's wife, Eliu, arrived, having flown in from Seattle. Hound's girlfriend, Glass, who'd returned to her Chicago home after being discharged from the Swiss clinic, was picked up in Maliha's limo. Glass was in a wheelchair but was working hard with a physical therapist. Hound said that with her determination, she'd walk again, and Maliha believed it. Amaro preferred not to involve his sister Rosie in their gathering. Rosie had been told little, for her safety, but suspected a lot.

It was apparent to all that Maliha had no special partner to invite. Jake was not an initiate into this group yet.

Much hugging and happy conversation followed, although for Maliha there was a pall hanging over the activities in the form of Fynn, who slept in the second bedroom, and the deaths he represented.

Yanmeng was thrilled with both the cake and the attention, but refused to confirm his age for the number of candles on the cake, and Eliu was mum about it. The group settled on seventy candles, even though they all knew that was a little low.

With the lights dimmed and the candles arranged in rows on the cake, Maliha handed Yanmeng the mysterious package that had arrived shortly after the bakery delivery. Inside was her present, a *jian*, a Chinese double-edged straight sword about nine hundred years old. It was an extremely rare sword, museum quality, beautiful and mysterious in its ancient past, perhaps a sword of royalty. Its surface gleamed from the thorough cleaning and polishing Maliha had given it.

Yanmeng was overwhelmed. His hands shook as he took the manta-ray–skin scabbard from her. When the candles were aglow, Yanmeng stepped up to the cake with the sword. The serious look on his face silenced the chatter.

"I use this honorable blade to mark our love and friendship. May we never be parted in spirit, as I will never be parted from this sword."

Yanmeng repeatedly swung the sword, as fast as a blur, then changed position and cut quickly again. Yanmeng bowed, and everyone clapped in delight when they saw the neat squares of cake, the burning candles undisturbed. Yanmeng cleaned whipped cream and cake crumbs from his sword, and they all ate their fill and laughed and talked late into the night.

I don't think anyone but I noticed that he wished that we would never be parted in spirit. He didn't say anything about our bodies. I'm going to have to ask him about that sometime.

Maliha viewed Yanmeng's aura, and found it just as soothing as when she'd rescued him from his prison cell during the Chinese Revolution. His aura was wide, swirling, and beautiful to see. Bright white mixed with yellow and blue, the aura revealed a man far along on his spiritual journey, a person who could be a great leader and teacher if he chose that path. Yellow was beginning to cluster near his head into a disk, and in the time she'd known him, it had gotten stronger. The disk, a floating aura of gold, was a common element in a number of belief systems, going back to the depiction of a glowing disk around the head of the Egyptian god Ra and later known as a halo. Painters and sculptors who drew and chiseled the disks may have been responding to what they were seeing in the auras of their subjects.

As she watched him, he suddenly turned to look at her. Tendrils of yellow surrounded his head, and a moment later she felt his gentle touch on her cheek. He was remote viewing her, though they stood ten feet apart, to share a private moment with her. His touch was an intimate caress given with deep love. She rested her hand where his touch had been.

How could the world ever lose such a magnificent man through aging and keep me, a flawed dealer in death, alive?

If Yanmeng lived another thirty years, it would be a long life for him. For her, the time might fly by as she worked toward her redemption and her larger quest of eliminating the demons from the world. Optimistically, she would add a decade or less to her apparent age during that time, while Yanmeng, from her perspective, sped toward death.

Could she love a mortal man as a husband and watch him age and die? How could she accept that? She didn't think so. What right did she have even thinking about drawing a mortal man into such an unfair arrangement? Mortal men were out of consideration.

Then there was Jake, the immortal. If she married him, her lifespan would be a small fragment of his. He loved her now, but his marriage wouldn't be a lifetime commitment to her. It couldn't be. He would go on to have many women after she died or ascended to Anu's paradise, her reward if she balanced the scales.

Get real. Nobody really expects a lifetime commitment today, anyway. That's Susannah talking.

She thought about Lucius. He was someone who understood the crisis of conscience that had caused her to give up her immortality because he was on his way to that crisis himself. He knew the risks she took every day, understood the thin ice she walked, where one misstep, one errant knife throw, one kick that didn't connect could send her plunging through to the depths of failure—he'd visited his demon's hell. She was undeniably attracted to him, and from their last kiss, she knew he had feelings for her. If Lucius were to break his contract, she would have a rogue companion, a man to share all parts of her life.

If there is such a thing as a true soul mate for me, that person might be Lucius, the man who might someday kill me. I am one screwed-up woman.

She brought herself back to the moment, seeing the faces of her beloved friends by candlelight. Maliha's eyes grew moist with the knowledge of Yanmeng's future passing, however far away, as she kept up with the birthday banter. Hound, a man who had seen too much death in Vietnam, met her gaze and gave her a small nod of understanding. No one else noticed.

With the bittersweet ceremony over, Maliha went in to see Fynn, and shook him gently awake. He was ready to talk. The others were still enjoying one another's company in the living room, so she pulled up a chair to listen.

"Do you still have the jump drive?" he asked.

"Yes."

"Good. That will back up what I'm going to say, because it's going to sound like I'm making it up. A couple of months ago I went to meet Amalia Ritter at the Tellman Foundation. She'd read a monograph of my latest work and thought that the foundation might want to support my project with a grant."

"What exactly was your project?"

He gave her an impatient look, as if she were a student who was trying to jump ahead before grasping the basics. "Are you familiar with nanites?"

"Assume I am and go on from there."

She was treated to a skeptical look, but he did go on. "I'm working with nanites that build human hormones, specifically insulin. Insufficient insulin in the body results in type 1 diabetes, or type 2 can result when the body doesn't respond well to the insulin it does have. Doyle was a type 1 diabetic with an insulin pump. Did he tell you that?"

"No. We didn't talk for long, and the conversation was about you, not about him."

"Did he . . . look well?"

"He did, and he was very worried about your disappearance. He'd devoted everything to finding you." She didn't see any harm in embellishing a little. Doyle couldn't dispute it, and there was nothing wrong with leaving Fynn with a good impression of his dead son. " 'Time to take care of the old man,' he said. Hired an investigator and everything."

"I'd always thought he'd follow in my footsteps and be a research scientist. He had the brains, you know." Fynn stared off into space. "Perhaps if his mother had lived. She was a good influence on him. On both of us. Jamie might have . . ."

"You were saying about hormones," Maliha said. She wanted to get the discussion back on track.

"Yes. Currently synthetic insulin for human use is created using recombinant DNA, a technique that uses bacteria to churn out the hormone. I had devised nanites that could manufacture insulin externally, in a dish. This is a valuable discovery in itself, but I wanted to take it one step further. I wanted those nanites inside the body, manufacturing insulin in a way indistinguishable in its results from the natural form. A cure, you might say, for diabetes."

"You were successful then?"

Fynn had warmed to his topic. "There was a problem with the nanites in the body. They were attacked by the immune system. My research focused on coating the nanites with a biological substance to make the immune system ignore them, so they could stay in the body for a lifetime. I had hoped the Tellman Foundation's grant would allow me to move the coated nanites, or c-nans, to market. The process from lab to patient use is brutally complicated and expensive."

"Several years at least, right?"

"A decade or more, plus millions of dollars for testing and large-scale manufacturing. But both the material and the human rewards were so powerful on this project. Once perfected, why stop with diabetes? Other diseases could be cured with nanites living contentedly in the body. How about Alzheimer's? It has complex causes, but at least the nanites could bust up the tangled neurons in the brain. On the phone the Ritter woman mentioned a hundred million dollars. There was no way I could resist going to the building with that sum dangled in front of me. It turns out they weren't interested in curing diabetes." His voice turned scornful. "They wanted my techniques, especially my biological coating, to insert nanites of a completely different sort in the body. Ones that tore apart cells instead of constructing hormones. A horrible prospect, and I had no choice but to go along. Remember, my family was at risk."

They were both quiet for a time. Images of ruined bodies floated through Maliha's mind.

"Have you ever heard of gray goo?" Fynn interrupted her visions. Without waiting for her to answer, he went on. "Nanites can take apart as well as put together substances. In this field there is a nightmare scenario where so-called rogue nanites become destructive and begin to take apart living or inert objects uncontrollably. People. Coal. Mountains. Marine life. The entire planet, turning everything we know into undifferentiated gray goo, including us. Can you imagine a more terrifying weapon, if it could be controlled? Targeted?"

Maliha shook her head.

"Now picture those gray-goo nanites in the human body, coated with my substance, undetectable, able to lurk for days or years until they are activated—in only the targeted people."

"I don't have to imagine it," Maliha said. "There have been two field tests of this weapon so far with, as far as we know, one hundred percent fatalities."

His eyes closed as he absorbed the idea, knowing his work had facilitated the real world tests.

"What? What are they planning to do, Fynn? Do you know?"

"I do. I found out, but they don't know about it. I found out a lot of things. I tried to take my life after that, but they stopped me."

"What's the route of infection?"

"Water. They dump the nanites in the water supply and wait for it to spread into the population."

"Hold on. I need to get the others in here. They have to hear this." Maliha went out into the living room and told the guests she had to borrow her trio of helpers. Glass and Eliu didn't mind—they were already deep into a discussion of Men and their Merits, or lack thereof.

After bringing the group up to speed, they peppered Fynn with questions.

"This TGEF is building these little rogue guys on purpose?" Amaro said.

"Yes. Not just any rogues. A very special kind that takes apart human cells. And they have been doing it for years, but they just got the final piece of the puzzle from me."

"Who are they targeting and why?" Maliha wanted to know.

"They are motivated by economics. Targets are countries with emerging economies like Brazil, India, China, South Korea, and the second-tier ones, like Vietnam, Chile, and Turkey. As to why, I have only a guess."

"Let's hear it."

"They consider those emerging countries to be parasites who built their success on technology, manufacturing, and other things the legacy countries poured their money and people into since the eighteen hundreds. Parasites that snatched the results of a hundred years of striving, then used the advantage of lax environmental standards, and are now beating the legacies at their own game. They cheated, in other words. At least that's what I think they believe."

"Jealousy is behind all this?"

"Jealousy, could be a factor, and anger. I believe they want to cripple those economies through population kills large enough to make them turn their full attention inward and stop competing in the global market. Major catastrophes in each country would let the legacies, like the U.S. and England and Germany, not only resume their world economic leadership but also keep it for a long, long time."

"Holy smoke," Hound said. "It sounds just crazy enough to work."

"I don't know if it would work or not," Maliha said. "The important thing is that they believe it will. Imagine the deaths worldwide."

"What sets these nanites off so they start chewing, or whatever they do?" Yanmeng said.

"I'm not certain about that," Fynn said. "If I were doing it, I'd use some special frequency of either light or sound. Widespread, quick."

"Who's behind this? Who's running this secret program of the foundation?"

Fynn smiled grimly. "I happen to have that information on a certain jump drive. She took it." He pointed at Maliha.

Chapter Twenty

Maliha produced the jump drive she'd taken from Fynn back in the Tellman lab. Amaro snatched it from her fingers and went to their isolation laptop. The computer had minimal software and no Internet connection. It was the first place Amaro took any questionable data source because if it turned out to be infected, the effect was confined to the isolation computer and couldn't damage anything else.

"What are we going to find on that drive?" Maliha said.

"Complete specifications for my formula, to start with," Fynn said. "I worked in isolation from the other scientists, so I don't have details on the nanites."

"We call the nanites hitchhikers."

"Good name. Once picked up, they can turn deadly."

Maliha shrugged. She hadn't been comparing the nanites to human hitchhikers, but more to something from nature, like burrs picked up walking through tall weeds. His allusion was apt, though, and definitely creepier than hers.

"Also on the drive is a lot of information I picked up at great risk. It took some doing, but I have some files from the TGEF computers."

Amaro whooped from the desk where he sat. "Good stuff here. Most of it's encrypted but not with killer ciphers. I can work with this."

"The most valuable thing in there is a list of TGEF's council members. They have two sets, a typical one for running the good work of the foundation in supporting the economies of developing countries. The secret council is running the nanite project. There are five members, but I only have names and photos for four. The other one is called the Leader. I had hoped to use these names and all the other information I collected in a bargain for my family's lives. You can see how that worked out."

"We're very sorry about what happened to your family," Maliha said. "But we'll still use your information to do something good. To stop this."

Once having spoken, Fynn retreated to mournful isolation and refused to be drawn into any more conversation. He had forced himself to enter the conversation long enough to pass on his story. Maliha knew it had taken courage to talk so factually in the face of his great losses.

When Eliu and Glass were gone and Fynn was again asleep—he claimed that he was not allowed much sleep while captive—Maliha held a meeting with her friends. Her group agreed that the best plan was a direct one.

They had to hunt down all the council members and kill them. They had four targets—from the United States, England, Germany, and France—plus an unknown fifth country, for the Leader. The information on the jump drive didn't have the current locations, so she'd have to ferret those out.

In the morning, Fynn wanted to leave. All of them tried to explain to him that he was in danger, that he should stay with them, but he wouldn't hear of it.

"I don't want any of you following me, either. My life is my own. I've given you everything I know."

He left her apartment with the clothes he was wearing and a few hundred dollars in cash that Maliha pressed into his hand.

"Don't worry about me," he said. "I want to go see my son's grave. And Jamie's, and my daughter's."

Unspoken at the end of his words was *before I die.*

When he referred to Betty Sue as his daughter, Maliha felt a great tug at her heart. He considered the girl his daughter, but he'd never had a chance to get married and be her father. She had a daughter buried, too. She hugged him and he walked out.

They were all silent when he left.

Then Amaro said, "Shouldn't we tie him up and make him stay here or something? You know we're sending him out there right into Mogue's hands."

Emotion was bursting in Maliha's chest. It wasn't right to let Fynn walk away to his death. He was despondent now. He might feel differently when time faded his grief, when he was able to contribute with his science studies again.

"Damn. I just can't let him do this, I don't care what he says about his rights."

Maliha left her apartment to the cheers of her friends. It didn't take long to catch up to Fynn. She slowed her pace and fell into step with him. He was surprised at her sudden appearance.

"We're going to go visit your family's graves and do whatever you want to do to pay your respects," she said, linking her arm firmly in his. "I'm going to do my best to keep you alive while you do that. Then you're coming home with me. The university hired me to bring you back. You're important to their alumni donor program. As a valuable commodity, you aren't allowed to go off and get yourself killed."

He tilted his head and looked at her. "I may be in mourning, but I still know bullshit when I hear it. Okay, come on, but you'll have to keep up with me."

"I won't slow you down."

Two days later, Fynn had accomplished what had been driving him. There had been no attempt on his life, but Mogue probably wasn't in a hurry. Whatever knowledge Fynn had was already passed on. Maliha installed him in one of her bedrooms, moving Amaro out to the living-room couch, and Fynn began living there quietly. Yanmeng sat with him for hours whenever he could manage. Maliha would have liked to know what they talked about; whatever it was, it seemed to be good for Fynn.

Planning began for the remainder of the hitchhiker case.

Over scrambled eggs and very flat biscuits, Yanmeng wondered if there wasn't another way besides murdering the secret council members.

"Global exposure. Get the word out," he said.

Hound shook his head. "Exposure does nothing. They'd still go ahead and set off the little fuckers and we'll have a lot of gray goo. There isn't time to develop an antidote."

"We're a cheery bunch," Yanmeng said. "All right, exposure's not the way to go. Back to practical stuff. What if there are secondary commanders in place? Kill the ringleaders, the seconds-in-command pop up, we're back in the same position."

"Highly unlikely," Maliha said. "A group like this doesn't want to share knowledge with anyone. In fact, they barely want to share knowledge with each other. And if they've been using working commanders, then there are plans in place to kill those people right when the hitchhikers are triggered. In fact, they probably have various plans to do away with each other, too. Multiple backstabbing plots. I've seen it before."

"Let's talk about the council members," Hound said. "Get into things we can actually do something about instead of this abstract crap." He took a big slurp of coffee.

The way he was sitting, the sunshine from the window lit up the scars on the side of his face. She had a sudden urge to run her fingers over the ruined portion of his face, from eyebrow to jaw, where the jagged line of pink scar tissue met his black skin. Hound somehow picked up the fact that she was thinking about him. He turned to her and winked. She winked back.

Amaro raised his hand. "May I speak now?"

"Very funny," Maliha said. "Hear ye, hear ye, Amaro has the floor."

Amaro pretended not to notice. "The American woman on the council is named Laura Bertram. It turns out not to be her real name, but the real name has no special significance. She's been using Laura most of her life after an adoption at an early age. Laura is a Boston defense attorney with a reputation for taking on high-profile cases and getting the accused off. She has strong political aspirations and the money and connections to act on them. Her public work as both an attorney and a political candidate for U.S. senator make her suspiciously easy to track down."

Maliha shrugged. "Maybe the Leader considers her most expendable. Or they're trying to get a political presence, someone in a position of power to step up when the country needs a new type of leadership. One willing to dump democracy in the targeted countries and establish indentured servitude as the new in thing."

"She has the best prospects of any of them. It makes sense," Yanmeng said.

"Something I don't get. If she's getting these high-profile guys off maybe on technicalities, in her attorney work, how come the public likes her so much? It seems like that would kill a political career, not boost it."

Amaro said, "Good question. One of the first things I thought of. I dug into Laura's casework and found that there's just enough ambiguity in them that she can spin it like she's making sure justice is served. She's never lost one of those cases, which is either damn smart or collusion with the prosecutor or judge or all of the above. Remember that middle-school principal accused of fondling little Susie's privates, the Lawrence Grove case? It got national attention just a couple of months ago."

They nodded.

"She got him off. It turned out little Susie was supposedly mental, supposedly due to supposed abuse by a dead cousin who couldn't be called back from the grave to defend himself. Gray areas are her specialty, and in the public's eye, she's a trusted truth seeker. Now how normal is a one-hundred-percent acquittal rate on cases like that?"

"Too many coincidences. That couldn't happen in all of her cases, unless she's one of those people who survive the plane crash and win the lottery the next day. The outliers on the natural distribution for luck—on the good side," Hound said.

"Wow—distribution. Outliers," Amaro said. "We're going to have to call you Professor Hound."

"Hey, I know stuff."

Amaro snorted.

"We're going after her first then," Maliha said.

Laura Bertram had a husband and two small children. Presumably those children loved their mother, even if the husband had his doubts about the woman he married. Or, love being blind, he might be devoted to her. Maliha decided it had to look like a political assassination, just so the father would have something definite, something the children could pin their understanding on when they got older.

Yanmeng had something to ask. "This is a grave situation we are in. Is it time to bring in government agencies, U.S. or otherwise? Interpol? How about the governments of the targeted countries?"

"Your reason?"

"Sheer manpower. You're one person. Others could be working in parallel. We have to consider it."

The audacity of her undertaking sank in on Maliha and her shoulders sagged under the weight of it. There was silence as the others considered it.

If I lose this I could end up a broken woman, just waiting to die and be punished by Rabishu.

There was a mirror across the room from her. She raised her head just enough to see her reflection. Before she'd broken her contract with Rabishu, she'd suffered through a period of seeing herself becoming a horrid old crone, more and more akin to him—but only in mirrors, as her private torment. She never knew whether he was showing her visions of herself rotting from the inside, growing claws, her skin splitting into fissures that dripped the same noisome liquid associated with him, the same nauseating smell. . . . Or whether the images sprang from within herself as a judgment of what she'd become, or even if her reality was altered by mental illness.

Her reflection in the mirror this time played out the guilt she would suffer, the physical decay, if she lost this challenge. In the scene people screamed and tore at themselves, trying to pull out the creatures tearing them apart from within. She saw her skin crawl with the exaggerated action of the nanites within her body, ripping this, dissolving that, as her healing ability struggled to keep her from dissolving as the others were. The Maliha in the mirror screamed soundlessly as portions of her body liquefied and sank to the ground.

Maliha closed her eyes. *Why shouldn't I pass this off to the government? I've done my best, I got this far, someone else can cross the finish line triumphantly—or pay the price on their conscience, not mine. Why not?* For a moment her spirits rose. *Why not?*

Then she realized that this was the life she'd chosen, to place herself in danger to save others. She started to say something when Hound spoke up.

"I've considered it long enough," Hound said. "And my vote is no. I'm involved in secret government work I can't tell you bunch of security risks about, and besides, you don't have any need to know about it. Let me tell you the first thing that would happen, be it our government or Interpol or whatever. They'd start pulling together their response team of scientists plus establish a military task force. The scientists would want to study the nanites and their effects—problem is, we don't have any. Mogue made off with the canteen, remember? Fynn would be pulled in for theoretical discussions. Are they going to find an antidote? No, because none of us knows exactly what the hell triggers 'em. The best they might do after a few months is find something that strips Fynn's coating off the nanites. Big whoop. The task force would start looking for the remaining members of the council. Their first action would be to raid the Keltner Building, finding nothing. Then they'd start sending around photos of council members in an effort to locate them. Do you see a lot of wheel spinning going on here? Given enough time, they'd probably get results. I say shoot the single arrow at the heart of the beast rather than slowly prick it to death with little needles."

"Hound's not normally that poetic, but he is right. I have to do it."

Yanmeng said, "It had to be asked. We should always question decisions that are so potent."

"Damn, that sounds good," Hound said. "Any sentence with *potent* in it gets my vote."

Maliha flew to Boston. There was a political fund-raiser coming up in three days, a benefit for Laura's campaign for U.S. senator. She stayed in her hotel most of the time, resting her ribs. She had to be ready for action by then. She went for an experimental run on her second day there and found that she could do a half mile in about a minute with no problem, but she was going to have to be faster than that. Fast enough to be unnoticed.

What I didn't tell my friends is that I'm doing this as the Black Ghost. Get back into assassination mode. One strike, one kill, as Master Liu taught me.

Maliha kept up with her practice runs until she could appear as a blur to human eyes. There was considerable pain, but nothing she couldn't tolerate for the short time necessary. Working through several links of a chain, Maliha was invited to the fund-raiser, sort of. One of the party officials had gone through a bitter divorce and wouldn't mind showing up with a beautiful woman on his arm to spite his ex-wife, who would also be there. With a little planning, he'd "bumped" into Maliha at a coffee shop.

On the night of the event, she left her long black hair loose, accented her green eyes with luminescent shadow, and shaped her lips with Kiss Me Now Red, going for a classy call-girl look. Her dress finished the effect. It was flowing black, cut low front and back—but covering the vestiges of her shoulder wound—and with a deeply slit skirt that showed a lot of thigh. Her shoes were barely there sandals with tiny black straps that crisscrossed their way up her calves. Her escort loved all of it, and all of her. It would make his ex livid. It was a practical outfit, too—slit skirts and no heels are better for running. He wanted his photo taken with her, and she obliged, managing to turn her face toward him so that a cascade of shiny hair hid her features. As for the rest of her body, there was nothing unique about what showed in the photo. She'd made sure of that.

Laura Bertram stood at the podium to make a speech. There was a spotlight on her and the room lights were dimmed. Maliha took a reading of the woman's aura, checking to see if there was any possibility that her information had been wrong. There was a dull black cloud around Laura, with fiercer, polished-looking black and red tendrils snaking outward. Maliha looked hard for Laura's loving nature toward her family, but it wasn't there, meaning the husband and kids were props in her political ascent.

She took note of the security arrangements in the room. Coverage was adequate but nothing special. She located all the plainclothes agents, including the two near the dais. None of them threatened her plan, and she thought the security barely adequate for a political event, much less one involving a member of a secret organization.

The council could be trying to get rid of her. This could be a trap for me.

Searching around the room using aural vision, she could find no streaks—no Ageless were here.

Maliha excused herself to use the ladies' room, stroking her escort's arm and smiling as she did so. He patted her hand while listening to the speech and she took off. The instant she rose from the table, she used her supernatural speed to make it to a bathroom stall.

After slipping on black evening gloves from her small handbag, she assembled the pieces of the plastic pistol hidden innocuously as stays in her skirt and added the few metal pieces needed, disguised in the hinged jaws of her evening bag. The single bullet she needed was part of the clasp of her bag.

When the ladies' room was empty, she dashed back to the meeting room, leaped atop a service table in the back, and shot Laura Bertram between the eyes.

Still moving fast, she dropped the weapon, stripped off the gloves and shoved them in her bag, and settled back in her seat at her escort's side in time to gasp along with every-one else as Laura slid down to the dais floor, dying.

Since everyone was told to remain seated, it gave her ample time to rest from the exertion of using extra speed and to let the pain of movement fade to discomfort.

It was a long evening of questioning and fingerprinting, but Maliha had come prepared with a solid identity based on undetectable "skins," sheaths covering her fingertips and heat-sealed to her skin. The worst part of it was turning her back and not crying out when her scale marked a reward. She managed to be in a corner of the room at the time and luckily, no one spoke to her right then.

She let her escort take her to his home when the police released them. To do anything else might have raised ques-tions as out of the ordinary. She got him drunk while hang-ing onto every word of his story about his divorce. When he fell asleep, she left her panties on the floor to make him think they'd been intimate and slipped out, satisfied with a job well done.

She didn't take the two thousand dollars he'd left for her on the nightstand. As she'd said to Jamie, she didn't work for money.

Walking the streets, her evening's kill a success, Maliha felt elated. The perfect way her plans had played out was exciting. Aspects of her Ageless life pulled at her. She was deliberately slipping into her Black Ghost persona to bring down the ones who were planning to use the hitchhikers. The Black Ghost came as a whole package of behaviors, why take just one behavior, like picking one cherry from a box?

After a successful kill, the demon's slave had enjoyed sex to take the edge off. Maliha was wearing a revealing black dress and shoes with tiny straps up her calves. She'd already lost her panties—so much the better. She ran her fingers through her hair, put some sway into her hips, and walked into a bar.

Chapter Twenty-One

Too easy. If Mogue was there last night, he could have stopped me or caught me afterward. So he's not guarding the council. Yet. After this initial strike, he might be.

By the next morning, Maliha was holed up in a downtown St. Louis hotel. Her guiding principle after shooting an up-and-coming political figure was to get out of Dodge. Walking a few blocks, she found a storefront McDonald's, drifted in for the pancake breakfast, and bought a *St. Louis Post-Dispatch*. On page one she found a headline about the slaying, attributing it to political motives. The article mentioned the victim's two surviving children, something that gave Maliha a pang of guilt. She'd changed their lives forever.

She checked the news on her computer, watching videos of the anguished husband. The anguished partner from her law firm. The anguished political figures who decried a life of public service cut short. It was assumed that it was "a vicious political slaying perpetrated by an ideological extremist," and the Department of Justice was looking into the murder as a hate crime because of the victim's stance on illegal immigration. Although according to Maliha's memory, there hadn't been anyone at the twenty-five-thousand-dollar-a-plate dinner who would have disagreed with Laura's stance on that topic, which was "Send them all home except my housekeeper and my nanny."

In other words, no one had any clue about Maliha's participation or motivation except maybe the other council members, and that depended on how much, if anything, Mogue had told them about her. One death out of a group wasn't enough of a pattern to be frantic about.

Maliha was beginning to regret taking the low-hanging fruit first. The others might go to ground even if they weren't convinced there was an active conspiracy against them, and would be harder to find. What did they have to lose by sequestering themselves? Since they had Fynn's advanced coating, they were surely in the manufacturing stage on the hitchhiker project, if not already into global distribution. And Maliha still didn't know two crucial pieces of information: what triggered the hitchhikers to begin turning their hosts' bodies into gray goo, and who the "Leader" was.

Her cell phone rang. It was Jake, texting her. He wanted to talk about Randy.

She and Jake had met through a blind date set up by Maliha's friend Randy, but Maliha didn't think he knew Randy well. According to her story, she'd only met Jake the day she set up the blind date. She called Jake right away.

"What's wrong with Randy?"

Oh no. Not Randy. Mogue didn't get to her. . . . Please, oh please, not Randy.

"She broke up with her boyfriend."

"Oh, you had me worried. That happens about every three weeks."

"She was falling for this guy, or already fallen. Said his nickname is now Dickhead."

She talks about nicknames with Jake? I thought that was our private girl talk.

"Did he used to be Power Balls before he got his new nickname?"

"Yeah."

"Why didn't she call me herself?"

"I think she's really hurting. I'm only so much good here. I happen to be of the same sex as the vile Dickhead. Can you come here and talk to her?"

She sighed. *Maybe I can talk her through it on the phone.*

"Can you get her to talk to me on the phone?"

"She threw her phone down and stomped on it. Then she locked herself in the bathroom. I think it would be best if you came in person."

"If this doesn't work, I'll be there in person, I promise. Give her your phone. Get her out of wherever she is and tell her that Doodles wants to talk to her. Then stay in her apartment but out of sight somewhere. Don't leave until she's okay. You let anything happen to her and I swear I'll rip your fingernails out, and that's for starters."

"You say that like you really would. Do I have to say Doodles?"

"Yes! If you don't, I'll . . ." He hung up the phone.

He hung up the fucking phone! She took a deep breath. *Calm down, he just went to get her. It's strange talking with Jake as if nothing happened between us. Only for Randy . . .*

Five nerve-wracking minutes later, her phone rang. She slid open the phone and shouted into it.

"You better have handled this right, you . . ."

There were some sniffles and blubbers on the line. "Doodles? Is that you?"

"Sweetie, it's me. Tell me everything."

"Listen, if you have something else to do, it's okay. I can manage."

I just have to stop nasty chewing things from eating peoples' guts, but what are friends for?

"You're number one for me, Noodles."

Randy burst into tears. It could have been from Maliha's declaration of loyalty or the actual breakup. Maliha, a.k.a. Doodles, waited a while, saying soothing things like, "Everything will be all right," until the crying lessened in volume. Then it was time to move in and make a difference.

"Where are you?" Maliha said.

"In the bedroom," she said between sobs.

Never stay in the bedroom where you made love after you break up with the guy. At least, not while it's fresh.

She pictured Randy's apartment. It was of modest size, but highly personalized. Randy was an Earth Mother type, and everywhere there were natural fabrics, wall hangings, posters, and small pieces of art from around the world, some of them given to her by Maliha as souvenirs from her research trips. In the living room there was a comfortable organic pillow grouping on the floor that Dickhead had probably never touched, since it would have put him eye level with a display of fertility dolls grouped on a table. Odd, since Randy professed not to want any children for another decade so she wouldn't waste her youth on breastfeeding and diapers. Cloth diapers, of course.

Perhaps the dolls scared Dickhead off.

"Would you do something for me?" Maliha said. She used her honey-sweet voice. This was the voice that had bought her entry to the home of European royalty when she arrived nude, wrapped in a thin blanket—no one there seemed to have heard of Cleopatra.

"Uh-huh."

"Take that box of tissues off the dresser, go on out to the living room, and make yourself comfortable on those floor pillows."

Gradually, the story came out. Randy and her latest boyfriend had gotten marriage-level serious, except that it turned out to be one-sided.

"I loved him. I knew it. We were going to move in together sometime soon, and then I wanted to go shopping for a ring after that. He got me a new TV for our three-month anniversary."

Maliha picked up immediately on "I wanted to go shopping for a ring," rather than "we," and figured Dickhead hadn't proposed. Randy was extrapolating the relationship. He had called her that morning and told her she was okay but he was moving on, and that she could keep the TV.

"Like that made up for everything. Stupid TV."

"Throw a pillow at it, one of the little ones."

Maliha heard a thunk coming through from the other end

of the phone. The TV, now a surrogate for Dickhead, had been punished. Randy was getting into the spirit of things. Maliha had to get some alcohol in her soon.

"He came by to drop off the key but he slid it under the door when I was asleep rather than talk to me."

"Ooh, that's cold," Maliha said. She heard another thunk, and hoped the TV was securely anchored.

"I hate men! I'm never sleeping with another man. They're just big brutes. Big, brainless, inconsiderate . . ."

The rant went on for a while. Maliha knew better than to deny anything Randy said. Her job was to hear anything and agree. She talked Randy into cleaning herself up with a hot shower and then donning her favorite pair of worn pajamas with stars all over them. She waited on the line.

Jake panicked about this. Either she was a lot worse around him or he's overwhelmed when it comes to women's emotions. He made it sound like he had her on a suicide watch. He's a seasoned field agent, not to mention Ageless. It just doesn't mesh.

Something else occurred to her. *He might have just wanted me back there. Maybe thought I'd come in person. In fact he asked me to, twice. Does he have any connection with the hitchhiker project? Okay, that's paranoid.*

"Noodles, do you have any wine?"

"I have organic wine. And that's another thing. He didn't respect my desire to surround myself with untainted products of nature."

"He wasn't good enough for you. Let's drink to that."

They clinked glasses on the phone. Randy's was full, Maliha's empty. It was all over not long after that. Randy was still very sad. She would be for a long time, since this was the first serious relationship she'd had since high school, the first time since then when she'd said, "I love you," and actually meant it. But she'd gotten her perspective back. She realized the tidal wave of pain would eventually pass and that no matter how hopeless things seemed now, there were other men out there for her besides Dickhead. The wine put Randy to sleep.

She was a bit ashamed she'd even considered that Jake might have something to do with the hitchhiker project and had called to deflect her from pursuing the case. Of course he wasn't much help to Randy. Few men would be. He just had a disadvantage in dealing with her at that moment, and it was in his pants.

Chapter Twenty-Two

Amaro had called Maliha with distressing news. An envelope had been found lying on the kitchen counter in her apartment. It was from Mogue: *I can get to Fynn and your friends anytime I want. Really, you're making this too easy.*

"The high-speed camera caught him coming and going, a blur I could slow down enough to make out a figure moving. That's it—no alarms or anything. That cinches it—Mogue's Ageless, if you didn't know that already. Fynn's whole family is wiped out and Mogue can't leave it at that. Bloodthirsty son-of-a bitch. Kinda scary. I didn't tell Fynn. By the way, Larry Maybry's still alive. He went to Bora Bora or someplace."

"I . . ." Fear shot through Maliha and transfixed her, as though a bolt of lightning had streaked from her brain to her feet. She was unable to talk, unable to move. The phone dropped from her hand.

Whole family wiped out. Mogue's done with Fynn's family. Now he's going to come after mine, to torment me before killing me—exactly the way he did with Fynn. She pictured herself holding Amaro or Yanmeng or Hound as he died in her arms. The thought was unbearable.

"Maliha?"

Eliu. Glass. Oh no. Rosie and her babies.

"Are all of you in my apartment?"

"What? Yes."

"Stay there. Lock the door. Put something heavy in front

of it that you can see and hear if it moves across the floor."
Useless, useless. "Tell Hound to get the weapons out. The
rocket-propelled grenade launchers, too."

When Maliha had remodeled her public apartment, she'd
put in a large gun safe and insisted that she train them all on
every pistol and rifle in the safe. For Yanmeng, she also let
him choose edged weapons and fighting sticks.

"Take shifts watching the door until I get there, at least
two at a time. Amaro, watch the high-speed camera. If anything shows up that looks like a streak or a blurred figure,
all of you get out of there."

There was a short silence on his end of the phone this
time. "Mogue's coming after us now, isn't he?"

"It's just a hunch."

"Hunch, bullshit! He said as much in his note, and
anyway, it's his pattern, start with the relatives and move
up, just like he made Fynn experience the pain of all those
deaths of people close to him."

"I think maybe you should gather everybody there.
Rosie, the kids, Alex, everybody."

She heard Amaro cursing under his breath and Hound
cursing loudly in the background. He'd figured out what
was going on from Amaro's side of the phone conversation.

"How about Randy?"

"Randy, yes. Do whatever you have to do to get her there
and keep her there, at gunpoint if you have to. Tell Hound to
fire the RPG as soon as whatever furniture you have in front
of the door moves. As soon as it moves. Take care."

"You too."

Maliha called the number for her private jet's pilot and
told him to be ready to fly from Chicago to Winnipeg the
next day. He thanked her for the advance notice, probably
the most she'd ever given him.

She bought a ticket for a flight to Chicago. She tried to
nap on the short flight so she'd be fresh when she got home.
She couldn't sleep, though. Every time she closed her eyes,
she had a vision of opening her apartment door and finding
a bloodbath. She told herself that Mogue wouldn't do that—

he'd want to drag it out and watch her suffer the effect of each individual death.

From the Chicago airport, she called Arnie and asked him to obtain a shuttle bus to take a dozen people to the airport together.

"Certainly, Ms. Winters. Is there luggage to be brought down now?"

"No. Don't send anyone up. Absolutely do not try to open the door to my apartment. Either of them." She hung up before he could react.

She got there, approached her door cautiously, and had Yanmeng ask her a couple of questions only she would know before opening the door. It was a practice she wanted them to put into place. Everyone was okay and ready to go.

Randy had been easily persuaded. It was a great adventure. She showed up at Maliha's apartment with suitcases full of clothes. Once Randy got a look at Amaro, nothing could have dissuaded her from going along. Total, high-wattage attention from Amaro was just what she needed after her breakup with Dickhead. It would build up her confidence, and Maliha knew Amaro wouldn't take advantage of her. With a wink at Maliha, Amaro put his arm around her and the two of them sat down on the sofa. He was in his element.

Maliha's jet flew out of O'Hare full of people who'd been told various stories for coming, including three young children who might or might not have thought they were going to Disneyland. At every interaction point where other people were around, she used her continuous-aura viewing, making sure Mogue wasn't among them. Her destination was outside the town of Yellowknife, in the Canadian Northwest Territories.

The jet landed in Winnipeg and she asked the pilot to hold it there for her—she'd be coming back through within the day. She hired a DeHavilland Twin Otter bush plane and loaded in passengers and luggage. Her safe house was underground near Great Slave Lake, which she'd always thought was appropriate, considering that she'd been a demon's slave. She landed the plane expertly on its skis.

Next came acquiring the unique key that would allow them to enter the safe house. She had to have it with her all the time, so she could make a rapid entry into any of her safe houses around the world. The easiest way to do that was to have it under her skin. She asked everyone but Amaro to leave the plane. Not that she was shy, but she thought the procedure might gross out the children.

Probably not, these days.

The location of the key varied. The last time she'd used it, it had been above her left breast. This time it was on the inside of her left thigh. She brought out a small kit she had with her, stood up, unzipped her pants, and let them drop to the floor of the plane. As Amaro watched, she used a scalpel in the kit to make a neat slice about half an inch long in her thigh, then wiggled and squeezed the area with her fingers until a thin, bloody wafer slipped out. She caught it in her hand and gave it to Amaro along with a four-by-four dressing to wipe it clean of blood. She cleaned the blood off her thigh with supplies from the kit and put a couple of butterfly bandages over the cut. It was silly, due to her fast healing and the small size of the cut, but she'd taken to humoring Yanmeng when he was around, and he wanted her to do it.

Normally the wafer would just be inserted in a special lock compartment in the door, but in this case the door was covered with snow. She had to use a remote control. She handed the remote control device to Amaro and he dropped the chip into it.

"What do you do if you want to get in and don't have that kit to get the key chip?"

"I usually have a knife on me I can use, and if I don't, I have fingernails." She held her hands out, fingers spread, like cat's paws.

"Ew."

Maliha shook her head. *If he thinks that's bad, then I have a lot of good horror stories for him.* "You're officially the remote man. Don't let the kids get hold of it. It has a self timer that closes the door in three seconds unless you press here"—she showed him on the remote control—"and the door closes really fast. More than watch-your-fingers fast. You don't want anybody casually sticking his head out to check the weather. Got it?"

"Got it."

The press of a button on the remote brought to life a powerful mechanism that opened a sliding vault door in the side of a granite mountain. Amaro turned off the timer and they all trouped in.

With the six hours of daylight fading, she saw them installed in the mountain hideaway, secure from any attack except a direct atomic bomb strike. If Mogue could summon that, then there was nowhere she had prepared she could hide her friends from him. She had fallout shelters in key locations, but this mountain vault was the closest she had to a direct strike shelter, and it wasn't nearly deep enough.

She'd used the place in the past as an asylum for political prisoners. It was spacious, two stories with a sleeping floor and a living floor, all outfitted for long-term comfort and safety.

The safe house was provisioned for twenty adults for several weeks, but she'd shopped extensively in Yellowknife for supplies for Rosie's children, including her youngest, less than a year old. As in all of her remote refuges, an operations manual allowed her to feel confident that Hound and the others could manage the systems that ran the generator, ventilation, water, trash, heat, and lights. An emergency button opened the bombproof vault door from the inside, but once closed, no one was going to get them from the outside.

Maliha wanted to talk to Hound, Amaro, and Yanmeng before she left. She corralled them all in a bedroom.

"Don't expect to hear from me often," Maliha said. "I can call the phone here because it's secure, but mostly I'll be operating quietly and quickly. I'll be using my old assassin techniques and you don't really need to hear about that, anyway. Keep everybody calm in here and I'll let you know when I'm successful."

Her three friends exchanged looks that she couldn't interpret. "What gives?"

"You're shutting us out. Do you need to work secretly?" said Yanmeng.

Maliha frowned. "If you want the job done and lives saved, then let me have a free hand."

"What exactly does a free hand mean? How do you operate with your 'old assassin techniques'?" Yanmeng wanted to know.

With no regrets, no looking back, and nobody getting in my way. Using any method to get what I want.

"Efficiently," she said. Her voice was cold. Unconsciously, she'd taken an aggressive stance: feet spread apart, her right foot slightly in front of her left, her left hand inches away from the gun in her hidden waistband holster.

"Whoa, back off," Hound said as he stepped in front of Yanmeng. "It was just a question. Shit, don't get all Rambo on us."

Maliha swung her arms to loosen them, and moved backward to sit on the bed. "What's with all of you? This is no different from other missions we've worked on."

Yanmeng shook his head. "Your attitude is different. You're slipping back to the way you behaved when you were Ageless, and it seems like you . . . want to."

What gives them the right . . . ?

"How do you know how I behaved when I was Ageless?"

"Because you've told us," Amaro said. "You also said that you never wanted to be that way again."

"I can handle this. It's temporary." Maliha stood up and left the room, cutting off the conversation. It was time for her to leave.

She double-checked the interior with her aura vision, looking for the streak that signaled an Ageless presence. Satisfied, she had Amaro close the mountain door while she kept watch. She felt a sense of relief and a rush of guilt that she was able to do for her loved ones what she hadn't done for Fynn's.

Back in Chicago, Maliha felt she had to warn Jake. Mogue might have seen them together, and even though Jake was

Ageless, he could be killed during a surprise attack from another Ageless person. She phoned him and asked if she could talk to him at his apartment.

"I have something to tell you," she said. "What I'm working on involves an Ageless, and he's shown himself to be brutal. He could be targeting people close to me, and that means he could be after you."

Jake didn't seem too alarmed about danger to himself. "Which one?"

"Mogue, although I think that's just one of many names he uses."

"Mogue," he said. "You mean Rasputin. Your basic nightmare among demon's slaves."

"*The* Rasputin?"

"Yeah, that one. Did some foul things when he was alive, not much of a leap for him to become an assassin. You should stay away from him."

"I'm doing my best to do that."

"Tell me everything. Maybe I can help."

"Do you mean you'd renounce your contract and work with me as a rogue?"

"Wouldn't I be more useful dealing with Rasputin if I stayed Ageless?"

"When your demon said you could do what you wanted, I doubt if he meant kill the slaves of other demons. If you go after Rasputin . . ."

"You're right. Idiptu would be very interested in what I was doing all of a sudden. Becoming rogue . . . I just don't know."

Here comes the familiar argument. "I'm so ancient that my scale would be impossible to balance." I've got an answer for that one.

"I'm a lot older than you. My scale—"

"Should be easier to balance than mine," Maliha said. "You told me you only killed for a couple of hundred years for Idiptu before he got tired of the whole thing."

Jake stood up, turned his back to her and crossed his arms.

Something's coming and he won't face me to say it. She stood up nervously and held her breath.

"I did say that about Idiptu. It's true, but it wasn't the whole truth. After I stopped getting assignments, I didn't stop killing until much later."

How could he? Maliha let out her breath. *How could he kill for . . . for fun?*

He turned to face her. His eyes were moist and his whole body sagged like a whipped dog's. "Give me a chance, Maliha. There are so many things . . . I love you. I don't want to lose you. Whatever you're thinking now, don't let it be the end for us. I swear I didn't want to hurt you like this."

He reached out to her, but she took a step backward, suddenly aware that she didn't know this lover of hers nearly well enough. She remembered what she'd thought about Mogue or Rasputin, whatever he wanted to call himself, not long ago. *What happens if a demon snares someone who is already evil, a true sociopath? Give that person a hundred years or thousands of years of unfettered killing with no consequences and it's a nightmare beyond imagining. Who's to say Jake isn't another Rasputin, just in a nicer package?*

She could almost hear her heart breaking, like the tinkling of glass shattering in the cold center of her chest. She couldn't think of a response.

"We'll have to talk about it some other time. I've got work to do."

She slammed the door and went for a run around the lake in McKinley Park. On her second time around at superhuman speed, she could finally put a few thoughts together.

There could be an explanation for this. He implied there was, but I don't know where we could go from here. I can't love a man who's a wanton murderer. If this is it for us, I wish I'd said something better than "I have work to do." I wish I'd thrown a plate at his head. Or sliced his neck with it.

Chapter Twenty-Three

She was on her way back from Jake's house when her phone rang. She wasn't going to answer it, since she was in no mood to talk, but when she saw that the call was a secure connection, she took it. It was Bernie, an information broker who lived in the Australian outback. She'd been to his place once, as probably one of the few human beings who'd set foot there.

She'd contacted a few outside sources that Rasputin would never suspect of working with her. With Fynn's family and Ty and Claire gone because of her information search, she needed to go further afield. She knew Amaro was frustrated at his lack of success in locating the council members so far. His techniques, while usually effective, hadn't come up with specifics.

Amaro doesn't supplement his computer work by talking to real people. He doesn't think to work that way.

Bernie had found one of the council members living in an underwater research station off the coast of Australia. She paid Bernie his usual fee by wire transfer, twenty-five thousand U.S. dollars now and an equal payment after "discovery." That meant different things to different clients, but in Maliha's case, it meant after she successfully located and killed Dr. Cort Maur.

Bernie was reliable. Maliha made plans to go to Australia. She begrudged the time it would cost her to get there and back—a full day each way. She had to go, though.

Maliha flew to Los Angeles and then to Sydney. In her mode of not calling attention to herself, she traveled as a last-minute addition to a tourist group bound for a fourteen-day guided tour in Australia. It nearly killed her. It turned out that she was the only one of the thirty tourists under sixty on the tour and consequently received an inordinate amount of attention from the traveling men. The women gave her the cold shoulder, which would have been okay with her, except that they speculated loudly on her background (a loose woman), why she was traveling to Australia (alternately to escape the law or to start a house of ill repute), and if those boobs were really hers (no) for the benefit of the men. The discussions inspired the men to pay even more attention to her.

Next time I'm not going to worry so much about attracting attention. If Rasputin wants to have it out right here on aisle 24, I think that would be better than traveling with this bunch.

On the longer leg of the flight Maliha checked in with her other sources. None of them had any news. She felt time pressure, and knew she couldn't wait for things to drop into her lap. It was time to call in a debt, the biggest chip she had to play in the intelligence business.

It had been more than thirty years since she'd last seen Abiyram Heber, once a shadowy commander in Mossad, the Israeli intelligence agency. Now he lived quietly in retirement. Maliha had worked with him on several occasions and had once saved his life when a plan went awry. Abiyram still had a solid network of connections, and they weren't confined to the Middle East, never had been. For a life-debt, he would do anything he could for her, and then his debt would be discharged. She needed information about the rest of the council and especially about the Leader.

It was six hours ahead where he was, making it late afternoon. He picked up on the first ring and inquired immediately about her safety. It was nice to know that somebody across the world had her back. She told him she would like to come to see him and he agreed.

Her itinerary was taking shape: get to Sydney, kill a man under water, visit Abiyram in the White City. The Black Ghost packed light on clothes, heavy on weapons. She was smiling with anticipation. Not because she was heading out to kill several bad guys—dealing death was no thrill to her—but because of the manner of her operation. She felt a freedom she hadn't felt in a long time. *With my friends stowed away I can operate with no attachments, no complications, as if I were still Ageless. Jake doesn't need any protection from me.*

Dr. Cort Maur lived and worked on a research station submerged in about ninety feet of water off the coast near the Queensland city of Mackay. It must have been a place where he felt secure, because after the first death among the council members, he had made no attempt to flee. Perhaps he believed he would be difficult to find, or that a hired killer wouldn't be able to get to him in the research lab. Maliha thought it was entirely possible that there were feuds among the council members, differing private agendas, and Cort may not have been disappointed or frightened to see Laura go.

He may have welcomed it and assumed one of the others arranged it. After all, this is a weird bunch.

Maliha bought scuba equipment from three separate stores, making her purchases less expensive and less remarkable. Something she'd brought with her, since it was so specialized that it would be remembered, was an underwater GPS kit. Acting as a college student wanting to write a paper, she obtained the location of the research lab from the Australian Institute of Marine Science. They didn't run the program because they had their own oceangoing research vessels, but kept tabs on other research in Australian waters.

This was a tricky mission. In the confined quarters of the lab, she had only one target, a man whose photo she'd studied, and didn't want to injure anyone else—otherwise, the simplest thing to do would be to blow up the whole thing.

She made her assault at night, dropped off by a fisherman she'd paid to deliver her and wait while she dived. She inflated the surface float antenna for the GPS, tossed it out into the water, and hooked the waterproof unit, attached by an umbilical cord to the float, to her belt. She went over the edge with barely a splash into the pitch-black water. With the lighted screen of the GPS unit leading the way and the cord playing out behind her, she found the undersea location, about ninety feet down. As she approached, she saw the lab's lighting, minimal at this time of night, but still enough to see by in the vicinity. She clipped the umbilical to the side of the lab, just in case she had the leisure on the way out to reattach it.

To enter the lab, a swimmer had to come up from underneath into a pool in a wetroom. There was a small positive air pressure throughout the station so that the water in the pool didn't rise up and flood the lab. She had no idea what she'd encounter when she popped up in the wetroom. Could be empty. For all she knew, she might interrupt some night expedition and the room could be full of divers.

Blood roared through her veins and her heartbeat thumped loudly in her ears. It was risky, impetuous, and exciting. *Like the old days.*

She slipped under the lab, which stood about ten feet off the sea floor on legs that made the station look like a giant insect from below. The well-lighted entrance pool glowed above her as a greenish rectangle.

Go for it.

When her head eased out of the water into the air of the wetroom, she saw one crewmember working among some boxes of supplies. He was wearing a pair of earphones while working, which was the best news she could get. She kicked her swim fins off and let them sink away from her in the water. She needed to be quick, and clomping across the floor with fins wasn't good enough. She put her hands on the edge of the pool, levered her body out of the water, and delivered a flying kick to his head. She stuffed his limp body in a gear closet.

Maliha hadn't been able to obtain a layout of the lab, the

glaring hole in her plan. With the need to move quickly on any solid information she received, she was going to have to forgo the thorough study of her target that she used to do when working for Rabishu. The need for haste added another element of tension. The missions would have to be done by the seat of her pants and not carefully plotted with support from Amaro, Hound, and Yanmeng. Maliha realized she was breathing too fast with excitement and slowed her breathing.

She left her gear behind a crate of supplies in the wetroom and moved quietly into the interior of the lab. There was no night shift working, and she'd eliminated most of the sleeping rooms by the time she found one with a plaque on the door: Dr. Cort Maur. Hoping to find him sleeping, she opened the door just enough to see in.

No such luck.

Maur was wide awake, busily typing at a computer, and he turned to face her as soon as she opened the door. She ran in, just in time to see him reach for a button on his desk. It was probably an emergency button that would bring a medic and other personnel rapidly. She threw a star at his arm, hoping to keep him from pressing the button, but his hand finished the movement just as the star bit into his flesh. She crossed the room quickly and pinned him against the wall. Even with the alarm sounding, she took the time to take a reading of Maur's aura. It wouldn't tell her specifically that he was a council member, but it would confirm that he had done and would do evil things. Should that not be true, she had to assume that the information that sent her here was false, and she would abort the mission.

With her knife poised above his heart, Maliha blocked out the developing commotion outside and let his aura come into view. As with Laura Bertram, she saw an overall dull black, but in Maur's case there were also red tinges of malicious hate.

She plunged the knife into his heart.

She heard noises, but on the station they had an odd, omnidirectional quality. She was sure they'd close in on her location, though, because the alarm emanated from this room.

How many people are on this thing? Two are down, maybe eight or ten more?

She made it to the door before anyone arrived. There were voices at the door, then three people entered the room in a rush. She slashed one across the arm as a distraction, knocked a head against a table, and gave the third an elbow to the jaw. She turned to find the man with blood dripping down his arm holding a taser on her. He was only a few feet away; he wasn't going to miss. That was his mistake—he was too close. She knocked a chair into his legs, jerking his lower body to one side, and the taser went skittering across the floor. As he tried to recover, she brought her hands together and swung them at the side of his face. He dropped instantly. Leaping over their fallen bodies, she ran back into the hallway. One man opened the door to his room just as she passed by. She grabbed the door and hit him with it, knocking him out.

One scientist she saw as she passed his room was retreating to a closet. She just got a glimpse of him as he closed the door. His courage had failed him. He wasn't going to be coming out until everything was calm again. Most likely, he'd be the one to find Maur's body.

Seven accounted for. How many will be at the pool?

The wetroom was silent when she got there. She couldn't see anyone waiting to trap her, but her scuba gear was gone. They must have thought the missing gear would keep the intruder on board until help could be summoned from the mainland.

Suspicious that she'd be attacked as soon as she showed herself, Maliha observed from a hidden vantage point for a couple of minutes. No change. She decided she couldn't wait any longer. Someone could easily have radioed for help, maybe the scientist she thought was heading for a closet. It could have been a communications room.

Nothing is as it seems here.

She made a dash for the pool, dove in and swam hard to clear the undersurface of the lab. Suddenly pain ripped through her calf. She twisted in the water and found a diver taking aim at her with another harpoon. The first had just grazed her leg. She didn't have much time to deal with him. He had a supply of air and she didn't.

With the underwater lab lighting their struggle, she picked a throwing star from her belt and released it at him, aiming for the arm that held the harpoon gun. It was a poor choice, one that she regretted as a waste of time. The water slowed and distorted the path of the star, and it went wide of its mark. He fired from about fifteen feet away. Maliha tried to twist aside but didn't quite make it—her movements were slowed in the water, just like those of her throwing star. The harpoon scraped her side and her blood trailed in the water. Her lungs burned in her chest. As he fitted another harpoon, she swam straight at her opponent and rammed into his belly. The harpoon gun fell from his hand and drifted to the ocean floor below them.

She started to swim up toward the surface and he grabbed her foot. She jackknifed her body, slid her last knife from her waist belt, and stabbed him in the shoulder. He released her foot and she swam urgently to the surface. There was no time for any precautionary stops to avoid decompression illness—all she could think of was filling her lungs. Her first gulp of air was a taste of life.

The fisherman's boat was gone. Maliha swam parallel to shore for a while, not wanting to come ashore in the place she'd started, in case the fisherman had decided something was fishy and called the police. Nausea and joint pain from her lack of decompression caught up with her. She'd experienced worse and knew she just had to wait it out.

Kill Number Two—Check.

She was struck midway in her swim with the movement of her scale. After unzipping her wetsuit, she floated on her back while a parade of figures painfully crossed her belly. Maur must have been a killer outside his council doings and her reward for dispatching him was generous. The pull through time barely registered.

She swam on her back and came to land some distance from the place she'd started. Her harpoon wounds were minor for her and the salt water had scoured them clean. When she got to shore, she bit her lip against the pain of the fresh scale balancing and splashed salt water on her bare chest. With the effect fading, she zipped up her suit and walked inland a few miles. She hitchhiked at the side of the Bruce Highway.

The first vehicle that happened along, a pickup truck with a male driver, stopped for her. She was barefoot, wearing a wetsuit with a couple of rips in it, and had no gear, but the man didn't say a thing about it. Maliha rode without fear with any human, since she felt she could handle any situation that arose, even weaponless. She wondered that the man, named Dac, wasn't afraid of *her*, a wild-looking apparition with tangled, damp hair and the smell of the sea on her.

Australian men are fearless. I want one.

Maliha went home with Dac and discovered that he made a living salvaging shells carried up on the shore by storms and selling them to tourists. She showered and changed into a clean shirt and a pair of shorts he set out for her. They were too big, but covered all the essentials. Dac came in and brushed her damp hair while they talked quietly about the sea and his goal of opening up another shop "unless I'd have to work too hard," which made them both laugh. He cooked her something delicious from the sea and they made slow, sweet love in his summer bedroom, outdoors on a screened porch.

Maliha woke a couple hours after dawn to the smell of coffee brewing and the sizzle of eggs frying. She'd broken her long-held rule of never staying the night with a casual lover.

"I hope you didn't need up earlier," he said. "You were sleeping so beautiful. The ocean does that, the rhythm of the waves. Me, I get up before dawn. Good time to walk the beach."

He looked her up and down. She'd slept in one of his T-shirts that said DAC SELLS SEA SHELLS.

"Your shop doesn't open for a few hours," she said. "How about taking me to Sydney?"

"How about taking that shirt off first?"

It didn't take Maliha long to decide that he had his priorities straight.

Later, he pulled up in front of her hotel. She felt a bit scruffy wearing his cutoff shorts cinched at the waist with a belt, a T-shirt pulled down over the belt, and oversized sandals he'd given her. He'd topped off the look with a straw hat that had been in his shop's lost and found for a year or two.

She started to get out and he stopped her with a hand on her wrist.

"You ever need a place to stay after a bit of night diving, you know where to come. You can stay as long as you like. I can make the place a lot nicer for . . . for a woman to live in."

She took it as a serious offer, one of the best ones she'd gotten, and so un-Jake-like.

Not that Jake had proposed. We didn't even have any kind of exclusive arrangement.

She hesitated for a moment, wanting to read his aura but not wanting to spoil the moment if he wasn't the man she thought he was. Curiosity won out. She focused behind him and let his aura come into view. His was beautiful. Clear bands of yellow and purple with areas of light pink that were the beginnings of love, the whole almost dancing about him. She slid close to him on the seat, kissed him in a lingering fashion, and then left.

In her hotel room, she changed clothes and folded the T-shirt up to keep.

Chapter Twenty-Four

Rasputin sat in the council's meeting room at the TGEF building in Washington, D.C. The meeting's start was ten minutes overdue. All of the monitors in the room were solid blue, showing no signal received. He was about to get up and leave. He had little patience for waiting for anyone.

That's it. If they want to have their little private discussions they can do it when I'm not warming a chair.

He was halfway to the exit door when three of the monitors came on.

"Going somewhere, Doctor?" It was the Frenchman, the one who irritated Rasputin the most of all of them for reasons he couldn't define. It wasn't anything superficial, like appearance or voice, because those were distorted by the monitor.

I think he's too damn smug. I'd like to get him on my operating table and . . .

"I didn't hear an answer."

Rasputin gritted his teeth. "Just thinking of getting a cup of coffee," he said, "since the meeting hadn't started yet."

"If you want coffee we can have some brought in. Or tea." It was the other man speaking, the one of indeterminate background, probably British. Even in his disguised form, Rasputin thought his cheeks looked hollower and his eyes a bit sunken.

Not sleeping well. Recent events, I imagine.

"Not necessary. Could we please get on with it then? Or are we waiting for the two missing members?"

"They won't be joining us." This time the Leader spoke decisively, or as decisively as one could with a garbled voice.

Rasputin already knew that, but thought he should appear ignorant of it.

"Status report, please."

Rasputin zipped through a list of countries and percentages of their populations infected with nanites.

"Your estimate of our time to activation?"

"Three weeks, maybe four."

"Cut it in half," the Brit said.

"There will be less penetration—"

"Something wrong with your hearing?" the Frenchman said.

"I was about to say there is no reason there can't be a second wave, as long as the first one is sufficiently damaging."

Rasputin wasn't surprised to hear that the council members wanted to move the timetable up, because they were worried about their own skins with an assassin running rampant among them.

The council had plans in place to swoop in to deal with the shock of losing the production and consumption capacities of the developing economies. Once set back with large population kills, the countries would be thrown into a recovery period measured in decades. Lengthened indefinitely, the council hoped, by new programs of suppression imposed from the outside. For their own good, the targeted countries would have to accept direct intervention from the outside. The council's plans were to shamelessly exploit that opportunity and move the devastated countries into indentured servitude, funneling all their wealth to the countries represented by TGEF.

But they knew that the global economy had intricate entanglements. Losing the targets would be a setback for legacy economies, too. Literally overnight, the inflow of cheap foreign goods would be halted. It would be a painful adjustment but one that according to the TGEF council was overdue, and could be smoothed out by advance planning.

They think they have plans in place to cope with all that. They are deluded fools who can't grasp the full extent of what they are doing. They are planning not just the demise of half a dozen countries but of their beloved legacy world, too, although they don't see it. Not right away, not as fast as the first rounds with the nanites. But it is a path to ruination and chaos that will spread across the world. Among all the Ageless, my achievement will be the greatest.

"Cutting the time in half requires substantially more money for distributors," Rasputin said. "Another one hundred million." It was a lot, but he knew he had them hooked. There was nothing they'd deny him now.

"Not a problem," said the Frenchman. "Money will be transferred to your working account."

"Agreed," said the Leader. "And I think a cushion of fifty million should be on reserve. Money should not hinder us at this point."

The other heads nodded.

Rasputin smiled, both at the thought of the extra money coming his way—only a fraction of which would be allocated to the nanite project—and the fact that both the Frenchman and the Brit would be dead soon—by the rogue's hand or his.

Chapter Twenty-Five

The city of Tel Aviv-Yafo perched like a majestic golden eagle gazing out over its dominion, the Mediterranean Sea. It was not lost on Maliha that there was an Israeli Desert Eagle handgun that was equally as in-your-face as the city she'd just landed in. A taxi to the White City took her through streets with office buildings, banks, and hotels that gradually yielded to cafés, parks, and the signature white concrete buildings designed by Jewish architects who left Nazi Germany.

Abiyram Heber's apartment building stood up on piers that let the desert wind sweep underneath it. She was about to enter the building when she spotted her friend working in the garden space set aside for residents.

She called his name, and he turned to look at her. He took his glasses down from where they were riding on his hat and looked again.

"Yes, it's me. Let's go somewhere we can talk."

"Come closer." He leaned on his rake.

He was about sixty years old. His hair had thinned and gone white. His cheekbones were sunken a little and his eyebrows had grown thicker, but his eyes were as sharp and intelligent as ever. There was still strength in his frame and he had the easy movement of someone long used to keeping his body in top shape.

"My dear." His voice was welcoming, but he didn't reach out to her. "It's been so long. What is it now, thirty years?"

"Yes."

He leaned forward and studied her face, his keen eyes taking in every inch. She knew he would question her appearance and would test her before he would accept her. She expected no less. She also knew that he was armed and would use his weapon if she didn't pass the test. Their meeting was like that of two lone wolves, each assessing the other. Abiyram's eyes scanned the vicinity for those who might be close enough to hear their conversation, even checking the balconies above. A few children played in the shade of the building next door, but other than that, they were alone.

"You are lovely, so lovely, just as you were when you danced with Oskar, what was his name, Oskar . . ."

He was referring to the minister of foreign affairs of East Germany in a mission with Abiyram in 1984.

"Mauser. I didn't dance with Oskar Mauser. I broke into his office while you regaled him with your stories of the arrest of the Butcher of Lyon the year before."

"Ah, of course. They say the memory is the first to go."

In your case I think it will be carved on your gravestone, "He never forgot anything."

"Remember when you smuggled that capsule to me right under Vatkov's nose? He never suspected that you dropped it into my drink. Hah!"

"We can reminisce all you want, Abiyram, but I know what you are trying to do and I don't blame you. I show up a lot like the woman you knew thirty years ago and you don't trust me. All right. Something that was not on any report, not known but for the two of us. When I passed you that tiny capsule, it was through a kiss. We were posing as husband and wife. You were so nervous that you bit my tongue."

"So I did, my dear. How did the unfortunate Louisa Kalb die?"

"Louisa Kalb burned to death in a car accident, but she is fictional. You made her up to have someone to blame for the loss of the Arkon papers that I stole from you, early on before we even knew each other well. You told me this later, the night I slapped your face for insulting Winston Churchill. Enough?"

"Why don't we get out of the sun?"

He took her to a fourth-floor apartment with a shaded balcony. They sat outdoors sipping wine.

"Tell me, how is it that you have remained so young?"

There it is. The question I'd hoped never to be asked. Three choices: lie, tell the truth, or be mysterious.

"I'm not at liberty to say."

"A medical experiment or reconstructive surgery?" He took her hand and held it in his, then reached out for her face. "You are about fifty-five now, yes?"

"About that, yes. *Give or take three centuries.*

"Tell me of this process."

"As Shakespeare wrote, 'There are more things in heaven and earth, Horatio, than are dreamt of in your philosophy.' Consider this one of those things."

He was silent for so long that Maliha thought he would soon kick her out as a lunatic. Finally he leaned over, pressed hard on her arm, and then poked her skin in a couple of places. Suddenly, with a small blade that appeared from nowhere, he made a cut on her forearm. She didn't flinch, but blood welled from the wound.

"You watch too many movies. I don't have green blood. I'm not an android. I'm not going to unscrew my arm or something."

"Let me get you something for that cut."

While he was gone, she kept squeezing the slit in her skin so it would keep bleeding and wouldn't close. He came back with a bandage and in a minute the wound was out of sight. He had made no apology for cutting her.

"What did you come here to talk about?" He reached for a bowl on a table between them and offered it to her. "Peanuts? I grew them myself."

She took a handful. "I want to ask a favor."

"I owe you my life. Ask, and if it is within my small power, I will do it."

"I need information on the location of three people and background on a fourth."

"That's all? You are spending a life-debt on such trivia?"

"It's urgent. I don't have time to network for this. I'm . . . active in the field." She knew he would interpret that to mean she was tied up on an assassination mission. "It's very important. Many innocent people will die if I don't find them."

"You have my full attention. Give me what you know."

She reached into her small handbag and pulled out an envelope. Inside were printouts of the photos from Fynn's disk. The thought of the scientist triggered memories of Rasputin's destruction of Fynn's family. *Mother and child are dead.*

She shook her head to clear the memory of Betty Sue sitting motionless, her throat slit. *The Black Ghost has no time for such things.*

"First, Vincent Landry, France." She handed over the photo.

"Don't know him. But I know someone active in France who might."

"William David Hall, England."

"I've seen that face, once, years ago. I might be able to get to him fast."

Maliha nodded.

"Third, a man or woman who goes by the name of the Leader and works with a secret council based at the Tellman Global Economic Foundation in Washington, D.C. I'm starting from square one on the Leader. No photo, no profile, no name."

"Tellman Global Economic Foundation. Go on."

"Last, I need background on a DEA agent, Jake Stackman, in particular on how he spent five missing years of his life." She gave him Jake's photo.

The white eyebrows pulled together and shadowed his eyes as he frowned. "Is the fourth related to the case of the others?"

Maliha lowered her eyes. "Stackman is not likely to be related to the others."

Jake had told her that he still wanted to talk with her about his admission of continuing to kill after his demon

no longer cared. He implied that there was a reason, and
without anything else to go on, Maliha had decided to look
into his missing years he'd asked her to take on trust. The
more knowledge she had, the better. If anyone could get that
information that Amaro couldn't find, it would be Abiyram.

"I see."

"I don't ask lightly."

"Then I will devote myself to finding the answer, as with
the others. And then I will dance at your wedding. You must
allow me that privilege."

She nodded. The word *wedding* tugged at her heart.

"Now I may have something for you, my dear. You collect certain archaeological items. Tell me about them."

"Another test? I network with archaeologists worldwide,
asking to be notified of any artifacts that are out of place—
they're too advanced or too primitive for their time, or they
simply don't belong in that location. Anomalies. If anyone
contacts me, he or she gets to be a character in my next Dick
Stallion book. The scientists love it. Most of what I hear
doesn't turn out to be the right stuff, but I give them credit
anyway. Did I pass?"

"What are you looking for? What is the right stuff?"

"Falls under more things in heaven and earth."

He sighed. "I thought it might. I came into possession of
a map that may be just such a thing a few months ago. Fate,
eh? That you should come out of my past now? I have been
studying it. Perhaps it will be of interest to you. I don't want
to be in one of your books, though. I've read one, though I
didn't know you wrote them. Dreadful."

"Most honest review I've ever gotten. Show me what
you have."

"Give me a moment."

He returned with a leather portfolio case, about a foot
and a half on each side. Unbuckling the briefcase-like fas-
tener, he displayed a piece of parchment with roughened
edges. "It's a rubbing taken from a stone, showing directions
to a location in the Omo Valley area of southwest Ethiopia.
Colors were added after the rubbing was done, so that it

looks like a painting. What is peculiar about it is that it is made of papyrus from roughly the year 1040, yet the writing on it is in various languages considered long dead by that time, including Sumerian. I am something of a linguist, yet one of the cuneiform variations isn't known to me. Odder still, the India ink used in those writings dates from a thousand years prior to the creation of the parchment."

"Where is the original stone?"

"Supposedly in a portion of the Sof Omar Cave, also in Ethiopia. It was embedded in the wall of a small room that was flooded by the Weyb River four hundred years ago and remains so today. It was that river that originally carved the underground caverns and it has, throughout recorded history, filled some of them and drained others, almost at whim. No one knows which room holds the stone, except that it is not in any of the presently accessible rooms."

"Has anyone else seen this?"

"Quite a few people. Copies are being sold in a curiosity shop in Addis Ababa. I was shopping for a present for a grandniece and wandered into a little shop. There was the map, in a glass case behind the counter. I asked about it and the woman said it was very old and that she had hand-painted copies for sale. 'A map to a priceless treasure,' she assured me. 'If I were not so old and my back so stiff, I would hunt for it myself.' It is beautiful, isn't it?" She held the parchment to the sun. The colors glowed warmly. "The shop owner wouldn't sell it to me, so I bought a copy. I waited a few days, came back, and stole the original. I left her a large compensation. She must have been satisfied, because she didn't report the theft. Is the map of interest to you?"

Maliha struggled to keep the eagerness off her face.

"I'd like to look at it. Probably isn't the right stuff." She reached out to take the portfolio. He hesitated for a moment, reluctant to part with it, and she could see why.

"What I search for is of great importance."

He sighed and handed it to her. "To your safe return." He raised his wineglass to her.

"To success, for both of us," she said, and clinked her glass with his.

"I will do my best."

Abiyram invited her to his bedroom. She didn't hesitate. There were perks to being the Black Ghost.

Later, at her hotel, Maliha pored over the map. The first thing she went after was the cuneiform that Abiyram couldn't read. Her contract with Rabishu had been written in the same form. Her heart beat wildly when she translated it.

Anu, son of Anshar and Kishar, leaves this for the children of the Great Above, should their wisdom grow.

It was exactly the same inscription that she'd found on an artifact from Peru, which had led her to the first shard she'd collected. She ran her fingertips over the markings as though they would leap from the parchment, the whole thing springing into the air in front of her, as her contract with Rabishu had.

That is the writing of Anu, either by his hand or by his direction. This is the being who tips my scale from afar, from the third sphere of existence, where distance and time don't matter, as Rabishu told me.

Rabishu had been talkative when it came to the Great Lens and the Tablet of the Overlord. But he'd kept from her their true purpose, which was dominion over the demons, including the option of killing them all by reading their individual weaknesses engraved on the tablet. This power was supposed to fall into human hands when humans advanced enough to figure out the purpose and location of the shards and tablet—and be able to retrieve them, a whole other story. In the attempts she'd made so far, she didn't see how anyone but a demon's assassin who'd taken the mortal path could do so on behalf of the human race. One of the Ageless certainly could—as Lucius had, by taking the shard she'd discovered—but they were bound to their demons and wouldn't act on behalf of the human race.

It seemed that Anu had set things up so that only someone who had been through the black years she'd experienced and then made a decision on the side of hope could ever free humans. Right now, it was her turn. There must have been others who tried, because Rabishu had said no others of her kind had succeeded in balancing their scales, let alone put together the lens and tablet. If she didn't succeed, the next opportunity might not happen for a hundred years or a thousand. Or ten thousand. She didn't know how often the Ageless gave up immortality.

Perhaps the others had made personal redemption their only goal and couldn't see beyond that. The way I see it, even if they had achieved balance and gone to the paradise of the third sphere, they would have failed. Failed the humans they left behind.

Alone in the world, she was carrying both the fears and the hopes of the human race, and very few even knew about it.

With the Great Lens and tablet in hand, she could control the demons or kill them. She thought for a moment what it would be like to be able to order Rabishu around, to have him do her bidding as she'd done his bidding for centuries. She could free Lucius from his contract with a snap of her fingers. She could make herself immortal without having a demon do it.

What's done with the Tablet of the Overlord and the Great Lens is the last test for the advancement of the human race. If they are used for petty reasons, we are still a child race mired in chaos, this time of our own making and not the demons'. If the demons are destroyed, we have a chance to move on. To what, I don't know, but it's gonna be a wild ride.

Too much time spent trying to give shape to the future gave Maliha a headache. Deciding that fresh air and some exercise would help her thinking process about the map, she went out for a run. Discovering quickly that no one else ran in the afternoon sun, she wandered onto the promenade and rented a bike. It was a grand trip on the wooden walkway, with the sun warming her shoulders, the Mediterranean to one side and the skyline of Tel Aviv to the other.

I should move here for a while. It's a wonderful city, wonderful climate. I could stay here to spend time with Abiyram, move when he is buried. Or at least spend ten or twenty years here. I don't have to pretend around him, and the more I was here, the more of my story would come out to him. He'd be another member of my family.

Stopping for a drink at a beachfront café, she bought lemonade that was strong enough to pucker her lips. A man stood next to the table she'd taken in the corner.

"You are a tourist, yes?" His English was lightly accented. Ulster, she thought, but it had been schooled out of him.

Ignore or engage?

He was in his thirties, fit enough for a guy who almost certainly had a desk job. Dark eyes behind wire-rim glasses, dark hair in a businesslike trim. An analyst, probably in a junior role looking to move up. She dropped her eyes and checked out his body in an obvious fashion just to see what he would do. When her eyes came back to his face, he just raised his eyebrows: *So what did you think?*

That level of attention from Maliha would fluster many men. Instead, he slid into the chair opposite her.

Either very smooth or very oblivious.

She thought about giving him a night to remember, but she found herself reverting to preferences established when she was the Black Ghost. If he wasn't romantic, powerful, rich, an incredible physical specimen, dangerous, or all of the above, she didn't want to fuck him. She was keenly aware that Jake qualified on all five, but the world was full of perfect fives.

Including Lucius. Okay, I've admitted it. In RandySpeak, Lucius is über hot. Then there's Dac, who only scores in the romantic category, maybe half a point as a good physical specimen but not incredible, yet my night with him is something that keeps popping into my head. I don't think I'll ever forget it. Does that mean romance trumps all the others?

"I was here to attend the medical conference. Cardiovascular research, at the Hilton." He jerked his head to the right, which as far as Maliha knew from her basic orientation in the city was wrong. He'd just indicated the old city of Jaffa. "I only have one night left before I go home to England."

Mmm. He's no more a doctor than I am a . . . beach ball.
She'd caught sight of some children outside the Lemon Tree
Café batting one back and forth.

"May I buy you another lemonade? They're really good
here. Or something stronger? My name's Scott, by the way."
He thrust out his hand. "And you are?"

She was reading his aura, finding it menacing and dark.
Very controlled, contained, possibly murderous. An aura
with a stain spreading over it. Her concern must have
flashed across her face.

"Something wrong?"

White Rabbit time.

"I'm late for a very important date."

She stood up, brushing past the arm he put out to block
her exit. It seemed like rejection didn't suit him. As she
was leaving, she saw him approach the table of another
lone woman and sit down. The woman smiled and started a
conversation.

A simple pickup or something much worse? Damn.

She reached for her phone to call the police, then considered. What was she going to say? *But Officer, you need to
arrest him because of his aura.*

She hesitated outside the door of the café. Her bicycle
beckoned. The sun was setting over the Mediterranean,
a sight lovely enough to wipe thoughts of Scott from her
mind. Almost. *The Black Ghost would walk away. If that
woman ends up raped and fed into a meat grinder, it's none
of my concern.*

They came out of the café together. His arm around her
waist looked a little too possessive, too soon. Creepy. *Oh,
to hell with the Black Ghost for now! Something's off here.*

She left her bicycle and followed them on foot. The
parking lot set back from the beach was crowded, so Maliha
didn't have to worry about him picking her out as following
him. Besides, he was totally focused on reeling in his catch.

Don't get in his damn car, you idiot woman!

He handed her the keys and she got into his car, in the
driver's seat.

Shit, shit, shit! It's as if he's using mind control.

She was aware of the experiments in China, North Korea, Russia, and the United States. But all of them required some sort of preparation of the subject. Unless this woman was a plant among the customers, previously prepared and susceptible to Scott's proposition, mind control wouldn't work. Or did Scott have something new here?

Hah! A plant in the Lemon Tree Café.

Maliha zipped along sidewalks or wove in and out through traffic when necessary, at a fast run or a blindingly fast run, whichever was called for. It was a long drive. The woman headed north into the wealthiest areas of the Tel Aviv District, home to the upper class of business leaders, the wealthy who made their retirement homes here, and a sprinkling of foreign diplomats.

I should turn back. This is a guy who got lucky and picked up a woman. So he has a dark aura. Lots of people do, like me, for example.

The car turned in at a narrow driveway. Maliha followed. When the car pulled into a circular drive and the two occupants got out, she was already poised behind a pillar near the door. Maliha picked up the woman's name, Florence. It was nearly dark and suddenly lights around the estate flickered on for the night. Maliha was hidden, but her shadow was not.

Holding her breath, she watched as Scott and Florence walked within a couple of feet of part of her shadow. She needed to remain in position because she was going to run inside when Florence opened the door, and had to be at the correct angle to make it in.

I can't believe I'm doing this. I should be back in my hotel room planning my expedition to Ethiopia.

Maliha was following a hunch and most of the time, her hunches panned out. Florence paused outside the door, leaning against the door frame.

Maybe she's having second thoughts. Run, Florence! I'll make sure he doesn't follow you.

Scott, trying to look cool, had one hand on the frame above Florence's head and was gesturing with the other as they talked. With the couple in that position, Maliha wouldn't be able to make it through the door without knocking them aside. She was close enough to hear the conversation, which was about Scott's export business. Finally, they turned to go inside. Scott opened the door, stepped in, and typed the password into the alarm system panel inside the door to disengage the alarm. Florence entered the front hall and Maliha followed as soon as she could without being seen. The door nipped her heel as she dashed in and found the first available room to hide in—an old-fashioned parlor for greeting guests. The couple passed her and leaned against the outer wall of the parlor.

Maliha heard some panting and moaning going on, and from her vantage point she saw articles of clothing flying onto the floor. There was low talk that she strained to hear but couldn't quite make out, and she couldn't stick her head out into the hall. Then, instead of their footsteps going upstairs, where she assumed the bedrooms would be, she heard a door being opened nearby. They'd disappeared into the lower level.

Maliha emerged from the parlor. The door they'd gone through wasn't fully closed and she sidled up to it to listen. She felt a bit ridiculous. Worse than the usual Peeping Tom, she was inside where the action was. She thought she heard sounds of lovemaking coming from the slightly open door to the basement. She quickly ducked back into the parlor.

Maliha had almost convinced herself to leave, when she was astonished to see Scott come up from the basement. He was nude, and she could see hundreds of small scars on his body, everywhere that would be covered by clothing. She got a queasy feeling in her stomach. She'd seen that before, only all the cuts were bleeding at once: an old Chinese method of execution known as *língchí*, death by a thousand cuts.

Scott came back with a large knife and went into the basement, confirming Maliha's fears.

She pushed the basement door open with her foot wide enough to see Florence, naked and spread-eagled, tied on a bed. Scott straddled her and began cutting with the knife. Cutting his own arms, letting the blood run down Florence's breasts.

What the fuck?

Maliha had the feeling that Scott was in his warm-up phase, and that soon he'd be cutting Florence rather than himself. She kicked the door open and ran down the stairs. Scott, still astride, looked over at the intrusion wide-eyed. He was just starting to react when she reached the edge of the bed and lunged for his knife-wielding arm. Grabbing his wrist, she twisted it and heard bones snap. The knife fell to the bed and Scott screamed in pain.

Yanking his broken wrist, she pulled him off the bed. She wrapped her arm around his neck, then pressed hard on her arm with her other hand, making a very efficient noose. She had him in a blood choke, compressing his carotid arteries. He raised his good hand to try to pull her arm away, but it was too late. In seconds, he was unconscious and she let him drop to the floor. If she'd continued the choke longer, he would have been dead.

Maliha drew a small knife from its sheath at her waist and cut the ropes binding Florence to the bedposts. Florence sat up with her legs over the edge of the bed, rubbing her wrists.

"He was going to kill me."

Maliha nodded. She didn't feel the need to explain that Scott would have killed her slowly, over two or three days, with hundreds of small cuts like the ones he bore on his body. "Here's what we do now. We go upstairs—"

Florence grabbed the knife from the bed and ran at Scott's unconscious body. Maliha blocked her.

"You don't want to do that."

Florence tried to slip by. "How the hell do you know what I want? Let go of me!"

"I'm not trying to minimize what you went through. Right now you can get counseling. Pull your friends around you and get your life back. If you kill him, he owns you. Even if you get away with self-defense, you'll think about him every day for the rest of your life. Put the knife back."

Instead Florence offered Maliha the knife. "You do it then."

Maliha inhaled deeply. She stared at the knife, which already had Scott's blood on it. She could easily add more. She could be the instrument of Florence's revenge and wouldn't lose a lot of sleep over it either.

"Your goal is to strike with no chance of recovery," Master Liu taught. *"An underhanded strike is always best. Point the tip up under the ribs, aiming for the heart. Be sure to enter below the ribs or the point may be deflected. A sudden jab overcomes the resistance of the skin and membrane beneath. Visualize the passage of the blade through the body as though you were guiding it with your mind. Continue upward until the heart is reached. With practice, you can feel this entry. Give the blade a twist to enlarge the heart wound. Always pull out the knife to allow a path for the blood to flow out of the body. If time permits, you may also slice the throat to speed bleed out."*

Maliha's brain played out the practiced movements in muscle memory. She started to reach for the knife.

Then she shook her head. "No. The law can handle this. Come upstairs with me, or don't."

She went up the stairs and into the hall. A few tense seconds later, Florence came after her.

"I didn't do it."

"I'll block the basement door. No, don't touch your clothes. Let the police give you a blanket." Maliha took a chair from the dining room across the hall and tucked the top of it under the doorknob to form a brace. "This is going to be a tough time for you, but you're a strong woman. You already showed that."

"What shall I say about you?"

"Say someone must have heard your screams. I'm going to break in the door so it will look like your rescuer came in that way and left before the police arrived."

Maliha went outside. It was a heavy door with a strong lock. She backed up about thirty feet, took a run at the door, and flew through the air to strike it with a powerful blow from both feet. She crashed into the hallway, with the door flat on the floor beneath her.

"Call the police now."

Maliha waited outside until she heard sirens, then started to walk to the hotel, thinking that maybe she should give up casually checking peoples' auras as she had in the Lemon Tree Café.

The pain started on her abdomen, and she sat down on a bench to wait until it passed. She leaned back as figures walked across her belly from one pan to another, leaving burning footprints in her skin, her reward for saving Florence's life and future lives that Scott would have taken if he'd remained out of prison.

Maliha wrapped the Black Ghost around her again and let it sink in deeply.

Chapter Twenty-Six

At the hotel, she cleaned up and slept for hours. In the middle of the night, she got up and spread the copy of the treasure map out on the desk to study it.

There were hundreds of map copies out there, maybe thousands, depending on how long the shop had been selling them. There was bound to be a certain small percentage of buyers who believed the woman's story and set off to find the treasure. The majority would have turned back after a few days in southwestern Ethiopia. There are some expeditions on the Omo River but nothing like the tourist tours on the Nile. And an expedition wouldn't go into the areas indicated on the map: up tributary streams and into the territories of tribes who have little or no contact with outsiders.

But there were plenty of adventurous treasure hunters in the world who could hire local guides and go off the beaten track. What if someone had already claimed the shard? It could be in some private collector's display case.

Or worse, in the hands of some demon? I might not be the only one Lucius is tracking. And what if the council reaches their launch point for the hitchhikers while I'm out running around in the wilderness? I could stay here and beat the bushes like everyone else. Try more long-shot sources. Abiyram's working on it, though, and that's the best I can do.

The pull to go to Ethiopia was strong, but there was a dilemma. On the one hand, there was the search for information on the location of the council members. On the other, a clear path, literally a map, to something that would move her closer to the greatest goal she could accomplish. Objectively, it was a tough decision, but her instincts had already made the choice.

She phoned Amaro and told him the basics of what had gone on with Abiyram. The conversation was a bit stiff but he didn't raise any of the complaints from their last talk.

"So you're on hold with the hitchhikers?" Amaro said.

"Until I come up with locations for the two remaining council members and the Leader, I guess so. I want you to keep digging."

"Oh, I am. Are you sure you should be doing this?"

"Going after the shard? I feel I have to."

Maliha's attempt to buy a packraft and go alone into the Omo wilderness was met with laughter by the outfitter in Addis Ababa, but money prevailed.

She had no time to spend days driving across Ethiopia to get to the point where she could begin using the map. Using Hound's contacts, Amaro rented a helicopter for her.

Her pilot was a Canadian nicknamed Cargo. He'd ferried food relief across Eritrea to starving Ethiopians in the mid 1980s famine and decided to stay on. He knew the countryside well. He kept up a conversation extolling his own adventures in Africa when he was younger. Now in his early sixties, he claimed he'd still be on those adventures if he didn't have a bum knee, which he slapped regularly during the conversation as if to punish it. Finally, he got around to curiosity about his passenger.

"Where you headed?"

"To do some white-water rafting."

"Eh, you could take one of the tours."

"I like the solo challenge."

He looked Maliha up and down.

"You done this kind of thing before?"

"I'm an old hand at wilderness adventuring. It's a wonder our paths didn't cross back in the eighties."

Cargo frowned for a minute, then burst out laughing. "A good joke! Okay, I'll stay out of your business. Just wanted to make sure you knew what you were getting into."

She gave him the coordinates for her drop-off and pickup spots. He shook his head.

"Drop-off's okay, pickup isn't. You need to be farther down, where the valley opens up into savannah."

"You tell me then."

They settled on a spot. "How much time?"

"A week."

When Cargo landed the copter, they were about a mile away from a put-in point. Maliha strapped throwing knives to her thighs and put the whip sword around her waist. The packraft, rolled into a tight bundle, rode low on her back with two backpacks above it. Last to go on were the foldable paddles on either side of the two backpacks. Cargo whistled in amazement.

"I guess you do know what you're doing. You got guns somewhere in all that stuff? This isn't the zoo, you know. The shit out here takes big bites out of you. What about fresh water? You drink that river water, you're gonna regret it."

"I've got everything I need. I'll see you downstream in a week."

She waited until he'd taken off, then started out at a fast walk on the path to the river. Maliha didn't expect to meet anyone because it was a little-used entry point, allowing practically zero float time before entering a stretch of rapids. Most tourists liked a combination of floating and running. She inflated her raft at the edge of the Omo River. Repeatedly filling the inflation bag, like blowing up a beach ball, she squeezed the air into the raft. She unfolded one of the paddles and tied it to the raft. The other one, a spare, was fastened in the bow of the boat with her other supplies. She made sure the map was secure in its waterproof container. The river's center channel was showing some rough water and rocks, and it was going to be difficult to get out there into a clear passage. With a packraft only five feet long, she wore it as an extension of herself as well as paddled it, meaning her body movement made a lot of difference. Out she went into the swirling river, paddling and maneuvering hard, and got the raft oriented before the water got worse.

The Crayne expedition is launched.

The first day was routine. The river passed through heavily forested hills. Between rapids, there were deep pools where hippos and crocodiles sunned themselves. Shrieks of colobus monkeys came from the trees and butterflies coasted lazily over the river. She spent the night on a sandy beach, but expected it to be the last beach she'd run across. She ate packaged food and drank from the river, in spite of Cargo's warning. The traveler's disease didn't strike Maliha. Her immune system wouldn't allow it.

The night under the stars was peaceful. She was comfortable with the jungle sounds around her.

In the morning Maliha sat cross-legged in the sand and examined the map. Her first key point was the mouth of a tributary and she believed she was close. If she didn't spot it today or at the latest tomorrow, she'd missed it and would have to start all over. It was unlikely she could hike back and put the raft in again in time, so that meant she'd lose her chance on this trip. The map was drawn in a rough three-dimensional manner, but not like an artist would render it accurately. It was more like a child's version, an attempt to use perspective to draw cliffs and hills and forests and the sheer-sided gorges that the river passed through.

She tried aura vision on the map, although she thought it was a long shot. Plants and animals had auras, subdued ones but there, but non-living things didn't. She turned the map over, held it to the sun, experimented with overlapping one portion of it onto another—nothing worked.

The map was simple. There were only two landmarks on it to get to the shard, not a complex series of them. At times her search felt hopeless—surely someone would have beaten her to the spot by now, with directions as simple as go to Point A, go to Point B, claim the prize.

There was something else she needed to be thinking about, but she wanted to wait until she'd passed the first milestone. She had to assume that somewhere out there, Lucius was following her, possibly running the riverbank as she ran the rapids, and that he intended to steal the shard if she found one.

Back in the river, she watched the shores intently. She entered a run of white water of a higher classification than she'd encountered the day before, probably a level V. Large waves pummeled her little raft, and it was hard to find the passage among the large boulders. It was the type of rapids she should have scouted first or even portaged, because she wasn't here for the thrills. The raft dipped and rose as she guided it expertly. Maneuvering around rocks, water flooded over her and she could barely see. Shaking the water from her face, her eyes widened as she caught sight of water pouring into the river from a narrow canyon on her left—the tributary!

She worked her way through the rest of the rapids and when the water calmed, she put in to shore on the west side of the river, where she'd seen the canyon. There was no sandy beach here, but a steep incline leading directly into the forest. She wouldn't be going any farther down the Omo until it was time to go to her pickup destination. It was late afternoon, but she broke everything down for trekking and loaded the packs on her back. With several hours of daylight left, she started walking back upstream. The noise of the rapids drowned out the jungle sounds, drowned out everything, including her thoughts.

She reached the canyon's edge and walked along it. Mist rose from the water at the bottom of the canyon as it tumbled over boulders on its way to join the Omo. The forest closed in around her and it felt like a primeval place, as it could have been—many archaeological finds had been made in southeastern Ethiopia. A leopard paced nearby, curious, close enough to take her measure but far enough away that she just caught glimpses of it. Birds called and flew and displayed their exotic colors. She spent the second night under a canopy of leaves so dense it was as if there were no stars.

How to keep the shard from Lucius? I could run with it but he can catch me. Appeal to his sense of fairness? Hasn't worked yet.

She had brought along with her something that she hoped might give her a chance. It was a tranquilizer gun, loaded with a dart that could be used on large animals.

Large animals. Giraffes. Hippos. Roman centurions? Would it work on him, or delay him long enough so I can break his neck again? I don't think he'd let me get close enough to do it otherwise.

She stopped for lunch, packaged hiker's food and bottled water. Afterward she examined the map again. Her next milestone was a cleft in the canyon wall shaped like a snake's head. That was it, point B, where the shard was hidden. She ran her fingers over the cuneiform writing, marveling again that Anu had in some fashion written it. To her amazement, the design on the map blurred as she did so, just like the writing on the Tablet of the Overload that spun by too quickly to read without the Great Lens. She watched it until her eyes hurt trying to follow the movement, and all of a sudden it stopped.

She blinked. Another section of the map had been revealed. The snake's-head cleft was the starting point of another journey. Maliha grinned. All those copies of the map that had been sold meant nothing. The heirloom that had been passed down in the shop woman's family hadn't done any of her adventurous family members any good. Nothing had. Not until Maliha, who had translated Anu's writing, brought the map here had anyone seen the secret portion.

Her heart sang, and it seemed like the jungle around her sang with her. The time was right and she was the right person to claim the shard. Quickly packing up the remains of her lunch, she was on her way. She might reach her destination before dark.

At the snake's-head cleft she turned south, away from the tributary. There was no need for her raft from this point on, so she left it at the canyon's edge, carefully concealed, along with one of her packs. Traveling lighter, she made better time even though the ground was rougher. She was descending into a valley that showed no trace of human influence. Even the animals were friendlier, crowding her with their curiosity. Maliha's excitement grew as she passed several more milestones. The conviction also grew in her that somehow, she would keep this shard from Lucius.

As the sun was setting, Maliha checked the map and put it away for the last time. The trail ended at a waterfall, and she could hear it ahead of her. On the valley floor, darkness would come quickly, and she wondered if she should wait until morning to retrieve the shard. Her excitement over-ruled her practicality.

The waterfall was a thin flow that cascaded in three stages. At the base, mist rose high and covered everything. Trees dripped, rocks were slick, and her skin was immediately coated with a fine spray when she drew close. The full moon, high in the sky, shone through the mist, giving everything a dreamlike quality. Maliha moved forward in the mist to the edge of the deep pool at the base. The spray was harder, her clothing was drenched, and her hair, braided down the center of her back, was plastered to her neck.

She left her backpack in a sheltered spot so she could move ahead unhindered. The only things she took were the dart gun in a leather belly pack and her throwing knives strapped to her thighs.

The shard was embedded in a wall of rock behind the curtain of the waterfall. It glowed as she approached, though it was impossible for it to catch the light of the moon in its location. She touched it, and it came loose in her hand immediately. She slipped it into a pocket.

She turned, and through the mist she could see an imposing figure waiting beyond the curtain of water—Lucius. She didn't think he could see her yet, but was waiting for her to emerge. She drew the dart gun and loaded it. She intended to fire the instant she was clear of the falling water.

Approaching stealthily, she reached her arm through

the curtain, reached a little more to fire, and slipped a little
on the wet rocks. She regained her balance right away, but
she'd given away her position. With nothing to lose at that
point, she fired the dart at the shape now coming toward her,
and continued moving until she was in the open.

Lucius was there, right in the path of her dart, and in less
than the blink of an eye, he wasn't. The dart flew on into the
night. She loaded another dart, but had lost her advantage
of surprise.

I will not give up this shard!

Maliha took off at the fastest speed she could manage,
her Ageless speed of old, through the fog. She knew she
couldn't outlast him but maybe she could trick him somehow, fire another dart, and get away. At any moment she
expected his arm on her shoulder, yanking her to a stop. She
wove among trees and rocks, over exposed roots, and cursed
the moon that had been her fortune up until now for trailing
her with a shadow.

"Stop . . ."

She heard his voice whispering like the wind to her, and
pushed herself harder. She threw one of her throwing knives
back over her shoulder in the hopes that he was close behind
her and it would slow him down. The sides of the valley
were steep, and she began panting. She was burning through
her resources. If she didn't find a way to outwit him soon,
she'd have no energy left to move or fight.

Maliha ran up the side of a tree, injuring herself on
branches that weren't aligned for that kind of stunt. When
she reached a good height, she flattened out on a thick
branch and tried to get control of her breathing and her
racing heart. She had run almost until she dropped, many
miles from the waterfall.

*I should hide the shard and lead him away from it. What
good will that do? He'll just follow me when I come to
retrieve it.*

All the buoyancy she'd felt earlier, all the wonder at the
way the map responded in her hands, had drained from her.

There is only one thing to do.

Slowly she climbed back down from the tree and sat at its base. She knew it wouldn't be long before Lucius found her.

He was there within a minute, walking forward, sword drawn. She stood up, leaning against the tree to hide her weakness.

"I follow the orders of Sidana," he said. "Hand me the shard and you can leave."

She shook her head. "Do you know about Rasputin and the people he is protecting? What their plans are?"

"Rasputin's plans don't concern me."

"You saved me when I was trying to stop Rasputin."

"Only so you could find more shards. My demon orders . . ."

"Fuck your demon. Listen to me for a change."

Lucius sheathed his sword. "Talk then."

She drew the dart gun from behind her back and fired. Lucius barely avoided it, then came at her at high speed and twisted the gun from her hand. He threw it into the forest.

"Will you talk or do you have more tricks to try?"

She explained to him about the nanites and the scheme to set back emerging economies. Although he was highly intelligent, living on his island and remaining mostly withdrawn, he had some catching up to do. He absorbed it quickly and asked pertinent questions. Then he thought about it and began offering his analysis.

"Isn't it good strategy to weaken your opponent for a battlefield advantage? This council is using war tactics that have been around for thousands of years."

"Where is the war, Lucius? The war is only in their minds. They are demented. Even if there was a battle here, there are honorable ways to fight it and then there is treachery."

He turned away at the sound of the word. She knew there had to be a personal meaning for him.

"Is that how you ended up as Sidana's slave?"

"My wife . . . As a centurion, I was gone for long periods of time from home. Sometimes years. My life was dedicated to the army. If she had taken a man for companionship, I would have understood. On those times when I could make it home, I would again have her heart. But she took to her bed a man who convinced her to marry him so he could have my lands. For her to marry him, I had to die. His name was Caius and he was once a friend of mine. We grew up together, then I became a soldier and he lived off women whose brave husbands were away. He killed me himself, one night in my tent while I was asleep. Gutted me with a short sword and made me die painfully, in a foul pool of my own innards. When Sidana pulled me to him I was ready to claim my vengeance. Was it this way for you?"

His story brought it all back. Losing Constanta, her husband stoning her, the satisfaction of taking vengeance on the woman who'd accused her of being a witch . . .

"Yes," she said simply. "But I found a way to change. You can, too." She reached out to him but he stood resolutely several feet away. "Join me. Or at least give me time to stop the horrible plot to kill so many innocents."

"Give me the shard."

"I intend to remove the scourge of the demons from Earth. I would sooner die than give it up. I ask you to return the shard you took from me."

"You would knowingly suffer Rabishu's eternal torment rather than give up on this dream of yours to possess the Great Lens?"

"It's not a dream." As she said it, the idea crystallized within her. *My redemption is only one step of my quest, and not the most important one.*

She saw sadness on his face.

"Then there's something I have to tell you. I have been ordered to force you to drop everything else you are doing in an effort to collect as many shards as possible in six months."

"Six months? It has taken me years to collect three—" she clutched the shard to her chest—"including the one you have. Why six months?"

"Because that is when I kill you."

She was silent for a moment. Everything had just fallen apart for her—her goals, her whole life. There was no way she could kill the demons in six months, so she would die at Lucius's hand. "That's what your heart tells you to do?"

"No. My heart is screaming—"

The pain of her failure made her lash out. "Damn you, Lucius! You're a coward! Stand up to your demon and spit in his face!" The instant she said it, she wanted the words back. It wasn't fair of her. He'd been an assassin so much longer than she had, six times longer, that there was no way he could balance his scale. She had no right to goad him like that, to ask that sacrifice of him. She dropped her head in shame. "I'm sorry."

Just as on his island home, she'd pushed one too many buttons with Lucius. He charged forward and pinned her against the tree, his sword at her throat. She barely managed to get her hands between the blade and her neck, and she'd had to drop the shard to do it. Her palms were no barrier. They were bleeding, and all he had to do was lean forward with his strength and her head would be on the forest floor.

His legs blocked hers hard, preventing any movement. There was no gimmick, no defensive move she could make. No argument she could make on her behalf after what she had just said. Her eyes overflowed with tears and they streamed down her cheeks.

Good-bye my friends. I love you all. I'm so sorry to have failed.

She closed her eyes.

His hand brushed her cheek. She opened her eyes to find him looking into her face. His eyes glistened with tears in the moonlight. Then she realized the pressure on her hands had let up and his sword was sheathed. He took her bloody hands and held them to his chest.

"What have I done? I almost . . ." He stepped back from her and dropped to his knees. His shoulders hunched as if a great weight had just settled on them.

"Hear me, Sidana! I defy your order! I despise you, you foul snake! I am no longer your slave."

Maliha fell to her knees and wrapped her arms around

him, ignoring the pain from her hands. She knew what would happen now. Lucius would be pulled into Midworld, where his demon could meet him halfway between the Underworld and the Great Above. She clung to him, not wanting him to go, wanting him to take back the words that she'd urged him to say just moments before.

It's my fault, it's my fault.

He started to fade and she hugged him tighter. Suddenly she felt the wrenching pull to Midworld, familiar to her but slightly different because she was being drawn into Sidana's presence, not Rabishu's. There was no time to think, and then she was there. She and Lucius were a tight package, and couldn't separate, just as she hadn't been able to move much when Rabishu drew her to Midworld.

It surprised her that both of them were naked.

The clinging, malodorous fog had a different feel. It seemed to get into her mouth, her nose, everywhere, and when it reached her stomach she felt nauseous. Unable to back away from Lucius, she turned her head and tilted her body as much as she could as she vomited. She heard him do the same.

She wondered how Sidana would appear. Her demon had taken various forms, each more hideous than the next, it had seemed to her. Nothing happened for a while, and when Maliha tried to tell him she was sorry, he wouldn't hear it. So they talked quietly of small things, anything that didn't have to do with what was coming.

Or rather, who was coming.

The stench of rotting bodies increased.

"The demon comes," Lucius said. "He appears as a snake."

As he said it, Maliha felt a horrible crawling sensation around her legs, a heavy, coiling shape that was warmer than her skin and dripping with slime. She shuddered. The snake came all the way up her back. She could feel the soft flicking of its tongue as it tasted different parts of her body. Finally, the demon dragged a heavy loop over her shoulder so he could look into her face.

The tongue darted over her closed eyelids, under her ears, and just when she was frozen with the thought that Sidana was going to invade her nose and mouth, Lucius leaned forward with great effort and covered her face with his, kissing her. She felt him flinch, but he didn't move until Sidana pulled back. When the kiss ended, Maliha saw that the snake had bitten Lucius in the cheek to punish him for blocking the way, and a bit of his flesh hung in shreds.

"Stay away from her, demon. She's not yours, just as I am no longer yours."

I make no claim on her.

The demon's voice came into her head, low and mean. Then Maliha was separated from Lucius as though a giant hand had scooped her up. Dumped several feet away, she found that she couldn't move from her new position, just watch.

You are another story.

Lucius was suddenly pulled upright, his arms over his head, his feet several inches off the floor. Blood dripped down on his chest from his torn cheek. As she watched, his feet remained in one spot but the demon was pulling on his arms, like stretching a piece of taffy. She tried to yell, but she could only emit a squeak. Before his shoulders were torn loose from their sockets, the demon let go. Lucius collapsed.

"Lucius," she said as loudly as she could, "fight back!"

Her words galvanized him. He looked over at her and regained the spirit he'd had when he first talked to the demon.

"I defy you and your orders. I break my contract!"

The snake rose up, standing on its tail, towering over them.

"Are you too ignorant to understand?" Lucius said. "I'm not your slave anymore! I demand that you send the woman back now!"

The demon blasted his anger in both of their minds. Lucius swayed on his feet.

"Stop this delay. I want to see my contract."

Blood shot from the circle on Lucius's chest, the de-

mon's mark, the point where Sidana extracted blood from
him to sign the Ageless contract. At every beat of his heart,
more blood flew from his chest. The demon dropped to the
ground, slithered to the spot where the blood had pooled,
and dipped his mouth in it. Maliha closed her eyes as the
demon drank.

My last taste of you, at least for a time.

The fog rose up in front of Lucius and flattened into a
wall. Writing in cuneiform began to scroll up it.

Your contract.

The demon breathed on the fog to slow the scrolling and
then to stop it.

*It says here that failure will not be tolerated. You may die
now at my hand or you may live a while longer in the Great
Above, but either way you will die. I will enjoy punishing
you for your insolence.*

Lucius can't read the contract, Maliha thought. She tried
to shake her head at what Sidana was saying and couldn't.
She forced some words out, barely able to whisper them as
her throat constricted. "You have . . . chance. Anu . . . says."

Rogue, the demon roared, *stop your interfering!*

Maliha was swept away, propelled to the Great Above
none too gently, and landed back at the tree. The sun was
shining, so hours must have passed even though she felt like
she'd been gone a short time. His weapons were there, as
were hers, and the shard.

Sick with worry, she hoped that Lucius would force the
demon into admitting what Anu had forced them to put in
the contracts, that each Ageless slave who rebelled should
be given a chance to earn back his soul. If Lucius took the
first bargain that the demon put on the table, as Rabishu had
tried to do with her, he would be doomed, with no scale.

He'd asked for her help before, asked her to talk about
how she left her contract when she was on his island, and
what did she do? Break his neck and leave.

She wondered whether to backtrack miles to the waterfall
and retrieve her backpack, with food, clothes, and the map

in it, or wait here for Lucius's return. She decided that it would likely be hours more before he came back.

Naked, her palms aching from sword cuts that had begun to heal, and with a heavy heart, she picked up the shard and started backtracking. It took longer than she'd anticipated because she'd covered a lot of ground in her panicked run. She had to pace herself to have enough energy to make the distance both ways. On her way back, she hurried, imagining Lucius there, dazed by the whole experience. She wanted to do everything she could to make his transition to the mortal path easier for him than it had been for her.

He did it for me. I can't ever forget that. He did it so he wouldn't have to take my life in six months, so I could continue searching for shards.

When she got near the tree, she was disappointed to see that he wasn't there waiting for her. He'd been there, though. At the base of the tree, there were bloody footprints—his, meaning that he was bleeding from his fresh scale carving. On the tree trunk, he'd left her a message, chipped out with the tip of his sword.

It was a heart with their initials in it.

Emotion overwhelmed her. Lucius, who had saved her life three times before and now had taken rogue status so that she could live—after all of that, he loved her. She dropped to her knees in front of the tree, clutching the shard to her heart.

Lucius, your sacrifice won't be in vain.

Chapter Twenty-Seven

Maliha was barely back in Tel Aviv, her emotions as raw as Lucius's new scale, when Abiyram notified her that he had news. She went to see him. Again they sat on the balcony.

He studied her closely. "You seem distracted, my dear. Or sad? What can I do for you?"

"Nothing except what I have already asked."

"The map. May I ask if you have had any success with it?"

"It was the right stuff."

His eyes closed and his face relaxed, she thought in pleasure.

"And did you bring it back to me?"

"No. I returned it to the shop woman in Addis Ababa."

"Ah! I paid that woman a great price! Now she has my money and the map."

"You stole the original from her, and it is back where it belongs. Consider instead that you paid a large price for the copy you have."

"You always could run rings around me. You are so much smarter than I."

"Catherine the Great always said that she praised loudly and blamed softly. Where is your soft blame?" Maliha said.

"You have already had it from me. You gave back the map that wasn't yours to give. Ah." He shrugged. "It's only money." He laid his hand atop hers, familiarly. "This mysterious process of yours. It is not something I could . . . become involved in?"

She hesitated. "Why would you wish it?"

He sat back in his chair. He was wearing a straw hat and sunglasses, and she thought he looked debonair.

There is nothing wrong with his age. He's healthy, and stubborn. He'll probably live another fifty years.

"I have lived a certain kind of life. A life dedicated to my country. You know, you are the same. I've done many things that don't give an old man peace of mind. It's not that I regret doing them. It's that I want to have another chance, another life in which I don't know and do these things. When I grow this old again and go to bed at night, I would sleep easily, except when I get up to take a piss. There are good things I could do."

She was quiet a long time, trying out and discarding different answers. "There is no process, Abiyram. My story is long and hard to explain. But I promise this to you. When I am done and can come back and take some time off here, I will tell you that story. You may end up joining me in something that I am trying to accomplish. And then you will live that life you are talking about, the one where you get to do good things. But it will not make you physically younger." She smiled. "I have a friend who would dispute that you are old."

"I'm intrigued. Let's put it all aside and get to what I have found. The Brit—I knew I'd seen him before and it didn't take long to track him down. William David Hall, former British Secret Service. Pushed out very quietly as a suspected mole, nearly executed, but calmer or stupider heads prevailed. Turns out he wasn't a mole after all, but by then the damage was done to his career and he couldn't go back to his undercover job. Didn't want a desk job, he liked the thrill. He doesn't seem to have held any grudge against England because the switch turned him on to a much higher lifestyle. He made a large amount of money in financial advising, and he kept his identity a secret from his customers. Some said he used inside knowledge, others that he was just a financial wizard. In any case, he must have loved the secret trappings of it."

"Where is he now?"

"He has a house in London and an office in Hong Kong, but he hasn't been at either of them for two to four weeks. He's in Latvia, in a ruined castle. I suspect he has some kind of personal fortification there."

"A safe room, in other words." She got the location of the castle from him.

"Anything on Vincent Landry or the Leader?"

"Nothing yet."

"Thank you. This helps immensely."

Abiyram waved his hand in dismissal. "This is the work of my life. This information is traded on the international market like eggs."

He omitted the fact that he was retired, making Maliha wonder if he really was. "Only if the trader is you, my friend."

Chapter Twenty-Eight

Maliha was on her way to kill William David Hall.

She hadn't had occasion to visit Latvia since the dissolution of the Soviet Union. If not for all of the other things crowding the top of her agenda, she would have stayed a few weeks or months collecting background material for a Dick Stallion book.

That was another thing sliding toward a deadline—her book *Too Big To Be True*. If she could manage to do one normal thing, she should phone her editor, Jefferson Leewood, and warn him that things would be close. Just the thought of dealing with Jeff, who lived his day from one crisis in his own mind to the next, was too much today. She could ask her agent to move the Dick Stallion series to a new publisher after the current contract ran out. The books were wildly popular. But Jeff had taken a chance on her when she was a nobody, so out of loyalty she'd stay with him. Besides, he sent her a fruit basket every year.

During her flight, she had some quiet time, and her thoughts revolved around Jake and Lucius.

She was holding the door open for Jake, at least a small crack's width, until she had her talk with him and learned more about him on her own.

I owe him that. Or do I? He's been so deceptive with me. She thought back to how she'd met Jake and how their relationship had gotten started. *But I can't say that I was honest with him either.*

Lucius was out there somewhere dealing with his new situation. He hadn't been in touch with her after the message carved in the tree, and she had no way to get in touch with him. She'd looked for L. A. Cinna, but he'd vanished. She could only assume he was back on his island, recuperating and planning what to do next.

The heart he'd drawn might as well be engraved on the inside of her eyelids. She saw it constantly and it was never out of her thoughts.

Well, almost never. Alarm bells were going off about the proximity of the full-scale launch of the hitchhikers, and she was ready for what was coming: the increasingly difficult tracking down and killing of the remaining council members and the challenge of finding their leader.

Her phone rang, and she was surprised to hear Yanmeng.

"Is Amaro—"

"Yes, he's wiping the call. Hello to you, too."

"Sorry. I was concerned about tracing or leaving a phone-company record."

"I'm concerned too, Maliha. All—"

"You're in a secure place. Nothing's going to happen to you."

"I mean about you—"

"I told you I can take care of myself."

"Would you shut up and listen for a minute?" It was the first time Yanmeng had ever raised his voice to her. She hadn't realized she'd been drowning out his words and genuine concerns.

"Sorry. Speak your mind." She had a feeling Yanmeng was not alone in making this call. She pictured Hound and Amaro sitting nearby.

Uh-oh. Did Yanmeng draw the short straw?

"We're concerned about the way you've gone off on a killing mission. Multiple kills. You're treating this like you're Ageless again."

"This again? How would you know how I'm acting? Are you watching me without permission?"

When Yanmeng remote viewed Maliha, she could tell him to go away with a hand signal. He was supposed to honor that and she always assumed he did.

"No. But if I did, what would I see that's made you so defensive?"

"I'm not defensive. We all agreed that the Tellman council needs to be wiped out. Now you're quibbling about how I do it?"

"You've got us locked away—"

"For your safety."

"Granted, for our safety. But you're slipping away from us on this. You want to operate in some kind of hidden mode."

You wouldn't understand, and you've just proved it.

"I have to find out who these people are and track them down. You don't think a little stealth is required?" Maliha was getting exasperated. She didn't understand Yanmeng's concern and resented the questioning of her methods.

"We just don't want to lose you."

"I always kill alone. I don't see you there helping. The burden's always on me. Now why don't you lose my phone number and let me work?" She hung up the phone.

And regretted it immediately. *What's gotten into me? I can't believe I treated Yanmeng that way, even if I don't understand why he's so concerned.*

She dialed the shelter, and this time Hound picked up.

"You can really be an asshole sometimes," he said.

"Yeah. Is Yanmeng still around?"

"He said he had a headache and went to lie down."

"What's going on there? Are you all getting paranoid or something?"

"Hell, no. We're all fine. What's with you and this secret shit?"

"I'm looking for the targets in old ways, that's all. Sources I can't reveal."

"Listen to you. Targets. Sources. You turned into a spook?"

"If that makes it easier for you to understand, yes."

"Spooks give up their humanity, you know. What's left of you if the human part's taken away? That's what we're worried about."

Arriving at the Riga airport, she rented a Škoda from the Europcar counter and left the city immediately. She'd brought with her everything she needed in her checked luggage. She was heading east, on the main road that crossed Latvia and went straight to Moscow. She'd have to go on country roads later, but for a while it was smooth going. Her destination was Volkenberga, the castle on Cloud Mountain.

She got to the ruined castle, a minor tourist site, after dark, and that was perfect for her purposes. It took nerve for a man to create a personal panic room in a tourist attraction. She wondered how many of them he had sprinkled around the world. She had about a hundred of them, but none were in tourist destinations.

Maliha packed carefully, both weapons and the padded cases she needed to get into the panic room. Then she climbed to the top of Cloud Mountain. The wooden steps the tourists used in the summer were covered with snow. She walked next to them, using snowshoes and pulling her supplies behind her over the snow. The pine forest she was in was dense enough to block out the stars. The weather in Latvia in November was bitterly cold during the long nights and her breath came in great plumes that tracked her progress through the woods. She checked with her aura vision to see if Rasputin was with her. All that showed were the smaller, pulsing auras of animal life nearby. She paused to marvel at an elk passing by, shimmering against the dark trunks of the trees. It scented her, startled, and was gone. Moments of beauty like this made her appreciate the unique life she led.

As an assassin, I travel the world and see things few people do. That underwater base aglow with lights, where I'd killed Cort Maur. A place of beauty, like Cloud Mountain. Death and beauty.

She searched the ruins, knowing that the crumbled stone walls were probably not the site of Hall's room. She wanted to make sure she wasn't leaving him a clear escape route. She looked for ventilation shafts, but suspected they would be too small to notice, especially in the dark. There would be a number of them, probably forming a network under the snow.

An assassin, that's what I am, demon's slave or not. Then I killed for chaos and evil, now I kill to save lives, but I still kill, kill, kill. Am I really different?

Satisfied that she'd done her best aboveground, she found the entrance to the catacombs. With a flashlight covered with her hand, she made her way down a dank passageway and found the steel door within minutes. Set to one side was the fake rock panel that normally covered it. She immediately used her dimmed flashlight to search for cameras in the wall and ceiling. They would be concealed, with just a small lens among the rough rock surface.

Not finding any, she turned her attention back to the door. The rest of the room's construction depended on when this room had been built. In the past safe rooms were made of concrete all around, but she couldn't figure out how Hall could have hauled concrete into a public site during the summer. It would be impossible to do it during the winter. If the room had been built recently, the steel door would be the same, but the ceiling, sides, and floor of the room would be protected with layered Kevlar fabric set into the rock. Now that could be smuggled in during the winter, with no one around.

With the flashlight on low and tucked into her coat pocket, she pulled a small ax from its sheath on her back and began chipping away at the rock next to the steel frame. The noise no doubt warned Hall, if she wasn't already in view on a camera she'd missed. She chipped past the frame and discovered a Kevlar wall.

She heard a click, like some gear turning in her direction, and she leaped away from the spot she was occupying. A bullet, fired from the ceiling, entered that spot.

She flicked off the flashlight and moved back down the passageway, she hoped out of range. Without light and having to move quickly, she stumbled several times and caught herself before falling.

Heading back into the passage, wary, her flashlight set on high, she scanned the walls and ceilings as she should have done instead of trying a stealth entry. She found four cameras on the low ceiling, including the one right outside the door, and destroyed them with the point of her knife. She found the weapon embedded in the ceiling and put it out of commission.

Now. Where was I?

She enlarged the exposed Kevlar area with her ax and then brought out one of the two special items she'd brought with her. It was a metal halide lamp, a super-high-intensity UV source. She set the lamp up at close range, put on special dark sunglasses, and walked back down the passageway until she rounded a corner before pressing a remote ignition.

Kevlar had a weakness. UV light degraded it, which is why it was rarely used in outdoors without a sun shield—such as the sun-blocking layer that covered it in applications like body armor. Degradation took time, but Maliha had put a focused industrial source three inches away from it, and she didn't need total degradation, just enough to yield to her ax.

In an hour, she turned off the light and went back. With a few swings of her ax, putting all of her strength into it, she dug through the first layer of Kevlar. Shine, repeat. In three hours she had a hole big enough to insert a flexible camera and get a view of the panic room.

Hall was in there, all right. He was staring back at the camera from across the room. It was small—only eight feet across—but packed with weapons and survival gear. The first thing she did was check his aura and was relieved to see that she hadn't put in all the effort to break into Hall's safe house to find that he was a sweet cherub of a man.

From all the supplies she could see, she wasn't going to starve him out anytime soon, and time was on his side with the hitchhiker project. He started to move, coming toward the camera with something in his arms she couldn't make out right away.

Oh. It's a . . . Her camera went dead. *Bolt cutter.*

In place of the camera, Hall shoved the point of a sharp rod through rapidly, hoping to catch her eye with it. She jerked away, caught the rod, and yanked it away from him. *This guy is pissing me off.*

Before he could get the idea to block up the hole she'd worked so hard to create, she slipped a blowpipe into the hole and shot a tranquilizer dart into his ass as he retreated.

From then on, with Hall not causing trouble, things moved smoothly. She blew the steel door off from the inside using C–4 inserted through the hole. Hall didn't die in the blast, but there wasn't a lot of killing left to do by the time she got to him. She snapped his neck. Unlike Lucius, Hall wouldn't be recovering from it.

She hadn't expected the mission to be so . . . *exhilarating.*

Being the Black Ghost is so much simpler than being Maliha Crayne, woman with a conscience.

Chapter Twenty-Nine

Maliha phoned Hound. They agreed to disagree on her method of work, at least for this conversation.

"Amaro found some info on the French guy, but he said the last group conversation didn't go so well, so he was hoping you'd check in. Then Randy dragged him off to bed."

"Really?"

"I mean, made him go to sleep. Alone."

"Oh. Is Glass okay there?"

"She's fine. She's stuck with me making her do her rehab exercises. She says none of the other physical therapists ever cursed at her before."

Maliha couldn't help smiling. "So you think she's had it too easy?"

"Damn straight."

"Before we get to Landry, let me say we can scratch William Hall off the list."

"Good."

"I'm getting nervous about not turning up anything on the Leader. I would bet he—or she—is the one with a finger on the button, or whatever it takes to launch the hitchhikers. Wiping out the rest of the council might be just what he had planned anyway, and I'm just an unpaid hitman. Tell me about Landry."

"Okay, Amaro's got notes here. Reading his words now. 'Very wealthy man, just like Hall. Interesting that you have picked up on this man. He is the grandson of a Nazi collaborator, one who was responsible for exporting Jews from France to the concentration camps during World War II. Not that Landry should pay for his grandfather's crimes, but he is a person of dubious repute on his own.' You know Amaro wrote that. I wouldn't say dubious repute in a million years. I'd say he was a . . ."

"Go on."

"There's more. 'Landry lives on a large estate, heavily guarded I'm told, in Normandy, near Les Pieux. The exact source of his wealth is unknown, but he is thought to be a major player in putting together illicit arms deals, a facilitator.'"

"I'm on it."

Driving through the Normandy countryside lifted her spirits. She turned off all of her concerns for a short time and enjoyed the sunshine. The weather was chilly, in the low forties, but cows roamed in pastures looking for the last green tidbits of summer and the bare branches of apple trees cast tangled shadows on the hillsides. She'd spent twenty years living here in a cottage overlooking the ocean between the two world wars. Rabishu hadn't given her an assignment during that time. She'd lived simply in spite of the vast wealth she had to draw upon, grew herbs in her garden, watched the waters of the English Channel, and gently turned away suitors.

Not all of them. There was Jules. Sitting outdoors with him, the sunset, wine, Camembert, fresh bread . . . I should do that again for a time. Go live with Abiyram. Sit on his balcony and drink wine and watch the world go by.

She approached Landry's estate. From the road, there was only a gate and a guard shack visible. The main home must be set back over the small hill she could see that had a driveway wrapping around it. She kept going, waving at the guard who, in a moment of unprofessional zeal, whistled at her.

There were several campgrounds in the area and that's

where Maliha stayed. Reading in her tent by the light of an LED lantern, she heard the conversations of neighborly campers outside and smelled the BBQ'd dinners they prepared. Someone "knocked" on her tent flap offering a glass of wine, but she said she wasn't feeling well, and was politely left alone after that. When the sounds died down in camp, she turned off her lantern. Time for reconnaissance.

Maliha ran through the night with her full array of weapons, her body a deadly bullet aimed at Vincent Landry. Crouching behind some bushes, she observed the guard shack. It looked like such a simple arrangement. One guard, carrying a sidearm, a phone on the wall in the booth, and controls to open the gate.

This is what Amaro reports as heavily guarded? There must be an inner perimeter.

She threw some rocks into the road away from her position. The guard immediately focused on the noise. She sprang from her position, ran as fast as she could toward the gate, leaped it, and kept going. The gate camera would catch her only as a momentary blur. If there was a motion detector, and she assumed there was, it would have gone off in the guard shack and in the central security area. Visual checks would show nothing except the camera blur. The verdict: An owl had swooped nearby, close enough for the motion detector, and left a shadow on the camera.

At least it sounded good to her.

At a full run she topped the hill in a couple of seconds, came to a stop, and crouched in the grass to look around.

The long, curving gravel driveway ended in the middle of a field of grass. No fancy mansion. No six-car garage. Not even another guard shack. Behind the area where·there would have been a home was a sheer cliff, shaped like a horseshoe, fronting the ocean.

The approach is by water then. No wonder the security out front wasn't too impressive. There probably wasn't even a camera or a motion detector. The guard who whistled— just some guy standing there to keep the tourists out.

She walked over to the cliff's edge, flattened herself

on the grass, and looked over. Because of the shape of the cliff, the water contained inside churned as waves bounced off the sides and collided. It wouldn't be an easy approach by water. She thought she saw some openings in the side of the cliff, but it was too dark to see clearly and they weren't exactly spotlighted. Her best approach would be to return with technical climbing gear and rappel down the cliff.

Maliha was at the top of the hill walking back when she heard the noise of metallic gears coming from the field spread out below her. She turned around to see a section of the earth lift and slide out of the way, not large, maybe ten by fifteen feet. Rising up was a platform that held a vehicle, a van. The vehicle's headlights were on, preventing her from getting a good look at the driver. The van pulled onto the gravel driveway and when it rounded a bend, she had a clearer view. There were no passenger windows and only the driver in the front seat.

If this happens often, I can ride down on the top of that van. Easier than flinging myself off a cliff.

She returned the next night with her bag of goodies, approaching cross-country this time, avoiding the dummy guard setup. She waited for several hours, hoping for a vehicle to arrive so she could ride down with it. Finally she abandoned the plan. She was going to have to reach Vincent Landry the hard way, by going over the cliff.

At the cliff, Maliha looked over and positioned herself above a point she thought was an opening in the rock. She set three anchors, stepped into the leg loops of her climbing harness, pulled it up, and fastened it securely at her waist. After attaching the relay device with a locking carabiner, over the edge she went, ready to make a controlled fall down the face of the cliff.

The opening she chose was a round ventilation shaft, but it was one of twenty or more that she could see honeycombing the cliff. There were so many because each of them was small, less than two feet in diameter. Not only that, the outside of each shaft was covered with a grate, and judging by the dead birds piled on the ledges below, the grates

were electrified. The mesh on the grates was small—small
enough to keep out bats. There was nothing to recommend
her chosen shaft over any of the others. It would be luck of
the draw whether it led her anywhere interesting.

She pulled up the end of her rope, which was dangling
down the cliff. Slicing off a length of a few feet, she threaded
one end of it through the grate. Very carefully, she reached
her finger through and tried to hook the end of the rope. If
she could just get enough of her finger on it to pull it toward
her, she'd have the rope looped around the wire of the grate.

Finally she got it. She evened out the ends of the rope,
yanked hard on them, and the grate moved a little. She had
to plant her feet on either side of the shaft and tug with all
her might, and the grate popped loose. It tumbled down into
the water below.

Her shoulders barely cleared the shaft's diameter. With
a piton in each hand, she maneuvered herself inside, head
first, and detached herself from the rope. Using the pitons
like clawed extensions of her hands, she pulled her way
forward into the shaft. For the first thirty or forty feet, the
shaft was rock, and not very smooth rock, either. It tore at
her clothing as she moved along. Then she came to a shiny
metal section. Still using the pitons, to punch holes in the
metal, she moved forward at a cautious pace.

*I feel like a mole in a tunnel. How long is this thing,
anyway?*

Just as she thought it, the shaft began to slope more
steeply downward. She started to slide forward on the
smooth surface, and the air around her became warm and
humid. She couldn't use the pitons any longer. They slid
away from her down the shaft and disappeared.

Uh-oh.

Suddenly she was dangling in the air, her hands grasping
the sharp metal edge of the shaft, about fifteen feet above
the floor. The metal was slicing her fingers, so she let go and
made the best of her landing, doing a parachutist's bend and
roll. She twisted her ankle a little but it was only a minor
hindrance.

Looking around, she found she was in a laundry room. Clouds of hot, steamy air issued from the washers when their doors opened and they tilted their contents into the yawning openings of industrial-sized dryers. The room was busy, but there wasn't a person in sight. Everything was automatic.

Out in the hall, moving cautiously, she found another automatic room—a bakery, going full tilt. A few fresh loaves of bread waited for the morning, and other items were in various stages of preparation.

Getting creepy. Does Landry run on automatic, too?

She was obviously on a utility level. Moving up a staircase, she expected to encounter armed guards. She came out into a warehouse filled with crates, presumably weapons bound for terrorist use, since Landry was a smuggler. No people, but the elevator she'd seen in operation led to this level. There were security cameras on the walls, missing from the lower automated level. Somewhere, in some security headquarters in this building, she was already on camera.

Is anybody watching?

She decided to try the elevator, which was a simple platform in a shaft, ideal for holding vehicles. The elevator was responsive to her press on the call button. There were four more levels in this place before the surface level.

She got on and pressed the button for the next floor. When the door opened, a dozen guards were waiting for her, assault rifles ready to cut her apart. Someone had been watching the security camera. She raised her hands in surrender.

She waited until they got closer to her and exploded into action. Side kicks to the temple put a couple out of commission immediately. As soon as she started moving, bullets started whining through the air. She took shelter behind a column as bullets impacted nearby. The guards didn't seem inclined to rush her, preferring to stand back and shoot. She pulled the whip sword from its sheath at her waist, flicked it to separate the two long, flexible blades, dashed across the line of fire at superhuman speed. She snapped the whip sword repeatedly, leaving arcs of blood and a trail of severed limbs as the fast-moving blades cut through flesh. The guards were just starting to scream when Maliha made another pass at speed behind them. This time the whip sword swept low, severing legs at the calf, leaving the stumps standing as the men toppled. In seconds, the area was the site of a bloody massacre. Maliha wasn't even breathing hard.

Something in her was protesting, but she shoved it down. *Too bad about them. They were in my way.*

She took a dead man's Uzi and slung it over her shoulder. She moved farther into the level, which encouraged her that she was on the right track by its luxurious appointments.

The next group didn't make the mistake of asking her to surrender. They just started firing as soon as they spotted her. She dove behind a large bar, but took a bullet in the calf as she went flying through the air. Behind her, liquor bottles shattered on their shelves, hit by the weapons fire. Maliha laid the guard's Uzi on top of the bar, squeezed the trigger, and raked it back and forth until the cartridge was empty. Any guard who wasn't under serious cover was dead. She peeked around the edge of the bar and earned a burst of gunfire. It seemed that there was only one guard left.

"I don't want to kill you," she called out. "If you want to live, put down your gun."

"You're out of bullets," the guard said. "Why should I give up now? I've got spare clips and help on the way."

"Why should you give up? Because I can do this."

Maliha had his location pinned down from his gunfire. She swung her arm up vertically over the bar and launched a throwing star. If he hadn't moved, he'd survive it.

There was a scream from the guard. She looked around the bar and saw that her star had landed in his arm, right at the elbow. A disabling shot. While he was staring at his wounded arm, she put another star in his other arm. The rifle clattered to the floor.

"I'm going to come over to you and if there's any prob-lem, I'll kill you."

She saw him nod vigorously. He'd pulled one of the stars out, causing bleeding. He stared at the blood and then at her.

She crossed the distance. "Where's Landry?"

The guard moaned.

"Where's Victor Landry?"

"Uh, next floor. Locked in. Nobody gets in there but the women he calls. You know, for sex."

"Women?"

"He keeps 'em locked up. Down that hall. Don't kill me. Please. I've got a daughter."

What if your daughter was in that locked room, waiting to service Landry?

Her knife went for his throat but at the last second, it was as though something inside jerked her strings like a puppet, diverting her hand. She knocked him out instead. He would probably be all right until help arrived later. She was tempted to visit the room of women and let them out, but it could be some kind of trap. Also, there could be women in there vulnerable enough that they'd fallen for whatever line Landry used, and were loyal to him.

There didn't seem to be any more guards on this level. She raided the extra clips of some of the dead guards and stored them on her belt for additional firepower. Limping back to the elevator, she favored the leg with the bullet in the calf. Maliha tore a piece of a guard's uniform and wrapped her leg tight enough to staunch the blood. She could feel the bullet grinding painfully against her bone, but there was nothing to be done about it now. She had to walk, run, and fight on that leg.

She thought of Lucius, moving off into the forest naked, with a fresh scale carving that must have been agony compared to her leg wound. In his pain, he'd taken time to leave a message of love and hope for her. It put her wound in perspective.

She rode the elevator to the next floor, prepared for a reception the same or worse as on the women's floor. The door opened to nothing but halls and rooms. Straight ahead of her, at the end of a long, dimly lighted hall, was a giant of a woman standing in a spotlight. She was at least seven feet tall, wore a loin cloth, a sword belt with two swords, and nothing else. Her skin was as tawny as a lion's and as burnished as the belly of a Buddha statue.

Maliha felt overdressed. She resisted the urge to cast off her clothing to match the giantess's level of undress. If they'd been alone, she might have done so. But she was certain Landry was watching, and she wasn't going to allow this encounter to give him any more enjoyment than what he was already getting from the nearly naked, muscular giantess. Her opponent drew swords that looked five feet long. Combined with her arm length, that gave her a reach of about nine feet.

Fighting sphere with a diameter of eighteen feet.

Maliha slipped the Uzi off her shoulder and sent a rain of bullets down the hallway. Just because the giantess was waving swords around didn't mean Maliha had to respond in kind. She'd seen *Raiders of the Lost Ark.* To her astonishment, right before the bullets were about to hit her opponent, they struck a clear barrier and fell to the floor harmlessly. It looked as though Maliha had to engage the giantess on her own terms.

Maliha threw down the Uzi and walked toward the barrier. When she got there, it slid into the wall.

The woman looked her up and down. "I have heard you are a great warrior. What you lack in size, you must make up in skill."

"Vincent Landry exploits you, as he does the women on the floor below for his pleasure. He is watching you now. Put down your weapons, and I will spare your life."

"You think that little toad shares my bed? Hah!" She spit on the floor. "I'm here because my lover thinks this man is doing something important. Soon it will be over and I will gut Landry myself. I despise his appetite for girls. A true man appreciates a true woman."

She arched her back and thrust out her breasts, and Maliha agreed: There was no doubt this was a true woman. A woman and a half.

Maliha was getting an idea she didn't like and decided to test it directly. "Tell me your name and the name of the demon to which you are beholden."

"What is this nonsense? My name is Duma and I am beholden to no one. My lover is my only equal and he is known as the Leader."

Maliha feigned disinterest, even though Duma had just admitted to being on intimate terms with the man Maliha had begun to think didn't exist.

"If he is your leader, then how are you his equal?" She thought she had a good chance to trip Duma up through her pride.

"He is the leader of these small-minded men whom he uses for his plans. To me he is . . ." Duma frowned. "Enough questions. The only thing you need to know is that I will separate your head from your body. Come, let us test each other!"

Duma didn't wait until she'd finished speaking. She lunged forward with one of her great swords, aiming for Maliha's midsection, and swung the other sword at Maliha's shoulder height. Maliha sidestepped one, ducked under the other and leaped toward her, getting inside the range of Duma's swing. Maliha used the techniques of Wing Chun for close-in fighting, particularly effective against a larger opponent. She made vertical fists and attacked Duma with short, powerful punches. She pummeled the core of Duma's body, the centerline where Duma drew all the strength for her massive sword thrusts. The fist strikes were meant to kill—the nose, the throat, and finally the solar plexus, but Maliha carefully controlled the force. She didn't want Duma dead yet. With the last blow, Duma had the wind knocked out of her and staggered backward. She dropped one of her swords.

Before Duma could recover from the spasm of her diaphragm, Maliha opened her fists and rammed both palms into Duma's chest, cracking ribs and sending the giantess over backward. Maliha quickly took up a position behind Duma's head and held a knife to her throat. Duma raised the sword she was still holding and tried to bring it over her head to dislodge Maliha, who easily kicked the sword away and sent it spinning across the floor.

Duma, trying to recover from the punches, unable to gulp air because of the searing pain of the broken ribs, lay on the floor in a very unaccustomed position of defeat.

"Who is the Leader, Duma?"

"You can't have the satisfaction of killing me!" Duma suddenly bit down hard on her tongue. Blood flowed and she gagged, then spit out a piece of her tongue that showed the remnants of a capsule that had been embedded in its flesh. Moments later, Duma started convulsing.

Maliha slit her throat, then used the knife to stab her in the heart. It was a quicker death than poison.

She stood up and turned her head away. Maliha felt as though she'd taken advantage of the dead warrior lying at her feet. Duma fought proudly with her strength and speed, and in this instance, Maliha had used it against her.

She felt like a female coyote, the trickster of Native-American myths. In some stories, Coyote was the bringer of death. At a time when death affected only animals, Coyote and Eagle went to the world of the dead to bring back their wives. The wives' spirits, along with many others, were collected in a box. When they left the land of the dead, Coyote heard his wife's voice coming from the box and was too eager to see her. He opened the box and let the idea of death escape into the world of humans.

Trickster or bringer of death—either one seemed to fit Maliha tonight. And she wasn't finished.

She made her way down the rest of the hall warily. There were security cameras but no guards. She must have exhausted the private contingent of security forces.

Somebody's watching me but letting me advance, or can't do anything about it.

At the end of the hall there was another of the clear barriers.

"Come in." A male voice offered entry and the clear door slid back.

She entered a darkened room with a panel of monitors

showing camera views of most of the places she'd been. On one wall there were huge images of outdoor Normandy scenes, playing in a slideshow. Behind the room they were in, she could get a glimpse of other rooms, a bedroom, exercise room, and some for which she couldn't determine a purpose.

Looks like Landry doesn't get out often.

"How do you like my snug little home?" he said. Landry was in his early fifties, pale, with small eyes and hair so fine and skimpy that at a quick glance he could have appeared bald. He reminded Maliha of some cave creature that never saw the light of day, and most likely he didn't.

"Your home's fine but your hospitality stinks. Not too happy with your harem, either. I've heard rumors that you like your girls young. Your pet warrior Duma didn't approve."

"What Duma thinks, or thought, I should say, doesn't matter. I assume since you've joined me that she's dead."

"You should know. You were watching her ass the whole time, you sick bastard." Maliha jerked her head in the direction of a couple of monitors that showed Duma's body from different angles.

"Did she say anything about me?"

"Yeah. She said you had the littlest dick of any guy she'd ever seen. Look, I'm not here to chat with you, Landry. I want to know who the Leader is and when the nanites are going to be set off."

"You're very desirable. I'm sure you've been told that. A little old for my taste, but I've been known to make exceptions."

Did I hear that right?

"Are you offering me information for sex?"

"You've been around. Can't be the first time."

"First thing in a confrontation," Master Liu said, "find out who is in charge. It had better be you."

"Let me explain something to you," Maliha said. "You can tell me about the Leader. Or not. But don't waste my time."

Landry began to reach for a gun hidden behind his desk. She spotted the movement, dashed over to him, and got him in a hold with his revolver pointed under his chin.

She hitched his arm higher, just short of dislocating his shoulder.

"Fuck you." Spit drooled down his chin from the vehemence of it. He'd put every bit of the pain he was feeling, his fear, his disgust at her entry into his private quarters into it.

With a strong elbow hold on him and his legs pinned against the desk, she pulled the gun away from his throat, released the latch and swung the cylinder out. With her hand inserted into the frame of the gun to hold it, she pressed her fingertips over three of the loaded cartridges and tipped the gun so the other three fell out to the ground. Closing the cylinder, she spun it and put the muzzle back under his chin.

"Tell me who the Leader is."

"No."

She pulled the trigger. *Click.*

Sweat broke out on his face. "You're crazy!"

"Feel like talking now?"

"You're crazy! I can't tell you anything! He'll kill me!"

"Then you'd better be ready to die now." She pulled the trigger again. *Click.*

Landry started shaking uncontrollably. He'd been so protected, shielded for years, in his cave home with his guards and his cameras and his warrior queen that the bravery of the man who dealt arms with some of the worst the world had to offer was in tatters.

Without saying anything, she pulled the trigger for a third time. She and Landry both lucked out.

"Been counting? I think the odds are pretty damn good, like one hundred percent, that your brains get blown out the next time I pull the trigger."

"Wait! I swear I don't know much. I don't know who he is. I swear I don't know who he is!"

Maliha relaxed the pressure on his arm a little, decreasing the pain. "What is it that you do know?"

"I know where his hideout is. It's in the Congo, in the jungle somewhere. I can give you the coordinates."

"Do it."

He rattled off the coordinates and as far as she could place them mentally, they were in the right area of Africa. They didn't sound made up on the spot, especially since Landry was standing in a pool of urine. He was a motivated man.

"When do the nanites get launched?"

"Two days from now." Landry allowed himself a sneer, no doubt thinking she'd never get there in time so his information was useless to her anyway.

"What sets them off?"

"I don't know, I don't know, he never told anybody! It's the truth. I told you everything! Now let me go."

Let him go? Did I say anything about letting him go? She thought of Landry's illegal gun sales to militias like the Janjaweed and his harem of underage sex toys.

She pulled the trigger.

Chapter Thirty

Maliha dropped the gun and Landry's body. She was looking around for something to clean the spattered blood from her face and arms when she suddenly felt the pull to Midworld. Rabishu was summoning her for a meeting, for the first time since she'd renounced her contract.

Midworld's fog and stench were as she remembered it from the numerous times she'd been pulled there to get her killing assignments. She wondered what form Rabishu would take this time. He'd appeared to her as many different creatures over the years, all of them horrifying. As the peculiar rotting smell that signaled his approach reached her nose, she braced herself for both his appearance and his assault on her mind. She decided to take an aggressive approach. She shouted at him before she could even make out his shape clearly.

"Demon, you have no right to call me here. I don't serve you! Send me back!"

There was a blast of sound inside her head in response. She felt like her head was splitting open, and for all she knew, it was. Her hands were pinned to her sides, or she would have checked to make sure her skull was intact. Then the roaring let up as Rabishu came into view.

He came this time as a nightmarish assembly of spinning blades, like the giant blades from a sawmill. Protruding at all angles from a central core, the blades were coated in blood and pieces of flesh. He had no discernible limbs or a head. Maliha watched in horror as a living human was spit out by the core and roughly tossed from blade to blade until there was nothing left of it to scream. A few seconds later, another person was ejected. Rabishu was shredding these damned people he brought along from his hell for his amusement as he talked to Maliha.

She wanted to curse him, but her voice died in her throat. Then she heard him in her mind.

You have not made much progress in balancing your scale. Stay your course and I will win. You will become my plaything forever.

"Enough with the plaything! I've heard that before. You don't scare me, and I will win! Why did you bring me here?"

You have come back to what I taught you. You stand there wearing the blood of a human you tortured in his mind. Your whip sword is as red as these blades of mine. Come back to me, servant. You will be immortal again. There is no need for you to suffer with these trivial wounds.

The bullet wound in Maliha's calf healed instantly. She'd forgotten how good it felt to heal that fast.

Let me put my mark on you and death will leave you, as before.

"Same contract?"

The same, signed anew with your blood. You will be my chief servant. There are privileges that go with that.

"The answer is—" She knew she should say no. She had friends who counted on her, she'd persuaded Lucius to go rogue. But it was tempting. *Am I crazy to even be thinking about this, or am I crazy to turn it down?* "Do I have to decide now?"

No, but I will not wait long.

She was thrown back from Midworld to Vincent Landry's bloody home.

Chapter Thirty-One

Ouésso, Congo, was on the Sangha River and about a degree and a half north of the equator. It had an airstrip cut out of the rain forest and a soccer park for enthusiasts, in a country where animist religions were practiced and it wasn't unheard of to have accusations of witchcraft during hotly contested soccer games.

From Maliha's viewpoint, it also sheltered in the nearby jungle the most important man in the world that day, the Leader. Vincent Landry had told Maliha that for many people the world would end in two days. Consideration of Rabishu's offer would have to wait.

Today was Day Two.

Maliha was running on empty as far as sleep was concerned. She'd taken a couple of fifteen-minute naps since then, dropping off on the plane when she was supposed to be planning her mission.

Following her GPS, she was walking through the forest looking for the Leader's headquarters. The sun had just risen and there was a break in the rain, though according to the humidity, it might as well have been raining. The sun peeked through a narrow opening in the clouds, lighting the tiny water droplets suspended around her and obscuring her view with a bright fog effect. It reminded her strongly of the forest where she'd last seen Lucius.

She pressed on. She felt Yanmeng's touch against her face. He was remote viewing her, and getting better at let-

ting her know. Previously, he'd told her of his presence
with a vague, feather-light touch on her face or shoulder,
easily missed in some circumstances. This touch felt like he
was standing next to her and had reached out to touch her
cheek physically. It amazed her to think that Yanmeng was
seventy-five hundred miles away inside a mountain. She
didn't resent his quick check. After what she'd reported to
them about Landry, they were rooting for her success and
worried about her.

When she had only a quarter of a mile to go, she stopped
and checked her weapons. She was a walking arms cache.
Wearing only shorts and a halter because it was too hot
for her usual black killing outfit, she carried her throwing
knives strapped to her thighs and a Glock 17 semi-automatic
low on her right hip. There was a small pack that held her
throwing stars within reach, a katana in a sheath slanted
across her back, and a sai bound to her belt with leather
straps on her left side.

The sai was a weapon with three unsharpened prongs,
with the round, center prong longer than the other two.
Normally, two sai were used, with a third on the belt in
case of damage to or loss of one of the primary sai. Maliha
brought only one with her. Weight was a consideration, both
for rapid travel and for fighting, and besides, it was all she
had with her in France.

The headquarters turned out to be a low building fitted
into the understory like it grew there: a squat mushroom.
Concrete block construction, but concealed with a trompe
l'oeil painting of the forest. No guards were visible so she
decided on a direct and low-tech approach. Standing about
thirty feet away, she heaved a rock at a spot on the door.
There was no response, so she moved closer and did it again.

A distorted male voice spoke to her.

"Come in. I've been expecting you."

"Why do you hide behind some computer squawk box?
Tell me your name."

"You'll know soon enough."

She was at the door, and tested it cautiously. It was open. She pulled the Glock from its hip holster, pulled the slide to chamber a bullet, and rested her finger lightly on the side of the gun's frame, ready to fire when needed.

With the door open, in front of her was a hallway that consisted of a round glass tube. Just looking at it made gooseflesh rise on her arms in the tropical heat. It looked exactly like the one in the Keltner Building, the one that had trapped a security officer and gassed him to death. There was a powerful urge not to step into that tunnel.

This is Day Two. Have I come this far to back out now?

"Scared? I assure you it's safe." There was a giggle after that, in the distorted voice.

It started to rain again, a thoroughly pounding rain. Maliha was already soaked. The prospect of getting into a dry building provided just the tiny boost she needed.

She took a deep breath, not that it was going to help if he left her in there for ten minutes, and stepped into the tunnel. Bright lights came on and the door snapped shut behind her. Maliha felt tingling all over her skin and wondered if it was the first effect of the gas. She ran to the other end of the tunnel and pushed on the door. It wouldn't open. The tingling on her skin became worse.

"Don't be alarmed. The tunnel's automatic. You're just feeling the bug cleaner. Mosquitoes, you know. Can't have those nasty things inside. Don't you hate that buzzing, especially at night? It'll finish when it detects no more bugs in the tunnel's air."

About ten seconds later the door in front of her opened and the tunnel went dark, an obvious invitation to move further into the house.

The room she entered was large and designed for the needs of one individual. There was a startling resemblance to her haven, but without the creature comforts. A wall of weapons, a practice floor, sleeping area, a basic kitchen, a basic bathroom out in the open. Utilitarian fluorescent lighting. The place was a self-contained box in the jungle where its owner could withdraw from society.

Like Lucius and his island. At least that was a lot pleasanter than this place.

One wall was nearly covered with maps showing Earth, with the target countries marked. Clocks timed down to an event about thirty minutes away. The rest of the wall was taken up with security camera views, including one of the now darkened tunnel she'd come through. There was a man seated at a desk with his back to her. She knew him in an instant by his lean form and lanky hair.

Rasputin!

Somehow, she had to stop one of the Ageless from throwing the switch, and she didn't think she'd be able to talk him out of it. Her plans immediately switched to different paths, different outcomes. Instead of hoping to walk away into the jungle after killing the Leader, she now saw her best possible result as mutual destruction.

With his back still to her, Rasputin was absorbed in the displays on the wall. She had a chance.

She dashed forward while squeezing the trigger on her pistol. She was an excellent shot, even while moving. If she could plug the seventeen bullets, or a good part of them, into his head and neck, Rasputin would be weakened enough that she could finish him off with a swing of her sword. Getting his head a good distance from the rest of him was her plan.

Halfway to the chair she knew her tactic had failed. Rasputin had vanished and reappeared to the side of the room, having used his Ageless speed, no doubt when he heard her wet shoes moving across the floor. Her bullets careened past the chair and hit the world map, creating showers of sparks and darkening entire countries.

"Interesting," Rasputin said. "It seems you have a penchant for destroying South America." He nodded at the darkened sections of the map. "You could join me and make that your dominion. I'm willing to share. Share my castoffs, at least."

"You never had any intention of sharing power with the other council members," she said.

"Ah, but it kept you busy, tracking them all over the world. It left only one thing for me to do, and that was getting rid of the naïve young man who pretended to be the Leader. I delivered his payoff." He smiled, no doubt remembering the man's painful death. "I do wish you'd left Duma for me, though. I had plans for her."

"There were only four members on the council then."

He waved his hand. "Forget the council. They were a means to an end."

Exactly what I thought about my method of obtaining this location. Hearing it from Rasputin's mouth makes it feel dirty.

"Don't you recognize me, now that we're standing still and having a conversation instead of fighting?"

"I don't know you from times past."

"You do," he said, switching to Russian. "We met in St. Petersburg. I was a penitent at the academy there. I tried to seduce you."

Maliha's free hand flew to her mouth. "Grigori Yefimovich. I do remember!"

"Kind of you not to use my nickname. I've never liked it."

"Rasputin." *Rasputnik* meant "lecher" in English.

"Couldn't help yourself, I see. I earned it, I suppose."

"Were you already Ageless when you were killed?"

Rasputin was a Russian peasant born around 1870. He found himself unwelcome in his village due to drunkenness, sexual conquests, and wild behavior. Roaming the Siberian wilderness, he was involved in obscure cults and became a hypnotist and mystic with a reputation for healing by hypnosis. He worked himself into the favor of the royal court by healing the Tsarina's ailing son, but court intrigue got the best of him. A group of men poisoned, shot, beat, and drowned him, later claiming that each successive attempt didn't kill Rasputin until he finally drowned.

"The body pulled from the Neva River wasn't mine. It belonged to some unlucky look-alike."

Maliha was inching closer to him. She didn't think he'd

let her get within sword's reach, but she had to try it. She glanced at the bank of clocks. Twenty-five minutes.

"So how did you become Ageless?"

"I was alone in the wilderness, hunting. It was in the spring, when the mother bears have their cubs. I was very careful, but also very hungry. I found a run of salmon and jumped in to try to catch some with my hands. Ah! I was so happy. I caught the fish, cracked their heads on the rocks, and threw them to the shore for later. Then I was lifted from the water by the claws of a great brown bear. She dragged me back to her den and left me there for her cubs, to learn to catch and eat for themselves. If I tried to escape, she would swipe my legs with her claws and bring me back. The little ones had full bellies from the salmon. They sniffed me, mauled me, but didn't kill me. After a couple of days, I was in terrible pain. Then one of the cubs caught me in the belly with its claw. For another two days I lay on the ground as the cubs put their muzzles into my guts and tore pieces and swallowed, or ate me alive in other parts of my body, and I could not die. That's when my demon came to me."

"You have been Ageless less than a century. Throw off your yoke and be your own man!"

"I will be my own man, and I will be Ageless, too. I will rule the humans as my slaves and kill the demons if they do not bend to my will."

He plans to have the tablet and lens!

She'd been keeping herself in check, trying to learn something that would give her an advantage. *Twenty minutes.* Maliha noticed on the wall behind Rasputin that the monitor displaying the tunnel showed the bright light of someone entering.

Lucius walked into view on the monitor.

The heart on the tree proclaiming his love for her flashed into her vision.

No! He can't be here! Her fear for him nearly overwhelmed her, making her knees weak. Somehow she kept the fear from her face and voice. As soon as she'd found out that the Leader was Ageless, she'd downgraded her chance of survival. Lucius was in the same position. He could no longer confront Rasputin as an equal.

"I know you have the nanites distributed in the water of the target countries. How do you plan to turn them on?"

"Distribution is not complete. That would take a year. What I have is barely adequate for a first strike. You have not figured out the key?"

Maliha thought back to what Fynn had said. "Some kind of broadcast?"

"Excellent! What kind?"

She shrugged. She could see out of the corner of her eye that Lucius had entered the room and was crouched behind a piece of furniture. "A concert."

"So close. Television is very popular in emergent countries. Where TVs have not penetrated, there are radios. Who would object to a patriotic advertiser who buys time to play the national anthem? No one. The trigger is a complicated series of sounds buried in the national anthems for each country. The ads are bought, the soundtracks submitted, and they will run several times over the next twelve hours starting in"—he turned to look at the clock—"eighteen minutes. There is a neutralizing sequence. It makes the nanites eat themselves. The council insisted on a last-ditch failsafe, in case the distribution went bad and the nanites got into their own countries. I thought it might be useful for blackmail." He pulled a jump drive from his pocket and held it up, then put it back in his pocket. "Might be fun to give them a scare after the first round of deaths. Contaminate London and New York, say, and offer to neutralize for a few billion dollars."

Maliha said nothing. Time was running out on the clock. She had to make her attack soon, regardless of what Lucius was planning, and she had to find a way to convey how the hitchhikers were going to be triggered.

"I have an interesting experiment you'll be participating in. Too bad you won't survive it, but you will contribute to my study of the nanites." He patted a strange-looking gun on his desk that was loaded with a vial attached to a dart.

Maliha figured out what it was, and she shivered.

"You're going to infect me."

"Yes. Wait . . ." Rasputin took a deep breath and tilted his head to one side. "There's someone else here."

Rasputin drew a knife and hesitated slightly as he used his senses to pinpoint Lucius's location. Rasputin's attention wasn't on her. Maliha pulled the sai from her waist and threw it forcefully. The point rammed through Rasputin's eye and came out the back of his head.

Instantly she saw Lucius take off at a run, and she heard one of his crossbow bolts whizz through the air. Hoping Lucius could take advantage of Rasputin's situation, Maliha quickly drew one of her throwing knives and raked the point of it across her arm. Dipping her fingers in her blood, she wrote TV AD on the floor. There was no time to write national anthem, so she wrote FLG and 15. Yanmeng, viewing her, would see the letters and tell Amaro and Hound. She could only hope they'd interpret them correctly, including the fifteen minutes left until the ad ran for the first time.

When she looked up, she found that Rasputin had pulled the sai from his eye and stabbed Lucius in the shoulder with it. She didn't know if Rasputin was blind in one eye or not, or if the brain damage had been repaired by his Ageless body that swiftly.

Lucius was on the floor. As she watched, she saw him yank the sai from his shoulder. Maliha reloaded her Glock and began firing.

Rasputin moved rapidly to her side, wrenched the gun from her hand, and brought his elbow down on her upper arm, breaking the bone. Her right arm was useless.

He turned his back on her and went back to finish off Lucius. He wasn't showing any sign of blindness or brain damage. She took two throwing stars from her bag and held them in her left hand, aiming carefully. She sent them flying at Rasputin's back. In midair they split apart, each taking its own path, and hit him in the back. One struck at the base of his spine, the other at the neck. A normal man would be dead or paralyzed.

Rasputin staggered a little, reached around, and pulled the stars out. He spun around and fired them back at her. She'd anticipated it and ducked down. The stars flew over her head and embedded themselves in the concrete wall. When she moved to reposition herself for another attack, Rasputin threw a knife at her. The knife impacted her thigh, and she stumbled.

Rasputin reached for the gun on his desk. He fired a dart at Maliha as she was trying to regain her balance.

Lucius dashed across the room, stretched as far as he could, and just barely deflected the dart with his sword. There was a cost. The second dart thudded into his chest.

"No!" Maliha screamed.

Cackling in triumph, Rasputin flipped a switch that flooded the room with the activation sound. Lucius fell, with the nanites rapidly attacking his organs.

"Stop them! Turn them off!"

"Once started, there is no way to halt the nanites. Just enjoy the show."

Rasputin did just that. He couldn't seem to take his eyes off the suffering man on the floor.

"You see, this is what's so interesting," he said. "His healing abilities are fighting the destructive power of the nanites. He's rebuilding what they are tearing apart, but inevitably, not fast enough. He is mortal, and he will die—just slower than other humans. I should be taking notes."

Maliha closed her eyes. She couldn't bear to see Lucius in a condition where there was no hope. She had to make his sacrifice for her mean something. Retrieving the first dart that had been aimed at her, she straightened out the bent tip and hurled it at Rasputin.

The dart landed in his back and injected him. Annoyed at another throwing star from Maliha, he reached around to pluck it out. When he got a look at what he held in his hands, his body became rigid with fear.

"Shut it off! Shut the sound off!"

The activation sound was still playing in the room.

"Enjoy the show, Rasputin."

Maliha moved over to Lucius. He was moaning and losing the battle. He was losing the fight for his life to the machines inside his body.

Then the nanites began to affect Rasputin. As one of the Ageless, Rasputin healed as rapidly as the nanites destroyed, but he couldn't gain an edge over them. Rasputin was helpless, his body stuck in a continuous cycle of destruction and renewal.

Maliha waited with Lucius. She cradled his head in her lap and kissed him gently. With effort, he tapped his belt with one hand, indicating that she should look there. In a small pocket sewn inside his weapons belt she found a key. She took it and held it up so he could see it.

"Is this for the shard?"

He wasn't able to nod, but his eyes told her that the key would allow her to retrieve the shard he'd taken from her in the Taklimakan Desert. Her heart overflowed with emotion and her eyes with tears.

She clutched the key to her chest. "I'll do it. I'll do it for us. I'll kill the demons and then we'll be together."

A tear slid down his cheek and she kissed it away.

She could have speeded his death, but she knew what awaited him: torment at the hand of his former demon master, because Lucius failed in his quest after stepping onto the mortal path. He did not balance the scale so recently carved onto his body. The only life saved to his credit was Maliha's, and while it counted for a lot, it wasn't enough to balance nineteen hundred years of working on the side of evil.

She could have been the one with the nanites coursing through her body. Would have been, if Lucius hadn't sacrificed himself for her.

That makes twice. When he gave up his immortality for me, then his life.

Portions of his body didn't look completely solid anymore, and she was certain if she touched those parts her fingers would sink in. She slipped his head off her lap before the last stages began. After Lucius took his last labored breath, his body disintegrated further and his heart failed.

Reluctantly leaving him, Maliha used Rasputin's communication equipment to contact Amaro and make sure that her message had gotten through about the TV ad. It had, and with Hound's connections in the U.S. government, the warning was taken seriously. The ads were pulled—awaiting, of course, a fabricated explanation to follow. Hound reported that a few deaths were reported among curious broadcasting personnel who listened to the ad in spite of the dire warnings, but those were quickly hushed up by their respective governments. Panic and mass deaths were averted.

Maliha went to the helpless Rasputin, who watched as she took the jump drive with the neutralization sequence from his pocket. The long process of detoxifying large numbers of people with the permanent deactivation sound would soon begin, and they wouldn't even know how close they had come to a horrible death.

Maliha tried something for which she didn't have much hope. She lay down as close to the position Lucius died in as she could and opened herself to experiencing the last impressions of his death. She hoped that somehow his spirit would coalesce around her, as in other cases, and that she'd be able to help him onto a different path, freeing him of torment.

She did slide into his death experience and her hope grew that she might be able to do something positive. She felt the kiss they'd shared from his point of view, and knew how much it meant to him.

His tortured soul did come to her, for a few moments only, and she felt the incredible agony of what he was going through. Then Lucius broke the contact. Maliha was sharing the pain of his torment, and he wouldn't permit it.

Maliha was tempted to leave the quivering, powerless Rasputin in his jungle hideaway for a few decades, stuck in the tortured space between life and death, as a partial retribution for the deaths he'd wrought. From the Sudanese and Nigerian villagers to Lucius, Ty and Claire, to Saltz's fiancée and child slaughtered in their apartment, to others who died in her pursuit of him.

Rasputin is a bloody nightmare.

Maliha felt stabbed in the heart by her own thoughts. A bloody nightmare—the same could have been said of her, until she set foot on the mortal path. And since then, she'd killed in the process of saving lives, people like guards. People like Duma, whom she may have befriended under different conditions.

People. Not targets. This is my burden to bear along with the deaths marked on my scale. Is it Lucius who achieved redemption with his act of sacrifice, even though he suffers now? Some potent questions to be considered. Yanmeng would be proud of me.

Maliha decided it was too risky to let Rasputin live. She came up to him, shoved him down on his knees, and with him watching but helpless to stop it, she swung her sword and sent his head rolling across the floor.

Freed of the immortality that was keeping them at bay, the nanites overwhelmed what was left of Rasputin and turned him into an ill-defined gray mass on the floor. Two of them.

A few minutes later Maliha, the only one left alive in the utilitarian concrete haven, convulsed on the floor. She was receiving the reward on her scale for killing Rasputin. A large number of figures moving into the "saved" pan left a rut across her belly from the acid of their footsteps. A noticeable shift in the balance of the pans resulted, and when the pull through time came, she felt as though a rope had yanked her forward, not that she was tugged gently by a cord.

A year, perhaps. Maybe a little more. Worth every second of it.

She bandaged her wounds as best she could. She forcibly straightened her broken arm, shifting the bones back into their approximate position since she had to travel. Using a sheet from Rasputin's closet, she tore a section to make a sling for her arm. The tunnel, indifferent to the death of the building's resident, ran through its cycle and let her out.

Chapter Thirty-Two

Maliha walked out of the rain forest to Ouésso and boarded a helicopter to the airport in Yaoundé, the capital of Cameroon, where jets frequented the runways. The jet from the clinic picked her up and took her to Switzerland.

Dr. Corvernis fussed over her broken arm and had to break it again under anesthesia, because it had begun to heal in the sling position Maliha used to hold the arm steady near her body. She woke up with a cast on her upper arm. He patched her other wounds and pressed into her hand a bottle of anti-malarial medication because she'd come from an area where the disease was endemic.

She had no need to worry about the disease. Her aggressive immune system killed the parasites injected by an infected mosquito before they had time to multiply in her liver and spread to her bloodstream. Finally, the doctor warned her to avoid coffee, a piece of advice he trotted out every time he treated her. She nodded, already craving her first freshly brewed cup of Kopi Luwak at home, made from Sumatran coffee beans that had been eaten and then distributed on the forest floor by civets.

During her initial recuperation, she had plenty of time to think about the way she'd handled the mission, escalating in violence until the slaughter at Landry's. She could see how Rabishu might get the idea she was ready to come back into the fold. In the calm and healing environment of the clinic, she began to see what had happened to her. She had been sucked in by the power her old life represented, the feeling of being in charge and on her own as she had been for over a couple of hundred years. It was a strong pull, but now she saw it for what it was—an attempt to recapture the feeling of being Ageless without the grim reality that went with it. It had backfired, caused deaths that might have been averted, and alienated her friends. It had brought her back to Rabishu's attention, and the very worst thing of all—the most shameful—was that she hadn't rejected the demon's offer immediately.

I'm going to be living with all of these choices for a long, long time.

She went to the safe house in Canada. Everyone was relieved to see her. She took her close friends aside for some private conversation.

"You ready to apologize for being an asshole?" Hound asked.

"I wasn't going to phrase it quite like that, but yes," Maliha said. "You three keep right on being my conscience."

"Let's skip the rest and go straight to the group hug," Amaro said.

"I'm not hugging him," Yanmeng said, pointing at Hound. "He hasn't showered since we came here."

"I forgot to bring my special soap. I have sensitive skin," Hound said.

"That is complete bullshit," Amaro said. "Remember that time in Iquitos when you took a bath in—"

"Ladies present," Hound said. "One of them, anyway."

Maliha drifted away as the conversation deteriorated. She hadn't told them about Rabishu's offer, and didn't plan to.

She took Randy and others out on snowmobile rides under the aurora borealis, had snowball fights, and gave the kids skiing lessons to make it seem more like a vacation. Randy told her she had a memorable time, and Amaro was mum about the whole thing, which made her think something was going on between them. Sooner or later, she'd worm it out of Randy.

She used downtime when the shelter was quiet to finish her book and send it off to her editor. Amaro dutifully tracked the progress of her new black Zonda F, currently at Dewey's Custom Security in a warehouse somewhere in New York City. Soon it would be finished to her exacting standards. She tried to contact Jake, but kept getting his voicemail. It didn't surprise her. When working on a case, he could be very single-minded. She knew that first-hand, from the intense way he'd investigated her when he thought she might be involved in a smuggling operation.

Maliha looked out over the sea from the reclining chair she'd awakened in when Lucius first brought her to his Mediterranean island. It was hers now.

Sun flooded the room she was in, and a breeze lifted the gauzy curtains. She glimpsed sparkling waves and olive trees with their trunks twisted like an old farmer's hands. With a silk gown wrapping her, Maliha looked like an ancient Grecian goddess. The smell of the sea was haunting, a call to adventure.

Not just yet.

Maliha was there to heal, her battered body and soul needing the peace of solitude. She meditated, fished for her supper, and lived simply.

I could withdraw from my quest and live here. Stop hunting shards, stop trying to balance my scale. Jake loves me and I love him. I could have a family with him. I'd wait until my children were grown and then go back to my quest, only if it didn't put my kids in jeopardy. And if I didn't succeed in balancing my scale, I know what would be waiting for me. So how much am I willing to sacrifice to have a family? Or is the whole idea all talk and no action?

She could put that plan in motion now. *Just pick up the phone and ask Jake to come to me. Lucius . . . is gone. I can't build a life around a man who isn't even in the Great Above.*

She'd told Lucius she would rescue him and bring him back. *A fairy-tale happy ending. How do I know what would happen if I kill all the demons? Even if I did rescue him, I might get whisked off to join Anu. I doubt if they sell diapers in the third plane of existence.*

A sweet memory of the kiss they'd shared before Lucius was swept into his snake-demon's hell was all that was left to her.

What am I thinking of, marriage, family, diapers? I'm the only rogue alive, the only one who has a chance to destroy all the demons and set humanity free to make our own path. Priorities! Damn.

Maliha had the Tablet of the Overlord and three shards now. At least she would have three when she used the key Lucius gave her as he died. Only four to go, and if Jake would help her, they might come into her possession quickly.

What motivation does Jake have for wanting the demons gone? He's doing well enough as it is. She considered his missing five years, something that gave her an uneasy feeling even though she loved Jake. A dear friend waited in Jerusalem who might have the information that would finally put those qualms to rest. She was due for a visit to Abiyram, anyway. She'd promised him that she'd bring him into the circle of friends who knew about her goals.

Maliha popped a freshly-picked and cleaned olive into her mouth from a bowl nearby. As she thoughtfully chewed it and looked out over the waves, something else tugged at her heart.

Hmm . . . I could spend some time gathering seashells on a particular stretch of Australian beach.

LYS2 1009

THE NIGHT HUNTRESS NOVELS FROM

JEANIENE FROST

 ## HALFWAY TO THE GRAVE

978-0-06-124508-4

Before she can enjoy her newfound status as kick-ass demon hunter, half vampire Cat Crawfield and her sexy mentor, Bones, are pursued by a group of killers. Now Cat will have to choose a side…and Bones is turning out to be as tempting as any man with a heartbeat.

ONE FOOT IN THE GRAVE

978-0-06-124509-1

Cat Crawfield is now a special agent, working for the government to rid the world of the rogue undead. But when she's targeted for assassination she turns to her ex, the sexy and dangerous vampire Bones, to help her.

 ## AT GRAVE'S END

978-0-06-158307-0

Caught in the crosshairs of a vengeful vamp, Cat's about to learn the true meaning of bad blood—just as she and Bones need to stop a lethal magic from being unleashed.

DESTINED FOR AN EARLY GRAVE

978-0-06-158321-6

Cat is having terrifying visions in her dreams of a vampire named Gregor who's more powerful than Bones.